A DATE WITH DEATH

 DEVIANT MAGIC BOOK ONE

Scott Colby

DEVIANT MAGIC BOOK ONE: A DATE WITH DEATH
Copyright © 2020 Scott Colby. All rights reserved.

Published by Outland Entertainment LLC
3119 Gillham Road
Kansas City, MO 64109

Founder/Creative Director: Jeremy D. Mohler
Editor-in-Chief: Alana Joli Abbott
Senior Editor: Gwendolyn Nix

ISBN: 978-1-947659-88-9
Worldwide Rights   .
Created in the United States of America

Editor: Gwendolyn N. Nix
Cover Illustration: Ann Marie Cochran
Cover Design: Jeremy D. Mohler
Interior Layout: Mikael Brodu

Printed and bound in the United States of America.

Visit **outlandentertainment.com** to see more, or follow us on our
Facebook Page **facebook.com/outlandentertainment/**

This is a work of fiction.
Any resemblance to real people or places
is a low down dirty shame.
For best results, serve with a snifter
of strong brown liquor.

— CHAPTER ONE —

A ttention Harksburg! I have news of the utmost importance that shall—*hiccup!*—change the lives of all gathered here today!"

Kevin Felton unleashed a mighty sigh as Oscar climbed atop the slab of granite used as a pulpit whenever one of them had something important to say. The abandoned industrial park known locally as the Works had seen more than its fair share of drunken proclamations over the years, most of which were prefaced with similar promises of substance. Usually they turned out to be pretty stupid. Kevin didn't doubt that his dumb friend would perpetuate that trend. He just hoped he wouldn't be involved in whatever was about to come out of Oscar's mouth; it was Kevin's welcome back party, after all, which made him a target for all manner of bullshit.

Oscar paused to cast a benevolent gaze across all those gathered, sticklike arms spread wide and welcoming, his battered Cubs cap straighter and lower than usual. The young man's freckled face, scraggly red hair, and wide, toothy smile often reminded others of a cartoon character. In the flickering light of their unnecessarily large campfire, Kevin thought his friend looked rather like a redneck messiah come to lead the faithful to the holy trailer park—complete with a 40-ounce bottle of Miller High Life duct taped to each hand.

"Get on with it, fucker," Waltman growled. "All day you wouldn't shut up about whatever dumb bullshit's about to come out of your mouth. Hurry up and get it over with before the keg gets warm."

Kevin glanced over his shoulder, trying to find Waltman in the crowd, but his friend was hidden somewhere in the gaggle of twenty-something men and women who'd come out for Kevin's party. Although he couldn't see Waltman, Kevin could easily picture the shit-eating grin on his beefy friend's crooked, acne-pocked face.

Oscar took a quick swig from the half-empty bottle attached to his left hand, then scratched his scraggly red beard thoughtfully with the lip of the bottle. "Ah, Waltman," he said softly, like a wise sitcom father trying to impart this week's lesson to his foolish-yet-well-meaning son. "Long have you tried to prove your superiority over me. The beatings in gym class, the wedgies on the playground, the theft of my prom date, that skunk you locked in the cab of my truck last week…"

"Yeah, so you're a fucking loser! Everybody knows that!" Waltman shouted, winning a chuckle from the thirty or so people gathered in the wooded outskirts of the Works. "Get to the damn point already!"

"Waltman," Oscar said again. "Poor, pathetic, small-minded Waltman. It is I who is…am…are…is better than you, as you'll soon see." At that point, he nodded to Kevin. "Sorry to steal the limelight at your welcome back party, but…" He paused for dramatic effect, favoring those gathered with one more loving glance. "I, Oscar Spuddner, am *immortal!*"

A collective groan echoed through the crowd. Empty beer cans rained down on Oscar, who found it hard to protect himself with a bottle taped to each hand. A tallboy clanged off his forehead and sent his cap flying. Kevin laughed under his breath. Some things never changed.

"Enjoying yourself yet?" Ren Roberts asked from his side. Kevin's ride had been missing for the past hour or so, ostensibly providing that cute redhead from the next county over with a grand tour of his Jaguar's backseat.

"Just like old times," Kevin replied with a smile. He'd forgotten how much fun these benders out in the Works could be, but he never would've ruined his reputation as the aloof city boy by admitting it. "Yourself?"

Ren took a quick sip from his snifter of Glenlivet. "Oh, a little romp among the bourgeoisie is always good for the soul." In his khakis, loafers, and blue velvet smoking jacket, Ren Roberts lent an air of melodramatic culture to the proceedings. His sandy blond hair, slicked back across his scalp with what must've been an entire bottle of gel, hadn't moved in six years. Since graduating high school, Ren had been a bit of an enigma. A smart, personable young man from a wealthy family, he could've gone to his choice of universities, but he skipped college completely and instead operated as an online day trader working out of his parents' home. That the one among them best equipped to leave Harksburg had never moved on was a topic of much whispered discussion among the locals. Some claimed that the only Roberts child suffered from a debilitating health condition that kept him living with his parents; others posited that there was a price on his head, that staying close to his powerful father somehow kept the wolves at bay. Oscar had even once suggested that Ren was an alien and the Roberts family's sprawling estate concealed a buried mothership. For his part, Ren seemed to find his status as a town legend quaint and amusing.

As the heckling died down, a squeaky voice cut through the night. "Oscar's telling the truth!" Doorknob shouted. "I seen it myself, right about ten this morning!" In the flickering firelight from the huge bonfire, Kevin could see that Doorknob's face was a pasty shade of white that shouldn't have been possible after three hours of hard drinking. Impossible seemed to be the theme of Doorknob's body: he was far too thin to have such a round beer gut, several inches too short to have such a long torso, covered in too much red hair and dappled with too many freckles to supposedly be primarily of Middle Eastern ancestry. Nothing about Doorknob made much sense, least of all his nickname, which no one could remember the reason for.

Tom Flanagan strode forward out of the crowd, still wearing his blue uniform and sidearm, though his hat was on backwards and he was missing his left shoe. "As an officer of the law, I formally request that any witnesses to this morning's alleged miracle who have not spent the last twenty-seven years shoved up Mr. Spuddner's *be*-hind come forward immediately!"

Junior Mullins stepped forward, handed Tom his missing shoe, then disappeared back into the crowd.

"Case closed!" Tom shouted.

"This is serious!" Doorknob squealed.

"Allow me to explain," Oscar cooed, once again in messiah mode. "This revelation of revelations came to me not long after breakfast, following closely upon the heels of an extra cup of coffee and a long, satisfying piss. I joined young Master Knob at our usual place of meeting, behind Old Mac Hurkin's barn where the day's pile of hay awaited baling. Also aaaaa-waiting my presence was an unsteady p—*hiccup!*—pitchfork unaware of its impending role in revealing my destiny."

"Awww!" moaned Jim Jimeson from his customary spot at Waltman's hip. "Did you and the pitchfork make love?"

A cheer rose up from the crowd. Tom Flanagan raised his missing shoe in the air and decried such man-tool relations as illegal. At Kevin's side, Ren washed down a groan with a sip of Glenlivet.

Oscar didn't miss a beat. "No, no. That pitchfork had much more devilish intentions—such as catching a stray breeze and tumbling straight through my heart!"

"So, you're saying you got some penetration?" Waltman hollered to the delight of the crowd.

Oscar grappled for the collar of his soiled Dale Earnhardt T-shirt, trying in vain to tear it free despite the bottles taped to his hands. Doorknob scrambled onto the ledge, took firm hold of Oscar's collar, and yanked. Though he failed to tear the shirt, he did succeed in awkwardly dumping the two of them off the back of the ledge in a tangle of sticklike arms and legs.

Another raucous cheer rose up from the ranks of Kevin's friends. He craned his neck back over each shoulder in turn to scan the crowd. Though he'd spent the first eighteen years of his life with most of this crew, he felt like an outsider. Four years away at school in Chicago and then three years in the workforce had effectively removed him from the group. He'd become a friend emeritus, a former member who only appeared for important occasions or at events where the free food promised to be good. Though Kevin was damn proud of the fact that he'd moved on to a new life, the realization that they'd all done the same was downright jarring. Both sides of the equation looked at each other with something akin to suspicion; neither quite understood why the sudden separation had ended or why things weren't the way they used to be. Regardless, the people gathered in the Works were Kevin's oldest friends and he was glad they'd come out to see him.

"He hasn't taken that damn shirt off in years. What made him think it would come off now?" Jenny Reilly said sagely from her perch atop the rusted bulldozer on the edge of their little circle. No one was quite sure what it was doing abandoned so far from the main buildings of the Works, but it was a great place to sit so none of them really cared. Jenny, a former cheerleader and vale-dictorian of the Harksburg High Class of 2002, reminded Kevin of the machine on which she sat: lopsided, falling apart, and mostly useless—a faded memory of better days. Despite the rough years, her blond hair, blue eyes, and confident smile still attracted plenty of gentlemanly attention.

"Normally when those two make out they do it with all of their clothes on," Jim Jimeson added with a proud belch. Waltman's second was a shorter version of his taller friend, broad and strong without definition, clad in dirty jeans and his favorite sleeveless flannel shirt. "Buttons and zippers are soooooooooooo hard!"

Everybody but Kevin laughed. Something about this didn't feel right. The fall wasn't a long one. Oscar and Doorknob should've popped right back up, red-faced and chagrined, weakly attempting to deflect the jokes and jibes raining down upon them.

He tapped Ren on the arm. "We should go check on them."

"Lead the way."

The scene they found on the other side of the granite ledge made Kevin gag and Ren turn away. Oscar had landed on his back, arms and legs spread, the four tines of a pitchfork sticking up through his chest in a spreading puddle of blood. His eyes were glassy and still. Both of his bottles of beer had shattered on the way down. Beside him was a tangle of arms and legs that used to be Doorknob, his neck twisted at an impossible angle.

"Flanagan!" Kevin shouted. He put his face in his hands, fighting the urge to sob.

The crowd surged forward en masse. Gasps and retches and exclamations of sadness and disgust echoed through the Works as Kevin's friends made a rough circle around the two corpses. Flanagan shoved his way through Waltman and Jim Jimeson and knelt beside Doorknob. "Well," he slurred, trying to sound officious. "What the hell were the chances of *that?*"

"Shouldn't have brought the pitchfork," Waltman added glumly. No one laughed.

Kevin rolled his eyes. "Flanagan, shouldn't you be calling for an ambulance?"

"Don't bother," Oscar said. The crowd gasped as he sat up, extricating himself from the pitchfork's gory tines. He plucked away a red, stringy piece of meat from the abused tool and examined it closely like a four-year-old investigating something he'd just pulled out of his nose. "That fucking stung." The hunk of flesh then crawled inchworm style down his finger, across his forearm, and disappeared inside the sleeve of his shirt.

"Tell me about it," Doorknob added, pulling himself to his feet and rubbing the back of his neck. Something popped ominously in the base of his skull. He glanced down at the bubbling puddle of cheap booze and blood at Oscar's feet. "Looks like cherry soda!"

Those gathered watched in slack-jawed amazement as the liquid slowly lost its red hue. It was as if Oscar's bare feet absorbed his blood but left the beer behind. Oscar, Kevin was sure, probably wished he'd been able to save the beer, too.

"The fuck?" Jenny asked. Beside her, Jim Jimeson fainted. Kevin seconded Jenny's sentiment with a nervous nod. He'd never been so relieved and so confused in his life.

"I feel like I should arrest the both of you for obstruction of justice," Flanagan said angrily. "That there was a murder-suicide, but now there's no fucking evidence. Don't do it again."

Oscar scrambled awkwardly to his feet. He paused to gaze wistfully at the remains of the shattered bottles still taped to his hands. "As I was saying," he declared proudly, "I, Oscar Spuddner, am immortal. And my power has spread to my bosom-est of buddies, Master Knob. You, too, can cheat death by pledging your love and support to my cause."

"Fuck you," Waltman spat. "Do it again and I'll think about it."

"Take your shirt off," Jim Jimeson goaded. "Prove this wasn't some kind of trick."

With his fingers finally free, Oscar succeeded in yanking his dirty T-shirt up over his head. Underneath, his blood-stained chest and stomach were pocked with light red sores clumped in groups of four. The crowd gasped once more.

"You tested it a few times," Ren said as he took a nervous sip of scotch.

"Duh," Oscar replied haughtily. "It may have taken me three years to finish eighth grade, but I'm not stupid enough to do something like this in front of you assholes unless I know it's gonna work."

Kevin stealthily excused himself from the ensuing drunken argument, ducking into the nearby woods. He couldn't keep himself from shaking. What the hell had he just seen? Reaching into his jacket pocket, he withdrew his smartphone and checked for a signal. Checking the score of the Cubs game—they were out on the West Coast, in Los Angeles or maybe San Francisco—would help him calm down.

"This is all your fault, you know."

He whirled to his left to face the unfamiliar voice. A short man in a long black overcoat leaned against a nearby tree, appraising Kevin with a scowl through a pair of slender spectacles. The tops of his ears ended in pointed tips on either side of his dark, close-cropped hair. "Your fault." He pointed at Kevin angrily for added emphasis, his handsome face twisted in an accusing sneer.

Before Kevin could react, the man disappeared. He simply faded away, melting into the shadows as if he were one of them.

Had Kevin just seen a ghost or some sort of stress-induced hallucination? Things just kept getting worse. First, he'd lost his job in Chicago with Noonan, Noonan, and Schmidt when the Griffin Group bought out the once-prosperous firm. His girlfriend, Kylie, ditched him for a man twice his age. With no money and no luck finding new employment, he'd done something he'd sworn he'd never do: give up his apartment in the city and move back to his mother's Harksburg home. Finally, at a party celebrating his return, Kevin had watched two of his oldest friends die and come back to life, only to be informed that he was the one ultimately responsible for whatever was going on.

It was too much to process. "Fuck this," he growled, spitting in the general direction of the mysterious messenger. Shoving his phone back into his pocket, Kevin hurried to rejoin his friends and find some strong liquor.

— CHAPTER TWO —

Kevin stumbled out of Ren's car, slammed the passenger door behind him, and lovingly flipped his friend off as the Jaguar sped away. The dark green Victorian home before him—his mother's—wouldn't come into focus. It insisted on splitting in two, then orbiting around the point where the sturdy front door should've been.

"Ssssstay in one ffffucking p-place!" Kevin growled. "Ssssstop being an assssssshole, house!"

Ren had not been happy to discover what had once been a mostly full bottle of Glenlivet made empty and sticking out of Kevin's jacket pocket. After what Kevin had seen—or, as he was coming to believe, merely thought he'd seen—getting absolutely shitfaced via someone else's liquor had seemed the only sane option. Oscar had not impaled himself on a pitchfork, died, and then woken up moments later. Doorknob's neck never twisted like a pretzel and then repaired itself. And that man in the woods? A figment of an overactive imagination stressed by job loss and the subsequent forced move to a less than desirable locale.

And, above all, none of it was his fault. Kevin blamed Waltman. It wouldn't have been the first time his friend had thought it a good idea to sneak shrooms into whatever they were eating in the

Works—although usually Waltman only did that to Doorknob, because that was hilarious.

Kevin stood on the cracked sidewalk and stared intently at the house, willing it to stop moving. It refused. He didn't like his chances at a quiet entry given his current state of intoxication. And any noise, any noise at all, would bring his mother running in her robe and slippers, armed with the rolling pin she kept in the nightstand for fighting off burglars, murderers, rapists, and atheists. As family, Kevin had much worse to fear than a blow from the rolling pin; he risked an annoyingly calm, heartfelt lecture reminding him of the evils of alcohol, decrying the quality of his friends, lamenting the state of today's youth, and musing on just how it was that his mother's peerless parenting skills had failed to keep him from becoming a miscreant. Having been on the receiving end of several such speeches, which always came spiced with a sprinkle of Jesus and a side of hellfire and brimstone, Kevin wished she'd whack him with the rolling pin instead.

He supposed it could've been worse. Abelia Felton always kept an even tone with Kevin regardless of how frustrated she became with him, like she knew he was a good person deep down who occasionally made a few mistakes and needed a little motivation to get things right. She didn't seem to have the same sort of faith in anyone else in Harksburg. Abelia Felton had stormed Waltman's front door more than once, and her dressing down of Doorknob at the town's annual Fourth of July fireworks eight years ago was the stuff of legend—even though no one could remember exactly what Doorknob had done to anger Kevin's mother.

The porch swing beckoned Kevin's exhausted body, the soft creak of its chains in the breeze a siren's song like no other. He eyed it suspiciously. Besides the fact that it, too, had decided to duplicate itself and spin, the swing had a reputation as a cold, hard mistress that had ruined many a nap and enjoyed leaving painful creases in the flesh of those who spent too much time in her steely embrace. Kevin knew better than to spend the night in the porch swing—chances were sleeping outside would only postpone the lecture until the morning, when his mother would surely discover him while coming out to retrieve the newspaper. He needed to get inside, to his own bed, where he'd be able to combat any accusation of impropriety with the simple, reasonable excuse that he'd come home at an appropriate hour and done so quietly and politely so as not to wake the other member of the household.

Kevin stared dumbly at the house for a few more moments before a brilliant idea twisted his drooping face into a big dumb smile: *the Pussy Hatch!* So named because he'd used it to sneak many a girl into his bed in his wilder, younger days, the ground-level window of Kevin's basement bedroom would get him inside safe and sound. It had never locked correctly except when it froze shut, and he thought that unlikely given that it was the third week of September. A quick jiggle and it would flip right open. He just hoped he could still fit through it.

"Ffffuck you, porch ssssswing," Kevin slurred as he staggered into the driveway. He skirted his mother's little white shitbox of a car as if walking a highwire in a windstorm, taking small, tentative steps as he wobbled precariously on the narrow strip of asphalt between the vehicle and the house. Banging against either, he knew, would bring his mother stampeding down the stairs, ready to clobber any ne'er-do-well she found traipsing about her property, an outcome that would ruin any chance Kevin had at getting close to a good night's sleep.

The Pussy Hatch was just beyond the car but prior to the garden hose dangling from an old metal hook that itself dangled from the side of the house. Kevin knelt awkwardly and examined the window. To the uninitiated, the lock would've appeared firmly engaged, but Kevin knew better. He pressed firmly against the bottom of the rectangular window, jiggled it to the right, then jiggled it back to the left. The Pussy Hatch opened with a soft pop, pivoting outward on hinges across its top, and he lifted it as high as it would go. *This must be what mail feels like!* Kevin thought as he slithered through the narrow slot feet-first. He inhaled deeply to squeeze his beer gut through. Kylie had warned him that he was getting a bit plump, but she was a dirty, two-timing slut and so her opinion didn't count and Kevin didn't miss her. Most of the time.

Kevin's feet sank into the lush carpet and he breathed a heavy sigh of relief. He turned, gently pulled the window shut, and reset the locking mechanism. *Mission fucking accomplished!*

Navigating in the darkness wasn't a problem. Kevin knew his way around that room like a concert pianist knew his way around a baby grand. To the right of the Pussy Hatch stood his desk, an ancient mahogany monster he suspected once belonged to his father which now played host to a broken PC and a pile of Cubs memorabilia. If he reached the shelves of soccer trophies on the far wall, he'd know he'd gone too far. The red lights of the alarm clock in the far corner to his left was a beacon beckoning him into the nearby bed—but he moved slowly, wary of the heavy chest at the foot of the bed on which he'd bruised many a knee. The faucet in the attached bathroom dripped at a familiar interval, a metronome of sorts that sped up whenever someone came down the stairs. He could've tapped and named each of the posters on the wall in turn blindfolded—Scarface, The Seven Samurai, Rounders—had anyone challenged him. Luckily, his mother had decided to leave his room untouched when he'd moved away. Sneaking in would've become prohibitively more difficult if she'd filled it with the Jesus crap that infested the rest of the house.

He shucked his jacket and his jeans and pulled on the flannel pajama pants he kept at the foot of the bed. Good, God-fearing children who go to bed at reasonable hours—soberly, by the way, and only after thanking the Lord for every breath, sip of water, and bite of food said children had partaken of that day and as such would not benefit from a stern talking-to—always put on their PJs.

Years of practice had made Kevin a master at avoiding his mother's attention. Sometimes he thought he should publish a book on the subject—under a pseudonym, of course. He didn't want his mother or Jesus to catch him.

As he settled into bed and closed his eyes, a warm, familiar arm settled across his chest and a gentle hand reached up to caress his cheek. "When I heard you were coming back, I almost couldn't believe it." Her voice was like silk, soft and smooth and welcoming.

Kevin rolled to his left and took the slender woman in his arms. As usual, she wasn't wearing anything. She sighed as he traced a finger down her smooth back and grabbed a handful of her soft ass.

"I missed you too, Nella."

Kevin must've fallen asleep as soon as his head hit the pillow. Nella was not real; her visits were a recurring dream he'd had since his teenage years. Oddly enough, it was a dream he'd only ever had in that bed. Never had he dreamed of Nella while napping on the couch, while staying with friends, while living in his college dormitory, or while working and living in Chicago. He'd given up trying to explain it long ago.

Definitely something in the fucking water. Something really fucking potent. Whatever it was had made Nella absolutely gorgeous, but also blue from head to toe, with glittering silver eyes, hair blacker than the surrounding night, and a set of gills that flared open in her neck when she came. He didn't know what his subconscious was trying to tell him with this one and he wasn't sure he really wanted to know.

Her eyes twinkling in the darkness, Nella leaned in for a kiss. Sparks flared in Kevin's mind as her supple lips caressed his own. He pulled her closer, letting the feel of her wash him clear out of Harksburg and onto another plane of existence.

So what if she was blue and a figment of his imagination? Kevin wasn't about to reject this: Harksburg's most redeeming quality.

— CHAPTER THREE —

Wakey wakey!"
Abelia Felton's high-pitched screech jolted Kevin out of a deep sleep. A list of sounds that would've been subtler tumbled through his groggy mind: the failing brakes of a semi truck careening down a steep grade, a family of squirrels dying screaming deaths in the blade of a riding mower, Doorknob's anxious pleas that someone let him out of his locker, a thousand sets of nails dragged down a chalkboard. Subtle, unfortunately, had run screaming from his mother's personality a long, long time ago.

Despite a throbbing headache, Kevin opened his eyes to a riot of color. At first, his vision blurred by sleep and alcohol, he thought he was looking at some twisted artist's rendering of a melting clown. As the image solidified, its pink cheeks gaining depth, its ruby red lips defining an impassable boundary around too-white teeth, its deep brown eyes framed in blue shadow and long, flowery lashes, Kevin realized what was looming over him: his mother.

This, he thought, *must be what Jim Bakker woke up to every damn day.*

"Up and at 'em, sunshine!" his mother squealed with glee. "The Lord has delivered unto us another day. Let's not waste it!"

"G'morning, Ma," he muttered, lest he receive a reminder on the importance of manners.

She swung herself off the bed, straightened her turquoise suit and skirt, and clasped her hands at her waist. Round but not overweight, Abelia was built like a fire hydrant: sturdy, low to the ground, and brightly colored. It always amazed Kevin how her hair, bleached blond and rolled into tight curls on either side of her cheeks, never, ever moved. It reminded him of a roof. Whether its unshakeable stability was thanks to gel or Jesus, he wasn't sure.

"Good morning, Poofy!" Kevin had been Poofy for as long as he could remember. He hated being Poofy. "Hurry and get dressed! Two of your friends are waiting for you upstairs!"

He sat up, stifling a groan, and checked the big red numbers on the digital alarm clock atop the nightstand: 9:34. Too damn early. "Tell them I'll be right up. Who is it?"

"That delightful Roberts boy and your economics teacher from college, Professor Driff."

Kevin had never heard of a Professor Driff, let alone taken a class with him, but he hid his confusion. Over the years, Ren had honed a particular talent at inventing identities for individuals that wouldn't pass Mrs. Felton's muster. He'd once slipped a pair of strippers past her by claiming they were undercover police officers being interviewed for a school project. Professor Driff was likely either Ren's new drug dealer, a pro-choice activist, or a Jew—all insufferable failures of character in Abelia's mind.

"Driff was one of my favorites. I'll be up shortly."

"Well, be quick about it! It's impolite to leave your guests waiting." Abelia paused for a moment, and when she continued it was at a slower pace, her words dripping with melodramatic warning. "Favorite or not, this Professor Driff gives me a bad vibe. You know how good my intuition is."

Abelia could spot Satanists, Mormons, evolutionary biologists, and many other species of heathen from miles away. Her great ability to identify and avoid associating with the wrong people was a blessing she truly cherished and never hesitated to brag about. Ren had found it very useful in locating loose women. Every Tuesday night he drove Kevin's mother to the grocery store. Ren pushed the cart and took careful mental notes about every harlot, tramp, and two-bit hussy Abelia pointed out. He'd had great luck with the two-bit hussies.

"All college professors are a little off," Kevin said as he swung himself out of bed. His stomach promptly executed a triple backflip, but he managed to resist the urge to vomit. "He's just another flaky liberal."

His mother put her hands on her hips and harrumphed, signaling that she still didn't like this Professor Driff character and, although she wouldn't go so far as to expel him from her home, she'd be watching him like a hawk. That was the best Kevin could've hoped for.

He covered the three steps from his bed to the adjoining bathroom in half a breath. "I'll be up after I shower!" he called to his mother as he shut and locked the door. The sudden motion set his stomach back into its gymnastics routine and he gasped hungrily for air to delay the bile threatening to explode up his throat. The thin door didn't stand a chance against puke noises, so he reached over and turned on the shower. The first splash of water cascaded onto the vinyl floor with a heavy crash just as Kevin turned and vomited into the sink.

That bathroom had saved Kevin from many a tongue-lashing. Small and a bit cramped by bathroom standards, it nonetheless included a pedestal sink, a toilet, and a narrow shower. The tile floor was cold, it needed a fresh coat of white paint, the crapper occasionally flushed on its own, and keeping the silverfish at bay was a constant battle, but its distance from the parts of the house Abelia inhabited made it a great place for rinsing away any and all evidence of wrongdoing. In that cozy little room, Kevin had hidden women, disposed of alcohol, washed temporary dye out of his hair, and secreted away a live badger—Buddy, Harksburg High's official mascot. He and that bathroom had been through a lot together, and he counted it as one of his best and most reliable friends.

He spat the last tangle of viscous bile into the sink and washed it away, marveling at how what had been a mixture of beer, scotch, and cheap hot dogs somehow came back out tasting like gin. Maybe Kylie was right; maybe twenty-seven was too old for drinking and carousing. But that couldn't be right, because she was a two-timing gold-digger and her opinion didn't count, even if it happened to be correct—perhaps especially if it happened to be correct. Examining himself in the cracked mirror above the sink, Kevin was pleased to find that he was still just as tall, blond, and blue-eyed as he'd always been. Partying had yet to ruin his slightly above average looks, which meant it was probably all right to keep doing it for awhile longer yet.

As Kevin undressed, piling his clothes atop the toilet seat in case any of the silverfish decided to take a morning stroll, he wondered what could've possessed Ren to come calling at such an early hour. Certainly, his friend was just as hung over. Maybe Ren wanted to confirm with Kevin that he'd also seen the strange incident with Oscar and Doorknob the previous evening—but he could've done that with a simple phone call, so why the visit? And who the hell was this Professor Driff?

Kevin hadn't expected his return to Harksburg to be this complicated. In no condition to think about things further, he wiped it all from his mind and climbed into the warm shower.

— CHAPTER FOUR —

K evin blanched violently when he met Professor Driff.
"G-g-good to see you again, sir," he stammered as his
fingers were crushed in a hard, firm handshake.

"Likewise. I'm glad life seems to be treating you well," replied
the strange man who'd scared the shit out of Kevin in the woods
the night before. He wore the same long black overcoat, but this
time the tops of his ears were round. Had Kevin imagined that
pointy bit?

Ren sat on the far side of the long dining room table, wearing
a smug smile Kevin wanted to scrape off of his face with a power
washer. He wore a tweed suit over a crisp white shirt. Wide-eyed
and alert, nothing in his bearing betrayed any lingering effects
from last night's activities.

Kevin and Driff took their seats at the table as Abelia trundled
in with a silver tray loaded with coffee and scones. "So, what
brings you to our fair town, Professor Driff?" she asked as she set
a steaming mug in front of each man.

Driff pushed his spectacles up on his nose and examined the
family pictures hanging on the nearest wall. "I've come to offer
your son a job."

Kevin almost choked on his mouthful of coffee. "A job?"

"A research position." Driff's attention had turned to the array of tiny Jesus figurines arranged atop a nearby hutch. He wrinkled his nose. "I'm investigating a rash of strange incidents in the Harksburg area. I've already retained the services of your friend Mr. Roberts, but I could use the assistance of one more good man."

"He pays promptly," Ren said in between mouthfuls of scone, "and he pays very well."

Kevin's mother regarded Driff with narrow eyes. "There can't possibly be anything worth investigating in our humble town, Professor."

Driff fixed Abelia with a steely gaze that seemed designed to expel her from the room, but she held fast. "Have there been any unexplained or otherwise notable deaths around here lately?" he asked.

Kevin froze. He'd seen two last night, prior to this strange man's first appearance, but the deaths of Oscar and Doorknob hadn't—for lack of a better term—stuck. Maybe those didn't count. He doubted it. So did his stomach, which threatened to leap back into action with a bone-rattling gurgle.

"Why, no," Abelia replied. "Harksburg hasn't seen a murder or a suicide in years, and that's the way we like it!"

Driff rolled his eyes—a dangerous move in front of Kevin's mother—and took a quick sip of coffee. "Nothing odd about the obituaries in the paper lately?"

"Seems the Lord is smiling on our little slice of Illinois," Abelia chirped proudly. "I read the *County Ledger* every morning. There hasn't been an obituary published since Sunday."

Driff locked his icy gaze on Kevin and smiled.

Sunday. Three days ago. The day before Kevin moved home. Surely that was just a coincidence. Surely whatever the hell was going on wasn't all his fault.

Surely this was all a giant crock of shit.

"No fucking way," he muttered.

"Kevin!" his mother hissed. "Language!"

"You saw it with your own two eyes," Driff said, "and the effect isn't limited to your idiot friends."

"He's telling the truth," Ren said between mouthfuls of scone. "Nobody in the county can die."

"That's impossible," Kevin snapped. He turned to Ren. "I can't believe you're buying this guy's bullshit."

Kevin's mother slapped him on the back of the head. "Language!"

Across the table, Driff sighed. "Well. In that case, let's just cut to the chase."

Suddenly, there was a revolver in Driff's hand, a silver six-shooter with a long barrel. Kevin never heard the sound of the shot or his mother's ensuing scream. A brief flash of pain signaled the bullet's impact with his forehead before the projectile ripped through his brain and put an abrupt end to all sensation. The force of the shot sent him careening backward toward the floor, taking the chair with him.

When Kevin's faculties returned a few moments later, he found himself staring down at his own corpse. Blood and brains oozed out in an expanding puddle around his head. The bullet must've passed clean through the back side of his skull. He looked oddly serene, he thought, for a man with a pair of holes in his cranium. Kevin himself felt weightless and buoyant, as if he were floating on the sea. Every nerve in his body burned red hot, but somehow it was comforting rather than painful. He felt free.

"Do you always have to be so fucking dramatic about that?" Ren asked Driff angrily. He took another bite of scone and washed it down with the rest of his coffee. "Do you know how much that fucking hurts?"

Driff stashed the revolver inside his coat. "I wouldn't have to keep doing this if you stupid humans weren't so stubborn about what is and isn't possible."

Abelia was on her hands and knees at his corpse's side, then, sobbing and praying and damning Driff to hell.

Fuck, Kevin thought. *I'm dead.*

That revelation brought forth a cascade of emotion—fear, anger, and a sensation of loss so profound it defied words. Kevin didn't want to be dead. He really, really didn't want to be dead. He'd never not wanted anything so much in his entire life. It overwhelmed his senses and his thought processes, wiping away Driff and Ren and Abelia and everything else in the room that hadn't once been a part of Kevin. Reaching out with every fiber of his spirit, he gathered up every drop of blood and fragment of bone and chunk of brain, willed it all back into his skull, and pulled with all of his might.

The world went black again.

Kevin sat up with a ragged gasp, choking for air and willing his blurry vision to solidify and his ears to stop ringing.

"Welcome back," Ren said nonchalantly.

Abelia swooned and fainted.

The healed entry and exit wounds were a bit warm to the touch, but otherwise Kevin seemed to be intact. A small trickle of blood disappearing into his fingers was the only evidence of the gore in which he'd laid. The hardwood wasn't even discolored.

"My hangover's gone," he muttered incredulously. It took a moment for reality to sink in. "You fucking shot me!"

Driff nodded. "Do I need to do it again, or have I proven my point?"

Kevin took a deep breath, fighting the urge to throttle the strange man. "Fine. So no one around here can die. Why?"

"We intelligent creatures are not good at dying," Driff said slowly. He grabbed a scone, took a bite, then ostentatiously spat it out on the floor—obviously not even tasting it. "We understand what it means, and in almost every case we are unable to accept it. Free will is a powerful thing, as you just experienced, and properly directed it can heal any wound. Obviously, the world would get a bit crowded if we were all allowed to live forever. That's where the reapers come in: distributed across the globe in strictly defined territories, they help us come to terms with death so we can let go and make room for the next generation."

Kevin couldn't believe the words coming out of Driff's mouth. His story was fucking insane. Death was a natural part of life; it was simple biology, the ultimate and unstoppable destiny of a body too old or too damaged to function. It was logical and rational and just flat out made sense. There wasn't anything supernatural about it.

Applying that line of reasoning to what he'd just experienced, however, left Kevin frustrated and a bit frightened. Logic and reason couldn't explain how he'd willed himself back to life. Nor could they explain how Doorknob had survived a broken neck or how Oscar had lived through several instances of being impaled on the same pitchfork. He wasn't naïve enough to think that science had taught humanity everything there was to know about the world, but he also had never been one to accept something new without solid proof.

He hated to admit it, but solid proof had blown his brains out all over the floor and then tucked them back inside his skull and patched up the holes.

"So," he said, putting together the pieces of Driff's explanation, "the local reaper isn't doing his job."

Ren clapped sarcastically. Driff nodded. "Word on the street is that it's got something to do with a woman named Nella. A different word on that same street says you know this Nella very, very well."

Kevin felt the blood drain from his face. Nella was a figment of his horny young male imagination. Or was she? Could she be real? That could explain why he only ever encountered her here in Harksburg. Kevin wouldn't have thought it possible the day before—but he hadn't died and resurrected himself the day before, either.

"I'll take the job," he said. All of this weird shit was intriguing, and at the very least it would be better than sitting around at home and feeling sorry for himself. "When do I start?"

"Right now," Driff said. "We're going to see Nella."

— CHAPTER FIVE —

Before they left, Driff checked on Abelia.

"You!" she snapped when the smelling salts brought her around.

Driff sighed and rolled his eyes. "Yeah. Me."

"You shot my boy! The Lord Jesus as my witness, I swear upon Peter, Mary, and all the Corinthians that I shall not rest until the proper authorities have locked you—"

Driff dropped a handful of silver dust into Abelia's face. She inhaled it with a heavy snort. Her eyes rolled back in her head, exposing their white undersides, and her body suddenly went rigid.

"No," Driff said calmly. "I did not shoot Kevin Felton. The four of us had a perfectly civil bit of brunch. I made a great first impression and you're excited that your son is going to be working with me. I'm not carrying a sidearm, I did not shoot anyone, Kevin did not come back from the dead because he was never dead in the first place, and from now on you're going to use buttermilk or yogurt in your scones so they don't have the texture of a pile of sawdust."

Kevin wanted to protest that his mother's scones were, in fact, fucking delicious, but he worried that any sort of attempt to interact with her would negatively impact the spell under which Driff had placed her.

Abelia's eyes righted themselves. She blinked a few times and looked to Driff, obviously confused. "Professor? What am I doing on the floor?"

Gone was the emotional maelstrom of watching her son get shot in her own dining room. When Abelia looked at Kevin, she did so without worry or suspicion.

Fuck me, Kevin thought. *He wiped her memories.*

"You had a nasty fall," Driff replied, his tone surprisingly concerned. "You hit the back of your head pretty hard."

She accepted Driff's hand and let him pull her to her feet. "It doesn't feel like I hit my head…"

"Lucky. You must've landed just right." He smiled unconvincingly, as if he hadn't gotten much practice lately.

"Damn elves always forget the details," Ren muttered under his breath.

Kevin bit his tongue. Elves? First people who can't die, then reapers, then Nella, and now elves? This was getting to be too much. He kept his mouth shut, though. Driff clearly wanted to keep Abelia in the dark, and Kevin didn't want him giving her any more of that silver dust.

He waited until the three of them were safely inside Ren's green Jaguar before speaking up. "You're a fucking elf?" he shouted from the backseat. Noticing the red welt on his forehead in the rearview mirror, Kevin leaned forward and touched it gently. The place where he'd been shot was tender, but it didn't hurt much.

Driff leaned around the passenger seat to face his accuser and rubbed each of his ears in turn. The pointy tips Kevin thought he'd noticed in the Works became visible once more.

"Don't ask me about Santa's workshop unless you want to get shot again."

Driff spoke with such malice that Kevin flinched. He forced himself to recover quickly. Showing any weakness to his strange new employer seemed like it would be a mistake. "Fine," he snapped, "but don't you fucking dare do whatever the hell it was you just did to my mother ever again! Not to her, not to me, not to Ren, not to anybody in fucking Harksburg!"

Ren snickered and turned the key in the ignition. The Jag came to life with a soft purr and rolled out onto Main Street. Kevin had always liked Ren's car. The heated seats were great in the winter, the interior was always spotless and the ride always smooth, and it attracted more easy girls than a movie star with a bucket of top shelf cocaine. Ren could be a ridiculous prick sometimes, but the perks of being best friends with the richest kid in town more than made up for it.

Driff, meanwhile, took a few seconds to consider his response. Kevin counted that as a victory. "The narii dust is a necessary part of my people's existence," the elf explained. He sounded almost embarrassed. "It protects us, and others as well, by hiding memories that might otherwise lead to unwanted repercussions."

Kevin decided to push his luck. "So, you're afraid of humans."

The elf's demeanor darkened. "My weapon carries six rounds. I've only used one today." He turned back around, putting a firm end to the conversation.

Kevin leaned back into the plush leather seat and took a deep breath. His return to Harksburg had taken a turn for the insane he never would've imagined. He'd been hoping to take a month or two to rest and recuperate and give himself time to miss the dog-eat-dog world of corporate finance before latching on with another big city company. Things so rarely went according to plan, however, as he'd realized after the buyout of and layoffs at Noonan, Noonan, and Schmidt, and so he felt like a bit of an idiot for expecting his time in Harksburg to be simple and quiet. Life was a lot of things, but simple and predictable weren't on that list.

Watching Harksburg roll past, he was struck by how little his hometown had changed. Sure, several of the businesses sported new names and owners and a few of the houses had been painted, but the community's aura remained the same as always. Harksburg was still an idyllic little postcard of a former frontier town that survived the winning of the West and mostly escaped the blight of industrial expansion. It was a place where people lived rather than worked, a place that wound up on lists in magazine sidebars with titles like "Best Towns to Raise Children" or "Top Ten Spots for Newlyweds!" The locals knew better, but no one ever asked them. Hiding behind the town's pretty façade and above-average school system lurked a bitter, isolationist streak that all of the residents decried but which none of them was willing to take responsibility for.

The Jag rounded the town common, an acre of boring grass and pretentious granite benches ringed with aged Victorian homes. Kevin leaned forward. "Ren, what smells like shit?"

Driff, busily cleaning his spectacles with a soft blue cloth, answered before Ren could. "The bags of garbage in the trunk."

Ren groaned and shook his head. "And so I ask you again: is that really necessary?"

"As necessary as a bullet between the eyes," the elf replied with an evil smirk.

Kevin ignored him. "So…uh…about Nella…"

Driff chuckled. "You don't honestly think the neighbors didn't see her sneaking in and out of this Pussy Hatch of yours, do you?"

"I…I didn't think she was real," Kevin stammered. He wanted to slap Ren; no one else knew what he'd named that window. Why was his friend so buddy-buddy with Driff? Kevin and Ren had been thicker than thieves since their first day of preschool. They grew up together and they'd always looked out for each other. Hearing something he'd told to Ren in confidence come out of Driff's mouth felt like a huge betrayal. What other secrets had he given away? Perhaps more importantly...what power did the elf hold over him?

Driff harrumphed. Ren snickered.

"Oh, next you're going to tell me my neighbor's a fucking troll!"

"Mr. Gregson is a pixie, actually," Driff corrected. "Your neighbor hates the rest of his kind, but he can't afford a better disguise. Functional limbs don't come cheap."

Kevin tried his best to picture fat, old, wheelchair-bound Mr. Gregson as a tiny man with wings and failed miserably. Surely Driff was fucking with him. Surely.

Ren turned north, guiding the Jag onto Sleeper Street. Here the homes were newer and further apart, the lots separated by thick woods. This was the part of town where the young couples sucked in by the magazine sidebars bit off pieces of the ancient deciduous forest so they could bulldoze everything in sight and drag the land kicking and screaming into the twenty-first century. Landscapers twisted the earth into gently rolling hills and replaced the native elms, oaks, and maples with slender foreign species with unpronounceable names. The grass looked too lush and too green to be real, the driveways blacker and smoother than any asphalt had a right to be. Lording over each plot stood a modern home, typically something glassy wrapped in some sort of vinyl or faux wood or fake stone and topped with strange roof lines. The locals called this area Plastic Hill; they did not use that nickname as a term of endearment.

"So, Driff—what's your interest in all this?" Kevin asked. "Don't tell me you're some kind of concerned citizen."

"I am, in fact, the leading investigator for an entire society of concerned citizens. We elves intervene whenever things get weird, contentious, or violent between the various forces and civilizations in the world. We keep the peace."

Kevin had always been skeptical of those who claimed to be altruistic. In his experience, such individuals and organizations all harbored some sort of secret desire or goal furthered by their good deeds. "What do you get in return?"

"As a people? A safer, slightly less screwed up world in which to live. Personally? Advancement up the sociopolitical ladder and a warm, fuzzy feeling."

"That's probably just gas," Ren said.

Ignoring his friend's stupid joke, Kevin continued his interrogation. "But why haven't I heard of you elves before? Or of these reapers or pixies or people like Nella?"

"You understand what I did to your mother, right? The whole memory wipe thing? That's why."

"That's not why. That's how. Answer my question: why?"

"Because most of us look at humans, both collectively and individually, as immature, short-sighted pains in the ass, and those in charge have decided you can't be allowed at the grown-ups' table."

Kevin didn't like the sound of that. "Bullshit. If the things you're doing affect us, we should get a say in them."

"In principle, I agree with you. In practice—can you imagine how difficult it would be to coordinate with every single one of your countries, religions, organizations, and interests? There are too many of you with too many diverse priorities. Often decisions must be made quickly; there wouldn't be time to make sure no one's toes get stepped on, that everyone felt their oh-so-important voice was heard. It wouldn't work.

"And then imagine what would happen when things go wrong. Your kind is terrible at evaluating risk and too good at assigning blame. One mistake and we're the bad guy—we're different, after all, and that makes it easy to cast us as villains, terrorists, heathens, or whatever threat-to-your-way-of-life happens to be in vogue at the moment. That probably wouldn't go very well for us."

Scratching his chin, Kevin considered Driff's words. His assertion that humanity was anything but a coherent whole certainly couldn't be refuted. Nor did his people have a sparkling record when it came to dealing with others who looked even a little bit different. Some would surely react violently to the sudden emergence of pixies or elves or whatever the hell Nella was—and those were the things Kevin knew were out there.

"It still doesn't sound right."

"What good is doing the right thing if it gets our civilization wiped off the map?" Driff asked. "Sometimes the right thing isn't the smart thing. Sometimes you have to settle for what sucks the least for everybody involved."

"That's a bit defeatist."

"It's for the best," Ren chimed in. "These people don't fuck around." He spoke as if he had first-hand experience with the subject. Kevin wondered again if there was more than there seemed to his friend's relationship with Driff and "these people."

"What the hell makes you an expert on the subject?"

Ren didn't answer. Instead, his sharp blue eyes drifted up to the rearview mirror to warn Kevin that it was time to drop the topic. He'd have to follow up with Ren in private, where pointy elven ears couldn't hear.

"Fine," Kevin grumbled, turning his attention to the window. "Leave me in the dark. Let's get this shit over with."

A wide turn brought the vehicle to a steep incline. Ahead and below, the forest gave way to a sprawling Midwestern plain bisected by a ribbon of sparkling blue: the Miller River. Once Harksburg's lifeline to the rest of the state and beyond, many of the old wooden buildings and rickety docks which used to service the steamboats of old still stood, fading reminders of a simpler age. Now, the land along the river was a game preserve held in trust by the town. Third graders at Harksburg Elementary learned all about the great industrialist who'd generously bequeathed the land to the community. Kevin couldn't recall the dude's name, but he'd never forget the man's awesomely bushy mustache.

Ren turned right down a dirt road that snaked along the base of the hill and back toward the center of town.

"Nella lives in the Works?" Kevin asked, surprised. He wasn't sure where he expected someone like Nella to live, but an industrial complex abandoned halfway through construction definitely didn't feel right. Kevin had been attending parties in the Works since his sixteenth birthday, not long before his first nighttime encounter with the woman he'd thought was just a dream. Had Nella been watching from the shadows all those drunken, hazy nights? Was that where she'd first spotted him?

"There's a lagoon just beyond the Works," Driff said. "That's where she makes her home."

Kevin knew the spot. Fornication Point, the townies called it, a secluded overlook above a serene pool in the Miller to which lovers and drunken hook-ups often headed during keggers in the Works. Apropos that Nella made her home there.

What the hell am I going to say to her? he wondered. She'd deceived him for years, and although he wasn't happy about that, he didn't want to drive her away. They'd had a lot of fun together, but their relationship was more than physical; he'd always felt a strong connection to Nella, stronger than he'd felt with a lot of women he knew for a fact were real—Kylie included. Letting his guard down around Nella had always been easy. He had thought she was a dream, after all, and dreams didn't exactly go spreading secrets around town.

Kevin wiped his sweaty palms on his jeans. Nerves. That didn't happen often, but he'd already seen stranger things that morning—and he was sure things were going to get even stranger before the day was done.

— CHAPTER SIX —

"F uture site of Harrison Co. Metal Works," proclaimed the black and white sign hanging limply from the rusted gate. Below that was a second sign, smaller and newer, that read "No trespassing." Underneath, an intrepid artist of great skill and cultural refinement had spray-painted a huge penis. Kevin would've known Waltman's handiwork anywhere; at one point that schlong had adorned the cover of pretty much every textbook in Harksburg High.

Ren left the car idling a few feet away and clambered out. The worst-kept secret in town was the $200 the police force charged for a copy of the key to the Works. Ever the shrewd businessman, Ren had talked Flanagan down to $50 and a date with Lily Walker, whom the officer had been in love with since sixth grade. Ren made it happen—he always paid his debts—and during the resulting seafood dinner with his beloved, Flanagan passed out from nervousness and shat all over himself. He and Lily had been together ever since and were engaged to be married the following May.

"It was cute," Lily explained to Kevin once. "He'd always been this big, tough, responsible guy—and there he was, reduced to a vulnerable, quivering puddle because I touched his hand."

Waltman maintained that Lily's interest in Flanagan resulted from a scat fetish. Whenever this theory was broached in Flanagan's presence, the burly officer just smiled and winked.

Ren unlocked the gate and pulled it open. The locals who hung out in the Works had taken good care of the gate, keeping its hinges clean and lubricated and even replacing them when necessary. It moved easily and freely without squealing or squeaking. When it's time to party, it's time to party—not fight with some broken gate.

"Why did the town leave this place to rot?" Driff asked.

"Locking it up and pretending it doesn't exist is cheaper than cleaning it out," Kevin replied. "Harrison leased the land from the town because Harksburg wouldn't sell it outright. The lease was terminated when the company declared bankruptcy."

The elf grunted. "Evitankari—where I'm from—would never leave something like this lying around."

"Good for Evitankari."

Driff ignored Kevin's snappy comeback. "We elves never waste anything we can find a use for."

"We aren't wasting the Works. On any given weekend, there are at least three keggers in here somewhere."

"My mistake. Surely this place is a jewel of your society."

Ren climbed back into the Jaguar and drove through the open gate. "I hope you two are behaving yourselves."

"Just discussing a few cultural differences. You missed quite the riveting debate," Kevin replied sarcastically. Driff snorted.

On the other side of the gate, Ren once again stopped the car and climbed out. He pulled the gate shut and locked it. There were two unwritten rules regarding the Works: lock the gate behind you, and don't light any fires big enough to be spotted from the street unless you're friends with the cop on duty and offer him a few beers. Visitors typically adhered to these rules. After all, if the cops didn't have reason to investigate the Works, they'd never find Waltman's plot of marijuana or the mushrooms he grew in the basement of one of the outbuildings, and that was in everybody's best interests.

Job done, Ren got back behind the wheel and eased the car forward. Harrison had never gotten around to paving the access road, so the Jag trundled slowly over dirt and stone and patches of brown grass. Towering oaks and elms loomed on either side, their branches trimmed back to allow the passing of larger vehicles. Not for the first time, Kevin wondered exactly what Harrison had seen in this location. It wasn't near any major highways or rail lines, and clearing the forest certainly hadn't been cheap. Word on the street was that the CEO had leased the land for a song thanks a few under-the-table deals with various members of the local government. Kevin knew better than to implicitly trust town gossip, but he'd heard enough of it to know that it usually contained a grain or two of truth.

The dirt road soon dumped them into a sprawling construction site, a work of human ingenuity frozen in time. To their left stood a row of six management trailers, rickety white and blue metal boxes with tiny windows. Riddled with bullet holes of all shapes and sizes, the nearest trailer was a favorite practice target for hunters heading off into the surrounding forest and for drunk idiots who wanted to show off the armaments their idiot parents had left unlocked. Kevin himself had sent a bottle rocket screaming and twisting through one of its windows years ago. To their right, like the rib cage of some long-dead behemoth, the naked superstructure that would've been the main factory of Harrison Co. Metal Works towered above it all. Pairs of steel posts as big around as Ren's Jaguar sprang up from the concrete slab in parallel every ten feet or so to support heavy girders perched twenty feet above. Graffiti covered the cross beams, a chronicle of every class to graduate Harksburg High in the fifteen years since construction was abruptly halted. Smaller outbuildings, simple metal squares in various states of completion, surrounded the main building like worker ants waiting to serve a larger queen.

Driff looked around with obvious distaste. "I'll never understand other species' need to vandalize any object that isn't under constant surveillance."

Kevin shrugged. "It's fun."

"That's what the gnomes say, too."

"Gnomes?"

"Ever had things randomly go missing or end up mysteriously broken? Your TV set to an input you never use? Your cords or cables twisted into a frustrating tangle? Pieces inexplicably missing from board games or puzzles? Then you've got gnomes. They live for that kind of thing."

"I *always* put the toilet paper on the roll so the next sheet goes over the top," Ren said. "Once I found a half-used roll with the next sheet going under."

"Gnomes," Driff said sagely, as if that explained it all.

"I know," Ren replied. "We had to gas the little fuckers. Haven't had any problems in years."

Kevin merely nodded. Gnomes. Surely Driff was fucking with him again. Surely.

Ren drove to the far side of the construction site and parked in his usual spot, underneath the boughs of a gnarled elm where the natural canopy could protect his vehicle from the ravages of the sun. He didn't have to worry about birds; most avian wildlife had learned that venturing too close to the Works was a great way to get shot. They all climbed out of the car and stretched.

"Get the garbage," Driff instructed.

"My pleasure," Ren replied. He popped the trunk and removed two big black bags stuffed full of rancid something-or-other. Flies assaulted him almost immediately. "Take this," he said, shoving a bag into Kevin's arms. Kevin gingerly shifted the bag into a loose grip and extended it far away from his body. It smelled worse than Flanagan must have on his first date with Lily.

"What the hell is this?" he asked.

"Garbage," Driff deadpanned.

"Specifically, that is a bag of garbage from the bottom of the dumpster behind the Burg," Ren replied, swatting away a fly that dared buzz too close to his face.

The Harksburg Bar and Grill—the Burg—prided itself on being the town's most popular eating and drinking establishment. That didn't mean a heck of a lot, given its status as the only sit-down restaurant in town, but that didn't stop Fran Kesky—owner, operator, bartender, and bouncer—from plastering it all over the Burg's awnings and menus. The Burg was the place to go when there was nothing better to eat at home, when the restaurants in the surrounding towns seemed too far away, or when frustrating constipation became too much to bear.

"Why did you have to go all the way to the Burg for garbage? Don't you have any of your own?" Kevin asked.

"I wanted the most vile, disgusting garbage in town," the elf explained.

Ren smiled mischievously.

Driff led them into the woods, taking the familiar path that would bring the trio to the scene of the previous evening's mayhem—and where Kevin had first met his mysterious employer. Fornication Point was maybe a tenth of a mile beyond that. Not a bad walk on a crisp, sunny autumn day.

"Hey, Driff! How much am I getting paid?" Kevin asked.

The elf didn't bother looking back. "Enough."

"How much is enough?"

"It's enough that you should shut your mouth and carry the damn garbage lest I decide a salary adjustment is in order."

The damn garbage was heavier than it looked—too heavy to carry at arm's length. Kevin had no choice but to shift it underneath his arm. He hoped it wouldn't leak all over him. If it did, he knew exactly which of his two companions would be getting a great big hug.

He and Ren were both breathing heavily ten minutes later when they reached the bulldozer and the slab of rock from which Oscar had proclaimed his immortality. The only evidence of the previous evening's activity was the pile of ashes in the fire pit. Doorknob always made sure he took all the empties so he could turn them in. Kevin eyed the bulldozer. No one quite knew how it had gotten here; there wasn't a path through the forest wide enough to admit a piece of equipment that size. He'd always wondered if maybe it had been airlifted in and deposited in the wrong place. Now he found himself searching the shadows in the surrounding woods for signs of gnome activity. Not that he really knew what to look for.

Several trails led away from the clearing in various directions. Driff steered them onto the northern fork, the best route to their destination. The elf certainly had done his homework.

"So…we've got reapers, elves, gnomes, and pixies. Anything else I should know about?" Kevin asked. He'd decided that bothering Driff with endless questions was good sport.

"Trolls, gnolls, dryads, vampires, werewolves, various species of nymphs, kobolds, Sasquatch, gremlins, ogres, unicorns, goblins, merfolk, demons—"

"Demons?" Kevin interrupted, bored with Driff's list.

"Demons," Driff affirmed.

"Nasty buggers," Ren added.

"Does that mean there's a hell or some similar place where they live?"

The elf shook his head but didn't look back. "The hell they inhabit is this very earth. When it comes to evil, you humans are like giant batteries. You can store a ton of it. Every vicious, selfish, horrible thing you do adds to your overall level of darkness. Build up too much and it takes over."

"Is there a way I can check my...err...level? Is there a meter or something?"

"Try shoving a dipstick up your ass," Ren suggested.

If Driff thought that was funny, he didn't let it show. "Do you feel evil?" he asked.

"I feel a little naughty," Kevin replied.

"That's normal."

Kevin took a moment to consider the elf's explanation, mentally listing all the bad things he'd ever done. He got depressed and gave up when his list became longer than Driff's litany of nonhuman species. Cheating on a math test in fourth grade hadn't really been evil, had it? What about convincing Doorknob his date to the spring semi-formal had syphilis? He immediately winced at the thought. He could almost feel his evil meter spiking a couple of percentage points.

The incline of the trail increased. Fornication Point awaited them at the top of the next rise. Though the weight of the garbage under his arm left him gasping for breath, Kevin didn't let up. "And then what? When the evil takes over, I mean."

"Depends on the individual and the nature of his or her sins. Most change shape radically, their features twisted by the vile energy they've embraced. Some gain the use of powerful magic— really black, dangerous stuff. Left unchecked, they go violently insane. That rarely happens nowadays, most demons are fully functional members of society who, with the assistance of their peers and families, keep their darker impulses in check. Most facilitate evil rather than engaging in it directly. Less chance of slipping into a murderous rage that way. You probably know a few."

Ren stumbled but quickly regained his balance. Kevin eyed his friend suspiciously. That private conversation couldn't come soon enough.

"But how do they keep themselves hidden? A demon would really stand out at parent-teacher night. A troll even more so."

"Magic," Driff replied. "Typically, nonhumans wear cloaking talismans whenever they're in your midst. In extreme cases, we apply the narii dust liberally to remove any memories that might complicate relations."

"That's the crap you threw at my mother?"

"Exactly."

Cresting the rise, they came upon arguably the prettiest view in Harksburg. The rocky ledge known as Fornication Point overlooked a crystal clear pool twenty feet directly below. Beyond, the Miller River snaked away through a lush forest before it split a set of rolling hills and disappeared into the horizon.

Driff strolled right up to the edge of the cliff, hands in the pockets of his long overcoat. Kevin somehow fought the urge to shove him into the lagoon. "Nella!" the elf called out nonchalantly. "I've come to have a few words with you!"

His voice echoed out and through the basin below. There was no response.

"Fine," he snapped. "We'll do this the hard way." He turned to Ren and Kevin. "Gentlemen, place the bags of garbage at my feet and open them up."

The two friends did as they were told, tearing away the knots at the top of their respective bags. Both flinched at the putrid smell and took a few quick steps back. The stench—that of rancid eggs mixed with piss and garnished with a few dollops of sour milk—reminded Kevin of an omelet he'd once had at the Burg. Ren must've snagged the remains of a week-old breakfast rush.

Kevin's pulse raced with anticipation. Nella was there, he could feel it. The lover of his dreams would soon be revealed as a real, live woman. But how was Driff going to draw her out of hiding? The elf would have to use magic, Kevin decided. Driff was going to use the garbage at his feet to fuel some sort of summoning spell. There'd be eerie chanting and exploding sparks and wild columns of whirling energy. The earth would quiver with every unintelligible word Driff uttered. Frogs would suddenly rain down from the cloudless heavens. The bags of garbage would erupt in towering gouts of black flame, and then Nella would appear, beautiful as ever, chained to the rocks of Fornication Point by Driff's tremendous power.

It was going to be awesome. Kevin was sure of it.

The elf reached down into one of the bags with his bare hands, pulled out a handful of something that looked rather like regurgitated French toast, and tossed it over the edge. It landed in the lagoon with a soft plop.

To say that Kevin was disappointed would be a severe understatement. "What the hell was that?"

"A warning shot. There's more where that came from, Nella! Show yourself!"

The blue woman didn't appear. Driff threw handful after handful of nasty sludge over the edge of the cliff and down into the pool below. Pretty much anyone else, Kevin decided, would've looked like an absolute lunatic, but somehow the elf made the act of hurling disgusting garbage into a beautiful body of water serene and hypnotic. Every movement was deliberate and controlled, a picture of precision and efficiency. There was no malice in Driff's relentless littering, just cold purpose. It was business, plain and simple.

"You might want to wear some gloves," Ren suggested. Driff ignored him and kept working.

Giving the elf a wide berth, Kevin approached the edge of the cliff. Below, the desecrated pool bubbled and frothed as if someone had cranked up the heat. Chunks of garbage swirled, submerged, and surfaced like the ingredients in some horrific soup. Worried that this activity might be a personification of Nella's ire, Kevin took several steps back.

He did so just in time. A tremendous spire of water burst suddenly upward, hurling all the garbage in the lagoon back onto Fornication Point. Ren ran for cover behind the tree line. Kevin ducked and covered his head with his hands—and watched in awe as Driff shoved his hands in his pockets and stood stoically as he was pelted with sopping wet garbage.

That, Kevin thought as something squishy caromed off his shoulder, *is a bad motherfucker.*

"Fucking stop it!" Nella shrieked. Kevin looked up to find her perched atop the tower of water, a nude queen sitting cross-legged in her aquatic throne. She'd never looked more beautiful.

More importantly, she was real. Kevin's heart fluttered. He wanted to call out to her, but his breath caught in his throat.

Ren poked his head out around the tree he was hiding behind. "Nice work," he hissed at Kevin, keeping his voice low so the others wouldn't hear. "Isn't a man alive that wouldn't like to tap that."

"I am Council of Intelligence Driff, representing Evitankari in a matter of great import," the elf said as he wiped down his spectacles with a blue cloth. He didn't seem to care about the wad of tissue in his hair or the globules of discarded food stuck to his jacket.

"I swear no fealty to Luminad VIII of Talvayne and pay no heed to the Treaty of Wreb," Nella replied haughtily. "You have no jurisdiction in my lands."

"You have no lands nor titles that I recognize and I couldn't care less what you think of those I represent," Driff replied. "What I do care about are all these humans who won't die no matter where I shoot them. I hear you might know something about that."

She snorted. "You must be shooting them in the wrong places. Try right between the eyes."

Kevin found some of his voice. "He...uh...tried that."

Nella's lustrous silver eyes settled on Kevin for the first time since her dramatic entrance. When she recognized him, her entire bearing softened. Gone was the regal woman protecting her territory, replaced by a teenage girl who'd spotted her crush strolling into class. "Kevin?" she asked softly.

"Hi, Nella."

A tendril of water reached out from the spire and slapped Driff across the face with a sharp splash. The elf took the blow without flinching.

"You asshole!" Nella screamed at the elf. The gills in her neck flared angrily. "You didn't have to drag him into this!"

Driff shrugged. "Probably not, but if you would prefer I tell the local reaper you broke off your engagement for this stiff...that can certainly be arranged."

She shook her head and stepped forward onto Fornication Point. Behind her, the tower of water lost form and plummeted back into the lagoon with a thunderous splash. "That won't be necessary." Nella ignored Driff and walked purposefully to Kevin. "I guess it's time we discussed a few things."

That, he thought, was a severe understatement, but the best he could manage was a weak, "Okay."

Nella took Kevin's arm in hers and led him into the forest.

— CHAPTER SEVEN —

Neither Kevin nor Nella spoke as they made their way through the thick woods. The things they had to say to each other were private and Driff had big ears. A little distance would make them both more comfortable and give them time to organize their thoughts.

Kevin's mind was a chaotic whirl of questions. Never had he seen Nella's face sagging with melancholy, her bearing defeated. She'd always been so confident and carefree, but now she walked as if heading for the gallows. Seeing her in that state was a bit of a shock to Kevin's system. His thoughts raced even faster, searching for a means of addressing the issue at hand without being mean or nasty about it. The last thing he wanted to do was scare her off.

Is she in some sort of trouble? Kevin wondered. *Why did she pretend like she had no idea what was going on? Why was she so afraid that Driff would tell the reaper about us? Does she ever put on any damn clothes?*

And, perhaps most importantly, one question desperately repeated itself again and again, louder and more insistent than all the rest: *We can still be friends, right?*

They walked for fifteen minutes before stopping. Nella lead Kevin down into a sandy hollow beneath the boughs of a gnarled, towering oak tree. She sat gingerly upon a mossy log and rested her clenched hands atop her knees. Kevin remained standing.

"The first time I saw you was atop Fornication Point," she said softly, her eyes glued to the loose earth at her feet. "It was late at night. The moon was full. I remember it had a sort of blue aura around it, as if it were the center of a great flower. Three or four of your idiot friends were lined up along the edge of the cliff with their pants down around their ankles and their asses aimed at my lagoon. They thought it would be hilarious to all shit over the edge at once and listen to the sound their excrement made when it hit the water after falling thirty feet. You told them they were gross and stupid, and then you whacked one of them on his bare ass with a switch and chased them all off."

Kevin remembered that night—vaguely. There were mushrooms involved. He was glad to hear that he'd maintained a bit of dignity even while stoned out of his teenaged skull.

"I came to you the next night," she continued. "I know it sounds silly, but I wanted to reward you for having a heart. Pretty much all the people who visit my lagoon are giant fucking assholes. But not you. Not you. Each time I came to visit, you were so nice to me, and…well…I love my home, but it gets a bit lonely out here, so I kept going back for more."

When she didn't go on, Kevin spoke, "I didn't think you were real."

She smiled sadly and looked up at him for the first time. Tears streaked down her blue cheeks. "When did I say I wasn't?"

He smiled back. "Fair enough, but you could've at least given me some sort of hint."

She shook her head. "It wouldn't have made any difference. They put shit in the water supply to preemptively suppress any memories you humans have of our kind, and then they use the television and the radio to trigger it. If I had told you, you would've forgotten the next day—and you may have forgotten me altogether.

It was better that you thought I was a dream; they don't use the dust to erase dreams."

"Driff shot me," Kevin said. "After I...came back...he used some kind of dust to remove my mother's memory of it."

"Same stuff." She sniffled. "By the tides, those elves are a bunch of assholes."

"I haven't been impressed with the one I've met."

She hesitated before responding, clearly debating whether to give voice to the words in her mind. "Kevin, you should run. Get far away from here. If Billy catches word that I left him at the altar to be with you..."

He raised his eyebrows. "Billy? The reaper's name is *Billy*?" He'd been expecting something a bit more ominous, something long and vaguely Biblical.

Nella nodded. "He was human once. Now he's just cold and dead inside. I started seeing him two years after you left for college. Without you, it felt like a part of me was missing. There was a Kevin-shaped hole in my heart. Billy could relate. We hit it off, and..."

"And now, two years later, I'm back for more than just a holiday weekend."

"He's not doing his job right now, but if he finds out about you, he'll kill you—and it won't be pretty."

That explained Driff's threat. If the reaper killed the man who stole his fiancée, he might go right back to work. So why had the elf dragged Kevin out to the Works to see Nella instead of dropping him off on Billy's doorstep? Driff was certainly a no-nonsense kind of guy. It didn't make sense.

"I can't run. I don't have anywhere to go." He paused, gathering the confidence he needed for his next statement. He couldn't believe his words even though he knew them to be undeniably true. "And I don't want to leave. This morning, I wanted to get the hell out of Harksburg as soon as possible—but this morning, I thought you were just a dream."

Nella's face flushed an even darker shade of blue. "That's sweet, Kevin. It really is. But *they* will never let it happen."

He wasn't so sure of that. Ren seemed to know way too much about what was going on to have only learned about all these hidden fairy people just recently. Kevin suspected there was a way to counteract the narii dust and that his friend knew exactly what it was. "We'll cross that bridge when we get there. For now, we have to deal with Billy."

"How? I doubt even your elf friend has any experience with heartbroken avatars of death."

Kevin scratched his chin, thinking. "We'll find him someone new. Avatar of death or not, he's still male and he *was* human once. He'll never be completely over you until he finds someone new."

She shook her head. "That's the dumbest idea I've ever heard."

"It's brilliant, actually," Driff said, materializing to their right. He stood nonchalantly, hands in his pockets, as if he'd been a part of the conversation all along. The garbage that had covered him previously was gone, his coat somehow spotless. "Even if I served him Kevin's head on a silver platter—I've been considering that, by the way—he might still refuse to do his job. If we find a woman who can pull him out of his rut, that problem's solved."

"Fuck you!" Nella snapped at the elf. "Were you listening the entire time?"

"Most of it." Driff furrowed his brow. "Did you really think I wouldn't be?"

Kevin shrugged. He had a point. "We'll need Ren's help." If Ren could hook a loser like Flanagan up with a beauty like Lily, surely he could find someone for a reaper named Billy.

Driff nodded, his attention still on Nella. "We'll need to know where Billy is."

She glared at Kevin. "I can't believe you're considering this. I'm not going to let you walk right up to him so he can kill you. He's a reaper. He can pull your soul out through your nostrils and tear it up into a million tiny pieces."

"He doesn't know about our relationship," Kevin said, "and we're sure as hell not going to tell him."

"No," Nella said. "No way."

Driff shrugged and turned to go. "I'll get the other bag of garbage. I'll be back with a whole dumpster tomorrow."

"No!" Nella sprang to her feet, tidal waves roiling in her eyes. Kevin was glad he'd never made her angry. "Fine. I'll give you his address if you promise me that nothing will happen to Kevin." She extended her right hand for a handshake that would seal the deal.

The elf paused. He considered Nella's offer for what seemed like far too long. It was a simple enough promise to make—unless Driff had other plans in mind for Kevin's fate that he hadn't mentioned. "Deal."

He took Nella's hand then, and the blue woman pumped it three times with what seemed like enough force to yank his arm free from its socket. When she let go, Kevin got just a glimpse of the new green hue to Driff's fingers before the elf shoved his hand back into his pocket.

"Lordly Estates," Nella said with a wicked smile. "Lot 22."

Driff nodded and headed back the way they'd come.

"What did you do to him?" Kevin asked when the elf was out of earshot.

"My kind take our promises very, very seriously," she explained, "and we have the power to enforce them."

"What...uh...what exactly...um..." Kevin stumbled over his words, embarrassed by his next question.

Nella took him in her arms and leaned in close. "I'm a water nymph."

A water nymph. Of course, Kevin thought sarcastically. He still had no clue exactly what that was, but it seemed to fit. His heart racing, he kissed her as hard as he could. Kevin had a reaper to visit, and he was going to be damned if his last kiss wasn't absolutely fantastic, just in case.

— CHAPTER EIGHT —

Had construction of Harrison Metalworks continued as planned, Lordly Estates would've teemed with the vast cadre of middle managers necessary for the facility's proper operation. Harksburg may have had a reputation as a great place to raise a family, but it was not even remotely on the radar of your average corporate ladder-climbing douche bag. To encourage its best and brightest to voluntarily relocate, Harrison purchased several dozen acres of land on what would become Plastic Hill and started building McMansions which it planned to include in its relocation packages. Like the industrial park it had been built to support, Lordly Estates stood incomplete, a vision of progress half-realized and half-baked.

Unlike the Works, Harksburg had found a buyer for Lordly Estates, a mysterious British gentleman known around town as Mr. Pemberton. Rather than completing the project and selling the finished homes, Mr. Pemberton lived there—alone, by all accounts, though Waltman often theorized that he had strippers and prostitutes airlifted in during the dead of night. Once a month, Mr. Pemberton drove his big black Lincoln into town to run errands. He'd stop at the post office to collect a massive heap of mail. He'd swing into the library to exchange last month's batch of seedy romance novels for an armful of new releases. Sometimes he'd visit the hardware store to procure various odds and ends. At his last stop, Herman's Grocer, he'd purchase several boxes of cereal and enough TV dinners for lunch and dinner until his next supply run. By all accounts Mr. Pemberton was a nice enough fellow, a quiet man who rarely started a conversation on his own but always responded politely and intelligently when spoken to. He always wore a crisp black suit, paid in cash, and adhered to the speed limit.

As far as the general populace of Harksburg was concerned, Mr. Pemberton was a complete fucking loon. Flanagan tailed him whenever he came into town. "That weirdo's up to something," the officer claimed, "and whatever it is ain't happening on my watch!" Kevin wondered what his friend would make of the news that Mr. Pemberton was consorting with the local avatar of death.

"We jokingly call them 'reaper keepers,'" Driff explained during the short drive back up Plastic Hill. He was careful to keep his hand in his pocket the entire time. "Helping friends, family, and even casual acquaintances accept death is not a fun experience. Most reapers withdraw from regular society to live as hermits. They're well paid for their work and each is assigned a servant to see to his or her needs and represent the reaper when interaction with the general populace is necessary."

"Hence why Mr. Pemberton's name is on the deed to Lordly Estates," Ren added. "Billy provided the capital, but he didn't want his name on record."

"Why does he care?" Kevin asked. His head was still swimming from his meeting with Nella; he suspected he was missing something obvious, and he wanted to know what.

"He was human once," Driff said. "He probably doesn't want to be tracked down by anyone he used to know."

"That could be a bit awkward," Kevin agreed. Telling people he hadn't seen in years that he was "in between things"—his preferred alternative to "unemployed" because it felt a little less desperate—was bad enough. Having to explain to someone that you're the avatar of death or look a friend square in the eye knowing that you're the only reason Grandma didn't climb right back into her body after that stroke would be absolute hell. Kevin certainly didn't begrudge the reaper his need for privacy.

A massive wrought iron gate set into a pair of towering stone pillars kept the riffraff out of Lordly Estates. Beyond, the forested road snaked around a corner, keeping the development itself out of view. The proletariat wasn't even allowed to catch a glimpse of the luxury inside without explicit permission.

Ren stopped the car in front of the gate. "I'll get us an invitation," Driff said as he clambered out and approached the intercom set into one of the monolithic supports.

As soon as the car door slammed shut behind the elf, Kevin leaned forward and took firm hold of Ren's shoulder. "What the hell's going on, Ren?"

His friend shifted into the contemptuous tone Kevin had only heard him use when he'd been caught red-handed. "Whatever do you mean?"

"You. Me." He pointed at Driff's back. "Him."

"He's our employer. And we're his exceptionally well-paid employees."

"I get why he wanted me along. But why you? Why'd he go to you first?"

Ren pursed his lips and considered this for a moment. "My reputation as a shrewd-yet-fair businessman must run deeper than I thought."

Ahead of them, hidden machinery pulled the two halves of the gate apart. Driff turned to make his way back to the vehicle. Their only chance to talk wasted, Kevin slapped the back of his friend's head. "You're an ass, you know that?"

"Yeah, but I've got a great car."

Driff yanked the passenger door open and climbed in. "Billy will see us."

Kevin rolled his eyes. "I'm glad he's willing to take time out of his busy schedule of not doing his fucking job."

"He knows who pays the bills," Driff said as Ren pulled the car forward. The gate closed behind them with an ominous clunk.

"You elves?"

"Among others. Anyone who doesn't want a world full of immortal humans—and elves—who refuse to let go when it's their time."

"Humans and elves. But not, say, water nymphs?"

The elf shook his head. "The fae do not need a reaper's help. They understand the way of things and they're at peace with it. When you live as long as they do, death is a lot easier to accept."

That explained why Billy, a recluse who spurned all human contact, was willing to become romantically entangled with Nella. Kevin found himself wondering what the reaper's work was like. How exactly did you go about helping someone die? A couple of days ago, his answer to that question would've been blunt and to the point. When blades and bullets aren't enough, what then? He flashed back to his own out-of-body experience after Driff shot him, to that overwhelming, all-consuming desperation with which he'd clung to life. What force on earth could possibly overcome such a powerful instinct? He wasn't sure he wanted to know.

The road banked sharply to the right, bringing them to the first row of homes. Lordly Estates was, above all else, a physical representation of the abstract social levels its intended inhabitants expected to climb. Smaller homes for lower-level executives were carved into the first row. Houses grew bigger and grander with each of the six tiers, culminating in the sprawling manse at the very top reserved for the regional vice president.

"My family's house is bigger," Ren said nonchalantly. Nobody cared.

Kevin shivered. Something about Lordly Estates didn't feel right. The empty driveways and curtainless windows made the place seem stillborn. Vacant overgrown lawns should've been strewn with tacky ornaments and forgotten children's toys. Halloween was only a few weeks away, and yet there was nary a scarecrow nor jack-o-lantern in sight. An eerie silence settled heavily over it all, interrupted only by the soft purr of the Jaguar's engine. The place felt dead—appropriate, Kevin decided, given its master. Nella never would've been happy in a place like this.

Ren took the direct route, easing the Jaguar up the wide street that bisected the lower tiers on its way to the reaper's abode. The number 22 beckoned in bulky gold figures on the marble mailbox at the head of the mansion's winding driveway. The building itself evoked memories of a Civil War era plantation Kevin had once seen in a movie: tall and white and foreboding and propped up with gargantuan white columns. Ren's family's home may have been bigger, but its silly postmodern lines weren't nearly as grand and imposing as those of lot 22.

As the car rolled to a halt before the front porch, Kevin leaned forward between the seats and looked to Driff. "So...uh...anything we need to know about dealing with a reaper?"

"If he goes for your nose, run," the elf replied as he clambered out of the vehicle.

Mr. Pemberton awaited them on the mansion's expansive front porch. "Good morning, gentlemen," he said, his deep voice emotionless and precise and annoyingly British. Narrow eyes and the pencil-thin mustache that traced his slender upper lip combined to give him a perpetual condescending frown. His age was as difficult to judge as his attitude. His long face was clean and unwrinkled, but his short black hair was flecked with gray and rapidly receding from his forehead.

"Good morning," Driff replied. "We appreciate your master taking time to see us."

"Representatives of Evitankari are always welcome in Lordly Estates," Mr. Pemberton said officiously. "As are their companions."

"Allow me to introduce Ren Roberts and Kevin Felton," the elf said, indicating each in turn. Ren offered Mr. Pemberton a slight bow. Kevin nodded and toed the grass awkwardly. He wanted to get this over with.

"Charmed," Mr. Pemberton said. It bothered Kevin that he couldn't tell if the damn Brit was being sarcastic. "Follow me, please."

The glass and gold front door, inlaid with the blocky Harrison "H," swung open automatically at their approach. Beyond, the cavernous foyer stood empty. Where Kevin expected to find ornate furniture and priceless art he found only empty marble floor and blank white walls. The balcony above, trimmed in gold leaf and repeating the company symbol, was similarly bare.

"Where's all the stuff?" he asked.

Mr. Pemberton sighed. "My master is a bit of a minimalist."

"Blew his whole wad on the house and couldn't afford to put anything in it," Ren whispered. "Typical new money. They ought to have a school to teach these people how to spend their dough properly."

Kevin snorted. "Yeah, because those portraits your parents had painted of you on horseback for your birthday every year are extra classy."

"Equestrianism is a dying art that deserves to be celebrated."

Mr. Pemberton led them across the foyer and into the far hall. The harsh glare of the ceiling lights against the bare walls and floor made Kevin feel as if he were walking into the mythical white light. Appropriate, he thought, if not entirely accurate. He'd been dead and he hadn't seen such a thing. Did that make the white light just an old wives' tale? Had he simply not been dead enough? Or... was his ultimate resting place not in the paradise beyond the light, but somewhere darker and less inviting? Like so many things that had crossed his mind that day, Kevin didn't want to think about it. He supposed he'd find out soon enough if he pissed off Billy.

An unnerving thought stopped Kevin in his tracks. "I'm...uh... not due for collection, am I?" he asked, the blood draining from his face. Technically, Kevin Felton wasn't supposed to be alive. What if the reaper knew Driff had shot him in the head and decided to set things right?

"Your soul is not a late library book," Driff snapped. "Let's go."

Upon reaching the double doors at the end of the hall, Mr. Pemberton spun around to face them. "Please forgive the state of the master's suite. He vociferously disapproves of any attempts at tidying up."

Ren shrugged. "When Death tells you not to wash his fucking socks, you don't wash his fucking socks," he said, looking to Driff for approval. The elf rolled his eyes and shook his head.

There was, Kevin realized, a rather unique smell emanating through the cracks of the double doors. He couldn't place it. Thick and sweet, it was spiced with undertones of blood and something spicy and humid. It was death, he decided, the stench of a dark, frightening creature steeped in violence and despair. After checking to make sure Driff and Ren weren't paying attention, he clandestinely took a step behind them.

Mr. Pemberton pushed the doors open, unleashing a wave of that unnamed odor. The room inside was dark, lit only by a single source of light in the far corner. Trying to force his eyes to adjust, Kevin blinked as he followed the others inside, stepping in something soft and squishy on top and hard and crunchy underneath. He took a deep breath and looked down, hoping against hope that the horror in which he stood wouldn't send him screaming from the room.

It was pizza. Half a pepperoni pizza, to be exact, exposed to Kevin's careless sneakers in an open box. Other pizza boxes mingled with fast food containers and dirty clothing to form an ankle-deep swamp of sorts that undulated across the entirety of the floor in wavelike heaps and clusters. Posters of pop punk bands with dumb names and even dumber hair covered the walls in layers like fliers on a popular bulletin board. Thick black curtains caked with dust and cobwebs were shut tightly over tall windows. The only light in the room came from the four computer monitors set atop a desk in the far corner. There the reaper sat, concealed behind the imperious black back of a tall leather chair. Kevin recognized the bulky medieval characters duking it out on the wide screens. His freshman year roommate had failed out of school because he wouldn't put that damn massively multiplayer online RPG down long enough to get to class. Not that it would've mattered, seeing as his roommate was an idiot, but a little bit of effort surely wouldn't have hurt.

"Master Billy," Mr. Pemberton called out, "allow me to introduce Ren Roberts and Kevin Felton of Harksburg and Council of Intelligence Driff of Evitankari."

Kevin was about to ask Driff why he was a Council and not a Councilor when a single tap on the keyboard brought the action on all four monitors to a halt. The chair spun slowly around, creaking as it went, to reveal the reaper. Kevin bit back an exasperated sigh. *Of course death is a scrawny little emo kid,* he thought. *Of fucking course.* In this new reality to which Driff had dragged him, Occam's Razor held no sway. The simplest answer was not the most plausible because the simplest answer was never fucking correct. When it came to magic and elves and fairy creatures and avatars of death, Kevin realized, the thing to expect was always the most ridiculous.

Billy glowered up at them through dark, watery eyes trimmed in thick black mascara. His swoopy black hair dangled across his eyes at a seemingly impossible angle. He wore a plain back T-shirt and plain black jeans at least two sizes too small. The studded belt wrapped around his waist was certainly more for form than function. Tattooed stars traced a path up his forearm and disappeared into his sleeve. Something about him seemed vaguely familiar, but Kevin couldn't figure out what.

Perhaps more importantly, he couldn't figure out what the hell Nella possibly could've seen in this guy. Billy was sort of handsome in a depressed-looking way, but that was all he had going for him. Kevin's departure must've hurt the water nymph more than he thought. At least he knew for sure Billy wouldn't be any competition, because really, why would Nella want this little twit when she could have a rampaging stallion like Kevin Felton?

Several moments passed in silence as the two sides studied each other. Driff finally broke the ice. "It's come to our attention that you've forsaken your duties."

Billy didn't give any indication of having heard Driff. He clearly wasn't pleased at having been interrupted. Maybe Nella had been right; maybe visiting the reaper was indeed a stupid fucking idea. At the very least Kevin was going to be scrubbing pizza out of his shoes all afternoon, and that was more than bad enough.

Driff continued. "Mind explaining why?"

The reaper just snorted.

"Fine," the elf snapped. "We know about the girl. We know she left you and you aren't happy about it, but that is no excuse for shirking responsibilities only you can perform and for which you are handsomely compensated." Kevin and Ren exchanged anxious looks. Neither liked how hard Driff was pushing.

Billy steepled his fingers and glared daggers over them at Driff. "Keep your fucking money," he growled. "I don't fucking want it."

"What *do* you want?"

The reaper's gaze flicked to each of them in turn. Kevin felt the hair on the back of his neck stand up straight. There was power in that gaze, dark and primeval. This Billy, despite his appearance, was not a creature to be trifled with.

"Before Nella left me at the altar, she made a little speech," the reaper explained slowly. "'I'm leaving you for someone kind, and warm, and all filled up in the places where you're empty. I'm leaving you for a real man. I'm leaving you for my best friend.' As she stomped away from me, tearing off her wedding dress as she went, I called after her: 'What's the fucker's name?'"

Kevin's blood turned to ice. She didn't. She couldn't have. There was no way she was that stupid. No way. Nella was blue and she lived in a lagoon in the woods by herself and she hated wearing clothes, but she wasn't an idiot. At least, he was pretty sure she wasn't an idiot. He didn't really know much about her.

"His name..." Billy paused and closed his eyes. He spat his next sentence out as if every syllable burned his tongue. "His name is Poofy."

Kevin almost threw up. Poofy. The pet name his mother called him when no one else was around. Thankfully. It was their little secret. He'd never told anyone about it—and he didn't think he had told Nella. So how the hell did she know about it? And what the hell had she been thinking when she said it to the reaper?

Driff cleared his throat. "Are you sure she was being serious? Maybe she just wanted to get under your skin."

"Anyone named Poofy is probably a big pussy," Ren added. "If she left you for someone like that—well, her loss."

"Yeah," was all Kevin could contribute.

Billy opened his eyes and rubbed his chin. "Find this Poofy. Bring him to me and I will *consider* going back to work."

Driff didn't leave any time for suspense. "You know I can't do that. Aiding and abetting a homicide isn't something my superiors would approve."

Kevin stifled a sigh of relief. He suspected the elf's reluctance had more to do with his newly green hand and his promise to Nella, but nonetheless he was grateful not to have been thrown under the proverbial bus.

The reaper spun his chair back around and reactivated his computer game. "Then this conversation is over."

Well, Kevin thought, *that went just perfectly!*

Driff's gaze swiveled over to Kevin and Ren to imply it was their turn. Ren took the lead, clearing his throat and sauntering slowly toward the reaper. "Billy, my friend, this is beneath you," he announced in his best used car salesman voice. "You're a reaper. Death, destroyer of worlds! The great equalizer! Along with taxes, you're the only sure thing in life." When Ren reached Billy's side, he grabbed the back of the reaper's chair with a friendly hand. "You, sir, are a man among men. Don't let a bad breakup bring you down!"

At that, the chair whirled around once more, knocking Ren on his ass. Fire burning in his eyes, Billy reached forward, grabbed firm hold of Ren's nose, and yanked with all his might. Ren's body went rigid as something dark and ethereal exploded out through his nostrils. That something slowly coalesced into a smoky version of Ren, tethered to his physical form by wispy tendrils that stretched between his ghostly feet and his real-life nose. Before anyone could protest, Billy let go. Ren's soul snapped back into his nostrils like a rubber band, launching him straight onto his back and slamming his head against the floor with a sharp crack.

Being told that someone can pull a man's soul out through his nose and actually watching it in person were two wildly different experiences. It took every ounce of self-control Kevin could muster to resist the urge to piss his pants and run screaming from the room. Driff and Mr. Pemberton both merely rolled their eyes.

Billy nonchalantly spun his chair back around and went back to his video game. Ren writhed like a fish out of water for a few moments, gasping and arching his back repeatedly as if trying to get his body going again. Mr. Pemberton took him by the hand, dragged him through the laundry and garbage littering the floor, and deposited him at Driff's feet. Ren rolled onto his side and looked up at Kevin. "Careful," he croaked. "That fucking hurt."

Oh, so it's my turn now, Kevin thought. He didn't want a fucking turn. Finding out which other orifices Billy could use to pull out a man's soul wasn't something he was particularly looking forward to, but if he didn't try, he might as well announce himself as Poofy right then and there and get it over with. There was no way to be sure who else in town knew; his mother had a big mouth, and despite her promises that the nickname had stayed between the two of them, it wouldn't surprise Kevin to know that it had slipped a few times. Nobody was going to save Kevin. He was going to have to take his fate into his own hands and save himself. So, what could he try that Driff and Ren hadn't?

The answer came to him almost immediately. It was so obvious that he knew it couldn't fail. The way to reach Billy wasn't to appeal to his sense of duty or to his pride. In his current state of mind, neither of those things mattered. Kevin knew that firsthand. Later, he convinced himself he hadn't acted completely selfishly, that he did what he did and said what he said because he genuinely wanted to help Billy. He'd been in the poor guy's shoes recently enough that it still hurt.

"A year ago, my company was bought out by the Griffin Group," Kevin said somberly. "I was laid off the next day. They gave me two months' severance, but I started looking for a new job immediately. That money wasn't going to last forever. I went on two, sometimes three interviews every week. Nobody bit." He almost couldn't bring himself to describe the next part. "Still, I figured it would work out. My girlfriend had a great job and we were living together, so I assumed things were going to be okay. I went on my last interview a month ago. It didn't go well—to put it lightly—and I came home earlier than expected. That's when I found Kylie screwing her fifty-seven-year-old boss on our living room couch."

Mr. Pemberton winced. Driff nodded and motioned for Kevin to go on.

Kevin had to pause and collect himself. This wasn't some story he'd made up to try to save himself; it was real life, his life, and it was still a raw, bleeding wound, even considering how happy Nella made him. "I threw the old bastard's pants out the window and chased him off with a Dustbuster. I wasn't trying hard enough to find work, Kylie told me. She couldn't take care of me forever. An unemployed boyfriend, she said, was basically social kryptonite. No one at the office could understand why she hadn't already traded me in for something better. It was only a matter of time before I wound up in retail, they reasoned—better to cut her losses now before someone important saw me greeting customers at the door.

"She packed a bag and left. I haven't heard from her since. I miss her—a lot—but if she tried to come back into my life I'd show her the fucking door faster than she could blink.

"I was broke as a joke. I couldn't feed myself or pay the rent. So I moved back here. Where I grew up. To stay with my mother and her umpteen Jesus figurines. I really hate those fucking figurines."

The video game froze. Billy slowly turned his chair to face Kevin. The reaper's expression had softened. He'd slouched back in his chair, defeated, as if listening to Kevin's story had taken a lot out of him. Kevin could sympathize; he wanted nothing more than to go crawl up in a corner and wallow in his problems. He hadn't told his tale to anyone in that much detail—not Ren, not his mother, not even Nella. Burying it and pretending it hadn't happened had worked just fine until he'd put it into words. Now it was all he wanted to think about.

But Kevin didn't have time for that. He'd successfully baited the reaper. It was time to set the hook. Luckily, he had a personal experience perfect for closing the deal.

"If I could just meet someone new—well, I'm sure the pain wouldn't go away immediately. But it would help."

Billy rubbed the stubble on his handsome chin, considering that. "Yeah, it would help."

"I could use a wing man. Even if we don't pick up any women, at least it's something to do."

The reaper nodded. "Better than sitting around here all day."

"Friday night at the Burg?"

"Friday night at the Burg."

— CHAPTER NINE —

After finalizing the details of Friday night's pending activities with Mr. Pemberton, Kevin and Driff carried Ren out through lot 22's automatic front door toward the waiting Jaguar.

"I still can't feel my fucking feet," Ren moaned. "Is that normal?"

"Will it make you feel better if I tell you that's a known side effect of having your soul ripped out through your nose like a giant snot?" Driff asked.

"A little."

"Then yes, numbness in your extremities is to be expected."

"You're a real pal, Driff."

When they reached the car, Driff snatched the keys out of Ren's pocket and left him hanging on Kevin's shoulder. Kevin stumbled to adjust to the added weight while the elf made a beeline for the driver's side door.

"Hey! No one drives my car but me!" Ren protested.

Driff lowered the keys and feigned confusion. "No one? But your feet don't work! In that case, I guess we'll just have to wait here until you're feeling well again. Maybe you and Billy can get to know each other a little better."

Ren's gaze darkened. "Fine."

"You know what they say," the elf continued. "You can pick your friends. You can pick your nose. But you can't pick your friend's—"

"Oh, shut up and get us the fuck out of here!" Ren snapped.

"Yes sir," Driff deadpanned as he opened the door and took his place behind the wheel.

Knowing the shit fit Ren would throw if he tried to put him in the back, Kevin instead crammed his friend into the passenger seat. Some battles weren't worth fighting, and he had more pressing things on his mind—like figuring out just how the hell they were going to find Billy a new romantic interest. The more he examined the specifics, the less thrilled he became with the idea. Hooking up someone that depressed and that different from the rest of Harksburg wasn't going to be an easy task. Kevin had no idea how long Billy's patience would last or how many fruitless evenings at the Burg he'd be willing to endure—and there would be no telling how the reaper would act out if he became frustrated. Getting his hopes up and failing to make anything happen might be worse than doing nothing at all. In the meantime, every day that passed was another twenty-four hours during which Billy might learn the true identity of his archnemesis, the mysterious man known only as Poofy. The margin for error in Kevin's plan was slimmer than Billy's hipster jeans.

I'm fucked, Kevin thought as he swung himself into the backseat.

"So, what's the plan, Casanova?" Driff asked as he guided the Jag back down the hill.

Kevin sighed. "Get him drunk. Get him talking. Get him laid. Hope whoever the girl is doesn't immediately run away screaming the next morning."

"Brilliant."

"You got a better idea?"

"Nope. This one will have to do."

"Glad you're here to impart that bountiful elven wisdom."

"Human, elf, reaper—a little action goes a long way with all of them. Each comes with a different set of consequences when things don't go according to plan."

"Tell me about it," Ren moaned.

Kevin tapped idly on the window, debating whether to voice his next concern or squelch it. In the end, curiosity won out over caution. "Why is it that dealing with this particular set of consequences is up to a single elf and his motley crew of human companions? Isn't there some sort of authority that can step in to strip Billy of his reaper responsibilities and give the job to someone who will actually do it?"

"It's complicated," Driff replied. "Billy's tied to his territory by a very old, very powerful magic that—quite frankly—we're all afraid to fuck with."

"So there's no way to remove him?"

"I didn't say that."

"Why not?"

"Withholding certain circumstantial information unnecessary to completing the task at hand could make things easier for me down the line."

"You're a real jerk, you know that?"

"So I've been told."

The remainder of the drive was quiet, save for Ren's occasional pathetic moaning. Kevin couldn't speak for his companions, but he kept his own mouth shut simply because he'd seen and heard enough strange shit for one day and wanted to go home so he could process it all. Occasionally he snuck a peek at the other two. Ren fell asleep quickly, his head dangling loosely against his chest. Driff, however, remained wide-eyed and alert, the wheels in his mind obviously spinning a mile a minute. The elf may not have been the college professor he claimed to be, but he was certainly a thinker. That was worth watching; he certainly had Plans B, C, and D prepared in case things didn't go as intended, and Kevin knew he couldn't completely discount the possibility of Driff sacrificing him to the reaper to get the job done.

They arrived in front of the Felton residence ten minutes after departing Lordly Estates. As Ren snored away in the front seat, Driff leaned around to offer Kevin some advice. "Make sure you're prepared for Friday night. We may not get more than one shot at this."

"I'm kind of assuming we won't."

"A pessimist. Good. Perfect attitude for this line of work."

Unable to determine if Driff's words were meant to be serious or sarcastic, Kevin merely nodded and exited the vehicle.

Abelia ambushed him as he walked through the front door.

"And how was that delightful Professor Driff?" she asked happily.

Kevin still couldn't believe the change the dust had brought about in his mother. Her suspicions about the elf had been washed away with a handful of crap and a few carefully placed words. It made him wonder what else that stuff could do—and what else it had already done to other people he'd met.

"Just like I remembered him," he replied as he kicked his shoes off onto the mat beside the front door. "Kind of a stuck-up jerk, but he's all right."

Abelia slapped his elbow playfully. "Just your type! What's this job he's offering you?"

"Research. He's writing a paper on Harrison Metalworks." Years of such interrogations had taught Kevin to think on his feet. This particular little white lie was an easy one to whip up; outsiders rarely came to Harksburg unless their visit had something to do with Harrison.

"Well, normally I'd say the town's skeletons are best left buried, but I'm sure Professor Driff will handle it with tact and class." She turned to go, heading for the living room to her right. It was about time for her afternoon dose of court shows. "Dinner's at six, Poofy! I'm making your favorite: lasagna!"

"Thanks, Ma," Kevin replied as he slipped down the nearby stairs and shut the door behind him. He still didn't like the idea of Driff wiping his mother's memory, but at least it might help keep her off his back while he dealt with the reaper. He just hoped the elf wouldn't see fit to give her another handful of that dust crap anytime soon.

The dull ache in the back of Kevin's head reminded him of the day's stresses. He headed straight for his freshly made bed when he reached the bottom of the stairs and collapsed atop the clean sheets, passing out almost instantly.

— CHAPTER TEN —

Dinner was indeed lasagna, and it was indeed Kevin's favorite. It had been for as long as he could remember. Abelia didn't make it often; it was a lot of work, so she saved it for special occasions or instances when her motherly radar told her Kevin needed a pick-me-up. It didn't matter that she couldn't remember watching her son get shot. Abelia knew something was wrong, and so she offered her support the best way she knew how. Kevin appreciated it.

After helping with the dishes, Kevin quickly retreated to his room. An evening of cheesy sitcoms and running commentary on the state of the casts' waistlines just didn't seem all that appealing. A trip to the only bar in town—the Burg, the lovely establishment to which he planned to bring the reaper Friday night—wasn't an option because he'd long ago made it a policy not to go to that dump more than once a week. That left one option: drinking alone in his basement bedroom.

Kevin was perfectly content with that.

He'd long ago gotten in the habit of keeping a bottle of Jim Beam attached to the back side of his headboard with a rubber band in case of emergencies. Mrs. Felton changed the sheets on that bed weekly whether her son used them or not, but she had no reason to look behind the thick headboard. The half-empty bottle was right where Kevin had left it during a weekend visit four months ago. Tangles of dust flaked off as he pulled it away, lingering in the air as if judging him. A quick sip warmed his stomach. He settled in to relax and let the booze work its magic.

He wondered what Driff was up to right at that moment. What did an elven spy do when he wasn't busy doing elven spy stuff? Driff looked like he enjoyed a good book, or perhaps unique art shows hosted in small, trendy galleries, or maybe evenings at posh cafés in tony neighborhoods. Was the elf a film buff, perhaps? Maybe a wine connoisseur? Or was there some other distinctly elven pastime in which he involved himself? It was an odd line of thought, to be sure, but it bothered Kevin how much he didn't know about these fairy people. What did Driff watch on television? Where did Nella go to get her hair cut? How did his neighbor, Mr. Gregson, a pixie in a Vietnam veteran's crippled body, really feel about local politics?

Kevin took a long drink of bourbon. *Mr. Gregson.* That gave him an idea. A terrible, stupid, horrible idea—but if it paid off, it might mean a better understanding of the new world in which he found himself. Any little bit of knowledge, no matter how small or seemingly insignificant, might mean the difference between a long life with a hot blue woman and having his soul yanked out through his schnoz.

After taking one last swig for good luck, Kevin stood and headed for the stairs. The alarm clock on the nightstand declared that it was 7:38; that meant Mr. Gregson would be on his front porch, enjoying his evening's cigar. A few questions—including what the hell a pixie was doing smoking Cubans—couldn't hurt, could they?

Although there was a pretty good chance his mother would be zoned out in front of a gameshow in the living room, it would be best not to raise her suspicions. Getting caught attempting conversation with their unfriendly neighbor would only lead to endless, extended interrogations that would break much tougher men. This was another job for the Pussy Hatch.

As Kevin stepped out into the clear, brisk evening, he couldn't help reflecting on his eighth birthday party. His mother's work at the church didn't pay much, but she'd managed to scrimp and save enough to put together quite the spectacular birthday party for her beloved young son. Their tiny backyard became a miniature circus of sorts, complete with a colorful tent, a few goats and sheep from a nearby petting zoo, and Boink-o the Clown. All of Kevin's friends were there, having a grand old time as their parents watched from the patio.

The party hadn't been in full swing for more than half an hour when the local police showed up to investigate a complaint. The squeaky rubber horn on Boink-o's tricycle, it turned out, violated local noise ordinances by several decibels. Boink-o did not take kindly to these accusations—Kevin would later learn that the seemingly benign clown was, in fact, an ex-convict wrongly imprisoned for grand theft auto because of police incompetence—and the cops were even less happy with Boink-o's suggestion of where they could shove their badges. A fight ensued. Bloodied and beaten, Boink-o was dragged to the waiting cruiser in handcuffs. That was the end of Kevin's eighth birthday party, thanks to a complaint from Mr. Gregson. The Feltons and their neighbor hadn't exchanged more than angry, suspicious glances ever since.

Local lore claimed that the events of that party first put the idea of becoming a police officer into Tom Flanagan's head. Young Tom spent the majority of the afternoon hiding in the bushes because he was absolutely petrified of the smiling clown. Most of the children were devastated when the police dragged Boink-o away, but Tom Flanagan couldn't have been more relieved. Those men in their snappy blue uniforms weren't there to ruin a birthday party;

they'd arrived to rid the world of a scary clown. Or at least that's what Waltman said.

Regardless, there was no neighborly reason for Kevin to approach Mr. Gregson. None whatsoever. Kevin almost turned around and went back inside, but giving up wouldn't accomplish anything. Surviving his current situation would mean manning up, pulling his balls out of his purse, and making something happen. It was time to do just that, even if it led to the occasional bout of borderline stupidity.

A plastic privacy screen obscured the side Mr. Gregson's front porch, but the tangy-sweet scent of a fine cigar wafted gently through the night air. Kevin's quarry was waiting for him. He straightened his jacket and strode confidently down the front steps, shoving his hands into his pockets when he reached the sidewalk. Calm, cool, and put together—that was Kevin Felton, despite the nervous energy coursing through his body that threatened to turn him into a quivering mess. *People are more likely to speak with those who appear confident,* he reminded himself as he sauntered down the sidewalk. He hoped that same rule applied to pixies secretly living as humans.

Mr. Gregson slowly came into view around the privacy screen. The old man stared right at Kevin as if he'd been awaiting his arrival. A thick black beard spilled onto his burly chest like a tangle of twisted moss down the side of a tree. His legs ended at his knees, leaving behind a pair of stumps sticking out just beyond the lip of his motorized wheelchair. One ham-sized hand clutched a half-smoked cigar, the other a can of cheap beer. Mr. Gregson wore his usual green military fatigues and a black baseball cap emblazoned with the word "Army" in big gold letters. Despite the man's disabilities, he exuded an aura of lethality that forced the town of Harksburg to treat him with respect. There, in the harsh glow of his porch light, Mr. Gregson appeared downright regal, an angry king surveying his lands and hating everything he saw.

Kevin had always thought he looked a bit lopsided; the man's girth listed to his right, as if that side of his body just couldn't deal with his weight.

And, Kevin realized suddenly, he'd always looked that way. Always. It had been twenty years since Kevin first laid eyes on Mr. Gregson, and yet there wasn't a single new wrinkle on the man's face or even a gray hair in his scraggly beard. The man hadn't aged a day—which made sense, if his human form was indeed just a disguise for something much smaller.

Kevin stopped in front of the steps to Mr. Gregson's porch. "Evening," he called out in what he hoped was a calm and friendly yet unavoidably confident and manly voice.

Mr. Gregson replied by sticking his cigar in between his thick bulldog lips and taking a long drag.

"I met someone today who said he knows you," Kevin continued. "Man named Driff."

His neighbor exhaled, blowing three perfect smoke rings into the night air. Mr. Gregson took his beady black eyes off Kevin to admire his handiwork.

"I was hoping you could tell me a little more about him. He— uh—offered me a job, and I'd like to know more about the man before I start working for him."

"Leave it alone," Mr. Gregson replied. His deep voice rumbled like a diesel engine.

"I'm sorry sir, but...leave what alone?"

"Driff ain't a man the likes of you ought to be getting involved with."

That's an understatement, Kevin thought. "So...so you do know him!" Relief washed through Kevin's body, warm and tingling. Coming to Mr. Gregson had been the right decision. "And you *are* a pixie!"

To say that Mr. Gregson froze wouldn't be quite accurate. His body merely stopped in place, his cigar halfway to his mouth, his eyes just beginning to squint, his lips curling mid-sneer. It was as if his flesh had suddenly turned to wax, or—and upon further review later on, Kevin would come to this conclusion—that he'd simply shut down, his pieces and parts locked in place like those of a robot that had suddenly lost power. Regardless of what exactly happened, Kevin immediately knew that he'd made a huge mistake.

"I'm sorry, sir, I didn't mean to offend you—"

Suddenly weightless, Kevin Felton floated a few feet up into the air. Although his heart pounded a mile a minute, he couldn't move any other part of his body. He couldn't fathom what was happening; one moment he'd embarrassed himself in front of his neighbor, a closet pixie, and the next he'd been lifted off the ground by an invisible hand that also rendered him mute and paralyzed.

Then it clicked. A soft "ooooooooooohhhhhhhhhhh" would've eased through Kevin's lips if he'd been able to move them. Mr. Gregson had called upon some sort of magic spell to forcibly remove his annoying neighbor from the premises.

I fucking hate this magic shit, Kevin thought as he zipped back above the sidewalk toward his own house. He'd always assumed that being telekinetically lifted would be much more complicated sensation. Outside of the cool air rushing past his face, it didn't feel like much of anything. It reminded him a bit of driving with the windows down, but even that was a stretch.

Mr. Gregson set Kevin down gently on the Felton family driveway. A thick, rasping cough erupted from behind the privacy screen. Magic, it appeared, involved a bit of cardio.

Kevin took the hint and went back inside through his bedroom window, relieved that he'd escaped with all of his pieces and parts intact.

— CHAPTER ELEVEN —

The next two days felt like two years. This was not because Kevin anxiously looked forward to spending an evening with Billy, far from it. He couldn't think of a worse way to spend a Friday night than chaperoning some moody emo kid during a night of drinking and carousing at a shithole bar in the middle of nowhere. No, the days dragged as badly as they did because absolutely fucking nothing happened. That lack of excitement, Kevin remembered, was why he'd left in the first place. Perhaps excitement was too strong of a word; life in Chicago hadn't always been exciting, but it had never been as mind-numbingly dull as his time in Harksburg.

Kevin spent most of his time poring through job listings in the local papers and online. He wasn't quite ready to take a job outside of the finance industry; someone, somewhere in central Illinois surely needed a junior business analyst with big city experience and a diverse skill set. There would come a time, he knew, when he'd tire of living with his mother and settle for a low-level clerical job, but he wasn't ready to give up. Not yet. Not after six years in school and three years at one of Chicago's hottest firms.

To get him out of the house, Mrs. Felton tasked Kevin with going to the post office to get the mail every day—a fair trade, he decided, for free room and board. That first day, Thursday, after getting dressed and mentally preparing himself to deal with the horde of chatty old biddies that infested the Harksburg post office during the weekdays, Kevin couldn't find his keys. They weren't on his nightstand where he usually left them, nor in the pair of pants he'd worn the day before. After half an hour of searching, he finally located them underneath his pillow. Briefly he wondered how the hell his keys had found their way into his bed—and then he became suspicious. He checked his headphones and the USB cables of his computer peripherals. All were indescribably twisted. He turned on the television and found it set to the VCR's input; he hadn't used the VCR in years.

Gnomes, he thought. *I've got fucking gnomes.*

Try as he might, he couldn't find the little bastards. The thought of a tribe of tiny men laughing maniacally at the petty annoyances they inflicted upon him really rubbed Kevin the wrong way. He was going to find his unwanted guests, and when he did there'd be hell to pay.

Kevin also invested several hours scouring the web for any trace of the man known as Poofy. Death via Google seemed like a miserable way to go out. The top hits for his nickname were weird Japanese fetish sites and some kind of overpriced teddy bear that told terrible knock-knock jokes—and neither topic, luckily, led back to Kevin Felton. An expert in cybersecurity, his mother had configured her email and social networking accounts to log in automatically, so he checked those, too. Nothing. Someone else out there *had* to know that Kevin and Poofy were one and the same— that's just the way small towns worked—but at least Billy would have to put some time and effort into sniffing out Poofy's identity. Hopefully that would buy Kevin the time he needed to hook the reaper up with a new woman that would make him forget all about Nella.

And just how in the hell was he going to do that? The question weighed heavier on him every time he pondered it. Billy didn't seem particularly outgoing, suave, or funny. He was your typical melancholy emo kid with dumb, swoopy hair and a few stupid tattoos. How the hell was Kevin supposed to find a girl for a guy like that in a town fifty miles from the nearest Hot Topic? Had he known what he was going to have to work with, he might've thought twice about proposing his plan to Nella and Driff. Maybe Billy would surprise Kevin by revealing himself as the biggest ladies' man in the county. Maybe his good looks would mitigate his long list of flaws. Maybe Ren's Jaguar would grow wings and fly.

Desperate to discuss both recent events and their plan of attack, Kevin called Ren two or three times a day. Ren neither answered nor returned those calls. That was not normal; Ren was one of the most conscientious people Kevin knew. He didn't think Ren had *ever* not returned one of his calls. Ren obviously knew more than he was letting on about all these crazy fairy creatures; but what did he know, and how did he know it, and why didn't he want to talk to his best friend about it? Whatever Ren was hiding, it had to be something personal. Maybe Friday night, somewhere in between working feverishly to hook the reaper up with someone willing and trying not to get his soul yanked out through his nostrils, Kevin would have a chance to corner Ren and find out exactly what the hell was going on. Somehow, he doubted it.

Nella didn't visit him, as they'd agreed. Kevin knew it was for the best. There was no telling what powers the reaper possessed that would give the two of them away, or what associates he might've tasked with keeping an eye on the water nymph. Regardless, Kevin missed her—a lot—and hoping that she'd suddenly appear in his room kept him awake most of the night, even though a few hours of fun with Nella could bring about his demise. Logically, he knew that was fucking stupid—but his heart wanted him to shove his logic right back up his ass.

Sometimes, when he was able to briefly talk himself out of thinking about Nella, he pretended to be asleep to try to lull the gnomes into a false sense of security. They didn't show. Either Driff had been pulling his leg, or the little bastards were really damn smart. He untangled his cables Thursday night and found them twisted maliciously the next morning. Gnomes or not, there were strange forces at work in his bedroom.

Life in Harksburg took an interesting turn about an hour after lunch on Friday afternoon. While Kevin was busy checking underneath the ottoman for gnomes, his mother stormed into the living room. "I just can't believe it!" she bellowed, her eyes dancing with hellfire and brimstone. "Have you seen what your friend, the Spuddner boy, has gotten himself up to?"

Kevin looked up at her from his hands and knees and shook his head. "What's Oscar doing?"

Mrs. Felton planted her hands firmly on her hips and harrumphed. "That little heathen's built himself an altar on the town common. He's *preaching!*"

For a moment, Kevin couldn't understand where the problem was. Typically, his mother wholeheartedly approved of any attempts to spread the good word. Then Kevin flashed back to the gathering in the Works four days prior, to Oscar's little messianic performance from atop the rock by the bulldozer. Mrs. Felton certainly wouldn't approve of *that*.

Neither, Kevin realized, would Driff. He didn't know what the elf would do about it, but he was sure it wouldn't be something Oscar would enjoy.

"I'll go see if I can talk some sense into him," Kevin replied, springing to his feet.

His mother nodded. "If he's still out there blaspheming when my laundry's done, I'm coming after him with the holy water," she said menacingly. Abelia kept a ready supply in the garage, in the kegerator Kevin's father had left behind. A tiny spray bottle in her purse served as a reliable weapon against barking dogs, rude heathens, and Waltman. She'd once told her son that any supernatural benefits were merely a bonus; getting spritzed by an angry old lady was usually more than enough to curb unwanted behavior.

"My old Super Soaker's in the attic," Kevin replied sarcastically as he brushed past her and headed for the front hall. In his haste to get to Oscar before Driff did, he put his shoes on the wrong feet. After correcting them, he couldn't make his fingers tie a proper knot. He gave up, threw a light jacket on, and shoved his way outside through the front door with his untied laces flapping in the breeze.

The crowd gathered on the town common across the street was the sort of motley collection of old people, creeps, losers, and stay-at-home parents you can only find out and about at one in the afternoon on a weekday while everyone else is at work. There was Sweatpants Bob, a homeless old duffer who wandered around town nonstop with an old bedpost he used for a walking stick and a giant hiking pack overstuffed with who-knows-what. Mrs. Robidas stood off to the side with her three-seat stroller, cautiously eyeing Jerry Flynn, an old veteran with a bushy mustache and thick glasses who drove the type of crappy maroon van favored by kidnappers and rapists. The staff of the nearby Harksburg Rest Home had wheeled several of their residents out to watch the proceedings. Waltman and Jim Jimeson were there, too, decked out in their WJ Construction sweatshirts even though they hadn't been able to find work in three months. There were ten or twelve others Kevin knew by face and reputation but not by name—the fat guy who used the library computer all day, the old woman who stole newspapers from the convenience store, the dude who sold home-grown mint in front of the post office every Saturday morning, and so on and so forth. The entire roster of local loons had come out for this one. Kevin refused to list himself among their number; his unemployment was just temporary, after all, and it would be only a matter of time before he was once again contributing to society—or so he tried to convince himself.

Tom Flanagan's police cruiser was parked right in front of Kevin's house. The beefy officer himself leaned against its hood, glaring angrily at Oscar's little show. Kevin stopped to say hello.

"Afternoon," Officer Flanagan spat as he shook Kevin's hand. "Quite the fucking shindig we've got today."

"How'd you get stuck playing riot squad?" Kevin asked.

"Short straw," Flanagan replied sadly. "Rest of the boys are out in the Works with some Mary Jane we took off Johnny T. last week. These jerks better behave. I've got a couple of gas grenades in the trunk an' I'm just itchin' for an excuse."

"My mother might get to them with the holy water first. How long have they been out there?"

"About half an hour. Believe it or not, Spuddner had the common sense to get a permit first. Nothing I can do 'less things turn nasty."

Kevin nodded. If Driff showed up—well, who knew how nasty things might get, and he didn't want to see Flanagan caught up in the middle of it. "I, on the other hand, am under no such restrictions."

Flanagan tipped his cap theatrically. "It's a free country, after all, but I'm sure local law enforcement would be mighty grateful if you got these idiots—I mean, these citizens exercising their First Amendment rights—off my damn common."

"I'll see what I can do."

Kevin left his friend with a final handshake and jogged across the street. There was no sign of Ren's green Jaguar—hopefully that meant word hadn't reached Driff and that Kevin had plenty of time to clean up this mess. That it was, in fact, *his* mess, there could be no doubt. His return had driven Nella to leave Billy at the altar, which in turn had caused the reaper to shirk his responsibilities, which meant that no one in the county could die and thus made it possible for Oscar to make a stupid spectacle of himself. Anything bad that happened to his friend because of it would be on Kevin's head.

He gave the contingent from the old folks' home a wide berth so as to avoid their strange smell, ducking between Sweatpants Bob and Waltman as he made his way to the front of the crowd. Oscar stood atop an overturned crate in the center of the gathering, smiling benevolently and making what Kevin could only term "Jesus motions" with his arms. He wore a baggy white bathrobe he must've stolen from a hotel. Doorknob stood to his right, standing guard over a metal trough of water with the infamous pitchfork in hand. A blue duffel bag by his feet bulged at weird angles.

"Brother Kevin!" Oscar said happily. "So good of you to make it!"

Part of Kevin wanted to fade back into the crowd and hide, but he couldn't do that. He had to talk some sense into his idiot friend—no easy task under normal circumstances, but certainly borderline impossible now that Spuddner thought himself indestructible. "Hey, Oscar. Whatchya up to?"

"That's Oscar the Immortalist to you, heathen!" Doorknob snapped in his ridiculously high-pitched voice, jamming his finger in Kevin's face. "You will show the proper respect!"

Kevin blinked and took a step back. Doorknob had never exhibited anything even remotely resembling a spine. Throughout his entire life he'd endured a never-ending stream of verbal and physical abuse with nothing more than the occasional meek, "C'mon, guys!" Waistband-snapping wedgies, hours spent trapped in his own locker, weeks without any lunch money, constant sabotage of his every public attempt to woo a woman— none of it had prompted any sort of aggressive outburst. It had taken nothing short of immortality to pull Doorknob out of his shell.

Kevin didn't like it. Recklessness would do Doorknob no favors in life. He was neither smart enough nor strong enough to deal with the consequences.

"First Acolyte Knob, stand down," Oscar said peacefully. "Brother Kevin is a good friend to the movement."

To Kevin's left, Waltman snickered. "First Asshole Doorknob."

"Good friend to the bowel movement," Jim Jimeson added with a sneer.

Doorknob eyed his tormentors maliciously, but Oscar ignored them. "Friends! Neighbors! Fellow Harksburgers!" he declared, sweeping his arms dramatically. "I come to you today bearing a gift—the gift of eternal life!"

"Bullshit!" Jim Jimeson declared.

"Do that trick with the pitchfork again!" Waltman shouted.

Kevin didn't want to think what might happen if Oscar stabbed himself in the middle of the town common. No way Driff would let that go unpunished. "Um, Oscar," he stammered. "I actually came out here to warn you about the weather. There's a really bad thunderstorm heading this way."

Oscar dismissed him with a gentle wave of his hand. "The Immortalist fears no storm. Neither lightning nor tornado nor water spout nor golfball-sized hail can silence his good word!"

"I bet a knuckle sandwich would do the trick," Waltman growled.

"Get on with the stabbing!" Jimeson goaded.

Oscar's brow furrowed. "Need we resort to such barbarities, gentlemen?"

"Yes!" Waltman and Jimeson shouted together. Beside them, Sweatpants Bob nodded.

The would-be messiah crossed his arms and pursed his lips. "If that's what it takes to spread the Word of the Immortalist, then it shall be done. All those who follow the Word shalt be forever safe from harm. First Acolyte Knob has embraced the teachings of the Immortalist and everlasting life has become his. Tell me, First Acolyte: are you prepared to give of yourself for the good of the Word?"

Doorknob bowed his head and put his hand over his heart. "I am, Immortalist. If a few moments of pain will save those gathered, I will gladly suffer so that they might accept your gift."

Oscar took the pitchfork from his friend's grasp and twirled it high over his head, a redneck Neptune ready to strike vengefully upon a sailor who'd defiled his sea. His sparkling blue eyes burned not with violence or hatred but with twisted love and psychotic empathy. The man had fucking lost it.

"Stop it!" Kevin shrieked, rushing to put himself between Oscar and Doorknob. "Is this really the time and place for this shit? Out in the Works is one thing, but here—in public?"

Anger flashed briefly in Oscar's face, but then firm hands took hold of Kevin's arms and shoulders—Waltman's and Jimeson's.

"Don't worry, Immortalist," Waltman said sarcastically as they dragged Kevin kicking and screaming out of the way. "We'll make sure this heathen doesn't interfere."

"Thank you, brothers," Oscar replied happily. "Perhaps I've misjudged you both." He hefted the pitchfork, testing its weight.

"Let me go!" Kevin screamed. He thrashed wildly, but his friends' grips were solid. "This is fucking insane!"

"Maybe," Jimeson whispered, "but it sure beats sitting at home watching Judge Judy all day."

"It's just a stupid parlor trick," Waltman added quietly, "and when we figure out how these dumbasses do it, we're going to have something to rub in their idiot faces forever!"

Kevin's only counter-argument would've been to expose the entire truth: that it was no trick, that anyone in the county could die and come right back to life. But having seen the way immortality had changed Oscar and Doorknob, he knew that wasn't an option. Who knew what forces—and what ridiculous, stupid, annoying delusions—the threat of death was keeping in check?

With no further ado, Oscar shifted his grip on the pitchfork slightly and then plunged the farm implement into his best friend's chest with all of his might, tumbling from atop the crate in the process. Doorknob, to his credit, didn't scream, moan, or express his pain in any way. He merely coughed up a thick gob of blood and fell straight back like a great tree brought down by a lumberjack's saw.

The stunned crowd didn't move or make a sound. Most of them appeared to have stopped breathing. All eyes were glued to Doorknob, lying spread-eagle on the ground with a pitchfork sticking out of his chest. No one came to help him. No one ran to get the police officer waiting across the street. Word of the miracles in the Works had spread quickly, and this was the rest of the town's chance to see it for themselves. This was high drama— the most entertaining thing to hit Harksburg since Johnny T. got caught trying to steal Bum Watson's prized collection of Three Stooges beer five years ago—and no one wanted to interrupt.

Oscar reclaimed his perch atop the crate and vainly tried to brush the dirt and grass stains out of his white robe. "Fear not, brothers and sisters!" he proclaimed. "No simple farm implement can overcome the First Acolyte's belief in the Immortalist!"

The pitchfork began to quiver. At first, Kevin suspected it had been caught in a slight breeze, but then he noticed that it was actually rising, pulling itself up and out of Doorknob's chest. It popped free with a gross slurping sound and fell away, cast aside by Doorknob's flesh. Doorknob sat up, alive and well and looking for all the world like he'd just awoken from a deep, restful sleep.

The crowd gasped. Several oxygen machines attached to the elderly in attendance whirred into high gear. Sweatpants Bob dropped to his knees and prostrated himself.

"Did you see how the fuckers did that?" Jim Jimeson whispered.

"No," Waltman spat. "Sneaky assholes. Any ideas, Felton?"

Defeated and angry, Kevin couldn't resist. "Maybe Death's taking some time off to deal with a few relationship problems," he suggested.

Waltman slapped him in the back of the head. "This is no time to be a cheeky son-of-a-bitch. This is serious."

"Sorry," Kevin deadpanned. "You're right. Those two are definitely up to something."

Doorknob clambered back to his feet, picked up the pitchfork, and took his spot at Oscar's side as the would-be messiah's potbellied honor guard. "That should silence the doubters, Immortalist."

"Indeed," Oscar said sagely. "But let us not hold our neighbors' skepticism against them. Forgiveness is the rock in which the Immortalist's message has been carved. The gift of everlasting life is available to all who wish to claim it."

Sweatpants Bob snapped upright. Tears streamed down his gritty, weathered cheeks, settling in his thick gray beard like dew in the morning grass. "Oh, Immortalist, I wish to claim it!"

Kevin would've slapped himself in the face if Waltman and Jim Jimeson hadn't been holding his arms back.

Oscar smiled like a proud father watching his son take his first steps. "Rise, Brother Sweatpants. The Immortalist is but a humble prophet, no better than any other honest man or woman. Rise, and let the world hear of your need for the Immortalist's gift!"

Leaning heavily on his bedpost-walking stick, Sweatpants Bob eased himself to his feet. The big man moved with the all the grace and speed of a continental plate, his stiff, grimy clothing crackling as it stretched back out. Not much was known about Sweatpants Bob. Harksburg's only homeless man lived in a camp in some undisclosed location in the woods. A friendly, easygoing fellow who went out of his way to help distressed motorists with flat tires or busted engines, no one knew Bob's real name, why he'd decided to live in the woods all by himself, or why he used the "Sweatpants" moniker when he only ever wore camouflaged cargo pants. Despite his amicable nature, there was a certain sadness in the man's face and bearing. It seemed he'd had a hard life, but he wasn't one to talk about it. Anyone who tried to press him for information was quickly added to Bob's shit list and never spoken to again.

Sweatpants Bob took a deep breath and closed his eyes. "My granddaughters," he said slowly, "live in California. Twins. They turn eighteen in April. I've never met them—my son-in-law refuses to let me near them—but I was hoping I could see them graduate high school next summer."

"A noble goal," Oscar said gently, eliciting a few sniffles and sighs from the crowd. "How will the gift of the Immortalist help you achieve it?"

The big man hesitated, clearly gathering himself for whatever it was he was about to reveal. "A month ago, I took the bus to the free clinic in Chicago. They referred me to one of the big hospitals. I have pancreatic cancer. I—I won't make it through the end of the year."

Kevin's heart broke. He physically sagged in his friends' grasp. Sweatpants Bob had been a friendly constant in town for as long as Kevin could remember. He couldn't imagine Harksburg without him. To make matters worse, Oscar and Doorknob were about to use that poor old man's fate as an excuse to sucker him into their dumb religion. The irony that Bob would only attempt the trip because he thought he was immortal when, in reality, leaving Billy's fucked up district would mean his own death was too much for Kevin to bear.

Oscar stepped down from his perch and wrapped his arms around the big man. "Never fear, Brother Sweatpants. The Immortalist can get you to your granddaughters' graduation…but there is a small processing fee. Fifty dollars."

Bob fished around his pocket and pulled out a small wad of bills. "I've got twelve bucks and a Burg sandwich card," he said hopefully. "Two more sandwiches and I get a free lunch."

The melancholy generated by Bob's sad story turned to boiling rage as Kevin watched Oscar doing the math in his head. "From a gentle soul such as yourself, Brother Sweatpants, that'll be more than enough," the Immortalist said softly, grabbing Bob's offering and shoving it into his robe's pocket. It wouldn't do to let the crowd think their new prophet was only in it for the money, after all. Never had Kevin been so disgusted. Here was Oscar Spuddner, a certified dumbass who'd barely graduated after six years at Harksburg High, peddling hope to the hopeless.

And it was all Kevin's fault.

He turned to Waltman. "Just let me go. I promise I won't interfere. I just want to go home."

Waltman shook his head. "You're a smart one, city boy. You're going to stay right here and watch so you can tell us how Spuddner's trick works."

That left Kevin with just one option. "Flanagan!" he shouted. "Officer! They're breaking the law!" Calling for the police made him feel like a bit of pussy, but what other choice did he have? He just hoped Flanagan would leave the tear gas in the trunk.

Jim Jimeson kicked him in the shin. "Flanagan left as soon as you showed up. Now stop interrupting the Immortalist!"

Kevin swore under his breath. Of course Flanagan had left. Kevin had told the officer he'd take care of Oscar's gathering, and in Flanagan's mind that would've freed him to join the other members of the police department in the Works for an afternoon toke. Kevin couldn't blame his friend. In Flanagan's shoes, he probably would've done the same.

Doorknob bent down and unzipped the duffel bag, spreading it open so those closest could see inside. It was full of green and beige striped paper—computer printouts produced using the shitty old printer in the Harksburg Public Library. They hadn't even bothered to tear away the edges. Doorknob grabbed one of the printouts and held it up high.

"In his hand, First Acolyte Knob holds the Scriptures of the Word," Oscar explained. "The Immortallia!"

"The genitalia?" Jim Jimeson asked. Waltman snickered. Sweatpants Bob shot them a fiery scowl that made it clear he'd beat both of their skulls in with his bedpost if they kept it up.

"The Immortallia!" Oscar repeated. Doorknob lowered the printout and offered it to Sweatpants Bob, who took it gently in his gnarled hands as if he were afraid it might shatter.

Waltman leaned close to Bob to read the printout around the big man's thick shoulder. "Is that a recipe for oatmeal raisin cookies?"

"The Immortalist's favorite," Doorknob replied haughtily.

Waltman frowned as he read further. "Cubs tickets, third base line. A carton of Marlboro Lights. Back rubs every day for a week. Miller High Life, bottles only. Red-headed virgins with a C-cup or better. Is this a holy book or Spuddner's dumbass Christmas list?"

"If one wishes to receive, one must also be willing to give," Oscar said warmly.

"You can have my granddaughter if it means I don't die in that dirty fucking nursing home!" one of the old ladies hollered. A few others echoed her sentiments.

"I'll bake you cookies every day!" Mrs. Robidas added.

"And I'll do the back rubs!" Jerry Flynn shouted.

The crowd erupted then, promising Oscar the world: drugs, sex, money, food, shelter. Whatever he wanted, whenever he wanted it, as long as he would protect them all from death. The Immortalist spread his arms wide and turned his face skyward, basking in the attention. Kevin could sympathize with his friend; mere hours ago, none of the people attempting to curry Oscar's favor would've given him the time of day, even though he was one of the friendliest individuals in all of Harksburg. Oscar's life as a loser was over. He was in demand. He was important. He was one of the cool kids for the first time in his life and he was enjoying it thoroughly.

But that didn't make his methods any less wrong. No one deserved to have their fear of mortality taken advantage of that way, regardless of how poorly they'd treated Oscar in the past. Kevin didn't like this twisted version of his friend. He had to stop him—and he finally had an idea of how to do it.

He turned to Waltman. "I know what they're up to."

"Oh yeah? Spill it."

"Let me go and I'll show you," Kevin replied mischievously. "Everybody here will see it. Just think how long you'll be able to hold *that* over Spuddner's head."

"Hmm," Waltman replied. "Not bad, Felton. Show us what you've got."

Finally free, Kevin stepped forward and grabbed the pitchfork in Doorknob's hands. His scrawny friend gritted his teeth and dug his heels into the grass and dirt, his knuckles turning white around the wooden handle as he fought to hold on.

"Give me the fucking pitchfork!" Kevin snarled.

"Fight him, First Acolyte!" Oscar shouted. "The power of the Immortalist will ensure your victory!"

Kevin rolled his eyes and sighed. He'd had enough of this shit. A heavy stomp on Doorknob's foot weakened the smaller man's grip just enough for Kevin to tear the pitchfork out of his grasp. Doorknob collapsed to the grass, whimpering and rubbing his toes.

"Watch this!" Kevin commanded, swinging the pitchfork high and aiming its tines for his own chest. He couldn't believe he was about to do this. "Spuddner, you're a fucking idiot! I'm not going to give you any money, any booze, or anything else—but I'm still going to get right back up after I—"

A familiar shriek interrupted Kevin's speech. "All right, heathens! You had your chance to leave peacefully! Now the wrath of God has come to wash Harksburg's common clean once again!"

A powerful burst of water struck Oscar in the face and sent him sprawling. Sweatpants Bob caught one next, then Waltman and Jim Jimeson, and all hell broke loose as the members of the crowd ran screaming in various directions.

Defeated, Kevin twirled the pitchfork around and plunged its tines into the earth at his feet. His mother rushed to his side, Super Soaker in hand, protecting him like the holy warrior she'd always pictured herself to be. The plastic tank on her back sloshed loudly with holy water as she moved. Kevin had forgotten how powerful that thing could be.

"I'm here, son!" Mrs. Felton said bravely as she turned her fire upon Jerry Flynn and sent the poor man stumbling for cover. "I've got Jesus as my wingman!"

Biting back a sarcastic response, Kevin gave his mother's shoulder a loving squeeze. Even though he was never, ever going to live this down, even though Harksburg would have one more tale of crazy Mrs. Felton to laugh about, even though he was disappointed that he hadn't been able to talk Oscar down on his own—he was damn sure glad that he hadn't been forced to pitchfork himself.

— CHAPTER TWELVE —

L eaving his mother behind to attend to her holy war, Kevin
headed for home. He needed a shower and a drink. He and
the bottle of whiskey hidden behind his bed were about to
become very, very good friends.

His trip was interrupted, of course, by the last man he wanted
to see. He'd almost reached the street when Driff materialized on
a bench to Kevin's left. The elf smiled and offered Kevin a slow,
sarcastic clap.

"Good show!" Driff called out. "You're lucky your mother's an
excellent shot."

Annoyed, Kevin turned on his heel to confront the smug elf.
"She's had a lot of practice. You saw all that?"

Driff stopped clapping. "Why do you continue to assume that
the man who can turn invisible isn't secretly watching your every
move?"

"It's taking some getting used to. Can't say I like it."

"Can't say I blame you." The elf patted the empty part of the bench
to his left. "Sit. Take a load off. Watch the grand finale with me."

Making sure to keep his distance, Kevin did as Driff suggested.
Harksburg's public benches were just as hard and unforgiving as

he remembered. He sat gingerly on the edge, afraid that he'd need to see a chiropractor if he leaned back into the wooden torture chamber's vicious grasp. Driff slouched comfortably, his ass and spine apparently made of tougher stuff than Kevin's.

Halfway across the common, most of those who'd gathered to watch Oscar's presentation had fled the scene, leaving trampled grass, wheelchair ruts, and a swirl of lost computer printouts in their wake. Alone in the center of the swath of green, Sweatpants Bob hobbled pathetically away from Kevin's rampaging mother like a wounded buffalo abandoned by the herd as it attempted to flee a hungry predator. A precision shot from the water cannon knocked Bob's bedpost out of his hand and sent him face first to the ground. Mrs. Felton pounced, raining holy water down upon Bob's copy of the Immortallia before the big man could protect it. Her work done, Kevin's mother turned to chase down Oscar and Doorknob, who were busy fleeing for the safety of the Immortalist's old Chevy pickup.

Driff chuckled. "Not a bad way to spend an afternoon, wouldn't you say?"

Kevin shifted uncomfortably, sliding away from a wooden shard he suspected of trying to take a chunk out of his right thigh. "Harksburg's fucking nuts. Something about living in a small town makes everybody freak out."

The elf snorted. "You really think if the reapers responsible for Chicago stopped doing their jobs that all those high hifalutin city folks would react any differently?"

Kevin's mind drifted, then, to Kylie and her friends and co-workers. She belonged to a social group based on one-upmanship and games of power and influence. If one of them suddenly could prove his immortality, he'd certainly use it to extort whatever he wanted from the rest. Especially Kylie, who Kevin suspected would use her newfound immortality to somehow bang every executive vice president in Illinois.

"People are the same everywhere, I guess," Kevin mused. "Selfish."

"*Humans* are selfish everywhere," Driff corrected. "Selfish and desperate to prove that they matter. What is a human's ultimate purpose? An elf knows his: to keep the peace, to safeguard the helpless. A demon is created to destroy. Nymphs tend their forests, lakes, or rivers—"

"Gnomes fuck around," Kevin added, thinking back to his tangled cords.

"Now you're getting it. But what does a human exist for? What's his lot in life? What's he supposed to be doing? Some say humanity's inability to answer that question is ultimately what keeps you from joining the greater community of races."

The elf's words struck something personal within Kevin, something he'd been wondering about himself since his return to Harksburg. Six years of college learning how to be a financial analyst had eventually led him to three years of actually being a financial analyst—and then all of the work and stress and sleepless nights and studying and schmoozing had been rendered worthless with a single pink slip. Without that job—without the desk and the suits and the business cards and the lunch meetings and the number crunching and the paycheck—he didn't feel like himself. But who was Kevin Felton, really? Was he the starry-eyed boy who'd left Harksburg for the glitz and glamour of the big city? Was he the stylish, smooth-talking analyst with the chic loft in the trendy gentrified neighborhood? Or was he the jaded, listless wreck stuck in Harksburg once again? The question made him squirm, the possible answers even more so.

All of which, he supposed, proved the elf's point and made it time to change the subject.

"What about all this stuff with Oscar?" he asked. "He's taking Harksburg's little death problem and putting it all out in the open. I thought you'd be mad."

"Mad?" Driff asked. "This ridiculousness is the perfect smoke screen. Rumors about people in the area not being able to die are bound to spread. If they're tied to your idiot friend, no one will think those rumors are worth a damn, now will they?"

"Maybe," Kevin said, feeling a bit foolish. He felt his cheeks warm with a blush and looked away. "But if you don't want word to get out, why not just use that dust stuff you put in the water supply?"

Driff's voice hardened. "How do you know about that?"

"Nella told me," Kevin replied sheepishly.

"Hmm. I knew I should've caught up to the two of you in the woods sooner. Your girlfriend's got a big mouth. For now, we've canceled the broadcasts that trigger that dust—in Billy's territory, that is. If anything happens that I need to know about, I want to find out about it before the television or the radio wipes it out of everybody's head."

That explained why Kevin still remembered everything from the last few days—Nella, the reaper, dying and coming back to life, Oscar's first performance back in the Works. He'd temporarily forgotten about Nella's warning and watched a few soap operas with his mother the day after. At first, he'd thought Driff had done something to keep Kevin's mind intact while he was in the elf's employ—the thought had given him hope. If Driff had made him temporarily immune to the dust, it stood to reason that Kevin could find a long-term solution so he could be with Nella. Sadly, that wasn't the case.

"And when this is over? When things go back to normal?"

"The broadcasts are turned back on and all this foolishness never happened."

"No one will remember? No one at all?"

"Nella. Your neighbor, the pixie. Any other nonhumans in the area." Driff's eyes narrowed, as if he'd just realized something. "I can't make you an exception to the rule, Kevin. That's not how it works. Rest assured that you will be well-compensated—as promised—even though you'll have no memory of our bargain. We elves pay our debts."

Kevin hadn't been thinking about the money. He'd been thinking about Nella, about how she'd turned out to be a real, live woman and not just a dream induced by some strange byproduct in Harksburg's air. Losing that connection they'd made in the forest by Fornication Point would be worse than losing any amount of money. She'd be a dream again, nothing more—and that hurt. Kevin couldn't tell that to Driff; he doubted the icy son of a bitch had a heart to which he could appeal, and he couldn't risk the elf taking decisive action to keep them apart. Once again, Ren seemed to be the only one who might be able to help Kevin beat the dust and the broadcasts so that he could retain his memories of Nella.

"Why drag Ren into all this?" Kevin asked. "I get why you needed me. I don't get why you went to Ren first."

"That is a private matter I'm not at liberty to discuss."

"Oh, come on!" Kevin said mischievously, smiling and leaning closer. The bench protested by jamming the head of an exposed nail into his hip. "Whatever it is, it's going to be wiped from my memory in a few days. Same deal for anyone I tell."

"It's neither my privacy nor that of my superiors which concerns me."

Which made it a matter of Ren's privacy, confirming to Kevin that there was more to his friend than he knew. But what the hell could it be? How had he gotten mixed up with Driff and his ilk, and why hadn't he told his best friend about it?

"Professor Driff!" Kevin's mother called from behind their bench. Kevin had no idea how she'd managed to sneak up on them. "Fancy meeting you here."

The two men turned as one to face Mrs. Felton. Makeup streaked from the exertion of her holy war, she leered at them over the barrel of the giant water gun strapped to her back, a crusader appraising a potential heathen threat.

Kevin tried to shoot her a warning look. *Don't do it,* he pleaded. *Please don't do it...*

"Mrs. Felton," Driff said coolly.

"Inquiring minds want to know what, if any, association you have with the Satanic gathering I just dispersed."

Kevin hated that tone of voice. He thought of it as her Inquisition mode; wrongs had been perpetrated upon Abelia Felton or someone or something she cared about and she wasn't going to end her search for justice until she'd punished every last party responsible—even if it meant blasting a pistol-packing elf in the face with a Super Soaker full of holy water.

Kevin couldn't allow that to happen. "Professor Driff's interest in today's proceedings was purely academic," he countered.

Abelia cocked her left eyebrow, a slender line of short, blond hair that had asked Kevin many a pressing question throughout the years. *Is that alcohol I smell on your breath? Did you really vacuum your room or am I going to find a pile of crud you swept under the bed? You and that girl were studying, huh? So that flaming bag of dog shit on Mr. Warren's porch put itself there of its own accord?* The gesture was a paralyzing, debilitating exclamation that Abelia wasn't buying his bullshit.

"Such spectacles are rare where I'm from," Driff said, returning Mrs. Felton's scowl—and daring her to call his bluff. "Luckily you arrived to put an end to it."

"So you simply watched? From right here? The entire time?"

"Yes."

Abelia's eyes narrowed. "And you didn't try to stop it?"

Driff shrugged. "I didn't think it was my place."

The blast of holy water leapt forth from the Super Soaker like a cobra striking its prey, drilling Driff square in the face. His head jerked back violently and sent his spectacles tumbling away. Water ricocheted off the elf's face like shrapnel raining down upon his clothing, the bench, the lawn, and the petrified, pale-faced young man seated beside him.

Recovering quickly from the initial blow, Driff leapt to his feet and swatted the Super Soaker out of Abelia's hands before Kevin could even blink. The elf's hand—now a solid shade of green from whatever hex Nella had placed upon him—darted briefly into the pocket of his overcoat and then up past Mrs. Felton's face. A heaping handful of silver dust exploded around her mouth and nose like a tiny star going supernova. Surprised by the speed and ferocity of her opponent's counterattack, she inhaled deeply and took what Kevin assumed to be a tremendous dose of the memory-wiping drug. Abelia's eyes rolled back into her skull as Driff leaned in close to her ear, his jaw working a mile a minute as he whispered instructions.

Kevin was too stunned and frightened to react. He couldn't hear what the elf said to his mother. Occasionally Abelia's mouth moved, her lips parting ever so slightly as if she were reading to herself. If she spoke, she did so in a tone too soft for Kevin to hear. Maybe she was answering questions posed by the elf. Maybe the movement of her mouth was a nervous reflex brought on by the dust. Regardless, interrupting a process that altered someone's mind seemed dangerous, so Kevin refrained from physical or verbal protest. What would happen to her memory if Driff stopped mid-sentence? Would his command simply go unheeded, or would the procedure fail and leave Mrs. Felton catatonic? Kevin didn't want to find out.

A few minutes later, Driff stopped muttering and Abelia's eyes rolled forward again. She glanced briefly to the elf and smiled the widest, most genuine smile Kevin had ever seen on her face. Gone was the perfectly manicured, thoroughly practiced smile she'd been favoring people with for years, replaced with a slightly crooked grin dripping with happiness and gratitude. She looked as if she hadn't a care in the world, as if she'd never known disappointment or tragedy or sadness or fear. She looked as if she'd found the heaven on earth she'd always hoped to create.

And all it had taken to help her find it was a pissed-off elf with a handful of magic dust.

Abelia let the Super Soaker fall from her shoulders, turned abruptly on her heel, and marched off home.

"What the hell?" was all Kevin could manage. His blood had turned to ice, his every nerve blunted. He was the man of the house, the alpha male responsible for his mother's well-being, and yet he'd been helpless to stop an interloper from rewiring her mind. A disappointment—that's what he was, useless and afraid and not up to the task.

Driff shrugged and picked up his fallen spectacles. "You don't have to thank me—just get the job done in the Burg tonight so I can get out of this dump."

With that, the elf faded away, leaving Kevin alone in a town he hated with friends he couldn't trust and whatever was left of his mother.

— CHAPTER THIRTEEN —

Kevin spent the rest of the afternoon in his bedroom. Having experienced enough drama the last few days to last him the remainder of his life, he was in no rush to discover what Driff had done to his mother. Despite all of Driff's talk of ethics and knowing better and racial superiority, the elf was a sadistic son of a bitch; whatever memories he'd torn from Abelia's mind would surely prove painful to someone. Kevin thought he had a pretty good idea who.

He hid downstairs, abandoning his search for the house's gnome infestation and skipping dinner and ignoring the sounds of activity echoing down through the floor. Every heavy footstep and groan of moving furniture made Kevin push his nose a little bit deeper into the high school yearbook he'd retrieved from his closet. There were few things Abelia took more pride in than her home. It had taken years of painstaking decorating and shopping and adjusting, but she always crowed about how the interior of her house was exactly the way she'd always wanted it. She hadn't moved so much as an end table since Kevin's first year in high school. A wholesale makeover could only mean that something profound had changed in Abelia.

The thought made Kevin want to punch something. Who the hell did Driff think he was, rewiring people's brains without their permission? Was such a drastic intrusion really the best way to maintain the peace between the races? What controls kept someone in Driff's position from going too far? Kevin decided he didn't care. All that mattered was that the elf was a danger to everyone and everything he cared about. Confronting Driff would do no good; he doubted he could beat the elf in a physical confrontation, and the last thing he needed was a snout full of dust and a fucked-up memory. The safest way to get Driff out of Harksburg would be to get Billy back to his reaper duties.

But how the hell was he going to convince anyone to go out with that miserable little fuck?

Kevin scoured the yearbook for an answer, studying it like a birdwatcher might a field guide. Most of his graduating class still lived in town, and many spent their Friday nights in the Burg. Using the alphabetized array of student photographs as a guide, he made mental lists of the girls he remembered as easy and those who might fall for Billy's loner schtick. Despite the large number of the former, his count of the latter was dishearteningly small. Harksburg's women, especially the attractive ones, tended to gravitate toward good ol' country boys who wouldn't recognize an emotion beyond "happy," "drunk," or "time for NASCAR" if it walked up and slapped them in the face. He took note of the female members of the drama club and moved on.

Next came the page and a half of superlatives. Best Smile? No. Most Likely to Work with Animals? Yeah, right. Friendliest? Definitely not. Most Likely to Become a Vampire? Looks Best in Black? Deepest Thinker? Unfortunately, the yearbook staff hadn't bothered with those.

Returning to the class photos, Kevin scanned through the men looking for people who might owe him a favor and who he remembered had sisters. He checked the teachers, trying to recall if any of them had been young enough and adventurous enough to show up in the Burg. He read each and every autograph lining the interior of the book's cover, searching for signs of possible sluttiness or desperation—a lowercase "I" topped with a heart, an overly wordy or effusive well-wishing, a general malaise toward the end of high school. All this work made his head hurt, but he didn't dare go upstairs to get an aspirin.

Eventually, he found his way to the list of sponsors on the last page. Most classes funded their yearbooks by begging the local businesses for donations. The Harksburg High Class of 2004, however, just asked Ren Roberts, who in turn asked his father, who in turn acquired the entirety of the yearbook's funding as a donation from his employer, the Tallisker Corporation. Below a quick paragraph thanking the company for its generous contribution, Tallisker's starburst logo filled the center of the final page, surrounded by the names of its smaller subsidiaries: Banner Holdings, Redmond and Co., the Griffin Group...

The Griffin Group.

The dirty sons of bitches that bought out Noonan, Noonan, and Schmidt and then laid off half the workforce, including a bright young analyst named Kevin Felton. He hadn't known of their association with Tallisker. He couldn't explain why, but the connection made the hair on the back of his neck stand straight up. Surely, it was just a coincidence. Surely. Kylie would've told him to stop being so damn paranoid; the world didn't revolve around him, after all. He flipped back to the class photo pages and banished the silly suspicions from his mind.

He napped for a few hours and then showered and shaved in preparation for the evening's festivities. Donning a black T-shirt, his leather jacket, and a pair of old jeans, Kevin exited through the front door and sat on the porch to await the arrival of his ride. The Burg was a fucking dump; he didn't want his good shoes touching the floor, he didn't want his nice pants touching the seats, and most of all he didn't want it to look like he had put any effort into his appearance. If anyone suspected he cared how he looked, it meant he was doing it wrong.

A cool breeze rustled through Kevin's hair as he looked up at the stars. He'd never learned the constellations—there wasn't much use for that kind of knowledge in a place where the local light overwhelmed that of the Milky Way—but as he zipped his jacket against the chill, he found himself kind of wishing that he had taken the time to do so, that he hadn't been in such a rush to advance his career at the expense of simpler pleasures.

I've got the time now, he thought. *When I'm not busy trying to thwart would-be messiahs, or playing matchmaker for Death.*

Ren arrived right on time at 7:45 sharp. The green Jag rolled to a stop in front of the Felton residence with effortless grace. Kevin was disappointed to find Driff in the front seat, and not just because of what the elf had done to his mother that afternoon. Despite all the unanswered phone calls, he'd still been hoping to have a private conversation with his friend.

"I didn't know we were going to have a chaperone," Kevin growled as he swung himself into the backseat. The car's interior was ripe with the sharp aroma of Ren's aftershave—specially imported from Paris, or so its wearer claimed, and supposedly laced with pheromones no female could resist. Kevin thought it smelled like olive oil.

"You didn't expect me to spend my Friday night sitting at home by myself, did you?" Driff asked.

"I figured you'd be busy stealing someone's memories," Kevin snarled as the Jag pulled back away from the curb, "and I'm not particularly thrilled about the prospect of bringing you into the Burg. You're an outsider. You're going to draw a *lot* of attention."

"Oh, I don't think that'll be a problem," the elf replied. "I'll leave you two experts to do your jobs. I'm going along to protect my superiors' investment."

"If it's any consolation, he's footing the tab," Ren said happily.

"What a guy."

"It's the least I can do," Driff said dryly. "Now buck up. I'm not familiar with the mating habits of the average American, but I doubt sulking and pouting is going to help you three with the local ladies."

"Tell that to Billy," Kevin replied.

"It got him into your blue girlfriend's pants," Ren said. "Assuming she ever bothers with pants."

Kevin rolled his eyes, shook his head, and bit back a retort about that time at one of Jim Jimeson's parties when he'd actually caught Ren wearing a girl's panties. It had been part of a dare, or so Ren claimed, and although Kevin didn't doubt it, he also wasn't one to give up an advantage when he had one. Normally Kevin wouldn't have held back even though Ren could occasionally be a prickly sort. His friend was known to get bent out of shape over things and avoid whoever he was mad at for a few days before suddenly showing up again as if nothing had ever happened. Pissing Ren off wouldn't help his situation any. He needed his friend's help with the reaper—and he needed answers he suspected only Ren could provide.

Ignoring the two men in the front seat and their continued conversation, Kevin watched the town roll past. The Jag eased around the elliptical town common and bore left to continue along Main Street. Harksburg's financial district—as town officials called this area, somehow managing to keep a straight face—was aglow with harsh halogen light streaming through the windows of Hucky's Gas-n-Go. Across the street, all five parking spaces in front of the squat general-store-like building that housed Big D's Liquors were filled with pickup trucks waiting for their masters to return with supplies for the evening's festivities. The town library next door stood dark and empty, abandoned for the weekend. Kevin couldn't help feeling that there was a bit of social commentary in the scene, but he dismissed the thought when he realized that he wouldn't be caught dead in the library on a Friday night either.

The view through the Jag's window darkened again, lit only occasionally when they passed a house with its lights on. Population density dropped dramatically outside the center of town, especially when traveling west toward the less respectable communities that rubbed up against Harksburg like the smelly homeless people who had always liked to stand too close to Kevin on Chicago's subway. The homes here along West Main were smaller—single-story ranches, simple split-levels—and older than those on Plastic Hill, inhabited mainly by people who'd spent all or most of their lives in Harksburg and likely weren't leaving anytime soon. Most of Kevin's local friends lived here. Narrow streets sprung off from the main artery every quarter of a mile or so, tunneling off into the woods and the labyrinthine network of even narrower streets therein. Neither nice nor dumpy, this area of town just kind of always was, always had been, and always would be. Those on Plastic Hill treated it as a sort of buffer, a DMZ between their idyllic existence and the riffraff in Norton and Edgartown.

A passing motorist who forgot to turn off his high beams snapped Kevin back to reality. Ren laid on the horn and flipped the other driver off.

"They have asshole drivers where you come from?" Ren asked Driff.

"Not really," the elf replied. "Evitankari's small, even compared to Harksburg, so we typically walk everywhere. And some of our more powerful mages can teleport themselves and others short distances."

"So there aren't any vehicles? At all?"

"There is one jerk who thinks it's funny to speed around town on a four-wheeler blasting classic rock from a boombox at four in the morning when he's had too much to drink."

"Sounds like one of the local losers."

"He's our highest ranking general, actually."

It distressed Kevin to see how well Ren and Driff got along. He had to admit that there was an element of jealousy to it; he and Ren had been best friends forever, but now Ren was telling the elf secrets he wouldn't tell Kevin. Driff had stormed into Harksburg and upended both of their lives, but Ren was treating him like an old friend. It didn't make sense.

Unless—and, as crazy as it sounded, it wouldn't be out of character for Ren—it was all an act. Unless Ren was playing Driff. Unless he saw some advantage in befriending the elf, something that could improve his own situation. Attempting to play someone as dangerous as Driff would take either a serious set of balls or a serious case of stupidity. Kevin had seen Ren excel in both roles. He disliked this possibility even more than he disliked the idea of his oldest friend and the elf becoming legitimate pals. Just one more thing to ask Ren about. The way things were going, Kevin was going to have to start writing all these questions down. He needed a damn drink.

Luckily for Kevin, the Harksburg Bar and Grill was waiting for them around the next bend. The Jag negotiated the deadly turn easily, giving Kevin a great view of the battered guard rail along the edge of the curve that had stopped more than its share of drunk drivers from plowing into the forest beyond. The Chaperone, they called it, because everything in Harksburg needed a fucking nickname. Kevin wondered how long it would be before the nicknames started getting nicknames and the original titles of things were lost forever.

The bright lights of the Burg filled the windshield. Kevin's vision cleared a few blinks later, revealing a silver structure of gently sloping lines trimmed in flashing bulbs. Neon signs blazed in every window, competing with each other for the rights to every patron's shitty beer budget. The Burg had begun life in the fifties as a diner, a narrow, streamlined former train car packed tight with a bar, a few booths, and a tiny grill. Fran Kesky acquired it in the seventies and began adding pieces and parts. First came the sign, a garish neon affair he would've built thirty feet higher and ten feet wider if the town hadn't put a stop to it for reasons of "taste." Next came the addition, a squat, square building tacked onto the back side of the original dining car that added a full kitchen, another bar, ten tables, a dance floor, and room for three pool tables and a dart board. Early in the 90s he added a patio with a mechanical bull and three pinball machines. The Burg was a garish, ridiculous monster of a bar and grill, the kind of place that didn't belong in a small town like Harksburg but would've been laughed right out of most bigger cities. The locals had nowhere else to go unless they wanted to go to lesser bars in Norton or Edgartown or drive an hour to Chicago—as most of the transplants living on Plastic Hill preferred—and so the Burg did a brisk, regular business in spite of the fact that everyone but Fran Kesky thought it was a dump with disgusting food, a shitty beer selection, and the kind of bathrooms you only use when it's too cold or too rainy to duck out into the woods. Ren occasionally did good business selling toilet paper and hand sanitizer in the parking lot across the street.

"Billy beat us here," Driff said as Ren turned into the parking lot. Mr. Pemberton's big black Lincoln sat idling on the curb right in front of the Burg.

"Hopefully that means he's excited," Ren said. "This'll go easier if he's in a good mood."

Kevin suspected the reaper's punctuality had more to do with Mr. Pemberton than with Billy's emotional state, but he kept his mouth shut. Billy in a good mood? Right. That miserable son of a bitch wouldn't know happy if it walked up and bit him in the ass.

The lot mostly full, Ren parked the Jag in the far corner, several spots away from any of the other vehicles. The spot wouldn't be convenient for a quick getaway, but Ren cared more about his paint job than he did about potential escape routes or the walking distance to their destination.

"Any last words of advice?" Ren asked the elf as everyone unbuckled.

"No," came Driff's disembodied reply from the front seat. He'd gone invisible already. "I'll be watching."

Kevin rolled his eyes as he clambered out of the vehicle. He didn't like the idea of not knowing exactly where that asshole was and what he was up to, but at least Driff's disappearing act would make it easier to pretend the elf wasn't around. The passenger door opened briefly and then slammed back shut seemingly of its own accord.

Ren and Kevin fell into step beside each other as they crossed the parking lot. It wasn't a walk they'd made often—three or four times a year, perhaps, when Kevin came home to visit—but it felt familiar nonetheless. Neither man had an actual brother, so each filled that role for the other. They were co-conspirators embarking on a familiar con, thieves returning to the scene of countless crimes. This time the excitement was gone, replaced by an unfamiliar tension that removed any sense of anticipation and boiled the event down to little more than a business transaction.

"So what's the plan?" Kevin asked.

"I'll take care of the girls. I've got several options lined up," Ren replied. He spoke of these women as if they were cattle headed for market. "You'll deal with the reaper. He seems to like you."

"'Like' is too strong a word."

"Fine. 'Tolerates.' 'Might think you're okay.' 'Can kind of empathize with.' Whatever you want to call his attitude toward you, he didn't try to rip your soul out through your nose."

"And if he tries that with one of the ladies?"

"I'll try to spin it as a mass hallucination brought on by fungus in Fran's tap lines, but we're probably fucked."

They crossed the street without looking, absorbed in their own thoughts. Mr. Pemberton climbed out of the Lincoln as they approached, his expression demure. He opened the back door and held it open for the reaper.

To his credit, Billy cleaned up relatively well except for his stupid swoopy hair, which had been spruced up with a liberal application of shimmering gel. His jeans, T-shirt, and leather jacket—all black—were clean and unwrinkled and wouldn't look remotely out of place in a dive like the Burg, where creative fashion meant wearing an old school Cubs cap. Billy had even spritzed on a bit of cologne. Kevin almost couldn't believe it; if the reaper had put this much effort into his appearance it could only mean that he actually wanted to come out to the Burg with them, that he actually wanted to meet a girl and make her like him, that he actually wanted this evening to be a success. Kevin suddenly felt a bit better about their chances.

"Evening," Billy said tentatively. He shuffled from one foot to the other and wouldn't look either Kevin or Ren in the eye. The reaper was *nervous*. Another good sign, as long as it didn't negatively affect his ability to make friends. An awkward, stumbling-over-himself-to-speak reaper could be even harder to work with than the silent, mysterious reaper they'd had to deal with in Lordly Estates. Kevin took the lead, offering Billy a smile and a handshake. The reaper stared at Kevin's hand for a few moments as if it were on fire, then he took it in a solid grip and pumped it three times. Billy's hand was like ice.

"Ready for this?" Kevin asked. Billy nodded.

"Gentlemen," Ren said suavely as he clapped a hand on each of their backs. "Let's go get some pussy."

Kevin and Billy exchanged an annoyed glance. Behind the reaper, Mr. Pemberton shook his head and got back into the car. Kevin thought he heard Driff sigh somewhere off to his left.

"Right, then," Ren stammered, stepping around Kevin to open the Burg's narrow metal door. "After you, fellas."

The front room of the Harksburg Bar and Grill was the old dining car, a spot known throughout town as the last stop before the Windy Pines Rest Home. Elderly men and women sat rigidly on the red leather-topped stools or leaned heavily on the stainless steel counter and tabletops, sipping cheap bottles of beer and picking at plates of the punchless buffalo wings that were half price every Friday night. Fran Kesky had left most of the original fixtures intact and installed replicas whenever something needed to be replaced. Behind the counter, cranky old Buck joylessly flipped burgers on the grill. The buzz from the back room was palpable, a dull roar of bawdy laughter and excited conversation underscored by the beat of the karaoke machine. None of the patrons moved when the three young men entered, but two dozen pairs of geriatric eyes watched their every step as they passed through. "Spring training for senility," Ren often called the place. Billy eyed the crowd nervously as if examining a lengthy to-do list he didn't want to tackle.

Crossing into the Burg's back room was like stepping into an entirely different universe. Gone were the old codgers waiting around to die, replaced by a younger crowd celebrating life. A morass of bodies swamped the bar to their right, conversing loudly or trying to catch Fran Kesky's attention to order a drink. Ahead, the majority of the tables were filled with drinkers huddled close together around pitchers of cheap beer. Smaller knots of people more interested in watching everyone else rather than talking among themselves leaned against the paneled walls. Beyond the pool tables and the dart board stood the stage, a rickety platform Waltman and Jimeson had built in exchange for five years of half-priced food and beer. There, a knot of younger girls Kevin didn't recognize crowded around a microphone and a monitor and butchered a Def Leppard song.

"Ren! Over here!" called a familiar voice Kevin couldn't immediately place. Then he noticed Jenny Reilly sitting alone at one of the longer tables near the bathrooms. *Of course!* Kevin thought. Jenny would sleep with anything for twenty bucks. The fix was in.

"First round's on me," Kevin said, detaching himself from the group. Even though the plan called for him to support Billy, Kevin figured the reaper would be more likely to talk to Jenny if his only other choice was Ren. Billy briefly made as if to follow Kevin to the bar before Ren placed a tentative hand on his back and redirected him toward the table. Kevin hoped everyone's souls would still be stashed safely up their noses when he returned with drinks.

The crowd between their table and the bar made no effort to make Kevin's progress any easier. Though drinks sloshed merrily in many hands—props waved for emphasis or just out of habit— their owners weren't about to give up the prime real estate they'd claimed in front of the bar. Those spots were like gold: convenient to the Burg's only source of alcohol with an excellent line of sight to every corner of the room and any debauchery, shenanigans, or brouhahas that might be occurring therein. Kevin elbowed his way between a douche bag in a Chicago Bears hoodie and a wobbling drunk in a Chicago Bulls jacket and took his place behind a forty-something couple waiting for a drink. The woman might've been his substitute math teacher a few times in elementary school, but he couldn't remember her name and her liquor-glazed eyes didn't register any sign of recognition.

Kevin scanned the crowd as he waited, hoping he'd find a few of the women he'd labeled as good prospects for Billy while perusing his yearbook that afternoon. He could put names to most of those gathered without much thought. A few nodded or smiled in his direction. He didn't return their greetings; he'd never been one to work a room that way.

He almost pissed himself when he spotted his mother at the end of the bar. Abelia Felton had spent the last twenty-seven years of her life running down anyone debauched enough to frequent "those damn gin mills." She'd spent one summer leading an outspoken but extremely short-lived campaign to make Harksburg a dry community—a campaign that made Kevin's sophomore year of high school a lot more difficult than he felt it needed to be. The only liquor to touch her lips during that time had been church wine and that only in very small doses. Yet there she sat, clad in some kind of red leather jacket Kevin had never seen her wear, watching the Blackhawks on the television as she nursed a Manhattan. Oscar leaned heavily on the bar beside her, still clad in his white Immortalist robe, working on a light beer and staring up at the very same hockey game. A few easy comments passed between them after a Hawks defenseman laid out one of Detroit's forwards. Abelia laughed and took a sip of her drink.

Kevin averted his gaze and wormed through the crowd toward the opposite end of the bar, putting as much distance as he could between himself and whatever the hell Driff had turned his mother into. What could the elf possibly have yanked out of her memory that made her go to the bar with a heathen to watch hockey and get drunk? The thought made Kevin shiver. He'd have to confront Abelia eventually, but he wasn't looking forward to it. Did she still love him? That, Kevin realized, was the question he was really afraid of. Abelia Felton had loved her son without question—and he loved her back, despite all her faults and general religious insanity. Kevin's mother had always been there when he needed someone, and she'd welcomed him home with open arms and a warm cup of cocoa when he'd had nowhere else to go. What if that part of her was gone? Could Driff and the elves exorcise something that fundamental from an individual's personality with just a handful of dust and a few strategic instructions?

Those thoughts made him thirsty. He sidled up to the bar as the two men in front of him—Fran Kesky's nephews, Lou and Ben, who occasionally filled in slinging drinks when their uncle was out of town—departed with snifters of cheap bourbon in hand. The bar itself was a sturdy wooden affair, its top tattooed with names and dates inscribed into the dark wood with car keys and pocket knives. The liquor shelves on the wall behind it were lined with blue Christmas lights and cluttered with keepsakes: a Jim McMahon bobblehead, a picture of Steve Bartman edited to give the infamous Cubs fan a black eye and several missing teeth, several horseshoes the workers found while excavating the addition's foundation, the bronzed baby shoes of Fran's eldest son, Rob. Nosy townies who knew such things claimed that the walls of Kesky's house were pure white and unadorned, that he hadn't bothered to put a single photograph on the mantel. The Harksburg Bar and Grill was Fran Kesky's real home. Kevin had always felt welcome there.

Kylie would've hated the place with a passion. "Why the fuck do you want to go to that dump?" she would've asked. "In the mood to slum it with the local yokels, maybe?" Kylie and her friends preferred modern, antiseptic bars with pretentious names like "Snack" or "Igloo." Places where everything was the same fucking color, usually a luscious maroon or a dark gray. Places where darts, billiards, and karaoke were all dirty words. Places where the drinks were named after turn of the century railroad barons or members of Andy Warhol's menagerie. Places they wouldn't let you into if you only had $20 in your pocket. Places without a soul.

Part of Kevin wanted to call Kylie up, drag her into the Burg, and tie her down to a stool until the place's unassuming vibe purged all the bullshit from her system. Part of him never wanted to talk to her again. If he could just find a way to make a life with Nella, he wouldn't have to worry about either option.

Fran Kesky was busy at the taps in the center of the bar, pouring a trio of pitchers for Betty Tuttle and the members of her bridal party. Kevin cursed, crossed Betty off his list of possibilities, and scanned the rest of the crowd. There was Harry Young, who sat in front of Kevin in fifth grade science, chatting up big Matty McGwire, one-time scourge of the back few rows of the bus. Waltman and Jim Jimeson stood with their backs to the bar, leering at Betty's crew like sharks deciding which goldfish to devour first. Laurie Nucent, Kevin's third grade crush, twirled her long blond hair while entertaining the advances of two younger boys Kevin thought were probably Doorknob's little brothers. The scene was strangely unnerving; for some reason, he flashed back to Mrs. Best's second grade class, to the day they'd gone around the room and announced what they'd all wanted to be when they grew up.

"An actress or a princess!" Laurie proclaimed happily.

"CEO of a Fortune 500 company," Ren replied disinterestedly. "With enough stock options to buy Monaco twice over."

"Astronaut," Waltman said.

"Astronaut," Jim Jimeson echoed.

"FBI agent," Tom Flanagan said.

"President," Jenny Reilly announced.

"Race car!" Doorknob said, picking his nose merrily.

"Do you mean a race car driver?" Mrs. Best had asked, smiling her best this-kid-is-fucking-stupid-but-I-have-to-be-nice-anyway smile.

"No! I want to be the car!"

Kevin couldn't remember his own answer. That troubled him. Had he ever really known what he wanted to do with himself? He'd gotten into finance simply because it paid well and the perks were out of this world. The work itself was fine, poring through ledgers and writing reports became boring and tedious at times, but it wasn't a terrible way to spend eight, nine, or sometimes ten hours a day. Still, it shocked Kevin to realize how little he actually cared for his old job, how he'd always cared more about the money, the benefits, and the prestige than he cared about the work itself.

When had his friends decided to give up their dreams? None of them had told Mrs. Best that they wanted to be an out-of-work handyman, the town's most infamous party girl, a fake messiah in a dirty bathrobe, or a regular at the Burg. Maybe it was wrong to tell children they can be whatever they want when evidence clearly pointed to the contrary. Maybe the difference between what Kevin and his friends had wanted to be and what they'd become didn't actually matter given that everybody turns out fucked in the end regardless of their title and position and how much money they have in the bank.

A burly hand clapped Kevin on the shoulder, shaking him out of his thoughts. He turned to find Fran Kesky's smiling bulldog face filling his view. Bald, fat, ugly, and damn proud of all three, Fran was probably the most gregarious and personable individual Kevin had ever met. He knew everyone in town by first name and always had a warm greeting for anyone he hadn't seen in a while. Underneath that friendly exterior, though, lurked one of the shrewdest businessmen Kevin had ever encountered. Kesky had single-handedly turned a failing diner into the social and political center of Harksburg. He could've given many of the investment bankers at Noonan, Noonan, and Schmidt a run for their money—and he never would've allowed the Griffin Group to take over.

"K-Felt!" Fran bellowed, his jowls quivering. "The prodigal son makes his triumphant return!"

Kevin couldn't help smiling. "It was a little less than triumphant, Fran, but it's nice to be back." He didn't really mean that, but there was a certain protocol that had to be followed. If Kesky picked up on it, he didn't let it show.

"Nasty business, that," Fran said, his demeanor suddenly demure and empathetic, "but it's good to see you. You coming back seems to have loosened your mother up some."

"It—uh—sure has." Kevin changed the subject quickly. "Two pitchers of your finest IPA, my friend," he said, slapping the bar for emphasis.

"Coming right up," Fran replied as he trundled off to fill the order. "This round's on the house."

As he waited, Kevin turned around and leaned back against the bar. He had to stand up on his toes and crane his neck to get a good look at the table at which he'd be joining his friends. He found Jenny talking a mile a minute at a rather stunned looking Billy while Ren played with something on his phone. It seemed like the reaper either wasn't able to keep up or didn't want to. Kevin shook his head and cursed under his breath.

Ten minutes. I've been here for ten fucking minutes and already I wish I were anywhere else. He hadn't been looking forward to moving back to Harksburg, but he'd never expected things to turn this fucking ridiculous. When had he become such a magnet for drama? Did he give off some kind of field that drew all these magical assholes straight to him?

Fran returned with two pitchers full to the brim with frothy brew and four warm, recently washed glasses. Kevin tucked the stack of glasses between his forearm and his chest, took a pitcher in each hand, and made a beeline for the table. The crowd parted slightly at his approach, affording him just enough space to squeak past with his heavy load. Ren stood and took the glasses from his arm as Kevin set the pitchers down.

"You put those on my tab, right?" Ren asked with a wink.

"They're on the house," Kevin replied. "A welcome home present from Fran Kesky."

Jenny took one of the pitchers and poured Billy the first glass. "Fran's a hell of a guy," she chirped. "My friends and I came here for my twenty-first. He comped everything, even the rim job he gave me in the bathroom."

Ren burst out laughing. Kevin chuckled, genuinely at first, and then more anxiously when he saw Billy's blank stare. The reaper looked absolutely petrified.

Thinking quickly, Kevin whirled into damage control mode. "So Billy, Jenny's really into heavy metal music."

"I just love a good, hard guitar," she said scandalously, leaning close to Billy and smiling brightly. Despite the extra weight and whatever the hell she'd done to turn her dirty blond hair a stringy, silvery white, there was still something alluring about Jenny Reilly—especially if you didn't know or chose not to think about the manic depression, raging alcoholism, and general lack of self-control that knocked the valedictorian and prom queen of the Harksburg Class of 2004 off of her pedestal and into the cashier's job at Hucky's Gas-n-Go. Kevin couldn't help feeling depressed at the sight of his old friend. The Jenny Reilly he'd remembered from school was a bright, pretty, hardworking girl who seemingly had the whole world ahead of her. What the hell happened to turn her into a busted, broken college dropout?

Billy shied away from Jenny and eyed his beer nervously. "I like the drums myself."

There, Kevin thought. *That wasn't so hard.*

"Say," the reaper continued. "Have you ever met anyone named Poofy?"

The girl cocked her head in confusion. "Poofy? Can't say I have. Sounds like a good name for a real pussy."

"Jenny, what was the last show you went to?" Kevin asked nervously, trying to redirect the conversation.

"I don't remember the band's name. Dragon-something, maybe. But oh my God, it was so much fun! We went backstage and did lines of coke off the bassist's Bowie knife!"

Billy's eyes widened so far Kevin feared they were about to fall out of his head and splash into his glass of beer.

"Hey, Jenny, what do you say we go look at the karaoke book?" Ren suggested.

Time to regroup, Kevin thought. *And not a moment too soon.*

Jenny didn't miss the hint. "Let's," she said happily. "Maybe we can find a song that'll put everybody in a better Friday night state of mind!"

Kevin took a long swig of IPA and watched them disappear in the crowd between their table and the stage. His mind spun, evaluating his options. He needed to find some means of encouraging Billy to come out of his shell—easier said than done, especially considering that the reaper still hadn't touched his beer. Nella never would've put up with him if he was all doom and gloom all the time. There was a spark in there somewhere. Kevin just had to find it.

"She's very...open," Billy muttered under his breath.

"Jenny's always been friendly," Kevin replied. "She likes to make sure everyone has a good time."

"Ah. One of those."

What the hell was that supposed to mean? Kevin ignored it. "She was the valedictorian of our graduating class. She's smarter than she lets on."

Billy chuckled and sniffed his beer. "Ha. So what happened?"

Kevin shrugged. "Life, I guess."

"Life does have a way of fucking up everybody's plans."

"I couldn't have said it any better myself." Kevin took another drink. Noticing Ren looking his way from a spot at the edge of the crowd, he shook his head once as slightly as possible to warn his friend away. If this was going to work, someone needed to get Billy talking in sentences consisting of more than two words. That someone was going to have to be Kevin Felton. "Life. Plans. You sound like you speak from experience."

The reaper's demeanor darkened and his gaze dropped to the table. His finger traced the rough edges of one of the names carved into the wood. "Don't we all?"

Come on, fucker. Open up. "Some more than others. Tell me, Billy: before you became—you know—what did you want to be when you grew up? A musician? A video game designer?" *A rich hermit with a manservant tending to his every need and an entire housing development to himself?*

Billy thought for a second. "Dead," he replied. Kevin blanched. "Before that, believe it or not, I wanted to help people. Social work seemed okay."

Dead. Social work. Oddly, Kevin mused, his job as a reaper gave him a mixture of both.

"And you?" Billy asked. "What did you want to be?"

"Race car," he said dismissively. "What kind of social work were you interested in?"

"I wanted to work with kids."

"That'll get you more attention from the ladies than a puppy," Kevin said happily.

Billy glanced anxiously toward the stage. Ren and Jenny stood to its left, flipping through the ratty, unbound stack of pages that constituted DJ Oberon's karaoke book. "Can I get that attention from someone a little less...intimidating?"

"Jenny's a great girl once you get to know her."

"I think she's a little too much for me."

Kevin scratched his chin. This reaper was proving to be a much more complex individual than he'd expected based on their limited interaction in Lordly Estates. Was he really a prude, or was there more to his dislike of Jenny? Kevin suspected the latter. Something about Billy wasn't quite right—beyond the obvious magical crap—and Kevin couldn't put his finger on it. Discovering and exploiting the cause of Billy's reluctance to interact with most people would be key to hooking him up with a new woman—and keeping Kevin's soul safely up his nose where it belonged.

He needed time to think and to send Ren a clandestine text. They had to get rid of Jenny before she did something Billy *really* didn't like. "Pardon me for a moment. Piss break."

The reaper frowned slightly but didn't protest as Kevin drained the rest of his beer and stood. Quickly skirting the trio of older women lingering behind their table, he made a beeline for the Burg's men's room. He'd always preferred to do his business inside, regardless of the facility's condition. Town gossip told of one too many people who'd literally been caught in the woods with their pants down.

Harsh fluorescent light streamed out through the open door of the men's room. Single occupancy, it was a tight space with little room to maneuver—but that hadn't stopped all manner of stupidity from occurring inside. A chunk was missing from the cover of the toilet's tank where Bobby Harman head-butted it in a fit of drunken rage in the eighties. Long scratch marks in the walls an outsider would've suspected were caused by some sort of wild animal were actually the result of a threesome involving Joe Marvick and a pair of Norton girls seven or eight years prior. The battered old vanity sank forward at a scary angle because Sweatpants Bob once decided to take a dump in the sink while the toilet was clogged. The Burg pulled in more than enough money to pay for repairs, but Fran Kesky claimed the damage gave the men's room a bit of character not found in most modern sanitary facilities. Word on the street was that he preferred to spend his profits on hookers and blow. Kevin figured the truth was somewhere in between.

He met surprising resistance when he tried to close the door behind him. Kevin pushed harder, but a small, feminine shape squeezed inside between the door and the jamb. Almost too pretty for words, she looked up at him with big doe eyes between locks of long raven hair. A wispy white sun dress hung off her shapely frame like gauze, leaving little to the imagination. She was barefoot—not a good choice in the Burg. Kevin's eyes were drawn to the pendant hanging just above her pale breasts, a silver crescent moon that glittered brightly in the fluorescent light.

Before he could protest, she smiled at him. Her mouth skewed slightly to the left, her two front teeth grazing her firm lower lip mischievously. Kevin knew that smile. He reached over her shoulder and slammed the door violently shut.

"Nella?"

In one lightning-quick motion she grabbed Kevin's hand and planted a heavy kiss on his lips. No doubt about it. That was definitely Nella.

"How? Why?" Kevin stammered, stunned by both her appearance and her welcome.

"I wanted to see you," she said gently, kissing his neck. "And I *love* karaoke."

"But...why aren't you blue?"

She rolled her eyes and fingered her pendant. "You don't think I'm wearing this thing because I think it looks pretty, do you? I don't know how you humans can bare to drape so much crap all over yourselves."

Nella lifted herself up onto her toes, grabbed the back of Kevin's head, and pulled his lips into hers. For a moment, all was right with the world. He wasn't stuck in Harksburg, wasting a Friday night in Fran Kesky's dirty old bathroom; he was wrapped in the warm embrace of a beautiful woman who smelled like lilacs and tasted like the crispest, cleanest spring water. The only magic that existed in the world was the warm feeling that started between his legs and raced outward through his veins. He didn't care about elves or nymphs or immortality or best friends with secrets. He didn't care about the personification of death waiting in the next room who would kill him if he could see what he was about to do to the woman who had left the reaper high and dry at the altar.

Actually, he did care about that last part. Taking Nella firmly by her soft shoulders, he put some space between the two of them so they could talk.

"If Billy catches us…"

"Don't worry," she cooed, leaning heavily against his grasp. "Reapers can't see through walls, silly."

"What about magic pendants?"

She shook her head. "I walked right past your idiot friend with the car and he didn't recognize me. No one will suspect a thing."

"Billy's not an idiot, and he's spent a hell of a lot more time with you than Ren has."

Nella frowned. "Billy's a juvenile little twit who never grew up."

Alarms going off in his head, Kevin froze. *A juvenile little twit who never grew up.* That was Billy's problem; that was why he looked so young, why he didn't touch his beer, why he was so afraid of Jenny's advances. He looked and acted sixteen because he was physically stuck that way. Becoming a hermit hadn't helped. All those experiences that turned boys into men—graduating high school, getting a job or going to college, starting to drink, moving off on their own, learning how to be comfortable around women— were things you couldn't get sitting in front of a computer screen.

Kevin took Nella's head in his hands and planted a wet, sloppy kiss on her forehead. "Nella, you're fucking brilliant!"

"No shit."

He yanked his phone out of his pocket and texted Ren: *Billy's still a teenager.*

"Tell me what made Billy like you."

Nella rolled her eyes again, then pouted her lip and put her left hand on her curvy hip. "Isn't it obvious?"

"Billy's afraid of women," Kevin said firmly. "*That* probably scared the shit out of him."

"Hmm. Explains why he never really put a move on me."

"Never?"

"Never. Boy's pure as the driven snow."

Kevin's smartphone vibrated with Ren's reply. *So what? We take him to Chuck E. Cheese?*

Find someone inexperienced and unassuming, Kevin typed. He looked up at Nella, thinking. The water nymph had bonded with the reaper because she missed Kevin.

And maybe a little sad, Kevin added in another text. *No shots, no dancing, and give Jenny $20 to go home.*

Tapping his phone against his chin, Kevin considered the situation further. He didn't know anyone in town who fit the criteria he'd given Ren. This place had a way of squeezing the innocence right out of people, of taking the most extreme traits of their personalities and twisting them into grotesque caricatures. Everyone in Harksburg was trying to be someone: the crusading avenger for the church, the lovable-but-shrewd bartender, the rich kid who claimed he was too cultured for everything around him, the party girl who was up for any and every vice. They were all putting on a show. That shit wasn't going to fly with Billy. Maybe there was a newcomer living on Plastic Hill who hadn't been twisted by the place, or maybe there was a local who had escaped the Harksburg personality grist mill unscathed. Hopefully Ren knew.

Kevin wondered if maybe his judgment of the community was unfair. Maybe his innate knowledge of the way everyone was *before* clouded his vision; maybe this slow degradation was just the way things proceeded, regardless of location. Maybe—

A heavy knock on the door interrupted his thoughts. "What the fuck is takin' so long in there?" a voice bellowed. It belonged to Mr. Yeardley, the town groundskeeper. "I've got a kid to drop off at the pool, and he's a fucking big mother!"

Kevin looked from Nella to the narrow window. She'd fit if he could jimmy it open.

"Oh no," she said, crossing her arms and glaring. "I'll be damned if I'm going out that way."

He took her shoulder gently in his hand. "I'm sorry. I have to get back out there and deal with Billy."

Then she did something Kevin never would've expected. Something he would not have recommended. Something that almost made him gag.

Nella stepped into the toilet. "Flush me."

"Um...what?"

"Water nymph, remember? This dump's septic system leaks into the nearby swamp. I'll be fine."

He wrinkled his nose and looked to the vanity. "Why not use the sink?"

"They both go to the same place," she replied mischievously. "Think of this as the express train."

"That's gross. You didn't like it when Driff filled your lagoon with garbage, but you're fine with swimming through a big tank of shit?"

"You might not mind walking through the dirt, but you aren't going to fill your house with it."

"Huh?"

With a sigh she reached back and pushed the lever down. Kevin watched, aghast, as her solid form turned liquid and merged with the flushing water.

"Good luck!" she chirped, offering a little wave as the rest of her melted quickly into her base element and was sucked down the drain.

Kevin shook his head, in dire need of another drink. Before leaving the bathroom, he unwound an entire roll of toilet paper and tried to flush it, hopelessly clogging the drain. He didn't like the idea of Mr. Yeardley's giant turd chasing Nella through the pipes, even though she was taking a one-way trip to the Burg's septic system. He hoped she planned on taking a shower or mixing a can of disinfectant into herself.

After taking a deep breath in preparation for dealing with Billy once more, Kevin slowly pulled the door open and stepped out. He found Sweatpants Bob waiting to use the bathroom. When he recognized Kevin, Bob's face twisted into a snarl reminiscent of an angry, rabid bear.

"You." The stench of gin rose off the old man in waves like heat from a sidewalk on a hot day. The big man's eyes, blurry and unfocused, boiled with rage.

"Hi." Kevin glanced left and right, but Sweatpants Bob was so big that there was no squeezing around him. He'd have to talk his way out of this—if Sweatpants started swinging, there wouldn't be much Kevin could do to defend himself. "I thought Mr. Yeardley was next."

"He decided to go in the woods."

"Oh. I think I saw the Immortalist over at the bar."

"I've got a present for your mother," Sweatpants Bob slurred. "A thank you of sorts. Make sure you give it to her."

Sweatpants was a lot quicker than his size or blood alcohol content should've allowed. Kevin dodged left, but he was too late. The big man's knuckles drilled Kevin in the chin and drove the back of his head into and then through the door behind him. The world went black. Kevin's evening ended on the bathroom floor, unconscious in a pool of water from the overflowing toilet.

— CHAPTER FOURTEEN —

Kevin woke with a groan. His jaw ached where Sweatpants Bob had tried to cave his face in and the back of his head burned from its collision with the Burg's bathroom door. Physics had not been his friend. He rolled onto his side and cursed Isaac Newton, gravity, inertia, and Kylie, who hadn't been there to catch him or talk him out of his dumb plan in the first place. He knew where he was without opening his eyes, He would've recognized that lumpy mattress and those scratchy flannel sheets anywhere. Being laid up at home was better than being stuck in a hospital, he supposed.

Try as he might, Kevin couldn't convince sleep to reclaim him. His mind whirled a mile a minute. How long had he been out? What happened with Billy? Did Nella manage to escape the septic tank, or was she still stuck in the Burg's pipes? Had any of Kevin's friends exacted upon Sweatpants Bob the revenge he'd been too unconscious to deliver himself? And, perhaps most importantly, when was life in Harksburg going to stop being so fucking ridiculous?

Half an hour later he gave up. Ignoring the waves of dull pain echoing through his skull, he sat up, swung himself out of bed, and stood on wobbling legs. A wave of nausea threatened to knock him right back down, but he swallowed and breathed deeply and fought through it. The last thing Kevin needed was a fucking concussion, so of course the universe—via Sweatpants Bob—had obliged. He supposed he was lucky not to have died in his sleep. Not that it would've been permanent. For all Kevin knew, he'd died seven or eight times and the delinquent reaper hadn't come to claim him.

A hearty breakfast and a cup of coffee would put him right back on track. His mother cooked up a feast every morning—pancakes or waffles, an entire henhouse worth of eggs, bacon and sausage and sometimes a pan of corned beef hash. Abelia took her cooking almost as seriously as she did her religion and she was damn good at it. The neighbors actually looked forward to the fruitcakes she dropped off during the holidays. Every funeral reception starred a Mrs. Felton truffle bowl, every wedding or first communion one of her famous pound cakes. Kevin often tried to convince his mother to go into business for herself, but Abelia was too humble and too focused on her work for the church to give his suggestions even a moment's consideration.

Climbing the stairs felt like scaling Everest. Kevin's knees didn't want to bend. Convincing his weak legs to push him up to the next step took a concerted force of will. The motion made his head spin, and he stopped every few steps to lean heavily on the thin railing and wait for the dizziness to subside. He wondered if Driff had any magic that could alleviate a concussion, then dismissed the thought when he realized it would probably involve rewiring his brain—or perhaps just shooting him, given what yesterday's should-have-been-mortal wound had done for his hangover.

Kevin paused when he reached the top of the stairs, catching his breath and letting his head and vision settle down. Maybe getting dusted when this was all over wouldn't be so bad. He didn't want to remember finding Oscar and Doorknob dead in the Works, or watching his mother chase people around the town common with a Super Soaker loaded with holy water, or the look of pain and terror on Ren's face when Billy pulled his soul out through his nose. He certainly wouldn't mind forgetting that time Driff shot him or the sensation of Sweatpants Bob's meaty fist impacting his face. All told, he pretty much wished the last week had never fucking happened.

But then there was Nella. Kevin probably never would've learned she was real if it hadn't been for Driff's intervention in the local drama. Suddenly more than just a recurring dream, he'd realized the water nymph was the real love of his life. Surely that would be the first thing the elf yanked from his memories.

Maybe that would be a fair trade. He wasn't sure.

Kevin dismissed the thought and stumbled down the hallway to the dining room. The good green china Abelia always used for Saturday morning brunch waited for him on the table, piled high with scrambled eggs, bacon, sausage, and home fries. Unfortunately, one of the seats at the table was occupied.

"What the hell are you doing here?" Kevin grumbled as he dropped into a seat opposite the unwanted guest.

Oscar Spuddner smiled meekly and buttered an English muffin. "I...ummm..." He wouldn't meet Kevin's eye, staring down at the pile of scrambled eggs and home fries on his plate instead. For some reason, Spuddner wore the pink bathrobe Abelia usually favored in the mornings. His red hair stuck out from his head in random tufts and his eyes were caked with sleep.

"Good morning, tough guy," Abelia chirped as she trundled into the dining room with a fresh skillet of eggs, wearing only a man's button-down shirt that barely covered the tops of her thighs. Her hair was pulled back in a loose bun and she had yet to apply any makeup. A lit cigarette dangled from her lips, adding an undertone of spicy smoke to the room. "How's your head?"

Kevin sighed. "It hurts." Truth be told, the scene in the dining room had made it even worse.

His mother dumped the scrambled eggs onto an empty platter and returned to the kitchen. "I'll make you a mimosa," she called back over her shoulder. "In the meantime, try to eat something."

For a few moments, the only sound in the Felton dining room was the steady scrape of Oscar's knife across the nooks and crannies of his English muffin. Kevin stared at the wall to his left, trying to subdue the tide of rage bubbling up inside of him. He frowned when he noticed the square spot of discoloration where Abelia's favorite portrait of Jesus should've hung. Glancing to his right, he found the shelves that typically held Abelia's ceramic Mary and Joseph figurines empty. The hutch in the corner stood devoid of the array of crosses that should've been propped up atop it.

Suddenly Kevin realized what Driff had taken away from his mother. He'd always wished she would spend less time on her religion and more time on the real world, that she'd somehow wake up and seize life by the horns and really make something of herself. This, though—this forcible removal of something she probably hadn't wanted to lose—felt wrong. For all of Driff's high-minded talk about responsibility, his ethics surely left a lot to be desired.

But there was a more pressing issue to address.

"I'm only going to ask you this once," Kevin said slowly so Oscar would understand. "Did you sleep with my mother?"

Deliberately, Oscar lowered the English muffin to his plate, set his knife down, wiped his hands on his napkin, and leaned forward to rest his arms on the table. Kevin could see the wheels churning in Spuddner's mind as he struggled to find an explanation that wouldn't get him punched in the face. "Your mother," Oscar said slowly, "is a grown woman capable of making her own choices. She's decided to embark on a journey of self-discovery that—"

"Cut the shit, Spuddner," his mother snapped as she whirled back into the room. She set a pint glass of mimosa down in front of her son. "Yes, Kevin, I fucked your friend. We were both bored and a little drunk and in need of a release, so I figured…why the hell not?"

Kevin's jaw dropped. This creature standing before him with her legs exposed and her face bare may have borne a passing resemblance to Abelia Felton, but this was *not* his mother.

"I actually propositioned that Mr. Driff first," she said thoughtfully. "The way he took down Sweatpants Bob after that big bastard knocked you out was *hot*. It was almost like he appeared out of nowhere. Whoever he really is, he's certainly a good friend to have."

Kevin fought back the urge to vomit.

"I was your second choice?" Oscar sputtered pathetically. "But you said I was special!"

Abelia snorted. "You were my first lay in twenty-seven years. I probably said a lot of things. For a consolation prize, I suppose you were all right. Now shut up and eat your eggs. I'm kicking you out in half an hour."

"Yes, ma'am," Oscar mumbled, returning his attention to his breakfast.

"How the fuck did this happen?" Kevin muttered as he lowered his face into his hands.

Abelia took a seat at the head of the table and inhaled a piece of bacon. Abelia *never* ate with her fingers, and she certainly never even looked at a piece of food without draping a proper napkin over her lap and saying a few words of thanks. "You know that conversation I had with Mr. Driff on the common the other day? It really got me thinking about things. Things I hadn't thought about for a long, long time—like life, the universe and my place in it, and what I want for myself."

"You always told me that God's plan was enough for you," Kevin said, "that His plan should be enough for anybody."

His mother harrumphed and rolled her eyes. "He should've put more sex and beer in His plan."

"Those both figure prominently in my plans!" Oscar said around a mouthful of scrambled eggs. Neither of the Feltons paid him any attention.

Kevin leaned forward and looked his mother square in the eye. He spoke softly and precisely, giving voice to a story he'd never told and only ever heard once. He didn't think his mother suspected he knew it. Uncle Fred, his tongue loosened by a few too many sips from the flask he kept tucked in the waistband of his wrinkled khakis, had told Kevin all about it at the end of his high school graduation party. "Twenty-seven years ago, on a warm spring evening, you left me on your sister's doorstep and drove, alone, to the Almeida Shopping Center. My father had just left you for that Kelly bitch he met in Peoria. You parked in the very last row, in a spot where you could look out through your windshield at the stars glittering over the mall's roof. You washed down a bottle of vicodin with a handle of cheap bourbon and went to sleep. The next morning, you were woken by the most beautiful pink and orange sunrise you'd ever seen. It was like the roof of the mall was on fire, you said, and in those flames, you saw your own rebirth in God's love."

"No, I didn't," Abelia snorted, wrinkling her nose and mouth like she'd just smelled a rancid fart. "What in the hell are you rambling on about?"

That was it, then—the memory Driff had taken away with his dirty fucking dust. Without that life-altering experience, Abelia's faith had no center, no foundation. Her religious fervor had flaked away like dead leaves in an autumn breeze, revealing the cold, hard ground beneath.

If the dust could destroy something as seemingly solid and unassailable as Mrs. Felton's faith, what chance did Kevin's feelings for Nella have?

"Never mind," Kevin said sadly. "Forget I mentioned it."

She already had. "Eat up, then. You start your new job in two hours."

Kevin blanched. "My new what?"

"After Mr. Driff tackled Sweatpants Bob, one hell of a melee broke out. I clobbered a couple of assholes from Norton myself."

"They wanted to hit me," Oscar said meekly.

"But I didn't let 'em, now did I?" Abelia said proudly, cracking her knuckles. "But old Buck got waylaid pretty good and broke his hip. Poor guy's out of work for the next few months—maybe for good."

"What's this got to do with me?"

Abelia smiled evilly. Kevin had never seen his mother look so prideful, so like a clever little girl who knew she'd gotten away with something sneaky that would bring her a huge payoff.

"That supposed 'job' you got with Mr. Driff ain't gonna cut it. I will not have any freeloaders living underneath my roof," she snarled. "You're the new fry cook at the Harksburg Bar and Grill."

— CHAPTER FIFTEEN —

Becoming a fry cook in a small-town dive had never been on Kevin's to-do list, but he decided that working at the Burg would be better than being trapped all day with that thing that used to be his mother. Fran Kesky personally drove his new employee to work in his cherry-red Corvette, jabbering merrily about last night's drama as his foot applied a little too much pressure to the gas pedal. "One hell of a donnybrook," he called it, and "exactly what the town needed to blow off a little steam." A few hundred dollars worth of broken glass and wrecked furniture and a disabled fry cook were worth it, he implied, if it meant giving his humble watering hole's reputation a kick in the dangerous—and therefore interesting—direction.

Kevin briefly considered pouring out all his troubles to Fran and letting the big man spin them into something positive. That threat of death at the hands of the local reaper? Just a story to tell the grandkids! But how would he be able to tell the grandkids without finding a way to evade that massive dose of memory-wiping dust waiting for him if he somehow found a way to survive? Well, at least he wouldn't remember that time he got shot by an elf! Best friend hiding a dark secret? That'll make Kevin seem more alluring and mysterious by association!

That got him thinking about Ren again. His friend had never been much good in a fight; he had probably bolted for the door as soon as the melee started. The thought reminded Kevin of an incident in third grade: that time Jerry Lyon and the Billups twins cornered Kevin and Ren on the playground. Ren took off like a rocket, leaving Kevin to take the brunt of the assault. But then two days later a gang of sixth graders broke Jerry's arm and sent the Billups boys screaming home. Ren paid them handsomely for their services and bought Kevin a new bicycle. People with grandiose ideas about morality and friendship probably would've vilified his friend's actions as a piss-poor attempt to make up for his cowardice, but Kevin didn't have a problem with it. Ren picked his spots, and he picked them well.

Which, Kevin realized, made getting back on the same page as his best friend all the more important. Whatever Ren was hiding, it had to be brought out into the open so they could deal with it and move on. Ren Roberts, Kevin knew, was the only person in town with a snowball's chance in hell of outsmarting that damn elf. Kevin's memories of Nella depended on it.

There was a small crowd of people waiting outside the Burg when they arrived, locals who came for breakfast every Saturday morning and had nowhere else to go and nothing better to do. They didn't look happy. Fran parked in his private spot behind the building and quickly shuffled Kevin in through the back door.

"I've never been a short order cook before," Kevin said. He felt the need to be honest with Fran, and he figured setting the bar low with his new employer would make his life that much easier.

"I'm sure an educated man-o-the-world like yourself will do just fine. Shit ain't rocket science. You think old Buck would've been able to do the job if it were difficult?" Fran said with a smile. His sad eyes betrayed his true feelings; he was going to miss his regular cook. "Just make what the menu says. Scrambled eggs and home fries is scrambled eggs and home fries. If people want spices, point to the salt and pepper and ketchup on the table in front of 'em."

Kylie would've had an aneurysm at the thought of ketchup as a spice.

The Burg's back room looked like it had been the scene of a bombing. Tables and chairs were scattered here and there and turned on their sides, save one set in the middle that had somehow survived the carnage. A splash of blood stained the blue velvet atop the pool table, and a heavy dent in the dart board looked like it would fit perfectly around a human skull.

"Going to hang that busted board behind the bar for posterity," Fran said as he tiptoed over a scattering of broken glass—no small feat for a man his size.

"Who's going to clean all this?" Kevin asked, a sinking feeling in his chest. He sure as hell didn't want to do it.

"I'll hire Waltman and Jimeson. Those two losers never have any work. Think they know which end of the broom to use?"

"They might be able to figure it out if you leave them the manual."

Fran guffawed and almost slipped on a piece of fabric that turned out to be a pair of blue boxer shorts. "Kids these days," he muttered as he kicked the shorts away.

The Burg's owner spent all of thirty seconds getting his new employee acclimated to his surroundings—"spatula's in the drawer, food's all pre-cut in the fridge, an' that hot thing's where you cook"—and then he unlocked the front door and disappeared through the back. While the regular customers streamed inside to claim their usual seats, Kevin helplessly watched Fran's convertible scream away down the road. Being left alone on his very first day of work was neither something he'd expected nor something with which he found himself particularly comfortable.

He wasn't sure how long he stood there gaping and staring out the window. Mr. Spicolli, a septuagenarian with a crooked smile and a wispy comb-over who'd been Kevin's second grade math teacher, snapped him back to reality with a polite sentence. "I'd like scrambled eggs with a side of bacon, hash browns, and wheat toast when you have a moment, Mr. Felton."

Kevin blinked a few times and took a deep breath, steeling himself. "Coffee with that?"

"Please," Mr. Spicolli said warmly, "and a glass of water."

"Coming right up."

Kevin whirled into action, taking care of his old teacher's beverages before collecting the orders of the various other blue hairs seated at the counter. Once everyone was set with a coffee or an orange juice or a glass of water, he turned his attention to the grill and got to work on the food.

The paper hat was surprisingly itchy. Buck's old apron, stained a splotchy shade of beige by decades of splattering grease, weighed heavily on Kevin's shoulders. The plastic grips on all the spatulas had been worn down to accommodate fingers narrower than his own. As Kevin tended the grill, staring intently at a mound of hash browns and a pair of the Burg's supposedly world-famous cheddar and Spam omelets, he could feel the judgmental glares of the patrons at the counter burrowing into his back. Kevin Felton was not old Buck; he knew it, and he'd be the first to admit it, so why did everybody and everything in the place insist on reminding him of it every damn second?

A few minutes later, after Kevin proved he wasn't going to immediately burn down the entire place, the regulars turned their attention to their primary pastime: kicking the infamous Harksburg rumor mill into high gear. The previous evening's festivities, such as they were, provided more than enough raw material.

"I hear Charlie Casserlin took out four boys from Norton all by himself," Mrs. Eichmann exclaimed to Roger Thorn, the groundskeeper at the elementary school. "And then he went home with Jenny Reilly!"

"Fran's going to have to tear down the entire back room," Bob Roman said sagely to no one in particular. "Structural damage. Can't be saved."

"Town jail was so full last night, they just left a few drunks locked up in the back of the cruisers," Willy Howard said in disgust. "Didn't even crack a window!"

"That crazy old bat, Mrs. Felton?" Cordelia Walton whispered to her husband in between bites of French toast—or, at least, *thought* she was whispering to her husband. "Word is she stopped praying to Jesus and started gettin' down on her knees for anyone that asks."

Without saying a word or even looking at the fat old woman, Kevin sauntered over to the Waltons' booth, picked up Cordelia's plate, and carried it back behind the counter. After scraping its contents into the garbage can, he returned to his work at the grill.

"Well, I never!" Mrs. Walton stormed out of the Burg and headed for the car. Her husband smiled at Kevin and kept eating his oatmeal.

Kevin quickly found himself getting into a steady rhythm. Take an order, cook, check for customers looking for a coffee refill or for their check. Lather, rinse, repeat. It wasn't hard work, but it demanded a certain constant attention to detail he hadn't needed to maintain while working in a cubicle. If a report was wrong or incomplete, well, most of his superiors were too busy to notice, but if someone ordered scrambled eggs and got fried, as accidentally happened when he delivered Mr. Loomin's breakfast—well, there was going to be a complaint, but that complaint wasn't trimmed in a politically-correct-sounding-yet-blatantly-passive-aggressive wrapper like those he typically received from his coworkers at Noonan, Noonan, and Schmidt. No, the complaints he received were just that: statements of wrongdoing, devoid of anything personal and free of bullshit beyond the occasional slight implication that Buck would've done it right. Kylie would've found their directness rude, but Kevin appreciated it.

Sometime around eleven, after the first round of customers had left and Mr. Spicolli had finished the third free mimosa Kevin had shoved in front of him, all conversation in the diner suddenly stopped. The soft jingle of the bell attached to the front door announced a newcomer. Kevin turned to find Driff approaching the counter, proudly wearing a bright shiner around his right eye. Magic rounded his pointy ears.

"I thought your mother was fucking with me," the elf said as he took a seat opposite the grill. "She knows you're working for me, right?"

"Unless you dusted that memory out of her, too," Kevin snapped. "Apparently she wants me doing something with better long term prospects than 'running around town with a freak show.' Who gave you that souvenir?"

"Sweatpants Bob is meaner than he looks," Driff replied with a scowl. "He got his elbow up just as I brought him down. Thought he broke one of my ribs, too. He's sleeping it off in the town pen."

"How'd you avoid that fate?"

Driff cocked an eyebrow. "Really?"

"Right," Kevin muttered. Dodging Harksburg's finest probably wasn't particularly difficult for a man who could turn invisible.

"Shouldn't you have handed me a menu by now?"

Kevin grabbed the greasiest menu he could find from under the counter and whipped it at Driff's hands. "Coffee?"

"Please," the elf said as he examined the sheet of laminated paper, holding it delicately at arm's length as one might a dirty diaper. His head suddenly jerked up and around to scan the silent room. Many of the other patrons looked away in embarrassment. "You can all go back to your business now. The stranger who kicked Sweatpants Bob's ass last night isn't going to do anything rash."

A low murmur returned to the Burg as the other costumers followed Driff's suggestion. Mr. and Mrs. Horton hastily left a twenty on their table and headed for the door.

"You don't seem happy with me," Driff said as Kevin poured him a cup of coffee.

"What gave you that idea? Cream and sugar?"

"No, thanks. I'm not the one who punched you in the face, you know. Nor did I give Sweatpants Bob the idea. You can thank your mother for that one."

"I'm pretty sure I can thank you for all the strange shit that's happened to me the last few days."

"You can thank me for pulling that grizzly bear off of you last night. You can also thank me for giving you the opportunity to save your own life."

Kevin turned back to the grill to flip Bob Peterson's scrambled eggs. He knew Driff was right, but he needed someone immediate at whom to direct his anger. He figured the elf could take it.

"What happened to Billy?"

"Ren got him out before things got too hot."

"Luckily for Billy, Ren's an old pro at escaping fights," Kevin said with a smirk.

"I'd say it's everyone else in the fight who was lucky," Driff corrected him. "I bet Billy's great to have on your side in a brawl, even if he's only got one good move. I'll take two over easy, by the way, with a side of sausage and wheat toast."

"Coming right up."

Driff continued rambling as Kevin bent down to remove the appropriate items from the refrigerator under the counter. "Oh, by the way, Ren wanted me to let you know he's going to be out of town for the rest of the week. Pressing family business in Minnesota. I'm house sitting."

Kevin froze and cursed under his breath. Ren's departure couldn't have come at a worse time. It ostensibly left Kevin alone to deal with both Billy and Driff without backup. His mind reeled as he considered his options—but then he realized he didn't have any. Oscar and Doorknob were loyal friends, but they possessed about three brain cells between them. Waltman and Jim Jimeson were devious sons of bitches who would surely play along until they saw an opportunity to screw Kevin over for their own enjoyment. Involving Nella would be too dangerous for both of them. His mother had become a wild card. Mr. Gregson, his only other link to the world Driff and Billy inhabited, hated his guts. For Kevin Felton, there was no one in Harksburg as capable and trustworthy as Ren Roberts.

"I take it Mr. and Mrs. Roberts didn't appreciate their son's attendance at last evening's festivities," Kevin said.

The elf's response was surprisingly hesitant. "I'm not sure. It seemed like there was more to it than that. Ed and Ellen were both a little nervous about the trip, and Ren looked like a man being led to the gallows."

Standing slowly, Kevin locked eyes with Driff. He wanted the truth. "And you had nothing to do with this? You aren't trying to separate us, are you?"

Driff raised his hands in mock surrender. "You got me. I realized that I am no match for a pair of small-town washouts."

"I'm not a washout. I've got *two* jobs right now." Kevin paused. "You think this is about those things you know about Ren that I don't?"

Driff pushed his spectacles up onto his nose and frowned. "If it is, then you and I had better get ready to pull ourselves out of a giant pile of shit."

Returning to the grill without acknowledging Driff's warning, Kevin focused on flipping the sizzling pile of hash browns awaiting his attention. He almost wished the elf had showed up simply to admonish him for the debacle in the back of the Burg; the fact that the seemingly unflappable Driff had come because he was nervous and needed an ally was somehow more disconcerting than any possible overt threat.

— CHAPTER SIXTEEN —

Monday morning, Kevin found Doorknob waiting for breakfast in the dining room. Oscar's sidekick blanched and fled the house, tumbling ass over teakettle down the front steps.

"Good riddance," Abelia mumbled as she trundled into the dining room and dropped a heaping plate of blueberry crepes on the table. She took a long drag from her cigarette and ashed it in Doorknob's abandoned coffee cup. "All that one wanted to talk about was race cars."

"That's kind of his thing."

The crepes, of course, were delicious, but unfortunately Fran Kesky's insistent honking put an end to any thought Kevin had of a second helping. The Harksburg Bar and Grill needed its new fry cook, even on a Monday. Shitty brunch waited for no man.

Fran greeted Kevin with a beaming grin and a dramatic wink. "There's my favorite new employee! Ready to sling some hash and make some cash?"

"Sure thing," Kevin replied as he climbed into the vehicle, forcing a smile. It was too early and he was too annoyed with his mother's newfound promiscuity to match Fran's gregarious attitude. He hoped he wouldn't have to deal with this crap every morning.

Kevin let Fran's yammering flow in one ear and out the other as the big man drove. His thoughts drifted to Ren and the Roberts family's supposed "urgent business" in Minnesota. He couldn't remember the last time Ren had traveled more than an hour two from Harksburg, strange, given that the affluent family could easily afford to venture anywhere on the planet. Ren's father, Ed, often traveled far and wide on business, but Kevin couldn't recall Ren and Ellen ever having been involved in any of those trips. He quickly checked his phone to see if his best friend had responded to any of the text messages he'd sent the night before, but Ren remained incommunicado.

The more he thought about it, the more Ren's departure concerned him. The timing couldn't have been worse, and it felt like it couldn't possibly be a coincidence. What did Ren's parents know of the situation with Billy? Was it something Kevin didn't know or didn't properly understand? And what of Driff's appearance two days before? The elf certainly wasn't the type to blow a potential threat out of proportion—unless, of course, he wanted Kevin to be nervous and out of sorts for some reason of his own.

All of which made Kevin miss Ren even more. Despite the danger of discovery, maybe it was time for a conversation with Nella. She, at least, was a part of the strange new world into which Kevin had been thrown. She might have some insight, even though she lived in a lagoon in the middle of nowhere. It was too bad that Mr. Gregson had turned out to be such an asshole.

"Hey," Fran Kesky tapped Kevin on the knee, pulling him back to reality. "You ever get a look at your mother's recipe book?"

"My mother's...what?"

Fran shrugged as he took the next corner. "They say she's the best cook in town. You got any of her secrets?"

Kevin frowned. Was that why Fran had given him this job? "She keeps it all in her head." That was a lie: Abelia's recipes were written down on index cards and stored in a little plastic box in the cabinet above the refrigerator. The last thing he needed was to be dispatched on a mission to steal the top secret formula to his mother's famous potatoes au gratin.

It was Fran's turn to grimace. "Ah, well. Maybe her culinary mastery is genetic! Want to try whipping up some fruitcake today?"

"Uh...I'm not really feeling up to fruitcake yet," Kevin stammered. *This entire fucking town is out to fucking get me*, he thought.

"Well, maybe tomorrow," Fran replied before launching into a rant about the rising price of the various bottles of cheap liquor the town drunks typically preferred. Kevin blocked him out once again and considered his options for getting in touch with Nella. Quickly concluding that a trip into the Works would be the only way to get the water nymph's attention, he lost himself in the passing scenery and blissfully thought of nothing as the world whipped past.

Fran parked the Caddy behind the Burg. "I smell a busy day!" the big man bellowed triumphantly as the two of them exited the vehicle. It was well-known that the Burg was basically a ghost town during the week, frequented only occasionally by groups of oldsters who missed out on Saturday or Sunday brunch and starving delivery drivers who couldn't bear the thought of driving another fifteen minutes to reach Mac's Pizza in Norton center. Kevin had been looking forward to a lovely day of reading the paper and occasionally wiping down the counter, especially given how hard he'd worked the previous two days. He really hoped Fran's interest in Mrs. Felton's cooking wouldn't ruin it.

"Hanging out here today?" Kevin asked.

Fran nodded. "Not that I don't think you can handle it, of course. No one died or called the health department this weekend, so you passed with flying colors." Kevin neglected to mention that the lack of breakfast-related deaths possibly had less to do with his skills on the grill and more to do with a certain magic local's dereliction of duty. "Waltman and Jimeson are on their way to clean up the back. They work better under a little bit of supervision."

Which, Kevin knew, was just a polite way of saying "If I don't watch those little shits, they'll walk off the job with several hundred dollars worth of liquor."

"You'll have a little more prep work to do today," Fran explained as they crossed the deserted street. "Nothing's chopped or mixed ahead of time like on the weekend. Tough to tell how many people we'll have on a day like today, and I'd rather nothing go to waste. Got your potato peeling shoes on?"

"Had 'em polished special for the occasion."

"Attaboy," Fran said with a dramatic wink, unlocking the Burg's back door without even looking at the knob.

After working together with Fran to move a sack of potatoes and a few other supplies up from the basement and into the cabinets under the front counter, Kevin was left on his own to tend to the grill while the restaurant's owner busied himself in the back room. Once Fran was gone, Kevin immediately whipped out his phone to text Ren about the Burg's basement. He'd never imagined the place having one, nor had he ever heard of anyone else in town mentioning it. His mind raced at the possible things that might be hidden in down there, from the bodies of Fran's enemies to a few redheaded stepchildren the Burg's owner didn't want seeing the light of day. Maybe a slightly less serious message would catch Ren's attention. Kevin's pleas for contact and an explanation certainly hadn't gotten the job done.

Text sent, Kevin put on his white apron and turned to the pile of potatoes he'd lined up beside the little plastic cutting board in his prep area opposite the warming grill. He'd always assumed that the Burg's food came in giant freezer bags, already pre-made. It was too terrible to be fresh; real meats and vegetables couldn't possibly be transformed into the radioactive slop old Buck used to sling. The thought gave Kevin a jolt of confidence as he picked up the peeler with one hand and hefted his first victim with his other. At the very least, nothing he did behind that counter could possibly be as bad as the status quo.

"Remember: ten potatoes for every onion!" Fran called out from the back room, his booming voice easily penetrating the cheap, thin wall separating the Burg's two halves. "Unless your mother would do it differently!"

"Got it!" Kevin bellowed in reply. "My mother would add in a lot of love, but I've got to hide all mine so no one knows I like the blue girl," he mumbled under his breath.

All was peaceful in the Harksburg Bar and Grill. Kevin quickly lost track of time as the repetitive motions of peeling and the rhythmic bass line of chopping lulled him into a state of semi-consciousness not all that different from that which had once gotten him through ten-hour days trapped in a cubicle. The thought would've sent him into an introspective tailspin had he been awake enough to acknowledge it.

Maybe an hour later, the telltale roar of a diesel engine snapped Kevin back to reality. He looked up from his cutting board just in time to see a familiar maroon van fishtail into the parking lot across the street. The vehicle arced around the lot once and settled into a crooked position that took up two of the parking spots closest to the road.

"Son of a bitch," Kevin muttered under his breath.

That maroon van belonged to Mr. Gregson, the Feltons' crotchety old neighbor. Kevin had never actually seen that particular vehicle on the road before; as far as he knew, it had spent the last twenty-seven years in Mr. Gregson's driveway, neglected except for its monthly washing. No one in town understood why a man who'd lost his legs had held on to that crappy vehicle. Some posited that it had sentimental value, that the man couldn't part with his car because it reminded him of a better time in his life. Most thought Mr. Gregson kept it simply because he was fucking nuts.

Staring intently through the Burg's front window at the ominous van, Kevin found himself hoping someone had finally stolen Mr. Gregson's precious vehicle. The alternative was too disconcerting to comprehend. Had the pixie come to the Burg, risking discovery by anyone who might recognize his van and start asking questions as to how, exactly, a man with no legs could operate something that relied so heavily on the use of one's lower extremities, simply to further screw with Kevin Felton? The glare on the van's windshield made it impossible to determine who was behind the wheel. Kevin found his heart beating in his throat.

The side door slid open with a harsh squeal audible even in the Burg. Mr. Gregson rolled his wheelchair out into the air, allowed it to hover for a second, then gently lowered himself to the ground. As he took a heavy puff on the cigar dangling between his bulbous lips, the door slid shut once again behind him.

Kevin flinched at the sound, his knuckles white around the handle of the knife in his right hand. "Fran!" he bellowed. Maybe Mr. Gregson would leave him alone if there was a witness around.

"What?" Fran's voice cracked as if he were straining himself. Kevin leaned his ear close to the back wall to listen. He swore he could somehow hear the big man sweating, but he had no clue what his boss was busy with.

Mr. Gregson, meanwhile, had scooted across the street and was making a beeline for the front door, leaving a wispy trail of gray cigar smoke wafting behind him. The town zoning board had forced Kesky to add a handicapped ramp to the side of his building, but Mr. Gregson apparently wasn't going to have any of that. What difficulty were stairs to a creature with telekinetic powers?

"Fran!"

"I'm busy! I'll be with you in a minute or two!"

The front door swung open on its own, violently ringing the bell attached above the frame. Mr. Gregson levitated up over the two steps and came to a silent, gentle landing on the Burg's linoleum floor. A triumphant sneer twisted his lips around the cigar, daring Kevin to make some sort of comment. He rolled toward the counter, letting the door slam shut behind him.

A deep, contented sigh echoed from the back room, followed by the soft roar of a flushing toilet. Kevin shook his head and rolled his eyes. He hoped Nella really had found her way out of the Burg's septic system and into the swamp.

Mr. Gregson forced his way between a pair of stools at the center of the counter. The big man and his chair fit, but just barely. Cigar ash littered his bristly black beard.

"Good morning, sir," Kevin said timidly. "I'm sorry, but you can't smoke that in here."

The window in the booth directly behind Mr. Gregson fell open. The old man took a quick puff on his cigar as if to say "How 'bout now?"

"Fine. Good enough," Kevin said as he grabbed a menu and slid it across the counter to his only customer. "Coffee?"

Mr. Gregson nodded.

"Cream and sugar?"

Another nod.

"Coming right up."

Mr. Gregson picked up the menu and held it close to his face, examining it through his beady little eyes. As Kevin turned toward the warming coffee pot, he wondered what a pixie would want for breakfast. How much could such a small creature eat?

How exactly did that disguise work? Was it a simple illusion like Nella's, or was Mr. Gregson some sort of magically powered shell?

"Are there any...um...allergy concerns I should know about?" Kevin asked.

Mr. Gregson responded with a glare that would've stripped the paint off the side of a barn. Kevin shrugged and examined the mugs from the shelf above the coffee pot. He didn't particularly want to deal with whatever his psychotic neighbor was up to, but the last thing he needed on his hands at this point was a severely ill pixie with an axe to grind against the hapless fry cook who'd inadvertently poisoned him with a borderline lethal dose of paprika.

Having selected the Burg's cleanest, whitest mug, Kevin turned to the coffee machine. The original carafe had shattered years ago and Fran had replaced it with a new one that barely squeaked in under the spigot. Taking firm hold of the coffee pot's plastic handle, Kevin gave it a sharp tug. It didn't budge. He tried turning it across the hot plate to see if he could pull it out at a different angle, but it wouldn't move no matter how hard he pushed or pulled the plastic handle. Exasperated, Kevin took a step back to examine the devilish device; it had been just fine the day before, even if it had been a little difficult to get it into or out of its spot atop the hot plate.

From the other side of the counter, Mr. Gregson snickered.

Fucking magic. "Do you want your coffee or not?" Kevin pleaded. On the next pull, the carafe finally came free of the machine.

Scowling, Kevin poured Mr. Gregson's coffee and wondered what the hell was keeping Fran. He needed backup, damn it, even if that backup wasn't going to believe a word he said about the dangers of the Burg's only customer. If he could somehow trick Mr. Gregson into revealing his mysterious abilities in front of his boss, surely Fran would kick the pixie out for being weird.

Coffee poured, Kevin delivered the steaming mug and a tiny basket of sugar, fake sugar, and tiny cream cups of indeterminate freshness to Mr. Gregson. The pixie eyed both items warily as if one of the two contained cyanide and he was required to eat one as part of some psychotic test.

"Can I get you something to eat?" Kevin asked.

"Eggs," Mr. Gregson grunted.

"And how would you like your eggs?"

"Over easy."

"Just eggs?"

"No."

"What else, then?"

"What else ya got?"

"It's all on the menu."

"Bacon."

"Toast?"

"Wheat."

"Butter or jam?"

"Blood."

"*Blood?*"

"Strawberry jam." Mr. Gregson blew out a thick puff of cigar smoke that briefly twisted itself into the shape of a strawberry, complete with leaves and a stem. The breeze wafting in from the open window quickly rent it asunder, turning the pixie's little work of art into just another wispy gray strand of noxious particles.

Exasperated, Kevin nodded and turned toward the grill. Were these fairy creatures always so difficult, or did they only become hopelessly ridiculous when dealing with humans? He couldn't imagine living in an entire city of magic yahoos, each one warped and demented in his or her own unique way. Perhaps that was why Mr. Gregson lived alone in a house in Harksburg and why Nella made her home in a lagoon in the middle of nowhere. Peace and quiet would be hard things to come by in a place full of magic bullshit. Alternatively, maybe Mr. Gregson found it preferable to be the lone whack job surrounded by sanity than to be just another nutcase awash in a sea of lunatics. There's something to be said for standing out, after all, even if you're hiding it a little bit.

After briefly holding his hand above the grill to make sure it was warm enough (and hoping to hell Mr. Gregson wouldn't telekinetically slam his palm into the hot surface), Kevin retrieved a carton of eggs from the refrigerator under the counter. Keeping one eye on Mr. Gregson for any sign of chicanery, he cracked two eggs onto the hot griddle. A sharp sizzle punctured the silence as the two dollops of protein and cholesterol heated. Kevin took a step back to survey his handiwork, satisfied that maybe, just maybe, Mr. Gregson had played enough torture-the-neighbor for one day and was content to eat his breakfast in peace.

Then, launched one by one like Fourth of July fireworks, each of the eight eggs remaining in the open carton on the counter behind Kevin rocketed up into the air and splattered against the ceiling. Mr. Gregson grunted as a long thread of egg drooled back down toward the counter like a massive stream of snot, that one simple sound somehow conveying a greater feeling of joy and accomplishment than a shout or a whoop or a touchdown dance possibly could have.

Frowning, Kevin returned to the grill, spatula in hand. He had to put an end to this before Fran found the front room trashed worse than the back. He was powerless to physically stop the pixie, but maybe standing up for himself would be enough to make Mr. Gregson think twice about fucking with him further. A plan formed in his mind as he watched the eggs cooking on the grill. It wouldn't be enough to run Mr. Gregson off—he fully expected the pixie to thwart it with his magic powers—but at the very least it would send a clear message that Kevin Felton was not going to take it like a big pussy—or like Doorknob.

Kylie, he knew, wouldn't have approved of his idea. She would've chided him for being immature, for acting his shoe size rather than his age, but her only solution to a problem had always been to bat her pretty little eyelashes at it and see what would happen.

Let's see you catch this, you son of a bitch.

Moving as quickly as his day's worth of experience working a grill allowed, Kevin scooped both eggs off the grill onto his spatula, whirled, and flung the still-sizzling mass at Mr. Gregson. His shot was a little off the mark—the trajectory of the eggs looked as if it would take them just over his target's right shoulder. At the last minute, however, the white and yellow glop swerved to the right like a left-hander's slider and slapped into the side of Mr. Gregson's face.

Kevin froze, stunned. Why had the pixie pulled the hot eggs into himself like that?

"Felton!"

Fran Kesky's angry bellow from the entrance to the back room was all the answer Kevin needed. Cursing under his breath, Kevin untied his apron and lifted it off over his head.

"I welcomed you back to Harksburg," Fran snarled. "I smiled and laughed when you and your asshole friends started a brawl that wrecked my bar. Then, when your mother came to apologize on your behalf and ask that I give you a job, I shook her hand and made you a part of my business. And you repay me by throwing food at a customer? You ungrateful little shit!"

Mr. Gregson pointed upward. Fran's gaze followed his finger and finally lingered on the mass of raw eggs dripping from the ceiling. Kesky's face turned a shade of purple usually reserved for children's cartoon characters.

"You're fucking fired!"

Kevin hurdled the counter, smoothly dodging the puddle of coagulating egg, and headed for the exit.

"You're fucking fired!" Fran repeated as Kevin opened the front door. "And you are hereby *banned* from the Harksburg Bar and Grill for the rest of your miserable fucking life! You are not welcome here, you little prick! You hear me? If I catch you so much as looking at my place they'll be pulling pieces of you out of the swamp for the next ten years!"

Kevin left without a word, resigned to the long walk home and what was sure to be a really fun conversation with his mother. He knew when he was beaten. Besides, he had more important things to worry about—like how the hell he was going to find Billy a new girlfriend without being able to take him to the only bar in town.

— CHAPTER SEVENTEEN —

The lonely road back to Harksburg would've felt like Purgatory to anyone unaware that civilization was just a few miles away. Although Kevin Felton knew that road well, he still felt adrift, a traveler stuck between worlds with no hope of latching onto anything solid. When life takes a turn for the patently absurd, what's to be done about it? To Kevin, brooding over a long walk and then discussing it all with an attractive blue girl sounded like the best and only possible option, even if it could potentially lead to his soul getting violently ripped out through his nostrils.

He was going to have to tell Driff about Mr. Gregson. With Ren out of town and possibly swamped with trouble of his own, only one person in Harksburg could help Kevin with his pixie problem. The elf had stood up for Kevin against Sweatpants Bob, hopefully he'd be willing to do the same to Kevin's psychotic neighbor, then dust Fran Kesky into forgetting that he'd banned Kevin from the Burg. Admitting his problems to Driff was going to be about as much fun as trying to teach Doorknob how to spell, but it didn't seem avoidable.

Very few cars passed Kevin as he walked, all of them heading out of town. He watched the dirty old sedans and exhaust-belching station wagons rumble past, wondering if he should cross the street and stick his thumb out. If he hit the road, traveling light and incognito, would any of these magical fuckwads actually be able to track him down? Could he escape by sticking to the slums and the shadows, by tossing his cell phone and his wallet out the window and starting a new life? He could let his hair grow out and maybe work on a beard. He'd be unrecognizable in a disguise of dirt and grime. Kicking a rock angrily into the woods, he dropped the idea. Life on the streets was no life for Kevin Felton. He yearned to be a success, to be a part of something, to enjoy the fruits of his labor. Just surviving would never be enough.

The low, predatory roar of an engine coming his way snapped him out of his reverie. Mr. Gregson's van rumbled past Kevin like a beast on the hunt, came to a squealing stop on the shoulder not ten feet ahead, and killed its engine. Kevin froze, his fight or flight instincts duking it out and coming to a draw in his head. Attempting to flee through the woods would be just as stupid as picking up a rock and charging the vehicle. If Mr. Gregson wanted to fuck with Kevin Felton that badly, he'd find a way to do it.

The van's back doors swung open with a harsh screech of poorly lubricated metal on metal. Inside, Mr. Gregson stared out at Kevin, chewing on the end of his lit cigar. The van's interior was trimmed in darkly stained wood. Cabinets lined either side.

"Get in."

"Why should I?"

"Because we've got shit to discuss," Mr. Gregson said matter-of-factly. "If I wanted to hurt you, I would've hurled you into one of those trees without even bothering to stop. Besides which, even if I did kill you, it wouldn't exactly be permanent, now would it?"

That set off alarm bells in Kevin's head. How did Mr. Gregson know about Billy's dereliction of duty? "True," he replied, "but that just means you *could* kill me over and over and over again. If you wanted to."

"If I wanted to, we wouldn't be having this useless conversation."

"Where are we going?"

"I'm giving you a ride home."

"I'd rather walk. I need some time to figure out how I'm going to explain to my mother that I lost the job she arranged for me. Thanks for that, by the way."

"You're welcome." A drawer in one of the cabinets beside Mr. Gregson jerked open and a manila envelope floated out to land in the big man's lap. "I imagine your first Tallisker paycheck will keep Abelia off your ass."

So that was it. Driff wasn't the only one keeping an eye on things in Harksburg. Tallisker had also recruited one of the locals. Kevin wondered if Driff knew Mr. Gregson was watching them. He doubted it.

Kevin took a deep breath and climbed into the back of the van. He still didn't trust Mr. Gregson—his interactions with the disguised pixie the last few days hadn't exactly been amicable or logical—but he needed answers. Kevin took a seat on the plywood floor beside Mr. Gregson and the doors slammed shut behind him. The vehicle suddenly roared to life and veered back onto the road to continue on its way toward the center of Harksburg.

Leaning around Mr. Gregson, Kevin tried to get a look at the front seats. The driver's side was empty. The steering wheel made slight adjustments seemingly of its own accord.

"Neat trick," Kevin said.

Mr. Gregson grunted. "First things first, Felton: we never had this conversation. Breathe a word of this to that fucking elf and I will personally cut off your testicles, bronze them, and wear them as a pair of clogs."

Kevin blinked, confused as to how that last part would be physically possible. Then he remembered that there was a tiny pixie hiding somewhere inside that massive, angry man. He nodded uncertainly.

"Good," Mr. Gregson growled. "What do you know about Tallisker?"

Shifting uncomfortably, Kevin fanned a puff of cigar smoke out of his face. "A lot more than I knew a few days ago. They're hidden behind a wall of smaller subsidiaries—one of which laid me off—and they're somehow involved with you magic...ah...people."

Mr. Gregson scowled, an expression not unlike those found on the angry cartoon bulldog mascots of several American universities. "Well, aren't you politically correct? Tallisker's the worst of the worst, Felton. They live fat off the rest of us who prop up their various companies and holdings. Your new elven friend's buddies in Evitankari ain't much better."

Kevin's jaw dropped. He hadn't been picked up by a Tallisker watchdog; he'd attracted the attention of the local conspiracy freak. He wasn't sure if that was better or worse.

"I've been watching your stupid ass since that pointy-eared sumbitch first came around asking about you," Mr. Gregson continued.

"If you wanted to know what was going on, you could've asked when I came to visit you a few nights ago."

"You annoy the piss outta me, boy. Y'always have."

"Sorry."

"Know why I came to see you today?"

Kevin had no clue. "Because you hate me?"

"See, it's that kind of dumb shit that makes you so annoying. I came to see you today because Tallisker's getting itchy. When Tallisker gets itchy, they start stickin' their noses in places they don't belong. That ain't something I need."

"Ok. But...how do you know Tallisker's not happy?"

The manila envelope in Mr. Gregson's lap sprung forward to collide with Kevin's face. Blinking, Kevin took firm hold of it with both hands and eyed it warily. There wasn't much in it, a few pieces of paper, maybe, or some sort of small book or magazine.

"I've been reading your mail."

"That's a federal offense, you know."

"Shut up and open it."

Kevin lifted the envelope's flap and emptied its contents onto the floor by his feet. Two things fell out: a fancy envelope monogrammed with the Tallisker sunburst logo and a paycheck, both addressed to Kevin Felton.

"Holy shit," Kevin said as the dollar value on the check sank in. "Driff wasn't kidding when he said I would be well compensated."

"Ten grand's pocket change to these assholes," Mr. Gregson snapped. "The real interesting part is that invitation."

Kevin picked up the fancy envelope and withdrew the card inside. The thick stock felt ominously cold to the touch.

"Your presence is requested this Wednesday night at the Roberts residence for a meet and greet with senior Tallisker staff," he read aloud. "Cocktail hour begins at 8 pm. Your RSVP has already been accepted."

The Roberts residence. According to Driff, Ren and his family had made an emergency trip up to Minnesota. Were they coming back for this dinner party, or were these senior Tallisker staffers just borrowing their home for the evening? Kevin really wanted to reconnect with Ren, but if there was more trouble coming Harksburg's way, he also hoped his best friend wouldn't have to be a part of it.

"Senior Tallisker staff," Mr. Gregson spat. "The worst of the worst. They don't climb off their big golden thrones for just anyone, Felton. They've got plenty of lackeys for dealin' with the riffraff. Those fuckers have something important to say, and they want to say it to you. In person."

A chill ran down Kevin's spine, but he tried to put up a tough front. "So? Maybe they want to commend me for a job well done."

"'Maybe they want to commend me for a job well done,'" Mr. Gregson repeated in a mocking voice eerily similar to Kevin's own.

He quickly shifted back to his usual gravelly baritone. "You are as fucking stupid as you are annoying. They hired you and the elf to do a job. You haven't been able to do it. What do you think comes next?"

"So why are they bothering with a dinner party? Why not just send out some big tough troll or something to break a few of my fingers?"

"Because that would be too easy. These sumbitches prefer to do things with style. They are evil incarnate, and they like to play with their prey a bit before they slice its throat."

Kevin wasn't buying it. By no means was he looking forward to Wednesday night's gathering, but he also couldn't see anyone—or anything—going to all that trouble just to send him a message. Besides, why would Tallisker bother cutting a check for someone they weren't happy with? If their leadership was truly as evil as their reputation, breaking a few labor laws wouldn't even make them blink.

All of which probably meant there was something even worse going on. Suggesting that to Mr. Gregson seemed like a bad idea.

"All right," Kevin said. "I'll be careful. But I'm still not clear about exactly what *you* want from me."

Mr. Gregson took a long pull on his cigar and shot twin streams of bluish smoke out of his nostrils. "Get rid of them. Do your fucking job so they'll leave this town alone. Stop fucking around with Sweatpants Bob and the moron twins and slinging hash for Fran Kesky. Focus on the reaper and get it done."

Kevin thought for a moment, parsing Mr. Gregson's words. There was something else, something his neighbor wasn't telling him. Something personal. Whatever it was, it had made him more desperate than angry. Kevin could barely detect it in the man's voice.

"That's going to be kind of difficult now that I'm no longer allowed in *the only bar in town*," Kevin said.

"There's nothing in that shithole for Billy and you fucking know it." One of the cabinet drawers beside Mr. Gregson slid open with a thunk. A matchbook wafted up out of it and landed atop Kevin's head. "That's where he met Nella."

Kevin pulled the little black matchbook out of his hair and examined its face. "'Donovan's,'" he read. The address beneath the neon pink logo put the place just over the town line in Woodville. "Never heard of it."

"You don't say."

After waiting a moment for Mr. Gregson to elaborate, Kevin pressed the issue. "Why haven't I heard of it?"

Mr. Gregson smiled for the first time, an expression somehow even more disconcerting than his various glares and scowls. "Because they don't really cater to your kind. They prefer mine."

— CHAPTER EIGHTEEN —

Sneaking into the house via the Pussy Hatch would only delay the inevitable, Kevin decided. It would be better to face his mother, show her the Tallisker paycheck, and get this whole ordeal over with. Judging from the old ten-speed bicycle locked to the porch railing, Abelia had company. She'd be less likely to cause a scene in front of a guest, he hoped, which meant he might be able to get his full explanation out before his mother had the chance to launch into an angry tirade.

But the sight of that bicycle also gave Kevin pause. He didn't recognize it, and he couldn't imagine his mother befriending whatever dirty hippie probably rode it, even in her newly altered state of mind. The thought of finding some grimy dude in Chuck Taylors and an ironic T-shirt bending his mother over the dining room table made him want to gouge his eyes out on the bike's rusted handlebars.

"Oh, just go in there, you big pussy," Mr. Gregson shouted from the porch next door. Kevin couldn't see his neighbor behind the privacy screen, but a thick tuft of cigar smoke proved he was there. "I promise you'll like what you find."

"You know whose bicycle that is?"

Mr. Gregson answered with a grunt but didn't elaborate. Kevin cursed under his breath and trudged up the front steps. His neighbor had made him more nervous instead of less, but he couldn't bear the thought of showing that crazy son of a bitch any further signs of weakness—even though he was now pretty sure the owner of the bicycle was yet another magical nut job come to torture him with some new and hitherto unimagined form of ridiculous stupidity.

Abelia and her guest sat at the dining room table, conversing softly over steaming cups of tea. His mother's eyebrows jumped up into her scalp as he strolled casually into the room.

"What are you doing home so early?"

Kevin heard her as if from a distance, her voice too faint to attract his full attention from the surprise seated at the head of the table. Nella—magically cloaked in her human form and wearing a conservative yellow dress with puffy shoulders—smiled up at Kevin and blushed.

"I thought it was time to meet your mother," she said shyly, as if she'd been caught with her hand in the cookie jar.

Try as he might, Kevin couldn't force his gaping jaw to close. He'd seen a lot of incomprehensible things these last few days, but finding his mother and his kind-of-girlfriend-who-he-always-thought-was-a-hallucination conversing over tea as if it were the most normal thing in the world somehow trumped them all. Perhaps it was because he'd known the two of them for an extremely long time and never seen them in the same place. Maybe it was because each belonged to a world he'd assumed could never interact with the other's. Or, given his more immediate concerns, perhaps he simply couldn't believe that Nella was taking such a huge risk by visiting his home after they'd agreed that they should keep their distance until the problem with Billy had been worked out.

"What are you doing home so early?" Abelia repeated, the surprised tone of her previous inquiry replaced with something dark and suspicious.

His mother's question shocked Kevin back to reality. "Turns out Fran only hired me because he wants your recipes," he replied. That likely wasn't so far from the truth. "We had it out, and then he fired me."

Abelia's eyes narrowed further. "You didn't give away any of my secrets, did you?"

"No ma'am."

"Good boy." Her expression softened and she smiled gently as her attention shifted back to Nella. "Nell here was just explaining your secret romance."

Blushing, Kevin pulled out the chair beside Nella and sat down. He needed to figure out what his mother knew and what lies the water nymph had told her as quickly as possible. Abelia seemed oddly approving of this arrangement, but she was no idiot; if their stories didn't match, she'd catch it and call them on it. Kevin really wished Nella had discussed this with him first so they could've built a solid game plan—and so he could've tried to talk his longtime lover out of whatever had gotten into her.

Apologizing seemed like a solid opening. "I'm sorry, Ma. I should've told you."

"Hush, you," Abelia snapped. "I understand that it can be more fun when it's secret, especially if there are no long term plans to make it serious. Honestly, I'm kind of relieved that you were with a girl all those times and not just masturbating furiously to some twisted porn like I always assumed. You two weren't particularly quiet, you know."

Blushing with the power of a trillion suns, Kevin suddenly wished he had Nella's ability to melt into a puddle and trickle away through the cracks in the floorboards. "You never said anything."

Abelia shrugged. "Boys will be boys, especially when they discover their willies are good for more than just taking a leak." An odd look came over her face then. "At least, that's what I think I thought. You know you're getting old when so many things turn so blurry. But enough about that. Nell, you were about to explain where you're from and what you do."

Oh, this ought to be good, Kevin thought.

Nella leaned forward, cradling her cup of tea in both hands. "I'm from Brazil originally. My parents are environmental advocates, so we traveled a lot, mostly to third world countries and developing nations, the kind of places where a few well-placed individuals might be able to make a legitimate difference. There was a... well, we'll call it a falling-out between Mom and Dad and their superiors, and we finally settled over in Woodville eighteen years ago. My parents are retired, but I've kind of carried on their work."

"How so, dear?"

"I freelance for the park service, counting fish and aquatic animals and insects, checking the water quality of the nearby rivers and lakes." Nella shifted uncomfortably. "It doesn't pay much, but I don't need a lot. Dad comes from money."

Listening intently, Kevin's mind whirled in a futile attempt to process which parts of that explanation were legitimate and which parts were pure bullshit. He suspected Nella's story was more true than false, that it was absolute fact from a certain point of view and with a few details stripped away. He suddenly felt bad for never expressing more of an interest in her past. It wasn't that he hadn't wanted to know more about her, of course—it was that he'd always thought the attractive blue girl who visited him on random evenings was just a dream. He wondered how different their lives and their relationship would be had he known all that time that Nella was, in fact, a real live woman madly in love with him.

"And how are the rivers and lakes doing these days?" Abelia asked.

"Fine, mostly. Every now and then I find a spot where some asshole's been throwing his garbage, but for the most part people around here respect the land. That's how I first met Kevin, you know, some of his idiot friends were about to soil the lagoon over in the Works, but he stopped them and ran them off." Nella turned to Kevin, the stars glittering in her eyes. Luckily it was physically impossible for him to blush any further. "It was love at first sight."

"Uh-huh." Abelia sounded skeptical of that last part. Just a few days ago, that sort of sentiment would've reduced her to a crying, quivering mess. "So tell me, dear: what are your intentions toward my one and only son?"

Nella took a long sip of her tea as she gathered her answer, and then she smiled the most genuine smile Kevin had ever seen. "I want to make him the happiest man in the world."

For several seconds, no one moved or spoke. Kevin continued to wish he could disappear. Abelia surely wasn't buying a word of what she surely saw as hokey crap designed to trick her into approving of her son's secret romance with a woman she'd never heard of. Visions of his mother going for the Super Soaker so she could wield it like a club as she chased Nella out of her home danced through Kevin's mind. This, he knew, would be the moment when life in Harksburg became completely intolerable, when the two people he cared about most turned on each other and made his existence a living hell.

"Do you know the answer I got when I asked Kevin's last lady friend that question?" Abelia asked deliberately.

Kevin somehow successfully fought the urge to piss himself. Nella shook her head, her eyes wide.

"She said she wanted to 'help him become a huge success' so the two of them could buy a condo in Chicago and a summer cabin in the Hamptons," Abelia said with a mischievous smile. "But she was a gold-digging skank. I like your version better, as unrealistically romantic as it may be. I'm glad you came to see me today, Nell."

The air returned to the room and the two lovers started breathing again. Kevin wanted to laugh but was still too shocked to make it happen. He'd never heard his mother speak ill of Kylie, but knowing that she shared his assessment of his ex-girlfriend made him feel better about a lot of things.

The water nymph smiled. "I'm glad I did, too. I think we're going to get along just fine."

Abelia stood, rolling her eyes. "Need a refill?" she asked.

"Yes, please," Nella chirped as she handed over her teacup. Abelia whirled and strode into the kitchen.

Kevin immediately wrapped his arm around Nella's shoulders and leaned in close. "What the hell were you thinking?" he whispered. "You know what happens if you get caught here, right?"

"We're not going to get caught," Nella whispered back. "Billy can't see through this disguise. Besides, the only reason you're risking your neck with that reaper is so we can be together. This is us being together. These are the kinds of things we're going to have to do to make that happen. You think Billy just…just up and leaves and never pays any attention to you ever again just because you hook him up with someone new? We're playing the long game here, Kevin, and we need to establish a solid cover as soon as possible."

Although Kevin couldn't get past the risk involved, he couldn't argue with her logic—and he rather liked the idea that they might be able to conduct their relationship in public rather than merely via secret late-night trysts. Not that he didn't enjoy secret late-night trysts, of course, but Kevin knew that being in a relationship involved a heck of a lot more than waiting for a woman to sneak in through your bedroom window and start taking your clothes off. He wanted to sit and watch TV with Nella until one or both of them fell asleep on the couch. He wanted to drive aimlessly around town with her in the passenger seat, singing along with whatever was on the radio. He wanted to go to the town fireworks with her on the Fourth of July. Without working Nella into the community and helping her gain the acceptance of the important people in his life, doing those things or any others like them would be downright impossible.

The thought left Kevin Felton absolutely petrified. Even if he found a way to take care of the reaper and somehow avoid getting dusted out of his skull by Driff, happily ever after would never be particularly simple. All the magic bullshit would never truly go away. It would always be part of his life, lurking under the surface like a shark circling a group of bathers. He wasn't sure it would be worth it...but he wanted to find out for himself.

Somewhere, he knew, Kylie was having a good laugh at his expense. She had never had much use for romance that didn't involve a fancy present or an expensive night out.

Abelia returned, bearing two steaming cups of tea. She set one down in front of Nella and leaned back against the side of her own chair, examining the younger woman as only a mother can.

"Will you listen to a piece of advice?" Abelia asked.

Nella nodded. "Of course."

"While you're busy making my son the happiest man on earth, don't forget about yourself," she said slowly. "I forgot about myself, and it took me twenty-seven years to remember. I think it may have only happened because I forgot a few other things that I thought were more important. Making up for lost time is fun, but it's also kind of a drag when you start thinking about all the things you missed."

Nella repeated her earlier nod. "I'll keep that in mind." Kevin knew her well enough, even in her disguise, to tell when she was thoroughly confused. This was one of those moments. He reached under the table and squeezed her knee reassuringly.

"And you," Abelia continued, pointing one accusing finger Kevin's way. He flinched back into his chair, accidentally squeezing Nella's knee hard enough to make her gasp. "Don't go getting all emotional and thinking what I just told your little girlfriend means I don't give a shit about you, dumbass. Oh, and you'd damn well better be good to this one when she needs some space. Lord knows you do enough stupid shit that she's going to need it eventually."

"Y-yes, ma'am," Kevin stammered. Nella shot him a wink.

"Good. Nell, dearie, how would you like to watch the soaps? Dr. Albert's been stuck on a deserted island for three weeks and hasn't been able to find a shirt."

With a bright smile, Nella bounced to her feet and plucked her teacup off the table. "Think he'll finally catch that Amazon that's been stalking him for the past four episodes?"

"Probably," Abelia replied as she hooked her arm through Nella's to guide her into the hall on their way to the living room. "Then they'll have a few episodes of island bliss before Mrs. Albert finds them together and all hell breaks loose."

"I can't wait!"

Left alone at the dining room table, Kevin put his head in his hands and sighed heavily. Although he was glad that Nella and his mother were getting along, he couldn't help worrying about the unholy alliance they'd formed. Assuming that things couldn't possibly get any more complicated, he realized, had become an exercise in futility.

— CHAPTER NINETEEN —

Kevin called the Roberts family's land line seven times before Driff finally picked up.

"Stop it," the elf growled.

"Driff."

"Felton."

Kevin didn't see a need to prolong what could turn out to be a very short phone call, so he got right to the point. "I think we should take Billy to Donovan's."

Driff paused before responding. Kevin thought he could hear the elf's eyes rolling. "And why do you think that?"

"It's where he met Nella."

"Your new grand plan is to drag the reaper to an emotionally charged location likely to unhinge him even worse than going out in public usually does, a place which—by the way—isn't particularly welcoming to either humans or representatives of the legitimate elven government. I assume this is all your little girlfriend's idea?"

It was Kevin's turn to pause and contemplate his answer. Would it be better to lie and implicate Nella or tell the truth and risk Mr. Gregson's wrath? In the end, he decided to change the subject and do neither. "Why don't the people at Donovan's like Councils of Intelligence?"

"Those of us who call Evitankari home aren't popular among the expat community. Any elves in Donovan's are either criminals on the run or the sort that think we shouldn't be doing the various things we're doing and felt strongly enough about it to leave on their own."

"Good. Someone I'll get along with."

"I don't think you get it. Donovan's is where these people go specifically to avoid humans. Management won't keep you from going inside, but the clientèle probably won't tolerate your presence."

"I'll have a reaper and an elf with me for backup," Kevin replied, swallowing his fear. He wasn't looking forward to the trip to Donovan's, but he didn't have a better idea given his lifetime ban from the Burg. Having considered the option further, he didn't want to ask Driff to dust Fran Kesky unless he didn't have any other choice. That shit had turned his devoutly religious mother into an angry nymphomaniac. There was no telling what effect it would have on the Burg's gregarious owner.

Driff sighed. "Despite the risks, it's not the worst idea I've heard—if we can get Billy through the front door. He's shown no interest in any human women. Maybe nonhumans really are more his speed."

"That's what I'm thinking." It really wasn't, but Kevin was tired of this conversation. "Get in touch with Mr. Pemberton and see if Billy's available tonight. I'll see if I can borrow my mother's car."

"Don't bother. I've got the Jag."

The thought of going for a joyride in Ren's precious vehicle without its owner brought an evil smile to Kevin's face. "Sounds like a plan."

"I'll call if Billy isn't available. Otherwise, expect me at eight." Driff slammed the receiver into the cradle and the line went dead.

That hadn't gone as poorly as Kevin had feared. He'd talked Driff into a trip to Donovan's without having to spill the beans about his earlier encounter with Mr. Gregson. Maybe this would work after all.

The door to Kevin's bedroom opened with a soft squeal. Nella shut it behind her and sauntered down the stairs, still wearing her human disguise.

"Your mother and I are not happy," she growled.

Kevin sat on the edge of his bed, his spirits sinking. He'd left Nella and his mother alone for an hour to watch a soap opera. What could possibly have come up between the two women in such a short span of time to turn them both against him? Kevin was starting to believe he'd been cursed. Given that the world had turned out to be full of elves, water nymphs, and magic, that seemed to be a distinct possibility.

"About what?" he asked tentatively, bracing himself for some new absurdity bent on making his life a living hell.

Nella sat down beside him, careful to leave about a foot of space between the two of them. She clutched her hands tightly together in her lap and glared daggers at him, her lips taut.

"Dr. Albert got eaten by a shark."

Kevin frowned, confused. "Dr. Albert..."

Realization dawned and Kevin rolled his eyes, feeling like a fool. He grabbed one of the pillows at his side and playfully threw it at Nella's face. Squealing happily, she ducked under it and dove forward to tackle Kevin, driving him down to the mattress and pinning him there, her slender hands on his shoulders. He could've thrown her off without much difficulty, but her mischievous smile froze him.

"What really happened at the Burg, Kevin Felton?" she asked.

"Fran wanted my mother's recipes," he deadpanned.

Her grip tightened. "And?"

Relieved that he wasn't going to have to find a way to broach the subject, Kevin told the story of Mr. Gregson's surprise visit to the Burg and his strange ride home. Nella listened intently, her expression unchanging. When Kevin finished, Nella lowered herself so she could rest her head on his chest.

"Things never get easier, do they?" she sighed.

Kevin had come to the same conclusion. "Usually not. Any advice?"

"Stick close to Driff. He's got his own agenda, but the chances he'll screw you have been…diminished."

His mind flashed back to that spot in the woods outside the Works, to the strange green hue of the elf's hand after he'd shaken Nella's and promised nothing would happen to Kevin. "Thanks for that, by the way. What else?"

"Be careful in Donovan's. Bring a few dollars in quarters and don't talk to Muffintop."

"Muffintop?"

"You'll know him when you see him. Oh, and one more thing." She shifted to look up at him, her dark eyes glittering with passion. "Don't let any of these motherfuckers win."

Every nerve in Kevin's body flared with warmth and a sly smile crept across his face. He turned the tables on Nella in one fluid movement, flipping her onto her back and kissing her passionately. As her soft lips welcomed him hungrily, Kevin realized he had something worth fighting for above and beyond his own survival.

— CHAPTER TWENTY —

T hanks for the ride," Kevin said as he pulled the passen-
ger-side door shut. "My mother's car isn't very reliable."

Driff didn't so much as look at him, his attention firmly
on the road as he made an aggressive U-turn. "I'd rather have this
thing," the elf said, "in case we need to make a quick getaway."

"Just what do you think is going to happen in this place?"

"I have no clue," the elf said somberly, "and that's the problem."

In the pocket of his leather jacket, Kevin fingered the Donovan's
matchbook nervously. What if this trip was Mr. Gregson's latest,
most convoluted attempt to fuck with him? Did the scheming
pixie hate Kevin enough that he'd send him somewhere legitimately dangerous? It certainly seemed possible. For a brief
moment, Kevin considered coming clean with Driff. If they were
walking into some sort of trap, the elf needed to know—if only
because he was Kevin's best and only possible form of protection
against magical threats. But Driff was already on edge and would
certainly be prepared anyway, so why bother risking his wrath?
Mr. Gregson had also demanded that Kevin keep their meeting
from the Council of Intelligence. Drawing the ire of both the elf
and the pixie would certainly make Kevin's life far too difficult.

Driff turned the Jag right onto Holland Street, heading south down the narrow road that would take them toward Woodville and the mysterious Donovan's. What would a bar full of magic assholes look like? Was it even inside of a building, or was it out in a field or a forest somewhere, hidden from prying eyes by deceptive sorcery? He should've asked Nella when she came to visit that afternoon, but at the time there'd been more important—and much more fun—things for the two of them to do.

Rather than stare out the window at the Holland Street version of Harksburg's scenery (which, by the way, looked just like that surrounding the town common: tall Victorian houses maintained reasonably well situated on moderately sized lots), Kevin decided to take advantage of this rarest of occasions and flipped open the glove box. He'd never been inside of the Jag without Ren's supervision, and there was no telling what manner of embarrassing paraphernalia his friend had hidden in that vehicle. Sadly, the glove box contained only an owner's manual and the vehicle's registration. Kevin slammed it shut with an annoyed grunt and leaned forward, reaching under the seat to continue his search.

"You won't find anything," Driff said calmly. "I looked."

Undeterred, Kevin continued groping along the rough fabric. "What gives you the right to poke around Ren's personal effects?"

"It's got nothing to do with 'right' and everything to do with making sure nothing in here was going to make my life unnecessarily complicated."

"You thought the Jag was bugged?"

"Or worse."

"Worse?"

"Worse."

"Like, gnomes?"

"Much worse."

Tallisker, Kevin thought. Driff didn't trust the Roberts family's business connections either. Sitting up, he shot the elf a conspiratorial glance. "Got any plans tomorrow night?"

"Let's focus on tonight," the elf said, his voice surprisingly warm—like a Little League coach giving his young squad a wholesome pep talk. "We've got a job to do, and we'll be that much better at it if we don't give in to distractions."

Kevin took the hint. Although Driff had searched the car to the best of his abilities, he wasn't completely convinced it was a safe place to talk—or perhaps he'd found some sort of bug he hadn't been able to deal with and thought it best to leave it intact. Regardless, Ren's Jaguar wasn't a good place to discuss strategy.

A palpable feeling of dread froze Kevin in place and drained the blood from his face. Assuming the car really was bugged, how long had someone been listening? He and Ren had discussed a lot of very personal things in that vehicle. Did Tallisker have a recording of that particularly bad LSD trip during which Kevin had become convinced that he was a hockey puck? What about that time he'd bared his soul to Ren and admitted that he may have gotten Holly Thompkins pregnant? The thought of Tallisker possessing a record of his private fears and most embarrassing moments was disconcerting to say the least.

"Stop it," Driff snapped. "I didn't find anything in the car. Your precious secrets are safe. I was serious when I said we need to take care of one problem at a time."

Kevin snorted derisively, hoping it would mask his relief—and his embarrassment. "I knew that. I was thinking about how angry Ren will be when he finds out we took the Jag without him."

"Sure."

The scenery around them turned treeless and expansive, the countryside opening up like a blossoming flower. Empty fields of rolling grass stretched toward distant hills on either side of the road. Kevin had seen small groups of cows and horses wandering the area on occasion, though there was no farmhouse or stable in sight. A full moon hung ominously above the forest ahead.

"So, what's a bar for magic people like?" Kevin asked.

"It's kind of like a bar for un-magic people, only the fights are more interesting," Driff replied.

"If there's a fight, I'll stand behind you."

"If there's a fight, you won't be able to see me."

"Brave."

"Smart."

Kevin chuckled and shook his head.

"What?"

"Sorry. It's funny how much you remind me of Ren sometimes— and it's not just the house you're living in or the car you're driving."

An oddly twisted smile crept across Driff's face as if he simultaneously wanted to choke his passenger and give him a high five. "I hope I haven't caught something."

The dense woods closed around them, blocking out most of the stars and the glow of the full moon. The Jag's headlights cut stark swaths across the battered gray pavement. An increased rattle from the tires signaled the town line. Woodville was sparsely populated in its center. Out here on the edges, houses were even fewer and farther between, set back from the road via long driveways and hidden behind the thick trees.

"This part of town's always been boring and it's always going to be boring," Kevin said to no one in particular. He'd always hated this stretch of road, though he'd never traveled it regularly. Uncle Fred and Aunt Tammy lived in Gratton, two towns and twenty minutes of bland, 40-mile-per-hour road past the other side of Woodville.

"Oh, I don't know," Driff replied. "It reminds me of a few places back home."

Kevin struggled to remember the name of the elven city. "In Elfertanki?"

Driff didn't bother to correct him. "I suggest we take a slightly different approach this evening."

"And that would be?"

"Let Billy take the lead. We'll play support roles. We're there for moral support and helping him sell himself to interested parties."

"Gosh, Driff, is dating always that romantic where you're from?" Kevin added a snort for sarcastic emphasis.

"Keep it up and you're walking home," the elf snapped.

"Throwing a fun, friendly woman at him didn't work so well last time. I suppose this is worth a try."

Satisfied that he'd gotten his way, Driff pushed his spectacles up on his nose and focused on the road. The Jag barreled down the razor-straight road at close to fifty miles an hour, but they'd passed two, maybe three driveways during that conversation and hadn't seen another pair of headlights since they'd left the center of Harksburg. That early in the week, there was little reason for the residents of either sleepy little town to be out and about at that hour.

The thought gave Kevin pause. If there were no humans out and about, did it stand to reason that all of the nonhumans had stayed home as well? The evening's excursion would be a complete waste of time if they were the only three people in Donovan's.

"Think it's going to be busy tonight?" he asked.

Driff nodded. "The sorts of people we're going to meet in Donovan's don't typically work nine-to-fives."

"Oh. So, what do they do, then?"

"In some cases, they do what they were meant to do—like your little blue girlfriend. Most of them just do whatever they want."

Kevin shook his head. That wasn't particularly helpful. He let the matter drop; learning more about the secret subculture Driff, Billy, and Nella inhabited had seemed important a few days ago, but it had proven to be difficult and confusing—especially when anti-social magic assholes refused to give him the whole story. He wondered if Driff and Mr. Gregson had attended the same class on giving half-assed answers. The two were probably old study buddies who still kept in touch on occasion.

Driff flipped his right blinker on and slowed. Confused, Kevin looked around. "There aren't any turns coming up."

The elf smiled, cranked the wheel to the right, and floored it. The vehicle lurched forward and turned, slamming Kevin sideways and back into his seat. He only had a moment to curse Driff and stare in wide-eyed horror at the thick stand of pine trees suddenly filling the windshield. Wincing, he jerked his arms up in a feeble attempt to protect his face and leaned as far back into the seat as he could go.

The Jag continued on its way, apparently unharmed. Kevin slowly lowered his arms so he could see. They'd turned onto a narrow road paved with some sort of sky blue asphalt that glittered in the bright starlight streaming down from overhead. The stars themselves seemed to have multiplied, the sky dappled with dense swaths of twinkling lights. On either side of the road, spindly trees with thick red leaves and narrow white and gray bark seemed to beckon them forward as they swayed gently in the breeze.

"You're a fucking asshole, you know that?" Kevin snapped.

"It's not my fault humans can't see through a basic cloaking ward," Driff replied nonchalantly.

"Are we still in Illinois? I've never seen stars like that. Is that the Milky Way?"

The elf nodded.

"But...how? We aren't near any major cities, but the light pollution still blocks a lot of the night sky."

"According to Donovan's dossier, he's a devoted amateur astronomer."

"That's why, not how. Are you saying there's no light pollution here because this Donovan dude...removed it?"

Driff nodded again.

"That's insane."

"And expensive. Supposedly that's why the drinks in his club aren't particularly cheap."

"Hmm. I only brought twenty bucks."

"Don't worry, we'll find a nice troll that thinks he or she can get into your pants by plying you with alcohol."

"You're a real pal, Driff."

Kevin leaned forward and watched the red and white trees whip past, his nerves still frazzled. The magic he'd seen thus far had been small and localized—and downright puny compared to that which cleared the night sky above Donovan's. He hadn't realized magic was capable of such things. It made him feel insignificant in comparison. How could someone without even a fraction of that sort of power hope to function in such a world and deal with its denizens? He doubted his charming personality would be enough to see him through.

And what chance, really, did someone like Kevin Felton have of keeping a woman like Nella? She'd grown up around magic, she'd dated a reaper, and who knows what else. Kevin possessed no power over life and death. He couldn't turn invisible, levitate annoying neighbors, or eliminate light pollution. Nella didn't seem like the kind of girl who would be impressed by his ability to balance a checkbook or make a snazzy pie chart in a spreadsheet.

"Can you teach me some magic?" Kevin asked. He immediately wished he'd stopped himself.

Driff responded with a sound that was something between a sigh and a growl and kept driving.

Embarrassed, Kevin crossed his arms across his chest and returned his attention to their surroundings. The narrow blue road became a wide parking lot, and Kevin was relieved to see a dozen other vehicles parked there. Beyond, a towering wall of red vines blocked the way deeper into the forest. As the Jag pulled into the parking lot, Kevin noticed that those vines were trimmed with thorns that looked for all the world like big, red shark teeth. Beside the wall stood a podium manned by a hulking figure in a black, pinstriped suit.

Driff pulled the Jag into an empty spot beside Mr. Pemberton's Lincoln and cut the engine. Billy, perched atop the Lincoln's trunk so he could stare up at the stellar light show in the sky, glanced back over his shoulder to nod a hello to Driff and Kevin as they exited Ren's vehicle.

"Nice night," Kevin said.

"Par for the course out here," Billy replied. "You should see it during a meteor shower."

Driff ignored their small talk and headed toward the wall of thorns. Billy slid off the car and fell into step beside Kevin, the two of them trailing the elf by a few paces.

"You come here often?" Kevin asked.

Billy nodded. "Several times a month, usually. I haven't been since Nella left me. This is where we met, you know."

Shit, Kevin thought. He'd been hoping that wouldn't come up. He needed Billy in as good a mood as he could possibly be, bringing up his former fiancée probably wouldn't turn him into a ray of sunshine.

"Don't worry," Billy said, noticing Kevin's discomfort. "She rarely ever came here on her own. We don't have to worry about running into her."

Kevin stumbled over his own feet but quickly righted himself. He hadn't considered that possibility. Nella knew they were planning a trip to Donovan's, so surely she'd be smart enough to stay away—unless, of course, she had some reckless plan to try to help, similar to her appearance at the Felton residence to meet his mother. "That's a relief. I...uh...don't want to drag you into an uncomfortable situation."

Billy zipped up his black windbreaker and shoved his hands into his pockets. "Wouldn't be your fault."

I beg to differ, Kevin thought, flashing back to his first encounter with Driff in the Works.

"Billy, my friend!" a deep, rough voice bellowed joyously. "Long time, no see! Donovan was thinking about putting the machine in storage!"

His eyes on the ground, Kevin had completely missed the doorman as they approached the wall of thorns. A seven-foot-tall, four-hundred-pound troll leaned casually on a wooden podium, smiling a toothy, tusky smile full of crooked teeth. A pinstriped suit strained against the beast's girth and an old bowler hat sat atop his head at a jaunty angle, looking three sizes too small for his massive cranium. A tiny gold plate attached to his suit above his heart declared his name to be Ulliver.

"What're you staring at, pal?" the troll asked, its black eyes locking on the human.

Remembering Driff's warnings about the place, Kevin tried to play it cool. "Your hat's crooked."

With a stubby finger the width of a shot glass, Ulliver tapped his hat a little to the left. The hard fabric moved across his thick, scabrous hide with a sound like sandpaper on stone. "Better?"

"Much."

Ulliver grunted. "Now that the fashion police has had their say, I need ID from everyone who isn't an avatar of death."

"I wasn't expecting an age requirement," Kevin said as he fished around in his wallet. "Can't imagine the state has any clue about this place."

"Who said anything about age?" Ulliver asked incredulously. "Here at Donovan's, we want to make sure we don't let the wrong kind of people in. You aren't the wrong kind of people, are you?"

"Depends on which ex-girlfriends you ask," Kevin replied as he held up his license so the troll could get a look, nervous Ulliver would break it if he actually took possession of it with his muscular hands. This would've been the point in the conversation when Kylie would've stamped her foot and insisted they relocate to an establishment where the help wasn't so mouthy.

"Hmm," the troll muttered as he scanned Kevin's ID. "Felton? Where have I heard that name before? Ah, right! Thisolanipusintarex's neighbor! The annoying little shit!"

"Thiso-whosits?" Kevin asked. Recognition dawned a moment later and he chuckled a little. "Ah, Mr. Gregson."

Ulliver nodded. "Anyone that gets that stuck-up twit's gossamer wings in a twist is okay in my book. Now, what about you, bookworm?"

As Kevin stowed his license, Driff handed the troll a little round badge made of some sort of blue metal. Ulliver ran his thumb over it carefully, then tossed it in his mouth and bit down hard.

"You ain't no ex-pat, buddy," the doorman grumbled in between bites. "I can smell a fancy pants city elf from a mile away. Every last one of you reeks like week-old pork. Show me the real one, please."

Kevin gave the air a quick sniff but couldn't detect the aroma the troll described.

"You're chewing on my *real* ID," Driff replied haughtily.

"Tastes like a phony. London—no, Manchester vintage, perhaps a 2004. Sulfur trim rather than phosphorus. Piss-poor workmanship, elfy. Probably shouldn't use this forger again."

"Killed him," Driff said nonchalantly. He clapped his hands together, held them there for a moment, then slowly drew them apart. As he did, he spread wide a bright band of blue light glittering with yellow and green specks. His name and title percolated into the band in fits and starts like bubbles rising to the top of a soda but never popping.

Ulliver leaned forward to sniff Driff's light show. "Now, there's the real thing! We don't get many elven politicians 'round these parts. Pardon my insistence on viewing your true credentials, Your Eminence."

"Can you make that show other messages?" Kevin asked, hypnotized by Driff's beautiful identification.

The elf glared at him. "The aurigh is a manifestation of my magical connection to the Combined Council of Evitankari," Driff snapped. He turned to the troll. "Forgive my companion. He's a little...behind."

Ulliver chuckled. "I kind of like him." He reached into his pants pocket and withdrew a thin slip of pink paper, which he handed to Kevin. "Here's a free drink, kid."

Kevin's eyes lit up as he snatched the coupon and shoved it into his own pocket. "Thanks!"

With a fist the size of a small ham, the troll hammered the top of his podium twice. In response, a roughly circular section of the wall of thorns slithered open with a soft crackling sound. One of the red vines beckoned them through coyly.

"No loitering," Ulliver deadpanned. "You're letting the heat out."

Billy waved back over his shoulder and headed on through, Driff close at his heels. Kevin hesitated, examining the entrance warily. Would it stay open long enough for everyone to get through? What if it decided to shut on him? Getting trapped in a man-eating bush but not being able to die in the process didn't sound like a particularly good time.

"Don't worry," the troll said reassuringly, "Sparky ate yesterday."

Kevin's gaze quickly darted from the vines to Ulliver and then back again. "I hope Sparky's a good boy."

"*She's* the best."

"Sorry, girl," Kevin muttered under his breath as he strode through the entrance as calmly as possible. His knees and hands quivered with every step he took until he gained the other side. The wall of thorns slithered together to seal the gap behind him.

Ahead, the strange blue pavement continued on, flanked on either side by the spindly white and red trees, until it came to a nexus of sorts around a circular bar surrounding a central glass column wrapped in shelves packed with liquor bottles. The bar itself was made of the same thorny vines as the entrance, capped with a thick wooden top polished to a bright sheen. Tiny wisps of soft purple flame floated several feet above the counter at every third stool, making the entire setup glow invitingly. Crystalline picnic tables sprung up here and there around the bar like mushrooms around the base of a tree, about half of them occupied. Other roads radiated out into the forest at various angles and disappeared under the gloom of the thick canopy.

"Nice place," Kevin said as he rushed to catch up to Driff and Billy, playing with the free drink ticket in his pocket. He looked back anxiously at the wall of thorns. "How do we get out? That door seems like a bit of a fire hazard."

"It's not," Driff replied. Billy just nodded.

As they emerged into the clearing surrounding the bar, Kevin felt every eye in the area lock onto him. A trio of short, spindly men seemingly made out of wood glared at him from a picnic table off to the left. To his right, a troll in a chainmail jacket smiled maliciously. At the bar, a stout woman covered in black scales and another with white hair and even whiter, semitransparent skin turned to watch his approach, whispering conspiratorially to each other. Kevin flushed and cinched his jacket tighter to his body, trying to make himself small. He knew those looks well; he'd given more than a few strangers who'd wandered into the Burg the same treatment. Kevin Felton's arrival in Donovan's was just as odd to those gathered as their appearances were to the human intruder.

"Billy," a warm, feminine voice called gently from behind the bar. "Welcome back, hon."

A tall, lean elf sauntered around the central shelving unit, casually wiping down a heavy stein with a white towel. Her high cheekbones and alabaster skin were straight out of a fashion magazine. She smiled fondly at Billy under piercing blue eyes and a thick mop of curly blond hair that dangled halfway down the back of her tight black T-shirt. The tips of her pointed ears barely peeked out from either side.

"Hi, Lil," Billy replied awkwardly.

"Chocolate or vanilla?" she asked.

"Mix 'em?"

"Coming right up." Lil winked and disappeared back around the other side of the central spire.

Driff and Billy settled onto stools at the bar. Kevin stood behind them, examining the bottles of liquor that covered the central shelves. Most he recognized, but a few were labeled using characters he couldn't interpret. A stocky blue bottle with two spouts contained a viscous, roiling liquid that reminded him of a tie-dyed T-shirt. Another, topped with an aerosol spray attachment, was infested with tiny turtles swimming to and fro.

"That one's not for you," Driff said.

"I was leaning toward a dry martini using that one," Kevin deadpanned, pointing toward a square bottle full of eyeballs that had decided to stare straight at him. "Billy, do you recognize any of the other customers?"

The reaper nodded. "They're all regulars."

"Know anything about them?"

"Not really."

"The wood nymphs over at that table are the Yrry family. Cousins, all born within a few years of each other. They're the county's biggest suppliers of locally grown narcotics and hallucinogens," Driff said softly. "Garganol—the troll sitting by himself—works dispatch for the Woodville PD. Janice Redding and Carolyn Peters went to high school together in Uncton. They stopped talking for several years when Redding's boyfriend left her for Peters. After he similarly abandoned Carolyn for another woman, the two made peace. They now traffic in a variety of magical charms and potions of questionable legality."

Kevin glanced suspiciously at the two women seated across from them at the bar. He recognized the name Carolyn Peters, but he couldn't quite place it—and neither of them looked particularly familiar. The pale one flashed him a smile full of pointy teeth and stirred her drink suggestively. He looked away quickly, returning his attention to Driff.

"You really did your homework, huh?"

The elf nodded. "Lil is not the bartender's real name. She was banished from Evitankari twelve years ago for interfering in the judgment of a shala'ni." He paused. "Tip her well."

Before Kevin could ask for an explanation, Lil reappeared. She handed Billy the biggest milkshake Kevin had ever seen, topped with a heaping mound of whipped cream and three cherries. "Here you go, Billy," she chirped.

The reaper took a long drag from the thick straw, turning the clear plastic pink as the cool liquid traveled through it. "Perfect," he said happily. Kylie would've thrown her hands up in the air and immediately demanded that Billy grow the fuck up.

"Good. Now, what can I do for my favorite reaper's scumbag friends?"

"Scumbags?" Kevin snapped incredulously. "Who're you calling scumbags?"

Lil leaned forward on the bar, her eyes gleaming maliciously. "Two people who can't possibly have a good reason to spend time with my friend here."

Kevin had never dreamed they'd run into someone so protective of Billy—or someone who'd so easily sniff out the possibility of an ulterior motive behind his friendship with the reaper. He frowned and curled his lip, hoping he appeared more insulted by her accusation than angry that she'd found him out.

Driff wasn't fazed. "My superiors are simply concerned about Billy's state of mind and sent me to investigate. Mr. Felton here is acting as a local guide of sorts. When we met Billy...suffice to say that he needed a bit of a pick-me-up, the reasons for which Kevin is able to closely relate to."

Lil's eyes narrowed as she examined the nervous human. "You havin' trouble with a little blue bitch too?"

That's one way to put it, Kevin thought. "Not quite," he replied. "The source of my difficulties is a gold-digging ex-girlfriend."

"Same difference." She took a step back from the bar, satisfied but obviously still concerned. "What'll you have?"

Kevin whipped his free drink coupon out of his pocket and presented it to Lil as if it were a Nobel Prize medal he'd won for curing cancer. "What will this get me?"

The bartender snatched the little piece of paper away and dropped it in the waste bin under the bar. "It's a surprise. You'll like it." She turned to Driff. "What about you, four-eyes?"

"Sidecar. Easy on the lemon."

"Coming right up."

As Lil grabbed a shaker and a bottle of cognac, Kevin turned to Driff. "That was anticlimactic."

The elf frowned. "Meaning...?"

"Meaning you're an elf who orders old man drinks! Wouldn't you rather have some sort of magic flaming margarita flavored with agave grown on the banks of a mystical spring?"

"Not on my budget, no."

"Meaning...?"

Driff pushed his spectacles up on his nose and glowered through them. "Meaning there are six such known springs in existence, all of which are controlled by a single corporation that artificially reduces the supply and thus drives prices through the roof."

Kevin's jaw dropped. "I wasn't serious..."

"It's really more of a special occasion beverage," a gravelly voice interjected. A distinct feminine lilt punctuated the deep, scratchy tone. Kevin and Driff turned to find the two strange women from the other side of the bar approaching them. The smaller, paler of the two led the way and did the talking. "It's not really appropriate for weeknight evenings out and about with random humans."

Something about Carolyn Peters and Janice Redding left Kevin feeling more unsettled than he'd felt around any of the other supernaturals he'd met. Though they seemed friendly enough, the two radiated a sort of chaotic danger Kevin couldn't quite put his finger on. The world around them felt darker somehow. Whatever they were, they certainly weren't people he wanted to mess around with.

He couldn't help feeling like he knew the pale one somehow. Up close, the curve of her face and the shape of her eyes were both frustratingly familiar. Perhaps he'd encountered her before in a magic disguise similar to the one Nella used around humans.

"Especially not this human," Driff grumbled.

The pale woman took a step closer, favoring Kevin with her pointed smile. "Oh, I don't know. He's grown into a much more attractive young man than I expected, but it's hard to tell just how someone's going to turn out in the fifth grade."

Squinting, Kevin examined her a little more closely, tracing her square jaw line up across her round cheekbones. "Carolyn Peters. We sat next to each other in math class that year."

Carolyn nodded, her vicious smile widening. "Thanks again for helping me with my long division."

Driff snorted.

Kevin couldn't take his eyes off his old classmate. She'd been a small, spindly thing back then, but she'd always had a healthy tan and a full head of thick brown hair. Her face seemed to have changed shape slightly, too, as if her nose had flattened and her eyes had spread farther apart. All in all, the effect chilled Kevin to the bone; being introduced to this version of Carolyn Peters was like meeting some mad scientist's attempt at recreating the real article.

"One sidecar and one house special," Lil called from behind the bar. "Shall I put the cocktail on the Combined Council's tab?"

"Combined Council?" Janice Redding snarled, a forked tongue flicking angrily between her scaly lips. "You're a fucking cop?"

"That's right," Driff said with an evil smirk as he took a quick sip of his drink. "Why do you ask? Have you been up to something I wouldn't approve of?"

Glowering at the elf, Janice took her friend by the elbow and dragged her away toward a table in the far corner. Carolyn smiled at Kevin one more time and mouthed "Call me."

"Are you always that good with women?" Kevin asked.

Driff shrugged. "Some people have no respect for law enforcement."

Behind them, Lil cackled dramatically. "Ha! Actually, your real problem is that most people have no respect for hypocritical know-it-alls with nothing better to do than stick their noses in everyone else's business."

As Kevin tried to parse the full meaning of that sentence, Driff turned and locked eyes with the bartender. The Council of Intelligence looked surprisingly disappointed, as if someone he'd trusted and respected had suddenly and inexplicably turned on him. Kevin knew that face well; he'd seen it in the mirror several times after Kylie left him. Seeing it on Driff in this particular situation made very little sense. Hadn't Lil just insulted him?

"I spent years on Poa," Driff explained flatly. "I understand better than you what's wrong with elven society. Evitankari's got its share of terrible problems, but it's still the most honorable power in the game."

Lil scowled and shook her head. "The biggest piece of shit in the bowl is still just a big piece of shit," she growled as she wandered around to the other side of the bar.

"What's Poa?" Kevin asked. He'd understood about three words in that entire conversation, but one thing had been made perfectly clear: the elves of Evitankari certainly weren't saints, and even their own recognized it. That fact made him wonder anew if there was more to Driff's involvement in Harksburg than simply straightening out the situation with the reaper.

"Drink your beer," Driff replied, handing Kevin the frothy mug Lil had left on the bar. The elf looked to Billy. "What now?"

Billy, obviously not expecting to be put in charge, choked a little on his milkshake. "Ummm...there's a clearing over there that's a lot of fun."

"Lead the way."

As the elf and the reaper took their first steps toward one of the paths radiating out into the woods from the bar area, Kevin paused to test his beer. As far as he could tell, Donovan's special was just the locally produced swill the Burg and similar establishments sold for two-fifty a pint. He wasn't sure whether to be relieved or disappointed, but he didn't have time to think about it; out of the corner of his eye, he noticed Garganol the troll watching him with the sort of hungry glare Kevin had only ever seen on nature documentaries. He hurried to catch up to his companions, spilling a few dollops of foamy beer on his shoes as he skittered awkwardly after Billy and Driff.

The only light on the narrow trail down which Billy directed them came from the stars above and the bar area behind. Kevin hadn't been able to detect any obvious difference between the trail they'd taken and the others they hadn't. There were no signs or markers labeling the paths or declaring their destinations. He wasn't particularly comfortable with that.

"Where are we going?" he asked.

"Cassiopeia," Billy replied.

"That's a constellation. It's kind of far away."

"It's one of the many clearings in Donovan's," Driff explained. "Each is named for the constellation it exists directly under."

"But...stars move."

"So do the clearings."

Kevin took a long drink from his shitty beer and tried to wrap his head around that. It implied that Donovan's whole setup—including the bar, the entrance, and all of the paths—turned like a wheel to match the movement of the heavens. And he had no idea how in the hell that could actually work.

"Who the fuck is this Donovan guy trying to impress?" he asked.

"He's got a large family," Driff replied cryptically.

Ahead, the trail forked. A narrow path led off to the right while the main walkway continued on at a slight left bent. Laughter echoed in between the trees, high-pitched and childlike. Kevin peered down the branching trail as they passed. Thirty feet away, the thick forest opened into a tiny clearing where about a dozen lights of various colors flittered to and fro above a shuffleboard game. Squinting, Kevin could barely make out the gossamer wings keeping the lights afloat.

"Pixies love that game," Billy whispered, "but I don't really see the attraction."

One of the pucks whizzed across the playing surface seemingly of its own accord, and Kevin's heart caught in his throat as he flashed back to his telekinetic manhandling at the will of Mr. Gregson. He wondered if his neighbor was there with the other members of his kind, cheerfully playing shuffleboard as a means of passing the time and an excuse to socialize. Somehow, Kevin couldn't picture the old curmudgeon out there among the other pixies—not that he would've recognized him without his Mr. Gregson disguise, of course.

Their path took a sharp curve to the right, one that Kevin swore should've sent them back the way they came, and then the trees around them opened up and the trio strode into the largest clearing yet. Cut into the side of a hill Kevin hadn't seen coming were three flat levels, widest at the bottom and narrower at the top, packed with glowing lights and logos of all shapes and sizes and colors interrupted intermittently by wooden staircases that allowed travel between floors. A mishmash of sounds and songs echoed down into the clearing, creating a strikingly electronic cacophony sorely out of place in their woodland surroundings.

Kevin paused. "Are those...arcade cabinets?"

Billy smiled happily. "Donovan's got one of the biggest collections in the state. Come on! Let's see if anyone's beaten my high score!"

As the reaper wandered off toward the nearest set of stairs, Kevin and Driff traded concerned glances.

"We aren't going to meet any women in here," Kevin said softly.

"Probably not. Humoring him for a little while might make him more pliable later, though."

"I'm sure he'll be really susceptible to suggestion after another milkshake or two."

Driff shrugged. "Got a better idea?"

"Fine. How are your pinball skills?"

"Bad," the elf said as he took his first step toward the array of arcade machines on the hill. "I was always more of a skee ball guy."

Looking up into the sky at Cassiopeia, Kevin shook his head and cursed under his breath. He hadn't come all the way out to Donovan's crazy ass bar with Driff and Billy just to play Centipede. Dumping a pocket full of quarters into Galaga or Revolution X probably wouldn't do much to get Mr. Gregson off his ass. And how long would Driff's patience with their ridiculous endeavor last? Granted, an extended effort to fix the reaper's broken heart would give Kevin more time to find a way to keep the elf from wiping his memory, but it also meant more time spent in danger of getting caught or pissing off the wrong magic asshole.

The situation was a real catch-22. He couldn't help flashing back to that time he'd decided to watch football all day rather than accompany Kylie to a new art exhibition featuring the latest from a blind, homeless lesbian who worked exclusively with drinking straws and chewing gum to create ten-foot-tall arches meant to symbolize the slow degradation of youth in the modern workplace. The more he ignored her calls, the more football he got to watch—but the angrier she became, to the point that she picked the lock to his old apartment, slapped him in the face with a box of souvenir drinking straws, then stormed out.

In hindsight, he really should've spotted the crazy a lot sooner.

Having already climbed to the top tier of the hill, Billy disappeared into a glittering, beeping array of the most modern machines in Donovan's collection. Kevin drained half of his beer and followed, stepping gingerly upon the narrow wooden stairs that jutted out of the earth like crooked teeth—and which certainly weren't up to code. He paid little attention to the first and lowest tier, a motley collection of ancient mechanical contraptions that would've been right at home in an episode of a reality TV show about crazy hoarders: pachinko, old school pinball tables, slot machines with mechanical reels. The next level featured machines straight out of the eighties and early nineties, dense, neon-trimmed cabinets offering a variety of entertainments still fashionable in certain circles who considered nostalgia more of a necessary accessory than an occasional indulgence.

On the third and topmost tier, after making a wrong turn and getting lost in a maze of Big Buck Hunter units of all shapes and sizes, Kevin finally found Billy feeding quarters into a shiny new Dance Dance Revolution machine, a double-wide model equipped with a huge screen and two dance pads. Nearby, Driff leaned against Street Fighter IV and sipped his sidecar, glowering at the scene over pursed lips as if attempting to locate the source of a particularly rancid fart.

"I wouldn't have pegged you for a DDR fan, Billy," Kevin called out.

The reaper continued pushing coins into the plastic orange slot. "Lil suggested it to me. She thought I could use the exercise."

"She's nice."

"Yeah."

"And she seems to like you."

Billy shifted uneasily, a motion not unlike a snake shedding an old, unwanted skin. "I guess."

"Billy doesn't want to bang any elves because they can't be trusted," a squeaky voice chimed in, startling them all. "Right, Billy? Remember what you said about that she-elf in the black dress?"

The source of this interruption was a short, squat-looking thing peering at them nervously from behind the nearest Golden Tee. Kevin guessed that it was some sort of stunted troll that had probably been dropped as an infant. The word "crooked" barely began to describe the thing. Its left eye bulged out of its brow as if its skull were trying to launch it like a missile, but its right was a mere pinprick of black surrounded by a thick, bony socket. A right leg shorter than its left skewed its posture in an unfortunate direction. Kevin couldn't help staring at the weird bony growth jutting out of the top of its skull at a funky angle. Shorter at the bottom and wider toward the top, the growth reminded Kevin of a muffin.

Remembering Nella's warning, he quickly averted his eyes.

"Hi, Muffintop," Billy said. "That was said to you in confidence."

"S-s-sorry, Billy." Muffintop's eye bulged out even further in distress. "Still friends? Who are these people? Are they your friends too?"

"Kevin Felton and Council of Intelligence Driff," Billy said, indicating each in turn as he positioned himself on the DDR machine's floor pads.

That brought Muffintop trundling out from behind the machine, a yellow smile spread across his burly face. He wore a pair of bright red shorts and a black Wild Jester Crew T-shirt speckled with gray and beige stains of indeterminate origin. "Oh, wow! I've never met a real live Council before!"

"I've met a *councillor*," Kevin muttered.

Driff squinted through his spectacles to examine the little creature more closely. "I wonder why."

"Me too!" Muffintop limped right past Kevin, paying the human no attention as he zeroed in on Driff. "Want to see my scrapbook?"

"No."

"Please?"

"No."

"Pretty please?"

"No."

"With sugar on top?"

"No."

"Aww, shucks." Muffintop visibly slouched as if Driff's denial had knocked all the breath out of his body.

Kevin understood why Nella had warned him to avoid Muffintop, but he couldn't help feeling bad for the little guy—nor could he resist the opportunity to mess with his elven companion. "Driff's just messing with you, Muffintop. Scrapbooking is his favorite hobby. He and I looked at mine for a whole hour on the way over here!"

Muffintop straightened as much as he could, standing a good five inches taller. Reaching inside the elastic waistband of his shorts, he pulled out a battered leather journal stuffed to the brim with random papers and photographs and presented it proudly to Driff. The elf glared slow, painful death at Kevin and violently downed the remaining half of his sidecar.

A puff of who knew what exploded out of the scrapbook as Muffintop opened it to a random page in the middle. "This is me and Sammi Too Swag at the very first Jester Jam. He invited me backstage and we threw shurikens at a life-size cutout of Warren G. Harding..."

Snickering and warmed by the triumphant sensation of a job well done, Kevin returned his attention to Billy. The reaper was already twenty seconds or so into his first song, some perky J-pop number that substituted various train noises for vocals as a group of cartoon teenagers wearing bathrobes and rabbit ears danced on the screen around the flow of arrows directing the player where to put his feet. It wasn't going very well: red X marks denoting missed steps littered the display, and the leading zeros in Billy's score refused to be banished regardless of how much the reaper flailed about. At the eye of that rhythmless hurricane of awkward hyperactivity, however, stood one of the happiest people Kevin had ever seen. A genuine smile stretched from one of Billy's ears to the other, his pupils dilated in ecstasy. Kevin stood back and watched, glad that his dour friend had found a release from his seemingly interminable depression.

An odd smell wafted into Kevin's nose then, a mix of peat moss tinged with sharp cologne. Someone tapped him on the shoulder. "Mr. Felton?"

Turning, Kevin found himself face-to-face with a technicolor caricature of the old businessmen with whom he'd once worked. Leaning heavily on an ebony cane topped with a glittering crystal, the man smiled up at him with perfect white teeth. He wore a purple suit of the sort usually reserved for Prince performances.

"Who's asking?"

"Donovan Pym," the man replied, extending his skeletal right hand. "Owner and operator of this fine establishment."

Donovan's handshake was heartier than Kevin expected. "'Fine establishment' doesn't quite cut it, sir. This place is amazing."

"You're kind to say so, Mr. Felton. I was wondering if you have a few moments for a private conversation."

Kevin knew a setup when he saw one. With Billy distracted by a video game and Driff waylaid by Muffintop—the conversation had shifted to a detailed description of a foosball game with Sammi 2 Swag in August of 2005—Kevin was easy pickings. The smart thing to do would've been to get the attention of his two friends, but pissing off an individual with the power to create and maintain the impressive space around them would probably be a great way to get hurt. Besides which, Kevin couldn't help being curious as to why such a person was so interested in a normal, boring human like himself.

"Lead the way."

— CHAPTER TWENTY-ONE —

Donovan Pym escorted Kevin up and over the top of the gaming hill, using a narrow dirt path hidden between an American Idol pinball machine and an NFL Blitz cabinet. Kevin didn't bother glancing back over his shoulder as they crested the rise; he knew Billy and Driff were lost in their own worlds and had completely lost track of him. He wasn't sure how to feel about that.

"Did I do something wrong?"

"I don't know," Donovan said playfully. "Did you?"

"Maybe I could've been nicer to the thorn bush at the front door."

"Don't worry about Sparky. She's got thick skin."

"Seemed like a tough old broad."

"Ha! Careful. The one thing she's sensitive about is her age."

Donovan angled them diagonally down the hill, toward a spindly apple tree growing all alone about twenty feet from the surrounding woods. Thick red fruit hung from its taut limbs like bombs about to drop on an unsuspecting city.

Kevin took a quick drink of his beer. "I'm sure you didn't go through all the trouble of dispatching the great and powerful Muffintop to distract my elven babysitter just so we can discuss the vagaries of magic bush psychology."

"Positive about that?"

"Kind of."

"Mmmm."

"Am I right?"

"What do you think?"

"I think I'm right."

"Mmmm."

Frustrated, Kevin took another swig from his glass of free swill. Donovan seemed set on not answering any questions about his intentions until he was good and ready, and there wasn't much Kevin could do about it beyond wait him out. For what felt like the millionth time, he wondered why all of these magic assholes insisted on being so fucking difficult.

He decided to approach matters from a different angle. "You're not human, are you?"

"What do you think?"

"You're not."

"Mmmmm."

"So, what are you, then?"

"I'm the king of this forest."

Of course you are. "I get that you own this joint, but what species are you?"

"I do not, as you put it, 'own this joint.' It owns me. Every forest must have a king."

Remembering that he was dealing with an individual with the resources to block out light pollution and maintain a secret bar out in the middle of nowhere, Kevin bit back a sarcastic retort. "Driff said you have a large family."

Donovan nodded. "Brothers, of a sort. All kings of their own forests."

"Do they all have such kickass bars?"

"Certainly not. Donovan's is one of a kind."

As they approached the lone apple tree, Kevin began to catch a weird vibe. The tree itself seemed devoid of substance, as if it were a hologram of sorts deployed in the middle of the woods. Its edges were simultaneously too soft and too ragged, its shape not quite round enough. As he watched, a ripe apple plummeted to the ground without making a sound or displacing the grass upon impact—it took over its new location like an unwelcome relative who slipped in through the back door and claimed the best seat on the couch when no one was looking.

With a tap on his elbow, Donovan guided Kevin around the tree in a tight counterclockwise loop. The scenery shifted suddenly; the surrounding forest closed in around them, the grass became thicker and shorter, and the temperature dropped several degrees. Disoriented by the abrupt change, Kevin stumbled forward and caught himself on the edge of a red picnic table.

"Careful, Mr. Felton," a familiar British accent cooed. "You know what they say about that first step."

Straightening, Kevin fixed a wary eye on Mr. Pemberton. The reaper keeper sat on the opposite side of the table behind a thick old book and a steaming cup of tea. Kevin had known all along that he was walking into a setup of some sort, but never in a million years would he have expected Mr. Pemberton would be involved. The man's appearance was even more surprising than suddenly teleporting elsewhere in Donovan's forest.

"We're still in Illinois, right?" he asked nervously. The clearing around them was barely big enough to contain Mr. Pemberton's picnic table. Dense rows of pines and firs hemmed them in as tightly as any solid walls could have. The strange apple tree behind him seemed to be the only way in or out. He glanced up at the sky but didn't recognize any of the constellations.

"In a manner of speaking," Donovan replied.

"Uh-huh. And you're sure I didn't do something wrong?"

"I don't know. Did you?"

Frustrated, Kevin redirected his question to Mr. Pemberton. "Did I?"

The old man closed his book ominously. "To tell you the truth, I've been wondering about that."

Before Kevin could reply, Donovan snatched his right hand in a death grip. "The King of the Forest knows the souls of all creatures," he whispered.

The hair on Kevin's arm stood on end as something that felt like static electricity flowed into him from Donovan's hand. "Let go!" he protested.

The strange old man held tight, his attention elsewhere. The wind picked up around them, flowing into and out of the tight clearing in a whirling vortex. Branches lashed back and forth against the neighboring trees, building in a drumming crescendo as Donovan hummed along. Beside them, Mr. Pemberton frowned as his teacup exploded and splattered its contents all over the table and the reaper keeper's perfectly pressed suit.

Kevin flinched as he felt something ethereal worm its way into his brain, moving deftly from neuron to neuron as it searched for its target. An array of smells—imaginary, perhaps, triggered by the intrusion into his head—assaulted his nostrils: peat moss, cedar chips, pollen, blood. The searching tentacle wrapped itself around something Kevin intuitively knew he'd done a shitty job trying to hide, and then it yanked. White light exploded behind his eyes and every muscle in his body screamed as Donovan pulled the information out of his mind.

When the pain faded and he could once again make sense of his surroundings, Kevin found himself lying atop the picnic table. To his left, Mr. Pemberton watched with interest. To his right, Donovan greeted him with a sigh and a shake of his head.

"Poofy," he mumbled, defeated. Reaching into his back pocket, Donovan withdrew his wallet, took out a hundred-dollar bill, and passed it across Kevin's chest to Mr. Pemberton.

"Told you," the old Brit replied sadly as he pocketed the cash.

Groaning, Kevin closed his eyes and banged the back of his head against the picnic table in frustration. That was it, then: the person closest to Billy had gotten hold of Kevin's secret. The difference between Mr. Pemberton discovering the true identity of the man with whom the reaper's fiancée had run off and Billy himself learning it was so miniscule as to be nonexistent. As of that moment, Kevin Felton was effectively dead.

And as a dead man, he really had nothing left to lose. "Did you two assholes *really* place a bet on me?" he snarled. Rolling onto his side, Kevin glared down at Donovan. "And what the fuck gives you the right to go digging around in my fucking head without asking?"

The King of the Forest was not intimidated. "You're a guest on my land, Mr. Felton. As such, you are subject to my rules."

"Fuck your land and fuck your rules, you crazy old fuck!"

"You don't mean that."

Kevin's face turned purple. "The hell I don't!"

"Mmmmmm."

Before Kevin could launch into another tirade, Mr. Pemberton placed a calming hand on his shoulder. The gentleness of the gesture shocked him into silence.

"I apologize for both the deception and the intrusion, Mr. Felton," the reaper keeper said. "I've had my suspicions, and I had to know for sure. Forgive me, but I didn't think you'd speak truthfully if I simply asked."

"Damn right," Kevin snapped.

Mr. Pemberton sighed. "I understand why you're concerned about Billy finding out that you're 'the other man,' but you're incorrect if you assume I'm going to run off to my master with that information like a child tattling on a sibling."

Kevin snorted and looked at his feet. "Right. Like that isn't your job."

"I'm responsible for the reaper's well-being, yes, but I'm not sure that task is best served by ruining his relationship with his new best friend."

"So why bother yanking the truth out of my head? Why not let things play out as they may?" The answer came to Kevin before Mr. Pemberton could reply. "You want something from me, don't you? And now you've got the leverage you need to get it."

"Of course. I'm human, am I not?"

"I always thought so." Kevin shook his head. "What do you want?"

Mr. Pemberton smiled. "As previously stated, I want what's best for Billy—and a little something for myself."

"Fine. Name it. Can't be worse than getting my soul sucked out through my nose."

"Oh, that'll depend on a variety of different factors. First things first, however: how do you really feel about my ward?"

"Best reaper ever!" Kevin said sarcastically. Still, he had to admit that Billy had grown on him a bit. "He can be a frustrating twit, but he's all right once you get to know him. He might actually turn out to be kind of fun if I can get him to open up a bit more."

Mr. Pemberton's eyes shifted to Donovan. "True," the King of the Forest said.

"Wait a minute," Kevin protested. "If this guy's a lie detector, why the fuck did he have to burrow into my brain like some kind of parasite from a bad B movie?"

Donovan cocked his head and smiled innocently. "How else did you expect me to set a baseline and calibrate myself to your particular thought processes?"

"I don't know. Ask me a few questions you already know the answer to, maybe?"

"Mmmmm."

"Did you seek out Nella upon your return or did she come to you?" the reaper keeper asked.

Telling the truth was obviously Kevin's best and only option. "She came to me. Before all this started, I thought she was some sort of recurring dream."

"Stupid, but true," Donovan said.

Mr. Pemberton paused, scrunching his face as if his next question were built of the most disdainful words he'd ever uttered. "Why the lies? Why did you befriend Billy? Why do you continue to string him along?"

Kevin shook his head. "I don't really want to have my soul stolen by my girlfriend's jilted ex. If you've got a better way for me to avoid that, I'm all ears."

"True."

"I wish I had a better idea to give you," Mr. Pemberton said. "I've tried talking Billy out of his crusade against the man called Poofy, but my words have fallen on deaf ears. I knew there had to be more to your involvement, Mr. Felton, but I never really suspected you of anything malicious. This meeting was designed merely to silence my own nagging insecurities, of which we all have many."

Eyebrows raised in surprise, Kevin exhaled. "You're really not going to turn me in?"

"No. In fact, I think you may be our best chance at dragging my ward out of his doldrums. He's already improved by leaps and bounds in the few days you've known him. However, there's still that matter of the little thing that I want. Rest assured, you're perfect for the task. I'll start the paperwork."

Before Kevin could press Mr. Pemberton for more information, Donovan grabbed his hand. A burst of hot energy rocketed up his arm and into his head and knocked him into oblivion.

— CHAPTER TWENTY-TWO —

Kevin woke feeling more refreshed than he had in days. Sitting up, he stretched, yawned, and glanced over at his alarm clock. Nine in the morning. He couldn't remember the last time he'd felt this good this early.

Then, as the events of the previous evening solidified in his memory, he growled a curse and violently dropped his head back onto his pillow.

"Just once," he grumbled to no one in particular, "I'd like to go to the bar and not get knocked the fuck out."

Food and coffee would help, as always. Rolling out of bed, he thanked whatever deity happened to be listening that Driff and his damn dust hadn't ruined his mother's penchant for cooking delicious breakfasts. Somehow that part of his mother had proven more fundamental to her identity than her previously stalwart faith. He wondered where it came from; Abelia had never told him much about her life prior to her conversion. She'd always politely brushed his questions aside, and he'd eventually given up asking. Maybe, given her change of attitude, it was time to try again.

Kevin pondered his trip to Donovan's as he climbed the stairs. He had no memory of getting home; the night ended after Mr. Pemberton promised to start some paperwork and that damn

Donovan Pim shocked him unconscious. As if his life hadn't already become complicated enough, now he had to worry about meeting the reaper keeper's demands—whatever the hell they might turn out to be. What could a man like Mr. Pemberton want? A generic stereotype of a devoted manservant, Kevin had never even imagined he might have an agenda of his own. Did he want help running errands or pressing his impeccable suits? Perhaps he needed someone to cosign on a loan for a new car to replace the Lincoln? It made no sense.

Abelia was waiting for him at the kitchen table, a cigarette in hand and three butts already deposited in a clam shell beside her elbow. Breakfast, to Kevin's chagrin, was nowhere to be seen.

"Need your help with something," she growled, obviously frazzled and annoyed. "There's one hell of a breakfast in it for you."

"Now what?" Kevin grumbled in return. He'd had enough vague implications of trouble recently to last him the rest of his lifetime.

Abelia replied with a forceful puff of smoke and a glare that would've stripped the paint off of a car.

"Fine. What can I help you with, oh dearest Mother?"

"Follow me."

Mrs. Felton led her son up the back stairs to the second floor. Kevin couldn't remember the last time he'd been up here. Consisting of a large master bedroom, two smaller bedrooms, and a large bath, the second floor had always been distinctly Abelia's—even more so than the rest of the house. As they traversed the narrow hallway that ended in the door to the master bedroom, Kevin was surprised to find the two other rooms completely empty. They'd once been loaded with antique furniture and Christian bric-a-brac, meticulously cleaned and cared for as they awaited guests who never appeared. More victims of Driff's insidious dust.

"I'm thinking about taking on some tenants," Abelia said dismissively. "Might as well use this dump to make a few bucks."

Kevin gasped. His mother never would've considered renting out her home, and she certainly wouldn't have ever called it a dump. He supposed he should stop being surprised by how the dust had changed her, but he couldn't help himself.

"What?" she asked, catching his shocked expression. "Would you rather pay the rent I could be making all by yourself?"

"Not particularly."

Reaching the end of the hall, Abelia whipped the master bedroom door open with a flourish. The once-immaculate space looked like it had been hit by a bomb loaded with clothes. Abelia's shirts, pants, dresses, and undergarments covered the floor like a second layer of carpet. The blue walls were speckled here and there with lighter colored spaces that marked where various pictures and decorations had once hung. Only the framed photographs of her son remained: four-year-old Kevin building a sand castle at the beach in Florida, Kevin in his pee-wee football uniform, Kevin looking gawky and awkward on his first day of high school, Kevin with Mickie Epstein at the prom.

"Oh, thank God!" Jenny Reilly said from atop the king-sized bed. "I thought you were never going to wake up."

Confused, Kevin frowned and surveyed the scene. What the hell was Jenny Reilly doing in his mother's bed? Why was she wearing such an ill-fitting leather corset? And why the fuck was she hand-cuffed to the bedposts?

"We lost the keys," Abelia said disinterestedly.

A rather loud voice in Kevin's head wanted to scream, swear, and stamp his feet. It wanted to tell Abelia to grow the fuck up, turn on its heel, and leave Jenny trapped right where she was for the rest of her useless fucking life because that would fucking teach her. Somehow, Kevin managed to tell that voice to shut up. His mother was a grown-ass woman and she could do whatever she pleased—and given everything she'd been through and everything she'd done for Kevin, she deserved his support, regardless of how much her activities made him want to vomit.

Besides, she couldn't keep this shit up forever, could she? Surely it was just a phase, a temporary side effect of having her memory microwaved by a self-important asshole with a pocket full of magic dust. It had to be. Right?

"I'll get the bolt cutters."

After Kevin freed Jenny Reilly, Abelia treated them both to a huge chocolate chip pancake breakfast. As the two women made innocuous, awkward small talk about the weather and traded gossip about the rest of Harksburg, Kevin kept his eyes on the table and tried his best to shrink into his chair. The day had certainly gotten off to an inauspicious start. He hoped it wasn't a sign of things to come, especially considering he was due to meet with Tallisker that evening.

Kevin spent the rest of the day online, researching the mysterious corporation behind Driff's mission with the reaper and the Griffin Group's buyout of Noonan, Noonan, and Schmidt. He wasn't able to find much of use. Tallisker's main website was a slick, classic example of a good marketing department's talent for using a lot of important buzzwords and stock photographs to pump up the company's success while revealing nothing of any real relevance. News and opinion pieces about Tallisker were complimentary to a fault. Analysts crowed about the company's bright future and the desirability of Tallisker stock, the price of which consistently ranked among the top ten in the entire world. Agile, socially responsible, and perched atop a solid foundation of excellence, Tallisker stood proud as a shining example of capitalism done right.

But Kevin knew a load of horse shit when he smelled one. No business could be that perfect. Regardless of how they operated, all publicly traded companies had their fair share of critics and detractors. That Tallisker had worked so hard to silence theirs indicated a deep insecurity—and, more likely than not, a terribly dark secret worth exerting considerable effort to protect.

After a quick tuna noodle casserole dinner, Kevin ransacked his luggage to find his best suit, the gray one with the pinstripes that Kylie had picked out for him at a downtown Chicago consignment shop run by some French guy in skinny jeans and a red beret. Harksburg didn't present many opportunities that required formal attire, so he hadn't bothered to unpack any. Upon finding said suit, Kevin cast it aside angrily and instead selected a plain black one he'd gotten on sale at Macy's, the one Kylie always said reeked of clearance rack. Kevin sniffed it tentatively but couldn't detect any particular aroma. He grabbed a blue-and-black-striped tie and a white shirt and got to work.

A shit, a shave, and a shower later, Kevin was ready to go. He stopped to check himself in the mirror hung on the inside of his closet door: conservative and inoffensive, just as he'd planned. A good little Republican. Perhaps a future CPA. Maybe a successful Cadillac salesman. No one who was going to rock the boat or question the authority of his betters. Perhaps most importantly, no one who deserved a thorough dusting or needed to be taught a lesson by finding his blue girlfriend's severed head waiting for him at the end of his driveway.

Dressed and ready to go, Kevin prepared to hoist himself up into and through the Pussy Hatch when an odd thought delayed his exit. Thanks to his mother's change of personality, there was no longer any reason to sneak out of the house. He could stroll right out through the front door and Abelia wouldn't even grunt. It was, he realized sadly, the end of an era. At least it meant he didn't have to worry about ruining his suit. With one last wistful look toward the tiny window that had served him so well over the years, Kevin headed upstairs. Exiting through the front door felt dirty, like cheating on a pretty, middle-aged girlfriend with a hot blonde supermodel ten years younger.

The Roberts estate wasn't far. Kevin quickly looked both ways before jogging across the street. He slowed his pace when he reached the common, watching the stars as he walked. There'd been so few above Chicago, and the novelty of a vibrant night sky hadn't yet worn off. After the sky he'd seen the night before in Donovan's, the simpler Harksburg iteration he'd grown up with was warm and reassuring. A strange thought furrowed his brow: somewhere out there in the cosmos, did one of those distant suns warm a planet teeming with creatures oblivious to their own shadowy subculture of magical assholes? Maybe, he thought, scientists searching for sentient life on other worlds should stop wasting their time on radio waves and start looking for bursts of ridiculous sorcery.

He wasn't surprised when Council of Intelligence Driff appeared to his left, matching his pace stride for stride. No words of greeting passed between the two of them.

"Be careful tonight," the elf said. "Our hosts are not to be trifled with."

Kevin snorted. "I figured. I'll be on my best behavior. This isn't my first fancy dinner with important business people."

"Who said they're people?" Driff asked.

Kevin didn't rise to the elf's bait; he'd been expecting the Tallisker representatives to be some kind of fairy such-and-such. "Whatever they are, what the hell is the point of all this? Why come all the way out to Harksburg just to meet me?"

Driff shifted uneasily. They reached the far side of the common and stopped to check for oncoming traffic before crossing. "I've been thinking about that. We're dealing with a pack of egotistical megalomaniacs who just *love* lording their superiority over the rest of us."

"Sounds familiar."

The elf sighed. "As I was saying, we're about to dine with a bunch of pompous pricks who revel in being pompous pricks. Thing is, they don't often make house calls. They usually prefer to make people come to them."

"So? Maybe they were in the mood to take a trip."

"I think they're in the mood to send a message. This is most likely a performance review of sorts, Kevin—and I don't think our employers are happy with our progress."

A chill ran down Kevin's spine. That wasn't so far from Mr. Gregson's assumptions. He attempted to cover up his fear with humor. "So we'll set some new goals for the next fiscal year and agree to an action plan. Business as usual."

"Right." The elf pulled a vibrating cell phone from his pocket and frowned at it. "I don't know how the hell your mother got my number, but tell her to stop calling me," he snapped as he stashed the phone back in his coat. "I'm not interested."

Kevin blushed. "You're the one who just *had* to dust her. Thanks again for that, by the way."

Driff shrugged. "She won't interfere with our affairs if she's busy screwing all of your friends."

"Fuck you."

They turned left onto Hampstead Street, the private way that lead to the Roberts estate. Square, squat lanterns powered by stored solar energy lit the perfect black asphalt with islands of strangely fluorescent glow, each pair spaced exactly twenty feet from the previous. The long pine needles that covered the ground along either side of the road somehow seemed *organized*, as if Nature herself didn't dare make a mess of the only route into or out of the Roberts estate. For as much as Kevin liked Ren, he'd always wanted to drop trou and take a big shit right in the middle of his fancy-ass road. *If things don't go well tonight,* Kevin decided, *I'll do just that.*

"Tallisker doesn't know about you and Nella," Driff said suddenly. "They think you're just a useful local I recruited to the cause. They don't know this bullshit is all your fault."

Kevin stumbled in surprise, quickly regaining his balance. He'd assumed that Driff was a staunch company man, a dutiful soldier reliably feeding every piece of relevant information to the corporate machine. The fact that he'd hidden that particularly important fact was reason for both relief and alarm. On the one hand, it would make him much less of a target in Tallisker's eyes. On the other, Driff surely hadn't withheld information from their superiors out of the goodness of his heart. The elf certainly expected something from Kevin in return.

"What's the catch?"

"No catch. I promised Nella I'd make sure nothing happens to you. I'm just fulfilling that promise."

Kevin was taken aback until he remembered the circumstances surrounding that promise. "What exactly did she do to your hand?"

"She joined my water to hers. Never, ever let that happen to you if you can avoid it."

"Sounds...sticky."

The elf snorted. "'Sticky' isn't the half of it."

"But why make that deal?" Kevin asked. "You don't seem like the type who'd bet his life on someone else's. If joining your water to Nella's was the cost of my assistance, why didn't you just feed me to Billy and go home, mission accomplished?"

"Because that's what those Tallisker fucks would've done," Driff grumbled. "I'm not above manipulating people to get the job done, but I'm not a murderer."

Kevin scratched his chin, thinking. He supposed that made sense. Elves, like humans, had to look themselves in the mirror every morning. Assuming, of course, that they had reflections.

"Who is Tallisker, really?" Kevin asked softly. They were still several minutes from the glittering lights of the Roberts estate, but he felt the need to be cautious. "They're obviously not just another huge corporation with a hard-to-describe business model."

The elf hesitated. He seemed to want to explain, but he didn't. "Better for now that you don't have all the details. If it seems like you know too much about them, they'll get suspicious. As far as you should logically know, they're the people employing you to do a really strange job." Driff smiled. "If you're interested, just ask them. It won't seem out of character, and they'll probably tell you. Like I said, they love showing off."

"Typical executives."

"Pretty much. How's your head?"

"Fine now," Kevin replied quickly. He didn't know how much, if anything, Driff knew about his encounter with Donovan Pim and Mr. Pemberton. "I guess Donovan's special was more than just shitty beer."

"Uh-huh," Driff replied, obviously not convinced.

"Muffintop didn't hurt you, did he?"

"I think he killed a few brain cells I wasn't using, but I'll live."

The blurry white light at the end of the private way on which the two of them walked began to coalesce into a sprawling McMansion. Built fifteen years ago when Ren's father was promoted to some esoteric vice president position, the Roberts residence put the homes in Lordly Estates to shame. Nine thousand square feet of dark red brick and stark white mortar rose three stories high from an immaculately groomed lawn. The architect had included all kinds of strange angles and clefts that served no useful purpose. The resulting structure was a jagged castle of sorts, either the imposing home of a mad scientist with a ton of grant money or an evil necromancer who'd hit the lottery.

"Looks like a prison I once visited in the fairy capital," Driff said thoughtfully.

"The neighborhood kids never want to trick-or-treat here," Kevin replied. Did elves celebrate Halloween? He wasn't sure, and Driff's non-reaction didn't give him any clues.

Soon they could discern a figure in the glare, standing maybe ten feet in front of the stairs leading to the front porch. A woman, Kevin thought, long and lean and wearing a silver gown that glittered in the mansion's harsh external lights.

"Who's that?" Kevin muttered. "It's too tall to be Mrs. Roberts."

"Is Mr. Roberts married to a woman half his age?" Driff asked.

"No..."

"Then that sure as hell isn't Mrs. Roberts."

Six-inch stilettos cracked across the pavement like gunshots as the woman sauntered forward to greet them. Kevin knew that stride. It meant business. It meant impatience. It meant its owner knew exactly what she wanted and how she was going to acquire it.

"Hello, Kevin."

Kylie looked just as beautiful as he remembered. Her dress hung loosely off her runner's body, her toned and tanned arms and shoulders on prominent display. Golden ringlets of blond hair dangled around her neck like taut springs in a style she only wore for important events.

Kevin's angry reply chickened out and dove back down his throat. He gagged and offered a weak wave. What the hell was she doing in Harksburg? Was she connected to Tallisker somehow?

Turning to Driff, Kevin covered his mouth with his hand. "Is she...magic?"

The elf didn't bother to lower his voice or disguise his response. "Magic? No, she's real."

Kylie sighed and planted her hands firmly on her hips. Kevin had seen that stance often enough to know exactly what would come next. Those beautiful brown eyes would slowly roll as she clicked her tongue and reached up to toss her hair with her slender left hand. Then her gaze would focus not on Kevin's face but at some far-off point just over his shoulder, as if she were addressing not a single frustrating man but lecturing an entire crowd of uncouth louts, and the pitch of her voice would drop two octaves as she steadily tore him a new one.

But she didn't do any of those things. The tightness in her shoulders and arms faded, and a gentle smile softened her face. "You must be Council of Intelligence Driff," she said warmly. "I'm Kylie Bonaventure. Kevin and I dated for several years."

"And then you abandoned him for some rich old geezer when he lost his job. I've heard the story."

The Kylie Kevin remembered would've cut Driff's balls off for that. This new version took it in stride and continued her greeting. "Tallisker and the Roberts family thank you for your attendance this evening. Please, follow me."

She spun on her heel and stalked away, one hand still planted on her provocatively swaying hip. Kevin put his hand out to stop Driff from following.

"Did you know about this?"

"No." The elf adjusted his spectacles. "Tallisker's just trying to get under your skin. They like to keep people off-balance and afraid. By bringing her here, they're merely trying to remind you who's in charge in their particularly convoluted way."

A disturbing thought occurred to Kevin. "Is she a hostage?"

Driff shook his head. "If she is, she's the calmest hostage I've ever seen. It's possible she could've been dusted, but that's not really Tallisker's style. They'd rather forcibly bend people to their cause than simply remove a few mental roadblocks. At first glance, I'd say she's here of her own free will."

Kevin scratched his head and looked back toward his ex, wishing he knew more about these shady Tallisker people. None of this made any sense.

"Be on your toes, Felton," Driff said as he brushed past Kevin and continued toward the Roberts estate. "I don't like this."

Kevin followed, keeping a few paces behind Driff so the elf was between him and whatever they were walking into. Driff's concern multiplied Kevin's own by a factor of a few dozen; his common sense told him that it was time to run, that he'd gotten himself in so far over his head that he'd never find his way out of the pile of shit into which he'd blindly stumbled. Forcing himself forward, he let his gaze wander to Kylie's long, graceful legs, his face flushing as he thought about how much he hated the woman they belonged to. His stomach twisted into a knot when he realized he hated Kylie simply because he missed her, her myriad faults be damned. He clung to his time with Nella like an alcoholic clinging to the last can in his six-pack, but a flood of doubts loosened his grip. What future could there be, really, for a human and a water nymph? Could two people from completely different species—hell, two mutually exclusive worlds—ever have anything remotely resembling a normal relationship? Kevin didn't really want to have to move to the middle of the woods, and he doubted Nella would be comfortable in a house. Would she accept having to disguise herself whenever he wanted to go out, or would she grow to resent him for dragging her to places where she had to conceal her true form? He hated himself for not knowing all the things he didn't know, for doubting all the things he doubted, for letting his confidence become shaken so badly by the woman—no, an open wound—he'd thought he'd never lay eyes on again.

Kevin shook his head, trying to focus. If Tallisker truly wanted to knock him off his game by thrusting his ex-girlfriend in front of him, they'd certainly succeeded. But why the fuck would they want to do that? Weren't they the ones ultimately paying for his assistance in bringing the local reaper back in line? Trying to work it all out made his head hurt.

Kylie smiled back at them as they climbed the marble steps leading up to the double front doors, sending a chill down Kevin's spine. He hoped he wouldn't have to sit next to her. He hoped Driff wouldn't leave them alone together. He hoped he'd be able to hide in a corner and watch her from afar. He hoped his suit pants were sturdy enough to conceal the boner that got harder the more he looked at her. In reality, though, he knew none of those things was likely to happen.

"This way, gentlemen," Kylie said as she thrust the doors open with a mighty shove. Kevin flinched away from the gold flash that burst out into the night from inside the Roberts estate, temporarily blinded by the sudden brightness. When his vision cleared and the scene before him solidified, he gasped and took a step backward. The room beyond the open entrance wasn't the expansive foyer of Ren's home, it was the small, cozy living room of a log cabin at some cheesy winter resort. Deer and elk were mounted on every wall, save for the spare real estate above the fake fireplace, which was adorned with a decapitated, snarling bear. To the left, a staircase led to a balcony and, presumably, a series of rooms on the second floor. Two dozen or so people filled the room, the scales tipped toward the male side by two or three individuals. The dress code appeared to be a choice between fleece or terrible sweaters trimmed with blocky snowflakes or crooked skis. Everyone clutched a steaming mug of cocoa, although their glazed expressions and slouched postures betrayed the heavy alcohol hidden in their seemingly innocent beverages. Raucous laughter echoed out into the night as they showed their appreciation for some joke the newcomers had just missed.

"Well," Driff said, "that's not quite what I expected."

"And my gold-digging ex is as overdressed as always," Kevin muttered.

Kylie whirled on Kevin, that nuclear glare he knew so well preparing to leap forth from her fiery eyes. "What was that, Kev?"

"The company you keep—I'm impressed, as always." It had been months since he'd had to pull something like that out of his ass, but the sudden softening of Kylie's features told him he hadn't lost his vaunted ability to placate her with total bullshit.

"They're lovely," she said coolly. "You first, boys."

Taking a step closer to Kevin, Driff placed an iron hand on his companion's lower back. "Might as well get this over with," he whispered. "Step through that doorway quickly, lingering on the threshold, or turning back, would not be good for your... consistency."

"Magic?" Kevin asked, his eyes wide.

"Yes," the elf said as he ushered Kevin forward. "Very expensive, very dangerous magic that'll sprinkle your molecules between here and wherever the fuck that is if you don't do as I say. Just another silly demon game."

The marble floor of the porch was too smooth for Kevin's heels to dig into as he fought to stop their advance. *"Demons?"* he snapped.

"Demons," Driff said. "We've been over this. Humans twisted by evil deeds into terrible new forms. But don't worry: most of them are pretty tame these days. Deliberate, purposeful evil pays better than random acts of violence."

Driff sent Kevin tumbling across the threshold with a quick push. Kevin bit back a groan as he passed through what felt like a wall of static electricity—the parts of him in the cabin losing and then regaining communication with the parts of him back in Harksburg, he assumed. The sensation was enough to ruin his balance and cause him to land hard on his side. Embarrassed, he pulled himself to his feet as quickly as he could.

Ed Roberts moved to help him. Ren's father had the look of an old weatherman: balding, short, but equipped with a bleached smile and a warm voice that could make a sunny forecast sound like a gift from the gods. Equipped with a mug of spiked cocoa and a terrible blue and white striped sweater over a pair of khakis, he fit right in with the rest of the crowd.

"Felton!" he shouted gregariously, as if announcing the winner of a horse race. "Glad you could make it, son!"

"Wouldn't miss it!" Kevin replied as he accepted Ed's vigorous handshake. *Because if I'd missed it, my liver would probably be the main course at the next one,* he added to himself.

Ellen Roberts appeared beside him, short and blonde and bubbly in pink designer ski wear. Red wine sloshed over the rim of her glass as she extended her own limp hand. "Good to see you." Her bright blue eyes shifted to something beyond Kevin's shoulder and she stood up on her toes to peek over him. "Ah, and this must be the Council of Intelligence!"

Driff was just stepping through the door when Mrs. Roberts swarmed him. He eyed the short woman like an art critic might a child's finger painting. "So I'm told," he grumbled.

Undeterred, Ellen hooked her elbow through the elf's and dragged him toward the rest of the party. Mr. Roberts nodded and winked at Kevin and followed.

"Tell me, darling, what's all the rage in Evitankari these days?"

"Well, I know a guy who makes a really interesting pound cake…"

Kevin took a deep breath as he tried to focus on the scene before him. He quickly scanned the room, trying to pick out the demons. The bearded, balding guy in the blinking reindeer sweater? The large woman picking at the cheese plate in the corner? The couple canoodling on the couch? The bored yuppie in a flannel shirt who looked like he'd rather be out on the golf course? And—the thought made Kevin shiver—what about Ren's parents, or even Ren himself? Or Kylie? Try as he might, he couldn't spot any sign that any of these people were anything other than what they seemed to be.

The door behind Kevin slammed shut, shocking him back to reality. He turned to find Kylie smiling at him mischievously, her hand lingering gently on the heavy brass knob of the thick front door. Through the windows on either side he could see a foot of snow on the cabin's front lawn. He certainly wasn't in Harksburg anymore.

"Northern Minnesota," Kylie said warmly. "The middle of fucking nowhere."

"Not really your kind of place."

She raised one slender eyebrow as she sauntered past, swaying close enough to ensure he got a thick taste of her familiar perfume. The scent of lilacs sent his head spinning. "Oh, you'd be surprised," she cooed.

Kevin couldn't help himself. "Anywhere there's money, huh?"

That stopped Kylie in her tracks. "Used to be," she admitted. "I always thought the money was what I wanted, but it turns out cash is just a means to an even better end. It's all about the power, Kevin, and these people have it all."

"Ren!" Mr. Roberts suddenly bellowed, his attention on the second floor balcony. "Your friends are here!"

A muffled curse replied from above. Had Ren been trying to avoid Kevin and Driff, or just the party in general? His best friend had a lot of explaining to do.

"Try to cheer your friend up," Kylie said evilly. "He's being a little bitch." And with that, she joined the rest of the party in the center of the room, heading for the gaggle of middle-aged ladies bombarding the befuddled Driff with questions about elven fashion.

Kevin shook his head as Ren made his way sullenly down the stairs. He'd dressed in a gray sweatsuit, his hair uncharacteristically unkempt.

"Someone's acting out," Kevin said.

"And someone's overdressed," Ren snapped, smiling tentatively. "Trying to match Kylie?"

"I was hoping to make her jealous so she'd beg me to take her back and I could tell her no just for the fun of it. Looks like that plan's a failure."

Ren nodded. "Unless you've got a tail, a set of horns, and a summer home in Monaco, you're probably out of luck."

They shared a quick laugh. Ren cut Kevin off before he could counterattack. "I'm sorry they dragged you into this, by the way."

"Dragged me into this?" He leaned in close and lowered his voice. "I'm the one who stole you-know-who's you-know-what. I should probably be apologizing to you."

Ren shook his head. "I don't think you understand. This little shindig isn't about you or Driff or Billy or any of that garbage we've been dealing with the last few days. It's about me, plain and simple."

A squeal from across the room interrupted Kevin's next question. "Strip poker!" a bubbly middle-aged blonde shouted gleefully as she led Ren's parents and two other couples toward the small table against the far windows.

"Now the party's really getting started," a conservative older gentleman with gray hair said as he approached Ren and Kevin. Deep wrinkles creased his square face, but his eyes burned with youthful energy. A happy snowman smiled dumbly from the center of his red sweater. "Charles Demson," he said as he extended his hand to Kevin.

The man's grip was tight as a vise and ice cold. "Kevin Felton."

"Ah, the young man helping out with Harksburg's little reaper problem. I hear good things about you, Felton. Very good things indeed."

Good things? Kevin had no idea what Demson was talking about, and he wasn't sure he wanted to know. "Thank you, sir. Just doing my part."

"As we all must." Before Kevin knew it, Demson's arm was around his shoulders and the older man was steering him toward the table of hors d'oeuvres in the corner. Kevin couldn't help feeling like he, Driff, and Ren were being intentionally separated.

"Caviar? Littlenecks? Perhaps a glass of champagne or brandy? I'm afraid we drank all the cocoa."

There was quite a spread on the table before him—various cured meats, strange cheeses, and enough liquor to fill an in-ground swimming pool—but the thought of sampling any of it turned Kevin's stomach. "I'm fine for now, thank you. So...ah...what's the occasion?"

"Success!" Demson replied. "They say such a thing is its own reward, but the people who spout such drivel have never been to a good party, eh?"

"You do have a point."

A triumphant shout from the poker game momentarily caught their attention. "I win!" Ren's father declared. "Off with your pants, Marie!"

A brunette with thick plastic lips stood up and unclasped her gaudy white belt. "I'll get you next time, Eddie!" she slurred as she shoved her jeans down around her ankles, revealing the black G-string underneath. Mrs. Roberts clapped wildly and smacked Marie on the ass.

"Your friends certainly know how to have fun," Kevin joked.

Demson chuckled. "If there's one thing we know, it's how to have a good time. That's why I invested in this little cabin. It's not much, but it's a great getaway spot."

"It's very nice."

Kevin's gaze wandered to Driff, who was now seated on the couch, surrounded by people peppering him with questions about his home. The elf had snagged some expensive-looking champagne and was keeping himself sane with regular deep draughts right from the bottle. Ren, meanwhile, had wandered over to watch the poker game.

Kylie had found a spot along the far wall from which she could watch it all. She felt Kevin's gaze lingering on her and turned to stare right back at him. Blushing, Kevin blinked a few times and turned back to Demson.

"Your ex-girlfriend is a very talented young lady. She'll go far with Tallisker."

The older man's inflection on the word "talented" told Kevin everything he needed to know about which of Kylie's abilities Tallisker prized. "How did she get involved with the company?"

"Oh, we've got an army of well-paid headhunters in all the major firms. If you're any good, we'll find you. Say, I hear you had quite the promising career in finance prior to your layoff."

The only thing that kept Kevin from causing a scene was his suspicion that his current companion might be a demon. "I was doing pretty well for myself, sure."

Their conversation was once again interrupted by a triumphant shout from the poker game. This time, the brunette had won. "Four jacks, baby! Take off your watch!"

Kevin wondered if he'd heard right. Did she really want Ren's father to take off his watch? Wasn't the point of the game to get to everyone else's naughty bits? He was about to ask Demson as a means of changing the subject when the scene before him made his jaw drop. As Mr. Roberts slid his watch off his wrist, suddenly there was a monster in his place—a big brown thing with scales, leathery wings, and some sort of sharp spines wherever it should've had hair. Everyone around the table hollered and cheered, save for Ren, who shook his head.

Well, Kevin thought, *I guess the watch thing makes a little more sense now.*

Demson drew him back into their previous conversation with a simple question. "Ever want to get back into the big time? Tallisker could use a man like you. There are always a few books that need to be cooked, if you know what I mean. We pay very well—as I'm sure you've noticed."

In spite of his reservations about the food's safety, Kevin quickly snatched a piece of hard cheese from the table beside them and popped it into his mouth, giving himself time to think. Up until a few days ago, this kind of opportunity would've been just the thing he was looking for. Networking was the name of the game, and he'd always been damn good at. He understood that it wasn't what you knew but who you knew that got you places in life. In a field where every job candidate had a degree from a good school and a perfect cover letter, one social reference made all the difference.

But there, in northern Minnesota, the thought of playing that game with these people almost made him choke on his cheese.

"Sorry, sir, but I'm not ready to leave Harksburg yet," he said, swallowing carefully.

Demson's eyes narrowed. "Why not?"

Why not, indeed? Because of Nella, obviously, and because he didn't particularly like the thought of working for the frightening group of twisted monsters that had cost him his last job in Chicago, but neither of those were reasons he could voice without endangering himself and others. His mind whirred through the events of the last few days, searching for an answer.

"It's a good change of pace." Kevin couldn't believe he'd managed to say that with a straight face, and he especially couldn't believe that he meant it. Being stuck in the middle of nowhere, surrounded by people who hadn't really made anything of themselves as defined by fancy businessmen with plastic smiles and holier-than-thou attitudes, had rejuvenated Kevin Felton. Hell, he'd even kind of enjoyed his dealings with all the insane magic assholes in the area, as much as he hated to admit it. He'd made new friends, solidified old relationships, and learned so much about things he'd never even imagined possible. After what Tallisker and Kylie had put him through, returning to Harksburg had pretty much been the best thing that could've happened to him. Except maybe for the parts when he got shot or punched in the face.

The other man chuckled. "Do changes of pace come with stock options and 401(k)s these days? This is a once-in-a-lifetime opportunity to play in the big leagues, my boy! I'd hate to see you turn it down because you were charmed by a few local yokels."

His gaze drifting to Kylie once again, Kevin took a deep breath. A once-in-a-lifetime opportunity at what? To be used and abused by whatever the hell these people were for whatever nefarious purposes they pursued? To be just another cog in their immoral machine? Life in Harksburg wasn't glamorous, but at least it was honest. Kevin felt his temperature rising and chose his next words carefully.

"I'm sorry, sir, but where was this attention when Tallisker gutted Noonan, Noonan, and Schmidt? If you'd wanted me so badly, all you had to do was give my pink slip to someone else."

Demson snorted. "You'd yet to prove yourself, my boy. Consider my offer; it won't be on the table forever. So, how do you think the Cubs will fare this year? We own a VIP box, you know."

Out of the corner of his eye, Kevin tracked Kylie as she removed herself from the far wall and integrated herself into the group surrounding Driff. She bent over to pick something off the end table beside the couch, which she offered to the elf. Driff wrinkled his nose, shook his head, and took a long swig from his bottle of champagne. A few of the other men in the group happily partook in whatever Kylie was passing around.

Kevin turned back to Demson nervously. "I try to get to Wrigley as often as I can, preferably along the first base line."

"You haven't lived until you've watched a game from right above home plate while an army of attractive waitresses services your every need."

"Sure sounds better than sitting in the bleachers, waiting for the beer guy to come around."

"Undoubtedly. Slumming it with the rabble can be...cute...from time to time, but people like you and me deserve our space and our comfort."

Kylie appeared at Kevin's side then, holding a wooden bowl up to his face. Kevin peered over the rim tentatively, expecting some sort of vile concoction these strange people would expect him to eat. Instead, the bowl was simply full of key rings.

"I drive an Audi these days," Kylie said with a wink.

Kevin's gaze settled heavily on the remote starter atop the pile, its blue and white logo blurring his vision as if he'd inadvertently looked right at the sun. These people really wanted him to join their little cabal and they knew exactly how to tempt him. A job was one thing; but Kylie, well, she was something else entirely. Would it really be so bad? What could they possibly do to him, or make him do, after all? This was his chance to get it all back and then some; he could leave Harksburg, get back together with Kylie, and enjoy all the perks that came with gainful corporate employment. No more living in the basement. No more nights at the Burg. No more worrying about Nella, the blue girl with whom a real life would likely be impossible. He could be himself again, the well-dressed, hardworking, ladder-climbing future executive with the gorgeous, successful girlfriend and the trendy apartment and all the other trimmings of a promising young professional, and all he had to do was pick up that key ring.

Driff snapped him out of his reverie. Clutching a half-dozen bottles of champagne to his chest as if carrying a cord of firewood, the elf leaned in close to Kevin's ear to whisper a few words of advice.

"Once they've got you, they won't let go."

Kevin watched, stunned, as Driff sauntered toward the exit, opened the front door—revealing the front yard of the Roberts estate—and left, abandoning him to choose his own fate.

He glanced over at Ren, who watched from the far corner of the room. His friend shook his head gently.

That was all it took. "I'm sorry, Kylie, but it's time for me to go. It was nice to see you again."

Without waiting for a response, Kevin turned and headed for the door. He didn't look back—not when Kylie tried to woo him with half-hearted platitudes, not when the men and women at the poker game started to laugh at him, and not when he stepped across the threshold and back into Harksburg, forsaking his old life forever.

— CHAPTER TWENTY-THREE —

Kevin found Driff sitting on the front lawn of the Roberts estate, sipping from a bottle of champagne as he looked up at the stars. The five other bottles he'd pilfered lay on the ground beside him.

"Welcome back to reality," Driff said, patting the lawn to his left. "Pull up some grass and have a drink."

"Don't mind if I fucking do," Kevin replied as he sat. He snatched up a bottle of champagne and started untwisting the wire that secured its cork. "What made you decide to leave?"

"My people spend enough time in bed with those Tallisker fuckers," Driff said with a snort. He'd begun to slur. "Besides which, I made a New Year's resolution against participating in demonic orgies. How's your old girlfriend?"

Kevin worked the cork out of the bottle with his thumb and fired it off into the night upon a burst of champagne. He raised the bottle to his lips to drink the cool bubbly rolling down the sides. "Just like old times. Hasn't changed a bit."

"Always been a greedy hanger-on, huh? Wonder what it was you saw in her in the first place."

"Tits. Ass. Style. Brains." Kevin shifted uncomfortably, pulled a twig out from under his ass, and tossed it aside. "The perfect fucking accessory for my urban professional lifestyle."

"Ha! A lifestyle. That was your first mistake."

For a few moments they sat and drank and looked up at the sky. Despite all he'd seen the last few days, he had difficulty processing the last fifteen minutes. Surprisingly, it was neither the demons nor Kylie that left Kevin feeling introspective; rather, he wondered what choice he would've made had Driff and Ren not been there. Would he have been strong enough to resist Tallisker's temptation on his own? He hoped so, but he wasn't sure.

"Ever think about the people you work for," Driff slurred thoughtfully, "and just ask yourself 'what the fuck?'"

Kevin turned to examine him. Driff was hunched over his knees, dangling his bottle of champagne between his legs and staring at the grass. Kevin wasn't sure exactly what had gotten into the elf—or why he kind of cared—so he just shrugged.

"The people who make the decisions...why do *they* get to decide how things go? What gives them the right?" Driff continued. "Why is it that anyone else who comes along who wants to be in charge and promises that things will be different inevitably ends up just as fucked as whoever he or she replaced?"

Kevin punched Driff playfully in the arm. "Aren't you some kind of big shot yourself, Councilor of Intelligence?"

"It's Council," the elf snapped. "Technically I was elected to 437 different Councilor positions. I am a Council unto myself."

"That's...really fucking strange. Why did *you* want the job?"

Driff finally looked up at Kevin. The elf's eyes were distant and quivered as he spoke. "It wasn't really my idea. I was part of...of a movement. My role was decided for me. And it's gotten a little out of control."

After taking a long swig of champagne, Kevin gave Driff the best advice he could think of. "None of us really has complete control over his or her life. That's probably what the people in charge really want, more desperately than the rest of us. We all have to do our best without crossing whatever line those fuckers in Minnesota stomped right over."

"Hear, hear!" Ren called out from behind them. He dropped himself casually to the grass beside the elf and grabbed his own bottle of champagne.

Kevin and Driff exchanged an awkward glance. Neither knew what to say to Ren. Given their history, Kevin figured breaking the ice was his responsibility.

"So how long has your father been a winged demon?"

Driff cackled and spilled champagne all over his right leg.

"He turned not long after my sixth birthday," Ren explained solemnly. "He came home from work one day and announced that he'd been awarded a big promotion that required him to attend a six-week training course in L.A. When he came back..."

Turning his attention back to the grass, Kevin considered Ren's story. He'd never met his own father; the closest facsimiles he'd known were the various dads on network television. Warm, smart, caring bastions of knowledge and guidance, he'd grown up assuming everyone's father was just like Cliff Huxtable and Andy Taylor: a role model, someone a boy learning to make his way in the world could look up to and emulate. It was a character Kevin had assigned to his own absentee father, attaching it with a steady string of silly rationalizations for the man's vagrancy. His father couldn't be with him because he was a CIA spy. His father was never around because he was in the Florida Everglades, searching for the fountain of youth. His father was one of the masked wrestlers Kevin occasionally saw on TV. Now a jaded, cynical adult, Kevin knew that no one was perfect and had long ago cast off those ridiculous daydreams, but the thought of Ren's own bubble of fatherly perfection having been burst at such a young age hurt—doubly so given how much Kevin and everyone else in

Ren's peer group had always idolized Ed Roberts. To all outside observers, Ren's father had always been perfect.

"My mother knew what was coming, I think," Ren continued. "She encouraged him. Pushed him. Asked him every day what he had done to take one more step up the ladder. When he first showed us his new form, she didn't even blink."

"Your mother's a hellfucker," Driff said with a chuckle. He pointed at Kevin. "Just like fancy boy's ex!"

Ren shook his head. "Thank you for your deep elven insight. Anyway, he never mistreated us. If anything, he was even better to my mother and me than he was before the change. These demons...they aren't what you expect. They're grounded. Focused. Running around being blatantly evil monsters all the time is a great way to get shot, so they stick to the shadows and manipulate others into doing their evil for them—a well-placed arms shipment here, a food shortage there, a bit of corruption in this church over there—so that they can live long, productive lives of luxurious bastardy. And to keep themselves from going off the rails, they maintain a connection to humanity: a family."

"That's fucking nuts," Kevin replied, washing down his statement with a mouthful of champagne and then punctuating it with a loud belch.

His friend laughed sadly. "Isn't it? But it works. These assholes live forever. That Demson jerk's almost four hundred years old. And he wants me to be his protégé."

Kevin gagged on his next drink. "You? The fuck why?"

"Better hope Daddy lives a *long* time," Driff added.

Ren shook his head and rolled his eyes at the elf. "My father did something that pissed him off once. There's some sort of convoluted professional rivalry between the two. I'm not real clear on it. Whatever it was didn't necessitate any sort of official censure. When there's a beef, the wronged party attempts to woo a member of the offender's family into the lifestyle—effectively stealing part of the perpetrator's connection to his sanity. Remember Carolyn Peters?"

"Yeah. In fact, I ran into her last night. She looked a little…pale."

"Well, now you know what happened to her. It wasn't just that thing with their shared ex-boyfriend that brought them together; Janice Redding's demon mother got involved and that was that. Luckily Demson can't act on me overtly as long as I remain in my father's presence or in his territory, so he has to resort to convoluted tricks instead." Ren took a long drink before continuing. "Like—"

"—like ruining your best friend's life by nuking his job, stealing his girlfriend, and forcing him to move back in with his Jesus freak mother, then sucking him into Tallisker's web with promises that he could have it all back and more," Kevin finished for him. "Then you turn that best friend into a demon to exert pressure on the real target. Like you said, tonight was all about you."

Shifting uncomfortably on the grass, Ren's eyes locked onto his shoes. "Yup."

"Well," Driff slurred, "that was even more awkward than I expected."

"It's not your fault, Ren," Kevin said quickly, hoping to head off any sort of confrontation and set his friend at ease. "It's not even your father's fault. It's Tallisker's. Harksburg is fucked up, and the things those demons can offer…"

Ren said nothing, but his shoulders seemed to relax. Kevin meant what he'd said, and he didn't blame Ren for having difficulty talking about it.

Driff regarded Kevin coolly. "You think this place is a mess? Where I come from, we've got a guy that once cut a lamp post in half with his broadsword because he thought it was looking at him funny. We've got a talking tree. I once saw a woman magically teleport a fart into the mouth of someone who owed her money. Harksburg isn't any more or less fucked up than anywhere else.

Some places just hide it better, and sometimes familiarity breaks down barriers that would be better left cemented in place."

Although he agreed completely with the elf's sentiment, Kevin never would've admitted to it. He'd encountered some truly screwed up people in Chicago, but as a big, important city, Chicago was somehow supposed to be better than a remote small town like Harksburg. In the city, local lunatics became beloved eccentrics. Annoyances became another part of that grimy urban charm. Still, he knew better, but the pride he took in having been one of the few to escape Harksburg for a place that supposedly mattered—albeit temporarily—stayed his tongue.

"How do you remember all this?" Kevin asked, changing the subject. "Isn't that dust crap in the water?"

"You know those allergy pills I've been taking twice a day since I was little?" Ren replied. "They neutralize the effect. They can't bring back memories previously blocked off by the dust, but they keep it from doing any more damage."

"Don't worry, Kevin. When this is all over, the dust will make it all better," Driff said melodramatically, like a doctor promising a child his boo-boo would heal up just fine.

Before Kevin could tell Driff where to shove his bottle of champagne, a vibration in his pocket alerted him to an incoming text. He pulled his phone out, swiped the screen, and quickly read the message. The smile on his face got bigger and bigger as he read it over and over again.

"It's from Billy. 'Had such a good time at the Burg the other night. Decided to go on my own tonight. Met the girl of my dreams. Don't wait up,'" he read triumphantly.

"And that," Driff said, "is a lot more anticlimactic than I expected."

— CHAPTER TWENTY-FOUR —

Buzzed and stumbling, Kevin nevertheless made the walk home from the Roberts estate in record time. Although Driff insisted he wanted to see proof that Billy was actually back on the job before he declared their mission accomplished, Kevin had no desire to linger within dusting distance after they'd each polished off two bottles of champagne.

He entered his bedroom through the Pussy Hatch simply for old time's sake, almost botching the landing as his inebriated brain misjudged the distance to the floor. A familiar giggle wafted up from the bed beside him.

"You are a picture of grace, Kevin Felton," Nella said. She activated the lamp on the nightstand, revealing her perfect blue body. Seated atop the comforter with her back propped up against a pile of pillows, she clutched a manila envelope over her breasts.

"And you are a creepy stalker," Kevin replied as he shrugged out of his jacket. "What the heck were you doing in the dark all by yourself?"

"Thinking."

"About?"

"About why the fuck Mr. Pemberton asked me to play courier."

Kevin glanced at the manila envelope. The reaper keeper had promised some sort of paperwork. He sat down at the foot of the bed and motioned for Nella to hand it over. She hesitated, expecting an explanation.

"Mr. Pemberton cornered me in Donovan's. He interrogated me briefly, then he told me that he knows about us and offered me some sort of deal."

Nella's eyes narrowed. "I don't like this," she said as she passed him the envelope.

Nodding, he put on what he hoped was a brave face. "I won't let him blackmail me if I can help it, but I need to know his terms."

Kevin tore the envelope open and dumped its contents into his lap. Two sheets of paper slid out: some kind of roughly photocopied form and a handwritten note on the sort of thick, fibrous paper usually reserved for resumes.

"*Dearest Mr. Felton,*" the note read in precise, flowing script. "*I apologize for taking over your evening at Donovan's, but I needed to be sure of several things. Please thank Nella for delivering the contents of this envelope. They should be most helpful, I would think.*

"*Long story short, I've decided a change of scenery is in order. I grow weary of my duties and desire a return to normal human life. My job has been most fulfilling and it has provided many a glimpse of things I never would have imagined or been exposed to otherwise. It is my sincerest hope, good sir, that you would pick up where I left off and take my position as Master Billy's assistant. You seem well suited to the task, and I believe he would find your company most agreeable.*

"*I shall continue in my current capacity until a replacement is found. I pray that you will consider my suggestion, and that you are successful in dragging Master Billy free from the doldrums in which he is currently mired. He is a good boy, albeit a bit overly emotional. He needs a friend—and I believe you, at the very least, have already satisfied that requirement.*

"*Please note that your involvement in this program also releases you from any obligations to Evitankari or Tallisker. You would become a legal part of the world in which they and Billy operate, with all the privileges and protections that entails.*

"Cordially Yours, Mr. Pemberton."

A stupid smile spreading across his face, Kevin put the note down and examined the accompanying form: it was a job application, already cosigned by Mr. Pemberton.

Billy lunged across the bed, scooped up Nella in his arms, and kissed her more passionately than he'd ever kissed anyone in his entire life.

"What is it?" she asked when he finally came up for air a few minutes later.

"Mr. Pemberton just dust proofed me!"

Nella snatched up the two documents and read them carefully. Kevin scrambled over to his desk, grabbed a pen, then sat back down on the bed beside her.

"Shit," she snapped as she handed the paperwork back to him. "You're lucky you're so fucking handsome, because your critical thinking and decision-making skills leave a *lot* to be desired."

"It'll work," Kevin replied, busily filling out his personal information.

"My kind have a saying," the water nymph continued. "Don't poke the troll unless you want it to tear your fucking arms off."

Kevin looked up at Nella in confusion. "Billy's not a troll."

"Right. He's something much, much worse."

He brushed her concerns aside and asked her assistance with the first question on the form. "What are my five strongest skills or qualities?"

"Drinking heavily, feeling sorry for yourself, getting punched in the face, and putting yourself into dangerous situations you should know better to put yourself into." She paused for a moment and squinted, thinking. "And fucking."

"Not bad, but we need to change the language a little: my strong work ethic, the ease with which I feel empathy for others, my strong resolve, my unflappable courage in the face of seemingly insurmountable odds." He mimicked Nella's squinting pause. "And my attention to detail."

The water nymph smiled that irresistible smile, setting his heart aflutter. "Fuck you, Kevin Felton," she said with a sigh. "I'm glad someone finds all this funny."

Setting the folder and the application aside, he leaned across the bed to take her hand in his. "If I take this position, Driff can't dust me," Kevin said softly. "This'll buy us some time. Billy won't be hung up on you forever."

She sighed again, tears in her eyes. "I suppose. But working that closely with Billy is an even bigger risk than the one you're taking now. I still think you should run, Kevin. Get the hell out of here and don't come back. If anything happens to you...I missed you. While you were gone. But at least I knew you were all right."

He gave her hand a reassuring squeeze. "Nothing's going to happen."

— CHAPTER TWENTY-FIVE —

Having gone to bed with a belly full of champagne, a satisfied libido, and the buoyancy of a man finally free of worry, Kevin Felton slept better than he had in months. He didn't dream. He didn't move. He didn't wake until his alarm went off at nine the next morning. Nella was gone, as usual, the only evidence of her passing the twisted sheets she'd left on her side of the bed. With a mighty yawn, he sat up and stretched his arms wide. He couldn't wait to get all the details from Billy. With any luck, the reaper's romantic encounter had already healed his broken heart and put him back on the job.

The dining room was empty, the table set with the usual two places. Kevin helped himself to a seat and a cheese danish from the plate in the center of the table, then opened up the newspaper waiting on his mother's usual chair. Skipping the national news, Kevin eagerly flipped to the local section to skim the headlines. He found what he was looking for in the bottom right corner of page fourteen, a tiny story shoved at the last minute into a spot reserved for a cheap advertisement: "R. Fredricks, Former Harksburg Councilman, Dead at 78." Kevin joyously slammed his palm down onto the table, rattling the place settings. Everyone in town knew

Fredricks had been confined to the Golden Dawn Rest Home on the far side of Plastic Hill. Billy was already back on the job!

"What's all the fuss about?" a familiar voice asked from the kitchen.

Kevin froze, every muscle in his body arrested in shock. He bit back a curse, hoping he was just hearing things.

Billy strolled into the dining room with a big smile on his young face, a heaping plate of scrambled eggs and fried potatoes balanced precariously in his hands. The reaper looked downright ridiculous in Mrs. Felton's pink bathrobe, but he didn't seem to care.

Oh, that fucking figures, Kevin thought as he tried to force his lips to make a friendly smile. His heart raced as he carefully closed the newspaper, folded it, and set it aside.

"Are you all right?" Billy asked as he sat down opposite Kevin, setting the plate in between them.

"Fine," Kevin stammered. Honesty, he decided, would probably be the best policy—and the best way to keep his soul in his body where it belonged. "I didn't expect to see you here."

The reaper blushed. "Well, your mother's a wonderful woman. We started talking in the Burg last night and sort of hit it off."

"Good. Good." Not good. Not good at all.

"Don't worry," Billy said casually as he shoveled a pile of eggs onto his plate. "I'll treat her right. And when we get married, I won't make you call me Papa or Father or anything like that. Sir will do."

Although Kevin felt like he was about to vomit, he managed an awkward laugh. "Thanks."

"Thanks...who?"

"Don't fucking push it, sir."

They shared a genuine laugh and Kevin relaxed. He began to think that maybe this could work. Maybe this was a one-time thing, a means of blowing off steam. Maybe, if it turned out to be something more, Billy and Abelia would find what they needed from each other and move on without any drama. Stranger things had happened—many of them in the last couple of days—and the reaper was certainly a step up from Mrs. Felton's other conquests. He'd actually give a shit about her, unlike Kevin's other scumbag friends. Things could get difficult, though, if "giving a shit" turned into "clinging mightily to Abelia's leg like she's the last woman on earth." For now, though, Billy was content with his life and back to fulfilling his reaper duties—and that, Kevin decided, made the situation worth the risk.

Abelia whirled into the kitchen wearing nothing but a Styx T-shirt that barely covered her thighs. "Who wants hash?" she chirped merrily as she dropped a steaming plate of the stuff on the table. "The meaty kind, not the green kind. At least not before noon."

"Thanks, Ma," Kevin said. Abelia Felton's pork hash was renowned throughout Harksburg. There had been a month back in eighth grade where Doorknob stopped by every morning to pick up a plastic container of it for lunch. That habit came to a screeching halt one day when Jim Jimeson dumped the entire container down the back of Doorknob's pants.

As the two young men eagerly shoveled food onto their plates, Abelia lit a cigarette. "That reminds me, Kevin. I got you a present. I'll be right back, boys!" She stormed into the kitchen, leaving a wispy trail of smoke swirling behind her.

"Your mother's so nice," Billy said in between mouthfuls of hash. "You're lucky to have her."

Kevin nodded and shifted uncomfortably in his seat. He wasn't one to talk about such things so openly. "What's your mother like?"

It was Billy's turn to look awkward. "Not like that," he said softly.

"Here we go!" Abelia returned from the kitchen carrying a plastic shopping bag stuffed with some sort of blue clothing. She quickly rounded the table to stand behind Kevin. "I had this made special when you still had a fucking job. They wouldn't let me return it."

Kevin continued to eat, ignoring the sounds of the crackling bag and unfolding fabric behind him. If whatever his mother was up to was going to make her happy, he could bear it. Probably.

"Stop eating so I can get this over your head properly!"

He set his fork and knife down on his plate and leaned back in his chair to let Abelia work. Something long and blue swooped down over his face and came to rest on his chest, held loosely against his body by a string that looped around the back of his neck. An apron.

"There!" Abelia declared, giggling to herself. "Everybody at the Burg would've loved it!"

Across the table, Billy froze. His eyes narrowed to mere slits, the very air around him seeming to grow heavy with malice. "Poofy," he snarled, spitting the word like a vile curse.

At first, the word didn't register with Kevin. Poofy? What the hell was a Poofy, and why was Billy so angry about it? The scene didn't seem real, it couldn't be real, because then the worst-case scenario for Kevin's future had come to its horrifying fruition despite everything he'd done to avoid it—and Abelia, who was still giggling, obviously found the whole thing very funny. He risked a look down at the front of the apron. "Hi!" it declared in big red letters. "My name is Poofy!"

Kevin reached up to cover his nose, but the reaper was inhumanly fast. Billy leapt across the table and jammed his fingers into Kevin's face, narrowly missing his target. Mrs. Felton cursed as the two of them crashed to the floor in a tangle of arms and legs. "I swear I didn't know she was your fiancée!" Kevin shouted as he deflected one of Billy's hands with his forearm. He assumed something akin to the fetal position, pulling his legs up to his chest and guarding his face with his fists and arms like a boxer. Billy responded by driving his knee between Kevin's legs and right into his balls. A high-pitched gasp signaled the end of Kevin's defense.

"What the hell was that?" Abelia demanded. "Fight like a man, you asshole!"

And then Billy's fingers shot up Kevin's nose and violently yanked out something important. Pain wasn't the word for the sensation that tore through his body; it felt more like his nerves were panicking because they didn't know how to deal with the information coursing from neuron to neuron. Once the reaper had firm grip on Kevin's soul, Billy threw himself backward with all his might. The straining threads that held Kevin's life inside his body snapped viciously. His perspective suddenly shifted a few feet forward so he was staring Billy square in the face. All sense of weight disappeared, as did the tearing sensation. He felt free, unbridled by the physical world. On one level, he realized that this was the sort of profound trip shamans and mystics of all sorts had pursued since the dawn of man, that he'd been granted a unique chance to experience an altered state of consciousness through which he might come to understand many of the world's mysteries. Those thoughts, however, were soon drowned out by a much louder chorus of overwhelming dread. His soul was no longer attached to his physical form—and that just plain wasn't right. Kevin lurched against the reaper's grip, desperately straining to return to his body, but Billy's grasp was impossible to break.

Abelia slapped Billy in the back of the head. "Put that back!" she snapped.

"I don't think so," he said angrily. "Poofy and I are going to have some fun."

— CHAPTER TWENTY-SIX —

Abelia Felton knelt beside Kevin's lifeless body on the dining room floor and glared up at the man responsible for her son's fate. "I mean it, you piece of shit. Put it back."

Billy shrugged, his attention locked on the disembodied soul wriggling desperately between the fingers of his left hand. "After everything my new best friend has done for me? I don't think so. Would you happen to have a Thermos or some sort of travel mug?"

"In the cabinet above the toaster."

"Thank you."

He left Abelia with Kevin's corpse and strolled purposefully into the kitchen. Kevin could feel the blood pumping wildly through Billy's hand and fingers, the heat of the reaper's anger seeping into whatever the hell his detached soul was made of. Ectoplasm, maybe? When Billy had pulled Ren's soul most of the way out of his nose upon their first meeting, what came out was a glowing, ethereal reproduction of Ren himself. Remembering that, he decided the word ectoplasm sounded far too sticky for what he'd seen and the way he now felt. His very being felt loose and transient, as if he were held together with strands of loose dental floss where once there'd been muscle and sinew. Weight held no meaning, but his sense of gravity had shifted drastically so that "down" had become the direction toward his soulless body. Although Kevin had more important things to worry about, focusing on and examining such minutiae helped ground his mind and stave off the desperate fear threatening to overwhelm him.

"Be afraid, you lying piece of shit," Billy muttered as he passed the old white refrigerator on his way to the cabinets on the opposite wall. He swung his hands as he walked, alternately giving Kevin a view of his surroundings and of his own hip. The odd angle gave him a great view of the underside of the kitchen's upper cabinets. Some sort of tiny gray spider had started spinning a web in the corner.

The reaper sighed. "You've got more important things to worry about."

So you can read my mind? Kevin thought.

"You don't really have a mind anymore," Billy replied as he opened the cabinet above the dishwasher.

On the counter below, a pile of neglected pancakes drew Kevin's attention. Funny how he already missed having a mouth that would water at the sight of his mother's cooking.

I'm sorry, Kevin tried, knowing it was his only chance—and that he meant it.

Billy hesitated, wobbling on his feet for a moment as he examined the cabinet's contents. "Whatever."

It was that or let you have my soul. Do you really blame me for the choice I made?

Blinking back tears, the reaper stood on his toes and reached for something on the top shelf. "Yes. Especially because you automatically assumed the worst."

You yanked Ren's soul out through his fucking nose!

"He was bothering me. I put it back," Billy replied defensively. There was no mistaking the mix of confusion and malice in his voice; the reaper's emotions were a mess, and so he erred on the side of malevolence.

Kevin worked quickly, hoping to mask the thought that he might be able to take advantage of the reaper's indecisiveness. *Ren can be an annoying shit, but let's focus here. I had no clue you were engaged to Nella. She came to me.*

Billy withdrew a Blackhawks travel mug from the cupboard and set it down on the counter beside the pancakes. "How many cups do you think this holds?" he asked, his voice quivering. "Two? Maybe three?"

Seriously, Kevin continued, pouring fear and regret into his thoughts. *What did you expect me to do, turn myself in so you'd do this to me?*

A low growl rumbled in the reaper's chest. "You never even gave me a chance. You presumed I'd hurt you and started lying."

Kevin couldn't believe whatever he had that still functioned as ears. Billy obviously didn't get it; his reaper powers made him so much more dangerous and unpredictable than the average spurned lover that dealing with him simply as such would've been impossible. Had he been dealing with a normal person without magic powers, Kevin would've manned up and taken whatever licks he'd had to take. A good right hook, however, was nothing compared to having his spirit violently exorcised from its own body.

"Well aren't you just a stand-up fucking guy," the reaper muttered as he unscrewed the travel mug's cap and sniffed its interior. "And Abelia, trust me when I tell you that you really, really don't want to do that."

Billy turned to face Kevin's mother, who'd decided to sneak up behind them. She'd unscrewed one of the wooden legs from a dining room chair and now brandished it like a club, her determined scowl making it very clear that she planned to bash the reaper's brains in.

"Give me back my son and I won't have to hurt you."

Yes! Kevin thought, mentally cheering his mother on. She never would've threatened someone with a weapon prior to her mental rewiring. Old Abelia would've appealed to Billy's inner goodness, citing scripture and insisting that the reaper's current circumstances were all a part of God's plan, another in a long set of challenges built to test his soul's mettle and prove the quality of his spirit. When that inevitably failed, she would've flipped the switch and triggered what he'd come to think of as Old Testament Mode, replacing her useless platitudes with an equally ineffective downpour of hellfire and brimstone. New Abelia, however, wasn't going to waste her time with any of that shit. She was going to kick some ass and take some names and then go smoke a cigarette, and then Kevin was going to go find Driff and plant a big wet kiss on the elf's meddling face.

"Don't worry," Billy said. "You'll get your precious Poofy back. He and I have some business to attend to first. Man stuff. You wouldn't understand."

Her eyes narrowed. "Try me."

Billy hesitated for a moment, considering. "My bride-to-be left me for this jerk when he came back to Harksburg. Rather than do the honorable thing and admit his involvement, he befriended me in a misguided attempt to save his own putrid skin by lying his stupid fucking head off."

"Sounds like something he would do," Abelia muttered, rolling her eyes.

Thanks, Ma! Kevin screamed. *You're a real pal. Just club the son of a bitch already!*

"And now he really, really wants you to hit me," Billy added. "Your son's an asshole."

Mrs. Felton nodded. "Yeah, but he's my favorite asshole, so you see where you and I have a teensy little problem."

That's it! Hit him! Knock his fucking head off!

"Actually," Billy said, "I was hoping we could work together on this one. Someone needs to teach your son a lesson."

"He has been a bit of an insufferable little bitch lately."

What? Damn it, Ma, you have no idea what I've been through the last few days! There are magic assholes everywhere and all they want to do is fuck with me for their own fucking entertainment! Do you have any idea how much my life fucking sucks right now? Hit the bastard!

"You should hear him right now," the reaper growled. "He's whining and crying like a teenage girl who just got grounded. He needs to learn to stand up for himself. If you club me for him, well…"

Abelia finished for him. "…he'll never learn."

"And if you beat me with that stick, let's just say that things won't go very well for you." Billy gestured toward Mrs. Felton with the travel cup's open mouth as if inviting her to climb into it.

She lowered her weapon. "Will it hurt?"

Like a motherfucker!

"It'll only if I let it—which I won't."

"And you promise you'll put both of us back?"

"When I've gotten my point across and Poofy's proved he's learned his lesson, yes."

Abelia shifted control of the chair leg to her left hand and raised her right, extending her smallest finger. "Pinky swear?"

No! No pinky swearing! Beat his punk ass up!

Billy smiled and wrapped his finger around Abelia's. "Pinky sw—"

He never finished. Mrs. Felton yanked him toward her, simultaneously jabbing her makeshift cudgel into his abdomen. The reaper collapsed, wheezing, as he tried to catch his breath. Feeling Billy's grip on his soul loosen, Kevin again pushed with all of his might against the cold fingers holding him in place. Though he had more room to move, the reaper still held tight.

"Fuck you, you fucking dumbass!" Abelia bellowed as she brought the chair leg down across her opponent's nose. Billy screamed as it broke, spewing blood all over his pink bathrobe and the white kitchen floor. Kevin strained against the reaper's clenched knuckles as they spasmed loose, screaming silently as he slowly tore free. Pain flared throughout his soul as he strained away from his prison one excruciating inch at a time, like a plant tearing itself up out of the ground while its roots held tight to the soil.

Abelia swung again, but this time Billy caught the chair leg in his free hand. The wood around his fingers turned black, the shiny finish flaking away in tiny chunks. The club warped and split as Mrs. Felton fought to pull it free before the reaper could transform it into a useless hunk of weak ash. Focused on freeing her weapon, Abelia missed the kick that took out her kneecap and dropped her to the floor beside Billy. Her agonized scream cracked something in Kevin's spirit.

You son of a bitch! Kevin screamed as his soul was violently sucked back into the reaper's fist. Billy cracked his fingers, giving him a clear view of his mother as she clutched her knee and writhed in pain. *I will fucking kill you for that!*

With an unimpressed snort, Billy leaned over Abelia and quickly shoved the fingers of his other hand up under her nose. Mrs. Felton's body tensed as she fought to keep her essence inside of her where it belonged, but she couldn't withstand the reaper's power. Her soul slid out of her nostril like a snake leaping out of its old skin. Billy flicked it around and hung it to dry like a piece of laundry, examining the spectral version of Abelia with a proud smile.

Now you're really fucking dead! Kevin's heart sank. His best chance at freedom had just been taken away. He sure as shit wasn't getting out of this on his own, and he had no means of getting in touch with Driff or Ren or anyone else who might be able to lend the necessary assistance.

"Don't worry, we're going to see them next," Billy said, his voice dulled by his broken nose.

Kneeling, the reaper shoved Abelia's soul into the Chicago Blackhawks travel mug where it had fallen on the floor, then picked the whole thing up and screwed the cap on tight. Kevin's perspective spun back and forth as Billy worked. He was glad he no longer had a stomach.

Billy then tucked Kevin into the breast pocket of Abelia's pink bathrobe, arranging things so he could peer out over the top. A great big gob of blood and snot dripped down past Kevin's view and splattered on the linoleum. Hoping the reaper had made a mistake by ending their physical contact, Kevin leapt anew against the constraints of his new prison, slamming into an invisible field and snapping right back into place like a ghostly rubber band.

"Now then," Billy said happily, tapping the side of the travel mug. "Let's go visit your friends."

— CHAPTER TWENTY-SEVEN —

After shoving a few tissues up his broken nose and snagging the keys, Billy commandeered Abelia's little white sedan. Three herky-jerky tries, a severely dented rear fender, and one chunk of siding taken off the house later, the reaper finally succeeded in backing the vehicle out into the street, only to drift into the other lane and narrowly miss getting sideswiped by a pickup truck coming the opposite way.

You might be the worst fucking driver on the entire fucking planet, Kevin thought. In the breast pocket of Abelia's fluffy pink bathrobe, Kevin had a front row seat to what was sure to become a brutal automotive accident.

Ignoring Kevin as he accelerated, Billy laid on the horn and flipped off the driver of the pickup truck.

At least you got that part right.

The car jerked as Billy braked suddenly, wound the wheel all the way to the right, and then gunned it once more to put the vehicle in its proper lane. The Chicago Blackhawks travel mug banged around ominously in a cup holder that was two sizes too big. Visions of it tipping and releasing its contents danced before Kevin's eyes. If Abelia got free, Billy would be in deep, deep shit.

The reaper sighed and depressed the gas again, exercising a bit more finesse this time. The car crawled forward for several moments at five miles per hour.

What are you pushing the accelerator with, your little toe? Kevin thought. He needed to get that travel mug rocking. *Give it some gas, you pussy!*

"Grow up," Billy snapped, maintaining the car's current speed and anxiously checking the mirrors.

We just got passed by three turtles and a sloth, Kevin tried. *I've seen octogenarians going to bingo drive more aggressively than you. At this rate, Ren and Driff will be dead by the time we get to them. You might want to get a move on before the car's inspection sticker expires and we get pulled over—the cops around here don't take kindly to transporting immortal souls in unlicensed beverage containers.*

Although Kevin could feel the reaper's heart racing, Billy kept his cool. He tried again to escape his pocket prison, hoping his captor's focus on the road meant inattention elsewhere, but the invisible influence keeping him in place remained impermeable.

As they rounded the edge of the town common, Kevin changed his tactics. *Never driven before, have you?*

"What do you think?"

That new tidbit fit well with what Kevin already knew about his captor. Combined with Billy's aversion to alcohol and his awkwardness around forward women, the reaper's inability to drive a car painted the perfect picture of a young man somehow frozen in adolescence.

Kevin poured compassion into his next question. *What happened to you?*

"Don't worry about it," Billy snapped, his heart pounding even harder. "I don't need your sympathy."

That was empathy, dumbass.

"Really? You're going to try to lie to an individual who can read every thought and emotion in your soul?" The reaper paused for a moment as he carefully adjusted course. "Empathy implies understanding. You couldn't possibly understand anything about my fucked up life."

Try me.

Billy slowly removed his right hand from the wheel and wrapped his fingers around Kevin's soul. "Fine. Just remember: you fucking asked for it."

The view of the reaper's hand exploded, replaced by a cascade of sound, images, and emotions that mentally knocked Kevin to his knees. The aftermath of a violent car accident, an entire family in various states of injury, all of them dead or slowly dying and raving hysterically. A man's soul staring down sadly at what remained of his skull after eating the end of his shotgun. An old woman passing due to liver failure, wailing in agony because she hadn't gotten the chance to say goodbye to children who lived on the other side of the country. Death after death after death streamed across the canvas of Kevin's senses, bombarding him with sorrow and regret. But he was so much more than an outside observer; the panicked thoughts and wild emotions of the dead and the dying flooded his mind just as they had the reaper's. He screamed in horror, trying vainly to block it all out.

In each and every case, the soul of the recently deceased immediately fought to restore his or her ruined body. The man who shot himself scrambled to put his brains back into his skull. An accident victim stuck her ghostly finger up into the torn artery through which she'd bled out, trying to staunch the remaining flow of blood. The old woman willed her liver to begin repairing itself. With their existences on the line, each awakened a torrent of inner power none had ever suspected they'd possessed.

And in each and every case, Billy put a stop to it. Sometimes all it took was a few kind words, reminders of a life lived well and good deeds done. Sometimes it took a bit more persuasion. Sometimes Billy simply grabbed hold of the offending soul and yanked, as he had done to Kevin and Abelia. Regardless, as each soul slowly faded into oblivion or the hereafter or wherever it was they either went or didn't, the reaper's own anguish at his role in events blocked out all else.

Billy's hand moved back to the steering wheel, restoring Kevin's view of the dash. "Get it now?" the reaper asked.

Despite his lack of lungs, Kevin nonetheless found himself hyperventilating. To call what he'd seen intense would be an understatement. What Billy had just forced into his mind were endings, irreversible and unstoppable. There was no pause and no rewind—and there would be no sequel. The purest expression of the finite. Kevin felt dirty, like the worst kind of voyeur, as if in experiencing their last moments he'd violated the dead in a most gruesome fashion.

Given the nature of the reaper's responsibilities, it was no wonder he was a little cracked. Hell, it was a damn miracle that he wasn't a raving lunatic. Kevin knew he wouldn't have held up half as well in Billy's place.

I get it, he gasped. *I'm sorry.*

The reaper started shaking. "Not yet, you aren't."

See, that's the attitude that made me lie to you about Nella.

Billy completed the turn around the common and straightened the vehicle, pumping the brakes unnecessarily a few times as he adjusted direction. He fiddled with the blinker, shifting it up and down until he finally found the right turn signal. The turnoff onto the private road that led to the Roberts estate was coming up quickly.

Kevin searched vainly for options he knew deep down just weren't there. Without any ability to manipulate the physical world on his own, he had no hope of escaping, rescuing his mother, or getting a warning to his friends. His attempts at tricking the reaper into a mistake had only succeeded in producing an episode of mental and emotional torture. Although he hated to admit it,

Kevin was completely fucking stuck. His only hope would be to ride this thing out and hope Driff could find a way to put it all right. Surely the elf had planned for something along the lines of this particular eventuality.

As the little white sedan sputtered right onto Hampstead Street's perfect blacktop, Kevin retraced his steps. Perhaps locating exactly where he'd gone wrong would serve some use. The problem, of course, was in choosing a starting point. It would be easy to say he'd doomed himself the moment he'd chosen to return to Harksburg, but how was he supposed to have known that in doing so he'd ruin the wedding of the local avatar of death? What about his decision to not run, but to stand his ground and—well, not fight, exactly, but to try to *do* something to change his fate? Should he have kept his nose out of Oscar's little revival on the town common? Had hurling eggs at Mr. Gregson sealed his inevitable doom? Would life be any different if he had succeeded in his quixotic quest to find the damn gnomes he was convinced had infested his home? Could he have handled things better with Sweatpants Bob, Muffintop, Lil, Fran Kesky, or any of the rest of the motley crew of lunatics and scumbags that had crossed his path?

He shook his non-corporeal head and corrected himself: the real problem wasn't choosing a starting point. The real problem was how consistently he'd fucked up.

A short burst of sad laughter from the reaper jiggled Kevin about his prison in Billy's breast pocket. *Stay out of my head!*

"Technically, your head is back on the dining room floor."

Something inside of Kevin snapped. Billy's comment, while not particularly insulting in its content, was far too glib for the situation at hand. It burned with overconfidence, with arrogance, with a conceited knowledge that he was in absolute control and he was going to enjoy it for as long as he could. It was just the wrong thing to say at just the wrong moment. Anger flooded through Kevin's being, hot and rampant. He couldn't punch Billy in the face as his instincts screamed at him to do, but maybe he could do something even worse.

Fuck off. Like poking around in other people's minds, do ya? Here, I'll give you a real fucking show!

Focusing intently, Kevin dredged up his memory of his most recent evening with Nella. He ran back through that night slowly, focusing on every tiny detail. He started with her coy smile as he pushed her down into the mattress and leaned in for a kiss, her breath warm on his face. He forced his mind's eye to linger on her soft lips and the weight of her legs as she wrapped them around his midsection, then he mentally moved onto the cool skin of her lower back. Their tongues danced across each other as Kevin slowly traced his fingers up her smooth sides and then across her breasts. At the moment of penetration, he focused not on his own pleasure but the smile on her face, the joy in her eyes, the gills in her neck fluttering open as he pushed himself deeper...

Billy slammed the accelerator to the floor, launching the little white car forward. Having not achieved such speeds in at least the last five years, the car protested with an ear-splitting whine more animal than vehicle.

Please crash, Kevin plead with the reaper. In his memory, Nella flipped him onto his back and started riding him. *Put yourself out of your fucking misery, you piece of shit!*

Moments later, just as Kevin had finished remembering the curve of his lover's hip in inexorable detail, Billy spun the wheel and slammed on the brakes. The car spun out with a squeal of shitty tires on hard asphalt.

Billy, Chicago Blackhawks travel mug in hand, was halfway out the door while the vehicle was still moving. Abelia's sedan came to a pained stop right at the edge of the cement walk leading to the Roberts estate's front porch, sputtering and rumbling like a fat man who'd run a mile on the treadmill for the first time in his life. As Billy stomped purposefully up to the house, Kevin fed him memories of a particularly good blow job. The reaper stumbled on the first step but managed to catch himself.

Which, Kevin realized, made little sense. Why hadn't Billy severed their mental connection the moment he'd started reminiscing about Nella? Without the ability to physically manipulate the world around him, those memories were the only real weapon in Kevin's possession. Either Billy was a super creepy voyeur, or he simply couldn't disconnect himself from his captive's mind.

The reaper's abrupt sigh was all the answer Kevin needed.

All you have to do to make this stop is let my mother and me go. None of us will ever bother you again.

Billy ignored him and rang the doorbell. A soft chime echoed through the house, but no one answered. Kevin shifted his focus to a romp in the shower, his attention on the soap bubbles dripping down Nella's slender blue back as she rinsed her hair.

Three increasingly angry rings of the bell later, the reaper visibly shaking with fury, Ren finally called out from somewhere inside. "Keep your fucking pants on! It's too fucking early for this shit!"

The sound of Ren's voice put a quick end to Kevin's mental assault. This was really happening; Billy was going to magically murder his best friend and there was nothing he could do to even try to stop it. He couldn't even warn Ren about what was coming. He'd hoped they'd encounter Driff first, but the elf didn't seem to be anywhere in the area.

See, I stopped. Please leave Ren alone.

Billy shook his head.

Please?

"No."

Leave my fucking friend the fuck alone or I fucking swear you will relive every last fucking night I spent with your ex. And I will make damn sure you don't miss how much fucking fun she had.

"No. You brought this upon yourself. You fucking deserve it."

So do you, asshole.

Before Kevin could queue up another memory, the door in front of him was violently yanked open. Dressed in his favorite pair of red silk pajamas, Ren appraised them with bleary eyes and a haggard look. He'd never been able to handle champagne.

"Billy?" he asked, his eyes widening as he realized what he was looking at. "The fuck—"

He never finished his question. The reaper's hand snapped up to his face, found the purchase it needed, and tore a ghostly duplicate of Ren Roberts out through the young man's nose. His empty body crumpled to the floor. Billy flipped open the travel mug's spout, shoved Ren's soul inside, and then snapped it back shut.

Motherfucker, Kevin moaned. He couldn't believe how quickly that had gone. Where the hell was Driff?

The telltale click of a revolver's hammer being pulled back into the firing position answered Kevin's question. Driff had snuck up behind the reaper while he'd been busy with Ren. Kevin smiled. The elf had a plan!

Billy didn't even flinch. "You're not going to do that," he said nonchalantly, as if dictating a law of physics rather than responding to the threat of his imminent death.

Of course he's going to do that! He's going to blow your fucking brains out if you don't let us all go!

"What makes you so sure?" Driff asked.

"Because you know the consequences."

Yeah, that'll stop him! Keep threatening him with paperwork! Or—gasp!—maybe he'll get fined! The horror!

"So do you. I'm sure a man in your line of work has been privy to many a gaping head wound."

Kevin flashed back to the time Driff shot him in his own dining room, focusing on and amplifying the brief burst of white hot pain as the elf's bullet tore through his skull. *He'll do it! The man's a stone cold killer!*

Billy spun on his heel to face Driff, the barrel of the long silver six-shooter now firmly against his cheek. "If you were prepared to pull that trigger, you wouldn't have wasted your time with all these idiots. You would've just done it."

Driff scowled, unimpressed. "Last chance."

"Same to you."

For several agonizing seconds, nothing happened. The two opponents stared at each other, waiting for the other man to make the first move. Kevin watched in stunned silence, unable to comprehend the fact that Driff hadn't simply blown Billy away and called it a day. How bad could things really get for the elf if he killed a reaper? Was there some big law against it that Kevin hadn't been informed of? As Billy had suggested, that certainly would better help explain why Driff had worked so hard to get him back on the job rather than simply removing him and installing someone new. Kevin didn't like the implications.

Billy moved first. He slowly raised his hand toward Driff's face, daring the elf to pull the trigger and giving him ample time to do so. Driff didn't even flinch when the reaper's fingers settled over his nose—but neither did he fire his weapon. Kevin couldn't understand it. What the hell was Driff waiting for?

"I won't give you the satisfaction," Driff said, the slightest quiver of fear in his voice.

The elf's soul slipped right out of his face like all the others. Driff's body collapsed, his revolver clattering to the porch with a sound that broke Kevin's heart. If the Council of Intelligence wasn't going to stand up to Billy and save him, who was?

The reaper shoved Driff's soul into the travel cup and closed the spout, stepping over Ren's lifeless corpse and into the Roberts estate as he did so. "Gotta make a quick stop to find something... special," Billy growled. "Then it's off to the Works to see Nella."

— CHAPTER TWENTY-EIGHT —

O minous gray clouds filled the sky above Fornication Point, blocking the sun and threatening rain. Although it was likely too late in the year, Kevin prayed for a raging thunderstorm. At this point, his best chance at escaping Billy's clutches seemed to be a lucky lightning strike.

Nella will know what to do, he reassured himself weakly. He didn't believe it. The water nymph had some interesting powers over her primary element, and she might still be able to make some sort of emotional appeal to Billy given their prior relationship, but Kevin wasn't holding his nonexistent breath. Somewhere Kylie was laughing and shaking her head.

Billy stared down into the lagoon for a good twenty minutes. Though he neither moved nor spoke, emotion rolled off the reaper in waves like heat rising off an engine. His shoulders crowded up against his neck and his hands were white-knuckled fists. Looking up from his vantage point in the man's breast pocket, Kevin was reminded of a cobra getting ready to strike. He decided it would be better to leave Billy to his own thoughts than to antagonize him further.

Nella's decision to remain hidden while Billy simmered surprised Kevin at first. It would be hilarious, he thought, if the reaper had come all this way only to discover that she'd left town, but it was more likely that she'd chosen to force Billy to make the first move. Letting him stew on the situation could make him more likely to commit an exploitable error. Kevin worried the delay would have the same effect on Nella.

"Come on out," Billy finally mumbled, his eyes vacant and his lips taut. "We've got some things to discuss."

Below, the lagoon the frothed and bubbled angrily in response. A thick jet of water launched skyward, bearing Nella's nude blue form atop it. She watched Billy from her perch for a moment, studying her opponent with a smoldering scowl, and then she strode confidently onto the land. The pillar of water plummeted back into the lagoon with a dramatic crash.

"Let Kevin go," she said, favoring his disembodied soul with a quick wink and a friendly smile. Kevin had never seen anything more reassuring.

Billy ignored her request. "You fucking left me." The pain in the reaper's voice would've sent a chill down Kevin's spine if he still had one.

Nella shrugged.

Gasping as if he'd been struck, Billy took a step toward her. "Why?"

Raising her eyebrows, Nella planted her hand firmly on her hip and addressed her former fiancé in a firm, no-nonsense tone Kevin had never heard her use. "Take a good, long look at what you're doing right now. That's why."

Billy's face flushed. "What I'm doing right now—"

"—is petulant and immature and unbecoming of an individual in your station and I *knew* it was only a matter of time before you flew completely off the handle just like this. Now you can't have what you want, so you're lashing out at everybody around you like a screaming five-year-old who can't get over the fact that his younger brother got a new toy. I left you because you are a fucking child."

Kevin couldn't help being reminded of his mother. He wondered if Abelia had rubbed off a bit on Nella. The thought was disconcerting to say the least.

"It was charming at first," Nella continued. "So many members of our peer group are so...dour. Sure, they've all got their eccentricities, but in the end, they're all slaves to the rules. You were different. You filled your role, but you didn't let it define you. You were Billy first and a reaper second. You reminded me of him that way." She gestured toward Billy's pocket. "But you are not half the man Kevin Felton is."

A low growl rumbled up from the reaper's chest. Kevin didn't like the way this was going.

This time it was Nella's turn to take a step closer. The narrow gap between them seemed to quiver with danger. "Kevin Felton knew what he was dealing with when he chose to befriend you. He knew there was a damn good chance he was going to end up right where he is, but he went through with it anyway. He is *nothing* compared to a reaper because he's human, but he did what he had to do. He acted not out of anger or some sort of delusional sense of vengeance but simply for his own self-preservation, and he did it with compassion. Did he lie to you? Of course. What choice did he have? But he never exploited you. He actually enjoyed spending time with you. He's *your fucking friend,* you fucking tool."

I tried all that, Kevin thought. *It didn't really work.*

"You're one to talk about friendship," Billy snarled.

"I never said I was perfect. None of us are."

The reaper snorted. "You say that as if it's something I didn't already know." Bending down, he removed the cover from the drywall bucket he'd retrieved from Ren's basement. "Get in."

"Fuck no."

"Get in, or I will make your precious little Poofy regret it."

"Leave Kevin out of this, Billy. This isn't his fight. Hell, it's not even his world. Let him go, and we'll settle this like the eldritch forces of nature we are."

I like the sound of that, Kevin thought. *Do that.*

Billy didn't reply. Suddenly, excruciating pain tore through Kevin's being. It felt like the particles that made up his soul were being pulled apart from each other. The world around him turned bright red, and he screamed in agony. Whatever it was that made Kevin Felton really Kevin Felton was being ripped asunder by an unseen force.

If he could've willed his own death to make it stop, he would have.

"Stop it!" Nella shrieked. Her hard eyes went soft and her combative posture melted into a panicked cringe. The stern façade she'd wielded as an anti-reaper weapon disappeared in a flash, replaced by a woman terrified for her man.

As Kevin's pain burned on, Billy pointed at the bucket. Her head hung low, Nella stepped inside.

"All the way," the reaper snarled.

With a sad glance toward Kevin's writhing soul, Nella's form turned liquid, then collapsed downward into the bucket. Billy sprung as soon as she passed the container's lip, slamming the lid on tight. The fiery pain in Kevin's soul ended as abruptly as it began. Billy got to work wrapping a roll of silver duct tape around the drywall bucket the long way to keep the cover in place.

What the hell was all that about? Kevin asked angrily.

"You haven't figured it out?" Billy snapped as he struggled with the roll of tape.

Enlighten me.

Finished with his work, Billy tore the tape and threw the remainder of the roll over the cliff and into the lagoon below. He tapped on the lid a few times, admiring his handiwork with a psychotic smile.

"I've taken all of the people you care about the most."

And Driff, Kevin corrected.

Billy chuckled. "And Driff." With his thumb and forefinger, he pulled Kevin's soul up out of his breast pocket and held it up so the two of them were face-to-face. "And if you ever want to see any of them ever again, you'll have to come get them."

Um...what?

With a sharp flick of his wrist, Billy threw Kevin's soul away as if ridding himself of a particularly gross wad of snot. Kevin registered his sudden freedom immediately and rocketed back toward his center of gravity—his soulless corpse. He traveled so quickly, so desperately, that the trip barely registered as more than a blink in time, a quick burst of kaleidoscopic color as he zipped through Harksburg at unspeakable speed to put himself back where he belonged.

— CHAPTER TWENTY-NINE —

The warmth and security of finally returning to his own body after an extended period away was like nothing Kevin had ever felt. It was joy, pure and unadulterated, better than all the sex he'd ever had all added together. But the feeling didn't last; his subconscious reasserted control over the body it had been built to maintain, kickstarting his heart and his muscles and obliterating his happiness with wave after wave of rippling pain. His lungs roared open to take in a mighty, ragged breath. His fingers opened and closed involuntarily, his legs thrashed, and his bladder and bowels unloaded before he could even think about stopping them. Banging the back of his head repeatedly against the hardwood floor as his entire body spasmed didn't help matters.

Although everything hurt like a son of a bitch, the fact that he could feel anything at all once again made him ecstatic. Every muscle contraction, every gasping breath, and every collision with the floor reaffirmed that Kevin Felton was once again alive, his soul safely residing in its proper vessel. Even the wet warmth of the filth in his pants was a welcome sensation. No shit had ever smelled as good as the shit soaking his drawers right then and there.

He lay on the floor for a long time, basking in the physical sensations as his body took its sweet time rebooting. He liked to think that it had missed him just as much as he had missed it. Except for that ugly mole on his elbow. He could've done without that thing.

When his fine motor control returned, he sat up and stretched his arms as far upward as they could go. Sitting felt good. Stretching felt good. Tracing his fingers down his chest to make sure it was really his felt good. He hadn't realized how much he liked his body until he'd spent a few agonizing hours without it.

The thought snapped him back to reality. There was a reason for that out-of-body experience. Its name was Billy. Billy was pissed because Kevin had stolen his fiancée, so Billy had taken his anger out on the people Kevin cared about most. And Driff. Then Billy had dared Kevin to do something about it. In response, Kevin had valiantly crapped all over himself and flopped around on his dining room floor like a dying fish on the bottom of a boat.

Panicked, he tried to spring to his feet and promptly fell right on his ass when his weak legs refused to hold his weight. He tried again, this time by first raising himself onto his knees then slowly standing, his hand on the nearby wall for additional support. When his legs stopped shaking, he made his way into the kitchen with short, tentative steps.

He found his mother's body on the linoleum where Billy had let it fall. The explicit wrongness of the scene was overwhelming; Abelia Felton, so full of life earlier that morning, had been reduced to a corpse by an asshole looking to prove a point. Kneeling beside his mother, Kevin checked her neck for a pulse. Nothing. Without her soul, Abelia's body lacked the capacity to take care of himself. How long could it last in that condition? Kevin knew the term rigor mortis but had no clue how long it would take to set in or when Abelia's body would begin to decompose. Could a human soul's innate healing ability repair such damage? He didn't know that either. He wondered briefly if he should find a way to shove his mother into the freezer to keep her fresh, then settled on simply moving her to the living room couch and covering her with a thin blanket.

Looking back at the winding trail of excrement he'd left behind him, Kevin considered his options. Whatever he was going to do, he needed to do it quickly.

"But what the hell am I gonna do?" he muttered to himself sadly.

What chance did he stand against an angry force of nature intent on royally fucking with him? A frontal assault would get him nowhere. Billy knew he was coming, and Kevin couldn't compete with the reaper in a straight-up fight. The trick, he realized, would be to outmaneuver his opponent somehow. He didn't have to incapacitate Billy; he just had to distract him long enough to release his friends. Freeing Nella would certainly even the odds if they could get Billy near a water source. But how could he keep the reaper occupied long enough to do that? He'd have to face Billy on his home turf, in Lordly Estates, which limited his options for making use of the environment. The one thing guaranteed to get Billy's attention was Kevin Felton himself.

Which meant he needed help. Unfortunately, all of his obvious options were locked away in a travel mug or a drywall bucket. Involving Waltman and Jim Jimeson or Tom Flanagan or any of his other friends seemed like a bad idea. Not only did he not want to put any of them at risk, but he also didn't think he could trust any of them to do the job properly. Besides which, how the fuck was he supposed to properly explain the circumstances so they'd believe him? He didn't have that kind of time.

Shaking with fear, Kevin glanced out the window at the house next door and knew he only had one option. Mr. Gregson wasn't going to be happy about the way things had gone down. He doubted the pixie would fight his battle for him, but if he approached Mr. Gregson with a solid plan that involved little risk to his own tiny person then maybe, just maybe, his crazy neighbor would agree to assist.

Although Kevin didn't want to waste a single second, he took a quick shower and changed into a fresh pair of clothes. Showing up on Mr. Gregson's front porch with a huge load in his pants seemed like a great way to get telekinetically thrown across the Harksburg town common. He absentmindedly lingered in the shower for a few minutes longer than he intended, lulled into security by the warmth and temporarily forgetting his troubles. After what he'd been through that morning, he couldn't help enjoying a moment of peace. He angrily turned the water off when it dawned on him again that the clock was ticking.

Clean and dressed in fresh slacks and a black sweater, Kevin headed for Mr. Gregson's. The front door creaked opened eerily as he scaled the steps onto the front porch. Kevin froze, a shiver running down his spine. He'd never been inside of his neighbor's house. Heck, he'd barely ever caught more than a fleeting glimpse of the interior through the thick curtains on all of the windows. That Mr. Gregson obviously wanted Kevin to enter in spite of his obvious preference for privacy was rather ominous.

"Hello?" Kevin called out nervously. "Mr. Gregson?"

Did the door open a little further in response? Kevin couldn't be sure. He began to wonder if this was just another part of whatever sadistic game Billy was playing with him. The reaper would've had plenty of time to travel from the Works and either incapacitate Mr. Gregson or recruit him to the cause. That latter possibility was especially frightening. Mr. Gregson would certainly be up for a rousing round of Fuck with Kevin Felton.

But that had to be impossible, right? Kevin had never mentioned Mr. Gregson's interest in recent events to Billy, so the reaper would have no reason to think his target would run to the pixie for help, right? Likewise, Mr. Gregson couldn't have found out on his own how badly Kevin had screwed up. The trick with the door was just another dumb game, and whatever new humiliation Kevin was about to suffer likely wouldn't be fatal—or even the kind of temporary-but-nonetheless-painful sort of fatal that had permeated Harksburg recently. It would just suck.

Taking a deep breath, Kevin eased the storm door open and stepped into Mr. Gregson's home. An intense sensation of not belonging washed over him as soon as he crossed the threshold, freezing him with his left foot inside and his right foot on the porch. "Mr. Gregson?" he tried again, his voice even shakier. Maybe the door had swung open simply because it hadn't been shut securely. Maybe Mr. Gregson wasn't answering him because he was asleep or showering or taking a dump. Maybe walking into his neighbor's house uninvited would be the worst mistake of Kevin Felton's life. Maybe he should turn around and find a way to deal with his reaper problem all on his own.

"Oh, fucking come in already!" Mr. Gregson's familiar gruff baritone commanded from some indeterminate point ahead.

Kevin about jumped out of his shoes and would've shat himself again had there been anything left in his bowels. He scrambled inside, the storm door slamming shut behind him with a sharp crash, and caught himself on the wall just before he would've collided with a small table. His flailing arms just missed wiping out an arrangement of framed photographs. Forcing himself to breathe normally, Kevin found himself staring at a panoramic image of the biggest waterfall he'd ever seen, a seven or eight tier behemoth interrupted here and there with rocky cliffs and small islands like a pod of dolphins breaching the raucous waves. Beside that hung a smaller image of a jungle, a scene thick with flora of all shapes and sizes, all of it trimmed with rectangular purple leaves. His eyes traced half a dozen similarly fantastic scenes—deserts of obsidian, mountains of pure quartz, lakes turned pink with dense vegetation. At first, he thought they couldn't possibly be real, that he was looking at some nerdy teenager's collection of homemade desktop wallpapers, and then he remembered Donovan Pim's magical forest and chastised himself for lapsing back into his former role as a stupid, naïve human. Set atop the table Kevin had almost crashed into was a tiny crystal castle, a glittering array of spiraling towers and soaring buttresses surrounding a sturdy central keep. Sunlight streaming in through the front door made it glow and dance as if on fire, its center a hot ember Kevin half expected to burn straight through the tabletop.

"From Talvayne," Mr. Gregson's voice explained. "My home. Before the bastards kicked me out."

The pure hatred in Mr. Gregson's tone sent a shiver down Kevin's spine. The pixie obviously thought he'd been wronged in a most terrible way. But what if he'd deserved it? What if he'd done something that warranted exile? In that case, Kevin's best hope for rescuing his loved ones was a hardened criminal likely capable of unspeakable things. He couldn't decide if that was a positive or a negative.

The telltale cheers and frivolous music of a TV game show trickled into the front hallway from the living room beyond, drawing Kevin forward past a thick set of stairs leading to the second floor. The worn hardwood creaked beneath his feet, scratched and pocked here and there by the wheels of Mr. Gregson's chair and looking for all the world like it had been attacked by some predator with ferocious claws. Ahead, Kevin could see the television's antenna above the back of a heavy old couch trimmed in classic 1970s burnt orange. Matching wallpaper speckled with paisleys completed the retro look.

He came upon Mr. Gregson from behind and to the left, circling around the shitty old couch. The pixie had parked his wheelchair on the opposite side.

"Mr. Gregson? Um, hi," Kevin stammered. Mr. Gregson ignored him, evidently hypnotized by a soap commercial with a cheesy jingle to the point that he couldn't move a single muscle. Annoyed, confused, and frightened beyond belief by thoughts of what nature was likely doing to his mother's corpse, Kevin bravely took a step in front of the TV—

—and promptly stumbled back in horror at the sight of the gaping hole in Mr. Gregson's chest. The man sat in his chair with his shirt wide open, exposing the empty cavity where his heart and respiratory system should've been. Upon closer inspection, it appeared his organs had been replaced with some sort of glass ball reminiscent of a fishbowl. Though he didn't move, Mr. Gregson's eyes glittered with awareness. Somehow, the pixie's shell was alive.

"Christ, that never gets old!" a small voice chirped.

A familiar force wrapped around Kevin and lifted him a few inches into the air. Although he couldn't move most of his body, his head and neck still worked. "G-g-great trick," he stuttered, his heart in his throat. The moment of truth surely wasn't far away now.

A tiny green light zipped out from under the couch to hover in front of Kevin's face. When his eyes adjusted, he found a tiny winged man in black sweatpants and a stained white tank top suspended in the middle of the glow, examining him with disdain as if his recent floor-crapping had somehow become common knowledge. The pixie's combination of sharp, aquiline features, five o'clock shadow, and thick beer belly would've been considered handsome in certain dirty biker bars Kevin had driven past but never thought worth visiting.

"Mr. Gregson—"

"That's Mr. Gregson," the pixie replied, nodding toward his empty shell. "I'm Thisolanipusintarex. Rex for short for stupid humans who can't say it right. What the fuck was the reaper doing in your fucking house?"

"Banging my mother." Kevin couldn't help himself, and he hoped his candor would break the ice and put the pixie at ease.

The little man scowled. "Have some respect for your elders, you little shit."

Kevin blushed, chagrined. "Sorry."

"And then the reaper stole your mother's car."

"You saw all that? Don't you have anything better to do than spy on me?"

"Where did he go?"

"To the Roberts estate, to take possession of Ren's soul. And Driff's. Then, he went out into the Works and put Nella in a bucket. He's got my mother's soul, too."

"And just why in the fuck would he do all that?"

This was it. "Billy knows."

Rex paused for a moment, the wheels obviously spinning in his tiny mind. Kevin braced himself to be thrown against the ceiling or out the nearest window.

"He's challenging you to rescue them."

Kevin nodded.

"And you came here to ask me for help because you're a pathetic human and Billy's an unstoppable force of nature."

"Yes, sir. P-p-please."

The pixie hesitated again. Behind him, his human shell's dark eyes glittered with anticipation.

"I'll help you," Rex declared.

Kevin's jaw dropped, his heart leapt, and a crushing weight slipped off his shoulders. He couldn't believe how easy that had been. Obviously, he'd underestimated his neighbor's desire to put everything back to normal and keep Tallisker's prying eyes off Harksburg.

"...on one condition," the pixie added.

All of Kevin's hope and joy suddenly fell off a cliff. "What's that?"

Rex smiled evilly. "I need new skin."

"New...skin? Like a graft or something?" That wouldn't be so bad. After all, how much skin could such a tiny creature really need?

"Something like that." Rex jerked his thumb over his shoulder to indicate the catatonic, wheelchair-bound man observing the scene.

Something like that, indeed. "Is he...still alive?"

"Very much so. I even give the poor bastard a few hours of freedom every now and then. Not that he can get very far on his own."

"And it's...permanent?"

The pixie nodded. "I'm the only thing keeping him alive."

It was Kevin's turn to stop and think. Rex's terms were extremely steep: a lifetime of unbreakable servitude in exchange for the safety of his loved ones. And Driff. He should've known the pixie's help wouldn't come cheap.

But could he do it? Could Kevin trade that much of himself to save his mother, his lover, and his best friend since childhood? And Driff? He quickly came to the conclusion that he couldn't. He wasn't that sort of selfless hero. The only thing Kevin Felton had in common with Captain America or Superman was that he sometimes wore blue. Self-sacrifice wasn't that high on his to-do list.

He was, however, kind of an asshole. Risking Billy's wrath by befriending him had come as naturally as speaking or walking. Although Kevin had meant no harm and had to come to like the reaper, he'd had no qualms about stringing him along. It had been his only option at the time, and he'd embraced it. Working a similar game with Thisolanipusintarex—playing along while searching for a way to flip the board and change his own fate— stood out as Kevin's best and only chance. He needed the pixie's assistance that badly.

And besides, after all the history between his neighbor and his family, after all the hell Rex had put him through the last few days, what was so bad about fucking the slimy little bastard over?

"After we rescue my friends," Kevin said.

Rex quickly shook his head. "Before. The last thing that son of a bitch will expect is a pixie popping out of your chest."

Kevin couldn't deny that logic, but such a progression would severely inhibit his chances of escaping the deal. "No way. Once you're...in charge, how do I know you'll help me?"

"Felton, when have I ever lied to you? You'll have to trust me."

Over the pixie's shoulder, Kevin thought he saw the man in the wheelchair shake his head ever so slightly.

"No deal. I'm leaving."

Rex sighed in mock disappointment. "Well then, just go!"

But the pixie's magic grip held Kevin in place. He struggled to move his arms and legs to no avail.

"Oh, that's right!" Rex chirped, snapping his fingers like he'd been struck by a fantastic idea. "You fucking can't! I'm in charge here, and if I say you're my new skin, there's absolutely fucking nothing you can do about it! Silly me! How could I have forgotten that? It's kind of important."

Though he fought with all his might, Kevin couldn't free himself from his captor's telekinesis. That overwhelming sense of helplessness he'd felt while in the reaper's clutches—a feeling he'd hoped never to experience again—came roaring back with a vengeance. "Let me go!" he screamed for what felt like the billionth time that day. "I will find a way to make you fucking regret th—"

And then his jaw stopped working, frozen by the same paralyzing magic that rendered the rest of his body useless.

"No, you won't," Rex replied. "In fact, I suspect I'm going to enjoy this. After we kill the reaper, we're going to disown your bitch of a mother, beat the ever-loving shit out of the Roberts twit, and fuck the daylights out of your saucy blue girlfriend. It's going to be a riot!"

Never before had Kevin wanted a flyswatter so badly. If he could've moved, he would've done unspeakable things to Thisolanipusintarex: torn off his pansy-ass wings, tossed him against the wall, ground the pixie's fragile little body under his heel until he begged for mercy. All Kevin could do was rage silently, partly angry at himself for being stupid enough and desperate enough to seek help from someone he knew absolutely hated his guts.

His captor magically dragged him into the adjoining kitchen, a tight space trimmed with cheap white cabinets and an island listing dangerously to the left. They paused long enough for the thin basement door to swing open and then they floated down the rickety wooden stairs. A rancid smell assaulted Kevin's nose as they angled down into the stone and mortar dungeon below. It reminded him of how bad he'd smelled upon regaining control of his body on the kitchen floor after he'd crapped and pissed all over himself, except ten times worse.

"Back for more, huh?" a smooth voice echoed from below. "What's it gonna be this time? I've had my thumb up my ass all day, so you're in for a real fuckin' treat if you want to chew on my hand again!"

In spite of his own predicament, Kevin couldn't help swearing to himself and wondering what the fuck he was being dragged into now. Because seriously, why the hell was there someone fingering his own asshole in Rex's basement?

They reached the floor and turned left, looping back around the base of the staircase. A trio of chicken wire cages jutted out from the far wall, speckled with rust but eerily intimidating despite the corrosion. In the left-most cage, a lone prisoner leaned arrogantly against the hard stone wall, glaring slow, painful death at the approaching pair. Because of his striking features, muscular build, and long blond hair, Kevin at first mistook the man for some sort of male model. Closer inspection revealed a pair of pointy ears barely sticking out from his golden mane. His white dress shirt and skinny black jeans were streaked with blood and grime and who knows what else. A cutlass dangled in a sheath at his hip, the guard trimmed with sparkling rubies. A single bare light bulb hanging from the ceiling by a thin wire illuminated the room.

An elf? What the hell? Kevin would've asked if he'd had the ability.

"Afternoon, Rotreego!" Mr. Gregson greeted cheerily. "How's the day treating you?"

"Fucking great! Just woke up from a nap on your cold stone floor and took a shit down the hole in the corner! I didn't miss this time, either!"

"Congrats! I know how you hate having to push it in with your foot!"

Kevin decided that he liked Rex a lot better as a gruff curmudgeon who rarely put more than three words together. He wondered what accounted for the change; perhaps he didn't like using his skin's voice for some reason. Whatever it was, he really wished the pixie would shut the hell up.

Thisolanipusintarex dropped Kevin into the right-most cell, leaving an empty unit between his two captives. The door slid shut behind him and locked with a sharp metallic squeal. The sensation of being released from Rex's magic grip was almost like breathing again after breaching the surface of a pool or a pond.

"You boys play nice, now," the pixie said. "I've got some supplies to pick up before we get to business."

"Hurry up," Kevin snapped angrily. "My mother's decomposing."

"Be back in two shakes of a lamb's tail!" Rex chirped as he zipped back up the stairs.

Alone, the pair of prisoners regarded each other coolly. The elf's face and arms, Kevin could now see, were pocked with what appeared to be tiny bites. Kevin hoped the basement wasn't full of bugs.

"He's been eating me," Rotreego explained. "Treats me like a giant granola bar. Pretty sure that kind of thing is what got him booted from Talvayne. Apparently, elf is good for eatin' but not for wearin'."

Defeated, Kevin slumped into an uncomfortable sitting position against the back wall. "What are you in for?" he asked.

"Stupidity."

"Same here."

"A victimless crime," Rotreego mused. "Unless you count yourself, that is."

"In my case, I ruined everything for three other people. And Driff."

Rotreego's eyes narrowed. "That jackass? He probably deserves it."

Kevin snorted. "His soul is being held captive in a Chicago Blackhawks travel mug."

"Deserves it." Rotreego stepped away from the wall and closer to Kevin, suddenly looking unsure of himself. He drew the cutlass from its sheath at his side. "Say…is my sword on fire?"

"Um…what?"

"My sword. Is it on fire? See any blue flames dancing merrily up the blade, ready to smite my enemies?"

Kevin squinted and looked closer. "I don't see shit."

"Damn," the elf replied, dejected. "I thought maybe it was just me, ya know?"

"Is it supposed to be on fire?"

Rotreego examined him for a moment, seemingly unsure what to make of the question. "Of course it is. I'm the Pintiri. The hero of Evitankari. The wielder of the Ether, the most powerful magic in the known world. I'm a leader! A statesman! An icon! Idol and role model to millions!" He sighed sadly. "Or at least, I was."

"Okay," Kevin was beginning to doubt his companion's sanity. Maybe he'd caught something from Rex's saliva. "I'm no expert on the subject, but...magic fire doesn't just go away, does it?"

The elf collapsed on the floor and tossed his weapon aside, hanging his head between his knees. "Only one thing can separate the Ether from the Pintiri: the Pintiri's death. That fucking pixie drove a railway spike through my heart a couple days ago. Killed me. Except...I didn't die. Well, I did, but I healed up in moments and came right back. At the time, I thought maybe he'd tricked me with a spell of some sort. I haven't been able to summon the Ether since."

Now that, Kevin thought angrily, *sounds too damn ridiculous to be a coincidence.* But then again, if someone wanted to separate the magic from Rotreego's sword, why not do it where it would be permanent? Maybe he was over-thinking things; life with all these magic assholes had certainly made him paranoid. "The local reaper's been...busy," he explained.

"Ah. Well, I guess everyone deserves a vacation every now and then."

Nearby, an old engine roared to life and backed out of a driveway. Thisolanipusintarex was on the move.

"I just wanted to make sweet love to what I thought was a hot-to-trot little blonde number with the tits of an angel, but it turned out to be that little winged bastard instead!" Rotreego wailed. "That's what I get for trusting an online dating profile!"

Cringing, Kevin frowned and examined his fellow prisoner, the supposed hero of Evitankari. If this guy was the best the elves had to offer, their race was in deep shit. He suspected there was more to it than that, though. Driff, for all his cold, heartless faults, seemed relatively competent. So how had this Rotreego asshole wound up in the position he'd reached?

He dismissed that line of thinking. He didn't have time for idle speculation regarding elven society. Kevin's priority at that very moment was finding a way out of there before Mr. Gregson returned and implanted a magic fishbowl in his chest cavity. Poking the chicken wire experimentally produced a shower of blue sparks and a burned fingertip, which explained why Rotreego had yet to hack his way free with his cutlass. The concrete floor and stone rear wall were both too dense to try digging through without appropriate tools. He eyed the exposed joists and plywood that supported the level above them, but there was no good way to reach them through the chicken wire cage.

"We're stuck here, man!" Rotreego moaned. "I checked all that shit. Fucker's a real pro. I'm going to spend the rest of my miserable life crapping in a hole and getting chewed on like a piece of beef fucking jerky."

"Beef? You sound more like a chicken to me," Kevin mumbled under his breath. He didn't quite trust the unstable elf's assessment and so he continued to search the room. Though he still felt like a moron for expecting help from Thisolanipusintarex, wallowing in self-pity wasn't going to do him any favors. Rotreego was living proof of that, and at the very least the elf's presence confirmed that Kevin Felton was, at worst, only the second biggest idiot in the world.

Wherever she was, he knew that Kylie probably disagreed. And he finally decided that he didn't give a shit what she thought.

The only thing in the room that seemed even remotely useful was the tiny window beside his cell. About the size of the Pussy Hatch in his own basement bedroom, the window was set into a notch in the foundation and appeared to open down and outward. Kevin could barely peer through it if he stood on his tiptoes. If he craned his neck while standing as tall as possible, he could see his own bedroom window up the driveway and to the left. As Rotreego tried and failed to conceal his pathetic sobs, the beginning of an incredibly stupid plan began to congeal in Kevin's mind.

"Do you do any magic?" he asked.

"I already tried forcing the lock, melting the cage, and making a fissure open in the floor," Rotreego whined. "None of it worked. I can't affect anything inside of this damn wire."

"Could you break that window?"

"Yes!" Rotreego snapped in a tone usually reserved for small children who've missed their naps.

Kevin waited a few seconds, but nothing happened. "Will you break that window?"

"Why?"

"Because that window breaking is an indescribably big part of my plan to get both of us out of here."

Rotreego hesitated, shaking like a leaf in the breeze. "We're not getting out of here."

"Not with that fucking attitude," Kevin snapped.

The elf looked up at him, his lip quivering below stone cold eyes. "Really, human? You don't think I haven't already thought of and tried every possible option available to us? You really think *you* can get me out of this when *I* couldn't do it myself?"

Kevin had pretty much decided that Rotreego deserved to be trapped in his cage, but he needed the elf's sorcery. "I think *we* can do it together."

"Hmmph," Rotreego growled, putting his head back between his knees.

"Even if it doesn't work, Rex is going to be really pissed that someone broke his window. It'll probably cost a fair amount to get it fixed."

That did it. The sharp crack of shattering glass made Kevin jump. He looked over his shoulder and found a pile of tiny shards where the window used to be. Rotreego hadn't moved a muscle.

"Will you shut up now?" the elf mumbled.

"Thanks," Kevin replied, rolling his eyes. He stepped as close to the side of his cage as he dared, took a deep breath, and yelled with all his might. "*Gnomes!*"

"Oh, what the fuck?" Rotreego moaned. "That's your grand plan?"

Kevin was sure as shit that no human would be able to open Mr. Gregson's cells, and magic cast from inside the cages obviously had no effect on their prison. That meant he needed sorcery from outside, and the closest magic assholes he knew of were the sneaky little bastards that had been tangling his cords, hiding his keys, mismatching his socks, and turning his toilet paper roll around—assuming they even existed and Driff hadn't been fucking with him, of course.

"*Gnomes!*" he bellowed again.

"That's not going to work," Rotreego grumbled.

"Better than doing nothing."

"Sure about that? A few minutes ago, I thought you were probably an all right dude. Now I think you're a raving idiot."

"Story of my life," Kevin muttered. "*Gnomes!*"

"Whaddaya want?" a surprisingly gruff voice replied. A tiny face peered around the window frame to look down into Thisolanipusintarex's basement. The gnome had the chubby cheeks and dark, scrubby beard of a low-level professional bowler. A pointy red hat sat atop his head at a jaunty angle.

Kevin's jaw dropped. He really hadn't expected that to work. "Um...hi."

"Eloquent," Rotreego grumbled.

"Hi yaself," the gnome said. "Whaddaya doin' in that cage?"

"Screaming for help. Rex is going to shove a snow globe into my chest and take up residence inside. And he's been chewing on Rotreego here."

The gnome did not look impressed. "So?"

"So, we were hoping you might be able to give us a little help."

"Like asking the termites chewing on your woodwork if they'll take the trash out," Rotreego muttered.

The gnome scratched his chin, considering. "I saw what happened to you this morning. Woke me up from my nap. Tough break, kid. Me an' mine have always enjoyed messing around with you an' yours. Yer mother always gets so deliciously pissed when I change the settings on the VCR. I'll talk to the missus, see what we can do."

"Thank you," Kevin replied, bowing his head. When he looked back up, the tiny man was gone.

"Like asking a tapeworm if it'll wipe your ass," Rotreego grumbled.

Kevin turned to face the elf. "What exactly is your issue?"

"My *issue*," Rotreego spat, "is that I'm the fucking Pintiri and I'm about to be rescued by a useless human and the disgusting vermin that have infested his shithole of a dwelling."

"If you'd prefer, we could just leave you here."

"No way. Just...don't tell anyone. I have a reputation."

So, it was a matter of pride, then. Kevin could kind of sympathize, at least to a small extent. He'd spent most of the day lamenting his own stupid decisions, but he liked to think he hadn't been as annoying about it as the supposed hero of Evitankari.

"But seriously, this is like asking the bacteria in your athlete's foot to paint your toenails."

"Beyond the minor annoyances, what's so bad about gnomes?"

"You don't find the idea of a creature that gets its rocks off purely by fucking around with everybody else to be inherently repugnant?" Rotreego asked, incredulous.

Kevin scratched his chin. "Well, when you put it that way... these gnomes don't sound all that different from you pain in the ass elves."

"Ooooooh, clever."

The gnome returned a few minutes later, this time accompanied by his equally tiny wife. The two of them floated gently down to the floor as if riding an invisible escalator. Squat, portly creatures with solid frames, their matching sky blue jackets and red slacks strained against their wearers' bulbous curves. The woman wore her long blond hair in an intricate braid under her pointy red hat, her cheeks flush with rouge. Kevin couldn't believe that something that small could have tits that big.

"I'm Yagor," the male said. He wrapped a loving arm around the woman's shoulders. "This is my wife, Iassonia."

She smiled a crooked, gap-toothed smile that immediately made Kevin forget the size of her chest. "Pleased to officially meet you, Felton. You've a lovely home, even with all the...um...changes, lately."

"My mother's having a bit of a midlife crisis," Kevin replied, blushing. "Thanks for coming."

Iassonia took a few steps toward the cage, rubbing her hands together awkwardly. Her eyes darted back and forth across the cage like she was watching a game of table tennis. "Interesting," she muttered, mostly to herself. "Your captor used a Parlava Cross overlaid with a Generian B-film to hide an underlying Red Quill. A rare combination, but not unheard of."

"Uh...what does that mean?" Kevin asked.

The female gnome closed her eyes, took a deep breath, and strode right through the chicken wire. She looked up at Kevin and smiled brightly. "It means he isn't as smart as he thinks he is."

"That's my girl!" Yagor crowed, waving to his wife. "Love ya, hon!"

"Love you too, sugar dumpling!"

Kevin gasped. "Can you...can you help me do that?"

"And me," Rotreego moaned, "but please don't tell anyone."

Iassonia nodded. "Easily."

"That may not be the smart thing to do in this case," Yagor added.

Confused, Kevin crossed his arms over his chest. "Why's that?"

"Have ya ever pissed off a pixie before, boy?" Yagor asked.

"Just this one."

"They're rabid, merciless animals," the gnome spat. "They don't forgive and they never, ever forget. You walk outta here and that little fucker will stop at nothing to find you, 'specially with what you seen him doing to poor Rotreego over there."

Kevin's blood turned to ice. "That...sounds like the last thing I fucking need."

"But don't worry," Iassonia chirped. "I've got just the thing."

— CHAPTER THIRTY —

Lying on his back on the cold stone floor, Kevin stared up at the ceiling and tried not to scratch his chest. The complicated sigil Iassonia had carved into it itched like a motherfucker.

"You're sure this is going to work?" Kevin had asked, wincing as the gnome dug the swirling pattern into his skin with a tiny but impressively sharp knife. He found himself wondering where people that small shopped for clothing and equipment. Was there a gnome store somewhere? Did they deliver by pixie? The world just kept getting stranger.

"Um, no, I'm not...completely sure," Iassonia admitted. She paused to drop a handful of herbs into the gently bleeding wound, as she had every few steps across his chest. "I've never done this before."

Kevin looked up at her in shock. "Never?"

She hesitated, looking a bit nervous. From his perch atop Kevin's left shoe, Yagor explained. "Iassonia is studying the gnomish dark arts as part of an online certification program. She's at the top of her class."

His wife blushed. "Thanks, kissy-berry."

"You're welcome, snugglepuss."

When Iassonia finished, she and Yagor promised to stay close and levitated back up through the shattered window. Iassonia weaved a quick spell over the gaping hole to make it appear as if nothing were amiss. From just the right angle, the fake window shimmered in a way that made its density suspect. Kevin hoped Thisolanipusintarex would be in such a rush that he wouldn't look at it too closely. Yagor had cleaned up all the glass shards from the real window.

Which meant all Kevin had left to do was wait and hope to hell that whatever Iassonia had done to him would have some effect on Rex. All he needed was a chance to get his hands on the little bastard. Even if the magic on his chest misfired, it might still be enough of a distraction to get the job done.

"That's never going away, you know," Rotreego muttered. He'd propped himself against the wall. His head hung between his legs, his long blond hair pooling over his kneecaps.

"What's never going away?"

"That little tattoo the vermin gave you. It's going to scar."

"I'd rather have a scar in my chest than a tiny winged asshole."

"Whatever."

Kevin still wasn't sure exactly what Iassonia had done, but there was no question she had done something. He could feel the power coursing through the winding line like some sort of parasitic worm roving back and forth under his skin. To Rotreego, he supposed, the analogy couldn't have been more appropriate. He kept it to himself.

Time passed, though Kevin couldn't tell how much and didn't care to guess. Hours, at least. The light streaming in through the fake window had lessened considerably when the rumble of Mr. Gregson's van signaled the pixie's return. Taking a deep breath, Kevin steeled himself for what was to come. The sigil, Iassonia had explained, was keyed to the beating of Rex's wings. He'd have to remove Kevin's shirt—or part of it, at least—to perform the operation necessary for implanting the glass container. When that happened, the gnome's magic would trigger, and then... well, Iassonia hadn't been particularly clear. She'd only recently completed her second lesson in gnomish blood scrawl and didn't quite have all the particulars down as of yet.

Regardless, Kevin couldn't have been more grateful for her help. For all the ridiculous ways they'd subtly annoyed him and his mother over the years, the gnomes infesting his home had turned out to be all right in his book. If he got out of this, he'd promised them he was going to buy five new extension cords for them to have their mischievous way with, which pleased Yagor a great deal.

Kevin cringed at the sound of the front door swinging open and then slamming back shut. Happy whistling trickled down through the floorboards. He couldn't quite place the familiar tune, but his pounding heart kept time anyway.

Something heavy came tumbling down the basement stairs, clanging dully against the old wood. The crystal ball ricocheted off the far wall and bounced toward the cages, finally rolling to an ominous stop against the front of Kevin's cell. Slender golden filaments spread through the glass orb like veins through flesh.

Rex zipped down into the basement and up to the cages, a brown paper shopping bag hovering behind him. "How's my new favorite outfit?" the pixie asked.

Kevin rolled his eyes.

"Yeah, it's always awkward at first. We'll get used to each other."

The shopping bag turned onto its side and dumped its contents onto the floor. A variety of tools, blades, and clamps Kevin had never seen clattered down to the stone, along with a loaf of bread and a plastic jar of peanut butter.

"I thought you might need a snack," Rex said.

"And that's the best you could do?"

"You could have some Rotreego if you like."

"I'll pass. Elf gives me the shits."

The cage door swung open and the pixie flittered inside. That familiar grip took hold of Kevin's body and lifted him up off the floor, rotating him forward to face Thisolanipusintarex. Kevin swallowed in a suddenly dry throat, mentally crossing his fingers that Iassonia's magic would work. If it didn't, he was about to lose some very important pieces and parts.

"Why's there blood soaking through your shirt?"

Kevin's heart skipped a beat. Though Iassonia had cleaned up her work when she finished, the wound must have reopened somewhere. He couldn't move his head to check.

Luckily, Rotreego stepped in. "Hey, pixie dick! Why are you so interested in that waste of meat when you've got a filet fucking mignon standing right over here? How typical! I'd forgotten that your species isn't exactly known for its intelligence or its attention span. Something to do with the size of your brain, you think? Can't fit too much gray matter in that tiny melon of yours, huh?"

The pixie frowned and his little wings beat faster. He sent Kevin flying into the hard stone wall with a wave of his tiny hand. Pain flared through Kevin's spine and skull as he collapsed onto the floor, the room spinning around him.

Rex zipped back out of Kevin's cage and into Rotreego's. The elf rose up off his feet, his body suddenly rigid as his captor's magic took hold. Hovering less than an inch from Rotreego's nose, the pixie crossed his arms and scowled.

"Don't worry, my pointy-eared entree!" he crowed. "Once I'm done with Felton's minor procedure, my new skin and I are going to throw one hell of a dinner party—and you'll be the main course!"

Shaking his head in a vain attempt to clear the stars from his eyes, Kevin fumbled awkwardly for the hem of his shirt. Iassonia hadn't been too clear about the range of her sigil, she'd merely said that Rex would have to be "close." Kevin suspected she didn't really know what that meant. Hopefully the eight or so feet between his cage and Rotreego's counted as "close."

"I think I'd rather be dessert," Rotreego deadpanned, stalling. "I'd make a great mousse. But what would a little shit like you know about gourmet cooking, anyway? Whaddaya got, maybe six taste buds?"

Sitting with his right shoulder against the wall and contorting his torso toward the other cage, Kevin's fingers found purchase on the bottom of his shirt. He yanked the thin fabric up over his face triumphantly, ready to enjoy the end of the evil neighbor who had tormented his family for so long. Nothing happened.

"Ah, fuck," he swore under his breath, defeated.

Attracted by Kevin's cursing, Rex turned and flitted to the near side of Rotreego's cell to get a closer look. "What the hell—"

The pixie's question was drowned out by the roaring blast of hot white light that erupted from Kevin's chest. It sounded like a tidal wave colliding with a cliff face and burned as if someone had lit a fire in Kevin's skin. Gritting his teeth, Kevin fought the urge to scream and watched over the hem of his shirt as Rex's tiny form writhed in agony amidst the storm of magic. Beyond, the spell collided with the far wall of the basement and stopped.

"Holy shit," Rotreego muttered, his eyes wide. He stepped away from the roiling maelstrom and pressed himself into the corner of his cell.

It was over a few seconds later. The light stopped as if someone had closed the valve responsible for holding it back. The searing pain in Kevin's chest faded to a dull ache. Rex plummeted to the floor, wisps of gray smoke wafting up from his body.

"My wings!" the pixie moaned, pushing himself up onto his elbows. "You took my wings, you motherfucker!"

It was true. Nothing remained of Thisolanipusintarex's pretty little wings. That wasn't exactly the end result Kevin had expected, but all things considered, it wasn't too bad. He couldn't think of anything worse that could happen to the puny son of a bitch.

Rotreego laughed, scrambling forward to snatch up the wingless pixie. "And without your wings, you're without your magic."

A look of pure fear twisted Rex's face. "Put me down, asshole!"

His eyes glinting maliciously, Rotreego smiled. "No wings and no magic. You must feel downright impotent right now, huh? But don't worry, friend! I haven't forgotten all the fun you and I have had together the last few days. It's time I returned your hospitality."

Before Thisolanipusintarex could protest, Rotreego shoved the pixie's head into his mouth and bit it off at the neck. Kevin winced at the sick crackle of crushing bone and tearing sinew as Rotreego yanked Rex's body out of his teeth like a piece of beef jerky. Bright red blood streamed out through the pixie's neck and dribbled down Rotreego's hand.

"That can't taste good," Yagor called out. The phony window illusion had disappeared and the two gnomes stood in its place.

"Tastes like shit," Rotreego replied. He spat the head out to his left and tossed the body away to his right.

Kevin made a point not to look at either, focusing on the gnomes instead. "Thanks again!" he said, waving to his tiny benefactors.

"D-d-don't mention it," Iassonia stammered, blushing a peculiar shade of purple. "Just happy I got to practice what I learned online."

"Don't forget all those cords you promised," Yagor said greedily.

Kevin scratched his chin, considering his next move. He still had a reaper problem to deal with.

"Say...what would it take to get a bit of help with Billy?"

The gnomes traded looks of concern—and perhaps fear. "That's your business, not ours," Yagor said softly.

"But—"

"That's your business!" Iassonia snapped in a tone that left no doubt the conversation was over. Kevin flinched, surprised at the previously meek woman's sudden explosion.

"See you soon," Yagor added as he ushered his shaking wife around the frame of the shattered window. "And good luck!"

Disappointed, Kevin sighed and turned to Rotreego. The elf shook his head. "Don't look at me," he said as he strolled out the wide open door of his cage.

Kevin couldn't help feeling like he'd missed an important piece of information about his situation. "Driff had the chance to put a bullet in the back of Billy's head," he mused. "Why didn't he do it?"

Rotreego turned. "Because a reaper is death incarnate. Take a guess where new reapers come from."

With a gasp, Kevin froze. His answer, if it were correct, would certainly explain Driff's reluctance to pull the trigger. It also made Thisolanipusintarex's plan to kill Billy a lot more logical. What pixie wouldn't want to ride around in such a powerful skin?

"Whoever kills a reaper takes its place," Kevin whispered, afraid to give the words too much power.

Rotreego nodded. "And this particular reaper seems to really, really want you to kill him."

— CHAPTER THIRTY-ONE —

No, I don't owe you for rescuing me," Rotreego called back over his shoulder as he and Kevin ascended the basement stairs. "I did my part. That shit-brained scheme of yours wouldn't have worked if I hadn't provided a distraction."

"All you did was call him names," Kevin snapped. "I'm the one who let a gnome turn his chest into a flamethrower."

"Your decision, not mine."

They topped the stairs and stepped into the kitchen. Glancing out the window above the sink, he saw that it was past sunset. Billy had been in possession of his friends' souls for more than six hours. Surely that wasn't good for their empty bodies or their sanity. The overwhelming need to return to his own flesh had nearly broken Kevin's spirit. He knew the agony his friends were experiencing and he wanted nothing more than to put an end to it—in a way that didn't result in replacing Billy as Harksburg's lord of the dead, of course.

"I figured the hero of Evitankari would be braver," Kevin goaded. His best option seemed to be finding someone else to do the deed.

"Brave's got nothin' to do with it. Nothing short of his own death is going to get that reaper off your back. Seen it before. It's the biggest 'fuck you' a reaper can give. He's going to make someone kill him, and it sure as shit isn't going to be yours truly."

"You could just...be a distraction. Like you were in the basement."

"You don't need a distraction. You could walk up to him with a knife in your hand and stick it between his ribs and he wouldn't try to stop you. Wouldn't even blink. He's checked out, man."

Kevin grabbed Rotreego's muscular shoulder and spun him around. "What the fuck do I do? I don't want to be a reaper either."

The elf's eyes hardened as he shoved Kevin's hand away. "Kid, you've got two choices if you want to rescue your friends before prolonged separation from the meat-space drives them permanently, irreparably insane: do the deed and take the job, or leave Billy's territory and kill yourself. That's it. No one's getting you out of this one. Sack up and do something about it."

Death or life as a reaper? Kevin didn't think that was much of a choice. He'd seen what the job had done to Billy, and he knew he wasn't strong enough to deal with the burden of shepherding the county's dying into the great beyond. If Kevin Felton became Harksburg's avatar of death, he'd inevitably be forced to do the job for his friends, his mother, his neighbors—everyone he knew in the area. How could he face them, knowing that someday he could be the last thing they ever saw? How could he live with himself? He'd end up isolated like Billy, or worse.

"And once someone's a reaper—"

"The *only* way out is death," Rotreego said quickly, cutting off Kevin's question before he could even ask it, "and if you don't do the job, Evitankari will either make you do it or remove you."

An exasperated grunt from the living room put an end to their burgeoning argument. Next came a bout of sharp, desperate wheezing. Someone was in a lot of pain.

They found Mr. Gregson sprawled against the back of his wheelchair, barely conscious. His head lolled to the side, perched precariously atop his left shoulder. Blood stained his chest, shirt, and pants, dripping from his limp fingertips to spatter on the floor. He'd managed to work the lip of Rex's glass sphere barely out beyond the skin of his chest before the pain became overwhelming, but the rest of it was still stuck tight.

The scene was hard to look at. Kevin directed his gaze to his shoes, considering his options. The man didn't deserve to be left like that, but helping him finish the job would both take time Kevin probably didn't have and be really fucking gross.

Rotreego made the decision for him. "You hold the chair steady and I'll do the rest," he said, drawing his cutlass.

Kevin couldn't resist. "Only if you help me with the reaper."

"Don't be a dick."

"Help me," Mr. Gregson growled weakly, his voice cracking. Tears streaked his face and spittle flew from his lips. "I will kill your fucking reaper."

Now there was something Kevin hadn't expected. He studied the old man for a moment, trying to judge if his offer were serious. He found nothing but hope in Mr. Gregson's eyes. Could the man actually do it, though? What chance did someone who couldn't walk on his own have against someone as powerful as Billy? Kevin dismissed those concerns, realizing that Mr. Gregson's apparent frailty could actually work to his advantage.

However...if Mr. Gregson killed Billy, he would become the new reaper. Could Kevin live with himself if he condemned his neighbor to such a fate? Of course he could. Mr. Gregson had volunteered, after all. If there was an ulterior motive beyond the immediate situation, Kevin could deal with it when or if it became a problem.

"All right."

Digging his heels into the thin carpet, Kevin took firm hold of the wheelchair's handles and braced himself. Rotreego examined his target, hefting his cutlass like a man determining how best to carve a Thanksgiving turkey. Slowly, the elf inserted the tip of his sword between the glass and Mr. Gregson's flesh. He worked the blade around the circumference of the sphere to gradually enlarge the hole and remove the muscle holding it in place. The wet sound of sharp metal slicing through live meat twisted Kevin's stomach into a knot. To his credit, Mr. Gregson didn't so much as flinch.

Rotreego stepped back to admire his handiwork. "I'm gonna need you to pull. On three."

Kevin nodded and adjusted his grip. Rotreego carefully positioned his sword between the base of the glass sphere and the flesh underneath and drove it in deep, eliciting a gasp and a fresh stream of tears from Mr. Gregson.

"One last fuck you for pixie dick," the elf snarled. "One. Two. Three!"

Kevin pulled back on the wheelchair with all his might as Rotreego pushed downward on the hilt of his weapon, working it like a crowbar. Sick pops burst from Mr. Gregson's chest as the remaining muscle holding the back side of the sphere tore and the glass began to move. Mr. Gregson screamed and pressed himself against the back of his wheelchair, lending what little strength he had left to the effort.

The sphere stretched the surrounding skin as its thicker middle began to push outward. Sweat trickled down Kevin's brow and his lower back began to protest. He wasn't sure how much longer he'd be able to pull. Rotreego, meanwhile, had adopted an expression of pained exertion usually reserved for those afflicted with extreme constipation.

And then the opposing force keeping Kevin on his feet suddenly disappeared and he fell backwards onto his ass. The sphere popped free, flew over Rotreego as he also toppled over, and crashed through a window, followed by a quick torrent of blood that caught the elf square in the face. Kevin yelped as Mr. Gregson's wheelchair rolled backward and over the toes of his left foot. Unable to compensate for the limp weight of its occupant, the chair capsized to its right and spilled him onto the floor.

"Uh...Mr. Gregson?" Kevin asked.

Rotreego, his face a crimson mask, spat out a gob of blood and crawled over to check for a pulse. "Nothing. But don't worry—he'll be back in a few minutes." The elf stood, plucked a pillow off the couch, and used it to try to wipe the blood from his face. The cheap fabric didn't absorb much.

Although Kevin knew the answer to his next question, he felt the need to confirm it. "But the pixie's dead, right?"

"The pixie's dead. He didn't need a reaper's help." Rotreego paused to pick a piece of Mr. Gregson out of his ear. "I'm taking a shower. If something strange happens...I don't know, call the damn gnomes or something."

Kevin watched Rotreego stroll into the front hallway and turn up the stairs, wondering if he should try one last time to enlist the elf's help with the reaper. He wasn't sure Mr. Gregson's assistance would be enough. He decided not to waste his breath, choosing instead a question asked by countless former co-captors in cheesy action movies throughout the ages.

"So what's next for you, Rotreego?"

The former Pintiri, however, was not one for cliché chatter. "None of your damn business! I was never here, this never happened, and we never met. If I had any dust, you'd best believe you'd be getting a schnoz full of it right now. If I find out you told anyone—and I mean *anyone*—about that time you and a couple of gnomes rescued the hero of Evitankari, I will cut off your balls and feed them to you. Catch my drift?"

The elf's burning anger momentarily stunned Kevin. "Got it," he replied meekly.

"Good!" Rotreego bellowed as he disappeared upstairs. For what felt like the millionth time, Kevin wondered about Rotreego's qualifications and how such an annoying twit had reached what sounded like a lofty station. He doubted Driff cared much for the guy.

On the floor, Mr. Gregson's body began to quiver, sending ripples through the blood pooling atop the cheap carpet. A soft crackling sound signaled the start of the healing process. Mr. Gregson's spirit was weaving his chest back together, tissue by tissue.

Kevin fought back the urge to vomit and took a seat on the couch, trying his best to ignore the sickening noise by focusing on the television. The weatherman on screen, equipped with the typical inoffensive gray suit, perfectly parted hair, and glittering smile, chattered on inanely about an early cold front that had locked New England in unseasonably low temperatures for the last week. Kevin was struck by how trivial the man's report seemed in light of everything he'd been through since returning to Harksburg. Part of him wanted to scream at the reporter, to wake him up to the strange reality beneath the surface of his banal existence. How would the weatherman's life change if he suddenly learned all the things Kevin now knew? Would he be interested in the world of magic, or would he cower at home and try to avoid it? How would he react to the knowledge that he could conceivably live forever if only the rules allowed him to do so? Would he quit his job if his corporate overlords turned out to be demons in disguise? Whether he wanted it to or not, exposure to that world would change the weatherman's life in ways no one could predict.

That alone was enough to make Kevin suspect the mass deception of humanity might actually be worth it. Turn one person's life upside-down and the potential drama is pretty minimal. Shake up billions of people all at once and everything would likely go straight to hell. His gaze glued to the reporter's hypnotic smile, Kevin suddenly envied the man's ignorance. There were so many things he wished he could unsee. Realistically, wiping all that away would be as easy as inhaling one handful of that damn dust. Driff would certainly be willing to help, but that would mean losing Nella, and Kevin had decided that was not a fair trade.

On the floor, Mr. Gregson gasped sharply, his arms thrashing about as his consciousness took control. Kevin watched closely but kept his distance. He didn't want Mr. Gregson to hurt himself, but he also didn't want to get too close lest he catch an inadvertent backhand across the face. His return to his own body still burned fresh in his mind, and he knew the one thing Mr. Gregson needed most was time. He hoped it wouldn't take too long.

The spasms ended a few minutes later as Mr. Gregson's soul and body finally got back on the same page. For several minutes, the man lay on his stomach, breathing heavily but at a regular pace. Kevin lowered himself to one knee and put a reassuring hand on his back.

"Mr. Gregson?"

"Call me Buddy," he replied weakly, rolling onto his side. He smiled warmly, an expression Kevin almost couldn't wrap his head around given its source. "Thought maybe that would fix my legs. Guess not."

Kevin looked away, embarrassed for his neighbor. "Here, let me help you into the chair."

Buddy shook his head. "I can do it. But I need you to go into the kitchen. Open the cabinet under the sink. Rex kept a stash of chloroform down there. Usually in a milk jug. You and Rotreego ain't the first people he's held in those cages."

Concerned, Kevin's eyes narrowed. "Why do we need that?"

"'less you've got a gun I can borrow, yer gonna have to knock that punk reaper out so I can get close enough to do the deed. Bangin' into him with my chair probably won't get it done."

It was Kevin's turn to smile. Buddy Gregson, previously such a problem for the Felton family, could very well turn into the best friend he'd ever had.

— CHAPTER THIRTY-TWO —

Buddy Gregson, now free of his tiny winged puppeteer, did not shut up. He rambled on and on and on about anything and everything, reveling in his newfound freedom.

"Fucking ramp was never right," he growled as he rolled down to the driveway. "Grade's too steep, and the thing's listing to the side. Wasn't attached to the house the way it should've been. Got maybe two more years before I gotta replace it. Shit ain't cheap."

Kevin replied with polite assent wherever necessary, just to let the old man know he was still listening. He supposed Buddy was simply overjoyed to finally be back in control of his own voice. After years spent under Thisolanipusintarex's control, Kevin couldn't blame him. He was painfully aware of how close he'd come to the same fate.

"...and that little bastard never washed the damn van right. For all his fuckin' magic, he never could figure out how to work a hose an' a sponge properly. Look at the rust along the bottom! Shoddy work right there, let me tell ya."

They found a couple of planks in the garage and used them to create a makeshift ramp into the back of Buddy's van. The old wood creaked and bounced as Kevin pushed the wheelchair across them, but they held. They stashed the planks in the back beside Buddy for use getting the man back out at Lordly Estates.

"An elevator. One more thing I gotta buy," Buddy moaned. "This reaper shit better pay well."

Realizing he still hadn't used his Tallisker paycheck, Kevin offered his assistance. "Kill that reaper and I'll buy you the nicest elevator I can find."

"I want one with diamond buttons!" Buddy declared happily. "And railings made o' pure ivory taken off some endangered elephants!"

Kevin couldn't help laughing. The man's enthusiasm was infectious. He reminded Kevin of Fran Kesky, sans the manipulative undercurrent. He'd never thought he'd see the day when Mr. Gregson turned out to be a legitimately nice, fun guy. The thought made him wonder how badly Buddy had suffered under the control of an evil, heartless bastard like Rex. Watching his body do things it never would've done under its own power must've been excruciating.

With Buddy secured in the back of the van, Kevin climbed up into the cab, positioned the half-gallon plastic jug of chloroform securely between his thighs, and stuck the key into the ignition. A quick twist of his wrist brought the engine chugging to life.

"Roll on out!" Buddy hollered.

Kevin carefully backed the van down the driveway and out into the street. He didn't like how far he had to push the loose accelerator to give the engine gas. A typical Harksburg weeknight meant he'd have little traffic to worry about, but he'd always been antsy behind the wheel of unfamiliar vehicles. The combined nerve-racking powers of his unease with Buddy's van and the anticipation of the looming showdown with Billy turned Kevin into a jittery ball of stress. He gripped the wheel with white knuckles, his arms shaking like a middle school boy asking a girl to dance for the first time. The world around him became a blur of dull color, his field of vision a tight tunnel between the driver's seat and the asphalt directly in front of him.

Buddy's deep baritone battered its way into Kevin's consciousness like an uppercut to the jaw. "That broad of yours is hot stuff. Where'd you meet her?"

"She lives in the Works at Fornication Point." Kevin smiled at the memory. "I stopped a bunch of scumbags from shitting in her lagoon."

"Ahh, the hero type! An' the pretty princess, safe from the rectums of evil, rewarded her white knight with a passionate kiss, huh?"

Kevin blushed. "To start with, yeah."

"Ain't love grand? She's got the Buddy Gregson seal o' approval, for whatever that's worth to ya. Nella never gave ol' Rexy the time o' day, no sir. Tried chattin' her up in Donovan's one night. She straight up told the little sumbitch to kiss her smooth blue ass!"

Laughing now, Kevin's vision cleared and he relaxed his grip on the wheel. He wasn't blind to what Buddy was trying to do for him, and he certainly appreciated the way he was going about it. Sometimes just being fun to talk to was the best assistance someone could offer.

"Nella's a major upgrade over that last one," Buddy continued. "What the hell was her name?"

"Kylie."

He'd brought her home for Thanksgiving a few years ago. In hindsight, he didn't know what he'd been thinking. Kylie and Abelia got along about as well as Godzilla and Mothra. Dinner was a tense, terse, uncomfortable affair during which the two headstrong women traded passive aggressive salvos like two battleships taking potshots at each other. According to Kylie, Mrs. Felton had no ambition, no vision, and no worth to civilized society on the whole. Abelia countered with punches at Kylie's greed, her complete lack of substance, and her future career as a very successful dirty whore. Kylie barely touched her meal and was back on the road to Chicago about an hour after arriving. At the time, Kevin chalked the drama up to a clash of two individuals with wildly different experiences, priorities, and philosophies. It was natural, he thought, an insignificant con made moot by the numerous pros of dating a woman like Kylie. One side of the fight let him play with her boobs, the other side was just his mother. Now he knew better. Like so many things about his youth, he couldn't figure out what the hell had kept him from properly understanding the situation sooner.

"Saw her walking to the car that Thanksgiving," Buddy said. "Wanted to ask her if she needed a hand pullin' that stick out of her ass."

Kevin laughed maniacally, almost swerving into the other lane. They still hadn't seen another driver. "That wasn't a stick. That was a great big wad of money."

"Hmmph. Well, to each his own, I guess. Sometimes I swear none of us can think straight when it comes to women on account of our dicks stealin' all the blood from our brains when they come 'round."

"Sounds like Rotreego had a similar problem."

"Pretty sure that jerk's a few bricks short of a load anyway. Strange business, that. Rex didn't bring me to the transfer. No clue where he came from."

"Think he'll give you any trouble?" They'd left the elf in the upstairs bathroom, primarily because Kevin was sick of dealing with his crap. There was a chance he'd still be in the house when Buddy returned, and interrogating Thisolanipusintarex's former skin might be his logical next move.

"If he does, I'm goin' straight for the fucker's nose!"

Buddy's joke about how he might use his new reaper powers brought Kevin back to the issue at hand. Sure, Mr. Gregson had offered to do the deed, but their unexpectedly positive interactions since forced Kevin to reevaluate whether he could actually allow his neighbor to take the fall for him. "Buddy...are you sure you want to go through with this?"

Mr. Gregson didn't hesitate. "I most certainly do, Felton, and don't you dare question it! I did a lot of bad things under Rex's control. I know it wasn't really me, but I still feel responsible. I made the decision to let him use me as a skin in the first place, ya know? So, everything that happened after because of that is on me. Think of it as a community service term." He paused, as if considering whether to continue. "Plus, those reapers live forever 'less someone kills 'em. I'd be lyin' if I said addin' a few healthy years to what I got left isn't attractive. I lost a lotta time to that fuckin' pixie. I want it back."

Kevin couldn't argue with that logic. With his sunny disposition, there was a chance Buddy Gregson wouldn't immediately spiral into a Billy-esque depression. "How'd Rex talk you into...all that...in the first place?"

Buddy's cadence slowed and became more precise. "I came back from Vietnam in a wheelchair. The bullets and bombs didn't get me, but the shrapnel did. My girl left me, I couldn't get my old factory job back on account of my condition, I ran out of money quick...and then here's this little magic asshole says he'll fix my legs in exchange for five years of my life. Seemed like a fair trade at the time."

Vietnam. That meant Buddy had been in thrall to Rex for decades. What must that sort of life have been like? How many times had he been forced to watch, helpless, as his body did things his mind didn't condone? How was it possible he hadn't turned into a raving lunatic? Kevin asked him as much.

"You know what kept me goin' all those years? Two things. First was the fuckin' absurdity of it all. There was a tiny Charles Manson with wings livin' in a fishbowl in my chest. How fuckin' stupid is that? Number two: I wanted a shot at redemption. I seen and done some bad things under Rex's control. Participated in the kidnapping and murder of at least a dozen people, most of 'em kids. Paid down-on-their luck women to do disgusting things. Ate all kinds of shit I don't wanna think about. Still, I always knew someday I'd get a chance to make good. I can't undo any o' what I done, but I can be better the rest of the way. Ain't no one movin' on to the great unknown without a great big smile on their face, I promise ya that!"

"You," Kevin declared, "are going to make one hell of a reaper." He unequivocally believed it.

"Yer damn skippy I am!"

They arrived at Lordly Estates a few moments later, the time and distance having been absorbed by their conversation. The development's gate stood wide open, inviting them to rush inside and confront the reaper. Kevin drove past and pulled over a few hundred yards down the road where a stand of thick trees blocked the view of anyone watching from the hill.

Killing the engine, Kevin leaned around the side of the driver's seat to face Buddy. "Ready?"

"One last thing. I always liked you an' your mother, Felton. You're good people. Or good enough, at least, given the general state of things. I know it ain't much, but I apologize for the hardships I caused you an' yours over the years."

Kevin's insides twisted into the shape of a pretzel. He turned his attention back to the windshield so Buddy couldn't see the stricken look on his face. "That means a lot, actually," he muttered softly.

After a few moments of awkward silence, Buddy slammed his fist down into the arm rest of his chair. "Enough with the mushy stuff, Felton! Get me out o' this piece o' crap so I can go give that reaper his pink slip!"

— CHAPTER THIRTY-THREE —

A s Kevin helped Buddy out of the back of the van, once again using the planks as a makeshift ramp, the two developed a hasty plan of action. The wild card in this situation, they agreed, was Billy's assistant, Mr. Pemberton. Neither fully understood the reaper keeper's role. Was he obligated to protect Billy, or did his duties dictate that he get out of the way and let things play out as they may? Regardless, it would be best to remove him from the equation. Mr. Gregson would enter Lordly Estates first—it would take him a little while to negotiate the hill, but he assured Kevin the incline wouldn't be a problem— and then he would roll right up to the front door of lot 22 and get Mr. Pemberton's attention. Kevin's job, meanwhile, would be to sneak around to the back of the mansion and find a way inside. Once there, he'd find Billy, chloroform him, and drag him out to Mr. Gregson, who'd be waiting with a switchblade they'd found in the glove box.

"I've never broken into anything in my life," Kevin said, concerned. "How the heck am I supposed to get into this place?"

"This dude is begging you to murder him," Buddy said. "Remember that open gate? I bet the back door's unlocked, too. He's going to make this as easy on you as he can."

"This is ridiculous," Kevin moaned.

"Welcome to real life, kid," Buddy replied with a smirk. "If there's one thing these magic fuckers enjoy, it's being giant pains in the ass."

Kevin laughed. "I'm glad I'm not the only one who came to that conclusion."

Their plan set, they traded a salute and then Mr. Gregson rolled away down the road. Kevin was supposed to wait fifteen minutes before following, then stick to the shadows around the other buildings in the development as he made his own approach. The only active lights in all of Lordly Estates belonged to lot 22, his ultimate destination, which would make it relatively easy to remain concealed.

He sat down on the van's bumper to wait, his thoughts drifting to the souls trapped in his mother's Chicago Blackhawks travel mug. If shit went south, freeing them would become his main priority. He didn't like the idea of leaving Abelia, Ren, and even Driff separated from their bodies any longer than necessary. Nella was another matter altogether, but he doubted she was in any real danger in that bucket. She seemed perfectly comfortable in her liquid form, though he had no clue how long she could stay that way. Probably a lot longer than a soul could function without its body, he guessed.

Big fat raindrops began falling from the overcast night sky. Appropriate weather for a final showdown, Kevin thought. He zipped up his jacket, wishing he had worn a hat. Just one more small entry to add to his list of recent regrets and things he should've thought of. The more he considered his situation, though, the more he suspected there wasn't much of anything he could've done to change the ultimate outcome. Could he have handled Oscar's little sermon on the town common a bit better? Certainly. Doing so likely would've kept Driff from dusting his mother, which would've ended her sexual renaissance before it even began, which meant she never would've picked up Billy at the Burg and inadvertently revealed the true identity of the fiancée thief known only as Poofy. But how long could Kevin realistically have kept up his charade? What were the chances, really, that he would've been able to hook Billy up with someone new anytime soon? Would Tallisker have intervened and thrown Kevin to the wolves if things took too long? He had no way of answering any of those questions, and so he decided none of them were worth worrying about. What was done was done and there was no changing any of it.

Fifteen minutes after Buddy Gregson departed, Kevin stashed a chloroformed rag into his back pocket and started down the road toward Lordly Estates. He considered cutting through the woods, but a tall fence of unscalable metal rods put an end to that idea. He'd be better off taking a more familiar route through the darkness anyway. Pausing outside the front gate, he quickly scanned the fence and the surrounding area for cameras. None jumped out at him, but he wasn't really sure he knew what to look for. He hunched down and darted through the open gate, sticking close to the left post. Once through, he stepped onto the grass and broke into a light jog, placing his feet carefully on the wet grass. His footfalls would make more noise on the asphalt, but a twisted ankle would put a quick end to this little caper. In the distance, lot 22 glowed brightly atop the otherwise dark and gloomy hill.

Not once in his life had Kevin ever seriously thought he'd end up participating in a first-degree murder. Make no mistake: although he was acting purely to defend himself, his loved ones, and Driff, there was no more accurate way of describing his intentions. Given the events in Mr. Gregson's basement, he supposed he was actually working on his second murder. Although he didn't doubt for a second that Rex had gotten what was coming to him, the situation with Billy felt murkier. Billy deserved to die, but he also kind of didn't. He was just a kid, wounded by the world, who'd struck back with powers far too dangerous for someone in his mental state. It was a combination that required action. Rabid dogs didn't deserve to die, but the job had to be done regardless.

Handing Billy over to Mr. Gregson still felt like taking the easy way out. Could the reaper be reasoned with? Would an apology and a long heart-to-heart negate the need for violence? Rotreego and Buddy certainly didn't think so, but Rotreego was an idiot and Buddy wanted Billy's job. The real problem was that any attempt at discussion would eliminate the element of surprise Kevin needed to knock the reaper out, which might lead to a more prolonged battle that forced Kevin to end things himself. He couldn't risk that.

"The fucker's got my mother, my best friend, and my favorite girl," he muttered angrily, trying to psyche himself up. It didn't really work.

He slowed as he neared the first tier of homes, searching for signs that Buddy had made it up the hill. Things would've been a lot easier if they'd had a means of either communicating or synchronizing their actions, but they'd had neither the time nor the know-how to figure out that sort of spy shit. Their amateurish best would have to be good enough.

An odd thought temporarily froze Kevin as he reached the corner of the first house: had it been like this for Billy? After all, the only means of becoming a reaper was to kill a reaper. Had Billy run afoul of his predecessor and been forced to act? Had he been tricked into the deed somehow? Had he known that murdering a reaper meant taking his or her place? Oddly, Kevin really, really wanted to know; the story would likely provide valuable insight into his target's character. Despite Billy's obvious capacity for cruelty, Kevin couldn't imagine the kid getting involved in that sort of physical violence. His nasty side felt raw and new, born from overwhelming emotion and years of depression rather than inherent instability or malice. So how had he offed the previous reaper? To a certain extent, Kevin regretted that his smash-and-grab plan wouldn't give him the chance to find out.

Unsettling during the day, Lordly Estates became downright creepy at night. The rows of unlit, unused homes adopted an air of frightening mystery. Were they really empty? Were they uninhabited for some terrible reason? Had anything taken up residence in them in the meantime? Kevin's exposure to reapers and pixies and demons had only made him warier of the dark. The possibility that something evil lurked in the shadows no longer seemed so far-fetched. He darted from home to home as he climbed the hill, careful to avoid even short glimpses through the bare windows lest he spot or be spotted by anything inside.

After ascending three of the development's six tiers, he could just hear Buddy Gregson's deep voice trickling down from the top of the hill. Part one of their ridiculous plan seemed to be working. Although there was no telling how long Buddy could hold Mr. Pemberton's attention, Kevin was willing to bet the talkative old man could manage a few more minutes at the least.

He made a wide arc around the outskirts of the last few tiers, trying to avoid the light of lot 22. Every room in the sprawling manse was lit brightly as if daring someone to try to sneak in. Kevin came upon the building from its side, keeping as much distance between himself and the front porch as possible. Peering cautiously into the closest window, he found he'd come upon what was likely supposed to be a large, formal dining room, a cavernous space with a twenty-foot ceiling and huge skylights, a glittering hardwood floor, and ornate trim—but it was completely empty. Billy obviously didn't need a well-furnished space for entertaining. Testing the window and finding it unlocked, Kevin gently raised the lower panel and clambered awkwardly inside.

Gaining access to Billy's home lifted a heavy weight off Kevin's shoulders. Finally, he could add breaking and entering to his ever-growing list of transgressions, a résumé item sure to raise his street cred throughout the Harksburg area. Things were going well; if he continued to be careful, that wouldn't change. He slipped off his wet shoes and left them by the window, thinking his socks would make less noise on the hardwood. He shrugged out of his jacket, too, and left it with his shoes. A trail of water would give away his presence.

He crossed the floor quickly, stopping beside the towering double doors on the opposite side of the room. Doors, he knew, were not likely to be his friend; they squeaked, they squealed, and they blocked his view of the next room. He tested the left's golden handle gently, slowly applying pressure until the mechanism inside clicked. The door slid open without a single sound of protest. Kevin peered around the dense wood and into the hallway beyond. Finding it also empty and silent, he eased the door open enough to squeeze through, gently closed it behind him, and moved on.

The floor became black and white tile and the ceiling dropped ten feet. The next pair of double doors stood closed about fifty feet away. Kevin ignored the smaller side doors and hurried forward. He couldn't help being impressed by how clean everything was. Although the mansion didn't get much use, Mr. Pemberton still kept it all in tip-top shape. Had Kevin taken over for the reaper keeper as planned, that likely wouldn't have been the case; he wasn't one for unnecessary cleaning. He wondered what would become of Lordly Estates when Billy was gone. Would Buddy inherit it somehow? Perhaps more importantly, would Buddy agree to bring Kevin on as his assistant? He should've insisted on that condition earlier; that reaper keeper job was his best and probably only guarantee against a future dusting, after all.

Leaning his ear against the door at the end of the hallway, Kevin could barely make out the voices of Mr. Pemberton and Buddy Gregson. The old Brit laughed heartily at something unintelligible—a good sign. If Kevin was where he thought he was, the hallway to Billy's room would be on the right side of the foyer, opposite the front door. That meant crossing behind Mr. Pemberton. If the reaper keeper had stepped outside onto the porch—which seemed likely, given that Buddy didn't have a means of ascending the front steps—that wouldn't be a problem.

However, Kevin suddenly realized that there was a rather large flaw in his plan: silently traversing the floor of Billy's bedroom, which was covered in garbage, would be downright impossible. He paused for a few moments, considering his options. With stealth out of the question, speed would be his next best bet. He'd have to rush the reaper and apply the chloroform as quickly as possible, a tactic certain to lead to slipping on an empty pizza box and falling flat on his face.

Like its predecessors, the next door opened without a sound. The glittering foyer awaited, as bright and white and empty as the rest of the underutilized mansion. Kevin kept a close eye on the wide open front door as he tiptoed across the marble floor. He couldn't see Mr. Pemberton, but he could hear the reaper keeper chatting up a storm with Buddy Gregson.

"Summer o' '68. Remember that shit storm?"

"I doubt I'll ever forget it. Never has there been a place and time more ill-suited to fighting a proper war."

"Swear there were mushrooms growin' in my fuckin' socks."

"Probably not far from the truth. The heat and humidity spawned all manner of nasty little beasties."

Bearing right into the short hallway that led to Billy's room, Kevin's throat tightened with every step he took. He pulled the chloroformed rag out of his back pocket. If it proved ineffective, his next best bet would be a solid blow to the head. He hoped it wouldn't come to that. Such physical violence could easily go too far, and Kevin really had no clue how hard he'd have to hit Billy to knock him out. If only Sweatpants Bob had been available for a consultation.

At the double doors to Billy's room, Kevin gritted his teeth and threw caution to the wind. He flung the door open and charged inside, plowing straight through the wave of garbage stench that slapped him in the face. The lights were off and the only illumination came from the flat-panel monitors on Billy's desk, each displaying a different computer game. The Chicago Blackhawks travel mug containing the souls of Abelia, Ren, and Driff stood ominously upon the front right corner of the desk. A ten-gallon fish tank filled with crystal-clear water sat on the floor to the left of Billy's big leather chair, crushing a few empty boxes of Chinese takeout.

Everything happened in slow motion. As Kevin stampeded through the morass of trash and discarded clothing on the floor, Billy turned in his big leather chair to face his attacker. Smiling like a saint in a Renaissance painting, the reaper spread his arms wide, inviting the killing blow. Kevin had never seen him so relaxed. Then his eyes settled on the chloroformed rag and the room itself seemed to darken as he recognized Kevin's intentions. Billy's lip twisted into a primal snarl as he stood and raised his fists to defend himself.

Thinking quickly, Kevin adjusted his priorities. He threw the chloroformed rag as hard as he could. It spiraled through the air and struck Billy in the face like a whip, staggering the reaper and knocking him back down into his big leather chair. Kevin zigged to the right as his enemy recovered, snatching the Chicago Blackhawks travel mug from the desk. The plastic cap fell away with a quick twist of his wrist. Three ghostly streaks burst forth from within and rocketed out the door on their way back to where they belonged.

Kevin didn't have time to celebrate. Billy's hand grabbed for his face, finding purchase on his nose before he could fight it off. An all-too-familiar pain wracked his body as the reaper once again ripped his soul free. Billy let go just as suddenly and Kevin's soul snapped back into his face like a rubber band, knocking him onto his ass and into a greasy pizza box. The room around Kevin spun violently as his consciousness settled back into his skull. He could hear Billy moving things nearby but couldn't focus enough to figure out what he was up to. One thing was for sure: his plan was fucked and it was time to get the hell out of there. He'd succeeded in freeing Abelia, Ren, and Driff, which meant he could come back for Nella with more help. She didn't seem to be in any imminent danger in that fish tank.

It took a concerted exertion of will, but Kevin managed to wobble back to his feet. The scene before him immediately vaporized his thoughts of retreat.

"Kill me," Billy snarled. He dangled a fully powered flat-screen monitor, taken from his desk, above the now wide-open fish tank. There was more than enough slack in the cord to keep it plugged in if he dropped it. "Kill me!"

Kevin's heart hammered against the inside of his chest. This was *not* how things were supposed to go. "Billy, let's talk about this—"

"Kill me!" the reaper screamed. Tears streamed from his wild eyes. "Kill me or I'll drop it!"

"There's got to be—"

"There isn't! This ends one way!"

"B—"

Billy opened his fingers. White-hot fear boiled up through Kevin's chest like lava about to burst forth from an erupting volcano. He sprang forward, driving his shoulder into Billy's torso as he groped uselessly for the falling monitor. Sparks flew as it hit the water. Billy, knocked off balance by Kevin's mad grab, crashed down through the fish tank and into the roiling storm of electricity, crunching the glass beneath his weight. Kevin stumbled backwards from the water spreading through the layer of crap on the floor as the reaper spasmed and sizzled. Billy finally fell still a few agonizing seconds later. In death, he looked almost happy.

Realizing what he'd done, Kevin fell to his knees in shock. He'd finally fucked up in a way he couldn't try to worm his way out of. Nella was dead. Kevin Felton would become Harksburg's new reaper.

— CHAPTER THIRTY-FOUR —

S omething deep in Kevin's skull popped, not unlike a ligament separating from bone. He knew immediately what it was. That was no muscle bursting; it was his own mortality. Whatever process would transform him into the new reaper to take Billy's place wasn't wasting any time.

Reality began to ripple. Every surface around Kevin undulated in regular waves like water in a windy harbor—except in every direction at once. The effect was most profound on and around Billy's corpse. The dead man's flesh rose and fell in rhythmic pulses, contorting his serene features into a series of ever more ghastly caricatures that reminded Kevin of a plastic action figure he and Doorknob microwaved back in middle school. Static electricity flared to life in Kevin's fingers and toes. His muscles refused to respond to his attempts to move. The sharp tingle spiraled up through his arms and legs and engulfed his torso, his neck, and finally his head. Helpless and scared out of his wits, he nonetheless laughed inwardly at his situation. What was good enough to kill Billy, it seemed, was good enough to enlist his replacement, albeit on a much less painful scale.

One by one, tiny sparks lit up in a deep, dark region of Kevin's consciousness. Each burned differently, labeling themselves as unique individuals in a way Kevin couldn't immediately describe. He could feel their relative health—or, in several cases, their lack thereof—as acutely as his own.

Souls, he realized. *Everybody in Billy's territory—in* my *territory.*

His new awareness was as awe-inspiring as it was pants-pissingly frightening. Try as he might, he couldn't turn it off. It was as much a part of his body now as his other senses. He chose one of the sparks at random and focused on it with all his will, testing the limits of his new power. No additional information manifested. Although he had a general feel for the spark's physical condition, he couldn't gather its location or its owner's identity. With those limitations, how useful could it really be? What good was knowing someone's health if he couldn't match that knowledge to an actual person? Was it a safeguard of sorts designed to keep him from abusing his abilities? He wished his new reaper powers had come with an owner's manual.

The rapidly vibrating world around him suddenly bounced, tossing him into the air a short distance before rising again to meet the soles of his feet. Reality settled back into its usual still form and Kevin found himself standing outside. Gone were the garbage and darkness of Billy's room, replaced by green grass and warm sunshine. A few feet away, the grass shortened around a slender flag sprouting up from a tiny round hole. Somehow, he'd wound up in the middle of a golf course. He counted four other holes between himself and the clubhouse looming in the distance, a massive postmodern log cabin sort of thing ringed in a wide deck covered with picnic tables. Dense stands of deciduous trees protected the course from the riffraff in the rest of the world.

"Motherfucker," he groaned.

"Yes, that's what they all say," a scratchy voice interjected from somewhere behind him. The man's accent was unmistakably Russian.

Turning, Kevin found three golfers getting ready to tee off at the next hole. The nearest, a tall, strikingly handsome man in designer slacks and a pink polo shirt, looked like he'd sprung to life straight off the cover of some magazine that routinely profiled important businessmen no one had ever heard of. Tucking his club in between his armpit and his round bicep, he pulled a white glove off his right hand as he confidently closed the gap between himself and Kevin.

"Ramsey St. Croix," he said through blinding white teeth, his voice friendly but firm. Crow's feet pinched his eyes and his jet-black hair turned gray at his temples. "Welcome aboard, son."

Stunned, Kevin limply returned Ramsey's well-practiced handshake. "Thanks. I guess. I'm Kevin Felton."

The trio's other male member oozed up beside St. Croix like a tentacle slipping into an anime character's nether regions. Kevin tried not to stare at the man's knee-length white socks, then his inappropriately short and tight sweatshorts, then the black leather fanny pack at his hip, then the bristly brown beard threatening to devour his neon green tank top. Everything about him screamed inappropriate, especially his wild eyes. Kevin couldn't meet his gaze, choosing instead to stare at his own feet as he shook the taller man's hand.

"Grigori Rasputin," he croaked in his Russian accent. "You can call me Griggy."

"Um...what?"

"Yes, I am that Grigori Rasputin."

"But weren't you..."

"Poisoned? Shot? Clubbed? Thrown into icy river? All of above, my friend! None of it matters when you've cut a deal with local reaper!"

That explained all the stories Kevin had heard about Rasputin's gruesome demise. "What did you give the reaper in return?"

Smiling like he'd convinced a small child to climb into his van, Griggy dragged his thumb across his throat.

"Ah. Right." Kevin leaned to his left, peering around Ramsey St. Croix to both examine the trio's third member and to put some distance between himself and the unsettling Russian. By the next set of tees, a young girl in a sky blue dress, matching ribbons in her curly blond hair, squatted down to poke at something in the grass. Ten years old at the most, she could've easily crawled into either of the two golf bags propped up behind her and left plenty of room for the clubs.

"That's Olga," St. Croix explained. "The oldest of us."

Kevin frowned as he parsed that sentence. "You're all reapers."

Ramsey nodded. "We're the Three, the oldest reapers in existence. We provide leadership, counsel, and—when necessary—discipline to avatars of death the world over." St. Croix spoke in a tone that implied Kevin should be awed or impressed. In truth, he was just confused.

And angry. And depressed. If the Three had done their jobs, shit wouldn't have gotten as twisted and out of control as it had—and Nella would still be alive. "Great work with Billy."

Shrugging, Ramsey slipped into that innocent middle manager mode Kevin had seen so many times working in Chicago finance. "You can't win 'em all, especially in this business. Our consultants did their best."

"Consultants?"

"Evitankari, via Tallisker. We're busy people. Got to induct two or three new hires every day. We've had to adjust our retention goals accordingly. Oldest trick in the ol' management playbook, eh?"

"I thought that was assigning blame elsewhere," Kevin snapped.

Ramsey St. Croix's face flushed an interesting shade of purple. Rasputin slithered around the businessman like a pick-up artist positioning himself to steal some poor sap's girlfriend. "Billy was boned at start. Had been ready to die for months before recruitment. Mistake, that one. Is hard to find good help these days, no?"

Kevin snorted. "That bar must be pretty fucking high if they let you in."

Griggy ogled him like a sketchy man in a van watching a playground. "Ah, this one gets it! Job requires few loose screws in just the right places. Is terrible thing we do, no? We end that which never end otherwise. Old, young, sick, healthy—it not matter. In most cases, dead man just unlucky. Is chance. Probability. Great big cosmic joke."

Nella's death flashed before Kevin's eyes. Could there have been a dumber way for her to go? Stuck inside a fish tank, electrocuted by her former fiancé's computer monitor. And yet she'd gone on her own, without any help from a reaper.

"But is not joke without punchline," Griggy continued. "Us."

Kevin couldn't help being reminded of Buddy Gregson's explanation for how he'd remained sane under Rex's control all those years. The absurdity of it all formed a sort of insulating shield against the gravity of the situation. Taking things completely seriously, after all, gives those things a sort of power, an influence that can't be denied, deflected, or ignored. Rasputin radiated that fuck-it-all mentality like a man without a shower gave off body odor.

Shaking his head, Kevin willed his outrage to return. "Tell that to the water nymph Billy killed trying to get at me," he snarled.

"Magic people? Magic people get it. No need reaper. Content with order of things, even with all screws in place."

"Not sure I believe that. No way Nella *wanted* to die."

"Want? Want have nothing to do with it. Is acceptance. Is recognition of greater force that not give a shit what people *want*. Trust me; she go peacefully."

Something tugged on the hem of Kevin's shirt. Looking down, he found Olga smiling up at him. The little girl pressed something into his hand and closed his fingers around it. She nodded once, then skipped away to look at something behind the golf bags.

Opening his hand, Kevin gasped at what she'd give him: a tiny heart, perfectly woven from blades of grass. "What the fuck am I supposed to do with this?"

"Olga hasn't spoken since 1913," Ramsey said gently. "She finds symbols to be a more powerful way to communicate."

"Less exact than words," Griggy added. "Carries more meaning."

Kevin wanted to move on so he could go home and sulk, so he stuck the charm into his pocket. "So what is this? Some sort of interview?"

"Some sort, yes," Rasputin replied. "Ramsey thinks we need standardize, but I prefer seat of pants approach."

St. Croix cleared his throat. "Tell us why you want the job."

"I don't fucking want the job."

Rasputin turned to his companion. "See? Is perfect. Take your spot someday."

Clearly exasperated, Ramsey shook his head and put his golf glove back on. "Fine. We've got a back nine to finish." Turning on his heel, he stomped over to the tees and examined the fairway ahead.

Griggy chuckled under his breath. "Retention rate for third spot in Three worst of all," he said conspiratorially. "Has only been reaper for thirteen years, with Olga and I for six months. Still thinking black and white, yes and no, love and lust. Misses dirty spaces in between."

Kevin couldn't help thinking of Kylie, Tallisker, and even the people he'd worked with at Noonan, Noonan, & Schmidt. People who thought there was one right way to do things. People who pretended the margins had no influence. People who, when you got right down to it, didn't have a fucking clue.

"I know the type," he said. "Hell, that used to be me."

"We all make mistakes," Rasputin replied. "Any questions about job?"

Kevin's gaze flicked from the mad monk to the stuck-up businessman to the tiny little girl. Each reaper had seemingly found a way to make peace with what was, really, a horrible situation—but they were all kind of fucked up in their own unique ways. What did that say about Kevin's chances of surviving the job? He wasn't sure which would be worse: quickly breaking under the pressure, or proving he was twisted enough to make it work.

"Is this...natural?" he asked. "The whole not-dying-without-help thing? Just doesn't seem like the way the world works."

Griggy stroked his beard like a serial killer running his fingers through the hair of his next victim. "Not sure. Some say it goes back to days of Axzar. Great demon lord. Covered most of planet with his hordes. He...broke us somehow. Rumors suggest he wanted death to be seen as reward and then made it so. No one knows for sure. Anything else?"

"I think I get it," he said. "Can I go home now?" He wanted to check on his mother, Ren, and Driff, then curl up in a ball somewhere and drink until he forgot all about Nella and his role in her death.

"Is simple, yes? Person dies, reaper makes it permanent. You will know what to do when time comes." Rasputin squeezed Kevin's shoulder like a drunk, overly affectionate uncle. "Quarterly pancake breakfast is December 3 in Birmingham. Hope to see you there."

Reality twisted again, melting the Russian's features and the golf course beyond into a real life post-modern oil painting. The mad monk's beard dripped into his neon green shirt and swirled around tendrils of his gray shorts and streams of darker green leaching into the mix from the surrounding landscape. Griggy's steely blue eyes, however, somehow fought off the power warping Kevin's view and maintained their size, shape, and position—implying, in a rather unsettling way, that the Three would be watching.

— CHAPTER THIRTY-FIVE —

When the world turned solid once more, Kevin found himself back in Billy's bedroom, standing in the exact spot where he'd watched the previous reaper—and Nella—die. Billy's body, however, was long gone, as was the shattered fish tank and a good chunk of the garbage that had once covered the floor. A motley collection of stains speckled the newly exposed carpet like a camouflage pattern, its original color long lost to time and the terraforming powers of takeout grease. He blinked a few times as his eyes adjusted to the light emitted by the recessed fixtures in the ceiling.

"Welcome back, sir," Mr. Pemberton said from Kevin's left. The old Brit, wearing blue latex gloves, shoved a pile of pizza boxes into a big black garbage bag already half full of crap. "I've taken care of the corpse."

Kevin wasn't sure he wanted to know how. "Thanks. This is... uh...awkward." He'd completely forgotten that his new gig came with a permanent assistant.

The reaper keeper sighed. "It always is, sir, but it will pass. Won't be long before you realize how quaint it is to have a British manservant of your own and ordering me about becomes second nature."

A wave of guilt washed over Kevin. He'd just killed Mr. Pemberton's master—no, Mr. Pemberton's *friend*—and the reaper keeper was duty-bound to accept Kevin in Billy's place. "I'm sorry. I…didn't mean to." His words felt useless, however, and his face turned crimson with embarrassment.

Mr. Pemberton paused, pretending to examine the black mold on the end of a formerly white sweat sock. "You gave Master Billy something he's wanted for years, something he couldn't bear to request of anyone else. Can't hold that against you."

Kevin was afraid of the answer to his next question. "Do you still want to retire?"

"More than anything," Mr. Pemberton replied immediately. "Unfortunately, my chosen successor found other employment."

"I'll get you out of this. I promise."

The reaper keeper wrinkled his nose. "I've no doubt you will, but there's no need to get annoyingly melodramatic about it."

One of the stars in Kevin's mental constellation of souls began to pulse wildly, stifling his response. Someone needed—no, demanded—his attention. The intense sensation overwhelmed and dulled his other senses, rendering him incapable of focusing on anything else.

"Someone's dying," he said softly, in awe of the feeling. "What do I do?"

"Let it take you," Mr. Pemberton replied, not without pity. "As for the rest…that's up to you."

Relaxing, Kevin let death's summons take control. A new scene overlaid itself atop his view of Billy's former room: a narrow forest trail, still muddy from the earlier rain, worming gently downhill between old growth and thick trees. It was like watching a 3D movie that had fallen woefully out of sync. When he closed his right eye, his view of the forest solidified; when he closed his left, the cool night breeze disappeared and all he could see was Mr.

Pemberton busily cleaning the floor. He shut his right again and examined his surroundings.

To his left, Sweatpants Bob sat propped up against a fallen log, leaning heavily on his right elbow. The homeless old man's chest rose and fell with ragged, gasping breaths. Blood oozed out of his mouth, trickled down his beard, and pooled in his shirt. If he knew Kevin was there, he didn't care.

The cancer, Kevin thought, his heart heavy. He kept his distance and watched, the memory of Sweatpants's rock-hard knuckles connecting with his jaw still fresh in his mind. He didn't doubt that his new reaper powers had given him a distinct advantage in any fight, but he was in no hurry to pop his pull-someone's-soul-out-through-their-nose cherry.

Sweatpants Bob coughed up one thicker gob of blood and then fell still. His eyes remained wide open, staring into the distance at something only he could see.

Kevin took a step forward and then hesitated. Was he supposed to do something at this point, or was there some other signal he needed to wait for? Not understanding his exact role here made Sweatpants's death all the more depressing. If Kevin fucked up, would it hurt the old man? Would his inexperience make Sweatpants Bob's final moments more excruciating than they needed to be? He shook his head and sighed, resolving to suggest that the Three create some sort of new reaper training program if he lasted to the quarterly pancake social.

Sweatpants's soul appeared beside his corpse, a spectral reproduction of the man's physical form. He looked down at his body sadly, his gray eyes full of longing and regret. Kevin knew he had to do something before Sweatpants returned to his flesh.

"Um…Sweatpants Bob?" he stammered.

The old man didn't even bother looking at him. "Felton. Looking for another knuckle sandwich?" Though his words were threatening, his tone couldn't have been gentler.

"I'm...uh...here to help you move on," Kevin replied through the lump in his throat. "It's over, Sweatpants."

"I know," he replied, biting his lip. "It's been over four times already. Barely made it ten miles. It's for real this time?"

Four times. How many others had died over and over again because of Billy's negligence? Kevin supposed he'd be finding out soon enough. Some maladies, it seemed, were too much even for the healing power of the human soul to completely expunge. A bullet to the head was surprisingly simple in comparison to terminal cancer. If the demon lord Axzar had truly intended to transform death into a gift, there could be no better case for it. "It's for real this time."

Sweatpants Bob finally looked up at him, the relief clear in his face. "So, what's the deal? Finally getting around to it now?"

"Just got the job a few minutes ago. My predecessor...had some performance issues."

"Whatever. Kind of glad it's someone I know and generally tolerate. Sorry I punched you in the face."

Kevin blushed. That made him feel a little bit better, but not much. "It's all right."

"I really wanted to believe Spuddner's bullshit. Anyway. How do we do this?"

Kevin felt the sudden urge to take Sweatpants's hand. "Something tells me we just shake on it."

"That simple, huh? Say...where's your cloak and your scythe?"

"Left 'em at home. Casual day." He offered his hand. "Any last words or...anything?"

Sweatpants Bob scratched his chin. "Seems like I should have something profound to say. I mean, this is one moment we all look forward to in our own way, right? But I've got nothing."

He closed the gap between them with two long strides and grasped Kevin's hand in his own huge palm and fingers. "Thanks, Felton."

As soon as their hands made contact, the old man's soul began to dissipate. It was like watching the image in a TV screen fail one pixel at a time. Tiny specks of Sweatpants Bob simply ceased to exist. Horrified, Kevin took a step backwards and tried to open his hand, but the muscles wouldn't respond.

"Good luck, kid," Sweatpants said, his voice garbled. Most of his lips and his right eye were already gone, along with a wide slash of his chest. "You're gonna fuckin' need it."

Moments later, Sweatpants Bob was no more. Kevin's body called his split consciousness back into Lordly Estates. Overwhelmed, he fell flat on his ass and banged the back of his head against the desk behind him.

"How was it?" Mr. Pemberton asked as he knelt down beside his new master. He gently set a steaming cup of black coffee on the floor by Kevin's left hand.

"Intense," Kevin replied, his entire body quivering. "Beautiful and terrible at the same time. That—that's not the way things should be."

The old Brit nodded sadly. "No, it's not. But it's the hand humans and elves have been dealt. It doesn't matter that the game's been rigged."

Kevin took a tentative sip of coffee and reflected on what he'd done. Sweatpants Bob, a fixture in Harksburg for longer than Kevin Felton had been alive, was deceased, gone, because Kevin kept the man's soul from returning to his body. The fact that Sweatpants couldn't completely fix his own cancer anyway was little consolation. What if things had gotten progressively better every time Sweatpants Bob died and came back? What could modern medicine have done for him with the knowledge that killing the patient didn't mean the end? There were far too many unknowns in this situation, and Kevin hated every single one of them. He felt like he'd put down the family dog and hadn't told anyone how the dog had passed. That was the real kicker.

Everyone in Harksburg would know that Sweatpants Bob had died, but no one would know that Kevin Felton had really killed him. The lack of responsibility felt somehow damning, like he was getting away with something—even though no one in town would ever believe him if he ever outed himself.

That right there was the thing that scared Kevin the most about being a reaper: the lack of immediate responsibility. Would the power go to his head? Would it twist him into a maniac in the mold of Griggy Rasputin? Would it wear him down slowly, like flowing water carving out a new canyon, until he became something completely unrecognizable? To say he'd already begun to dread the future was an understatement. Life as a reaper held far too many terrible possibilities and not nearly enough happily-ever-afters.

And it would only get worse. Sweatpants Bob had made things easy for him. The old man knew it was time to go, regardless of how tightly his subconscious clung to life, and he just needed a little help getting there. Billy had shown him just how difficult the job could get when he'd streamed his own memories through Kevin's soul while collecting hostages. He wasn't looking forward to doing the deed with someone who wasn't ready for the end, and the thought of working with children sent a shiver down his spine.

Another soul went haywire in Kevin's mind. This one was a lot closer and somehow different from Sweatpants Bob's. "I think...I think an elf is dying."

"Ah," Mr. Pemberton replied, "that's likely the result of the hullabaloo on the front lawn."

"The...what?"

"Miss Nella is none too happy with that Driff fellow. I daresay I wouldn't be either if I'd spent the last few hours confined to the toilet tank in one of the spare bathrooms upstairs."

Kevin couldn't believe his ears. "Wait...Nella's not..."

Mr. Pemberton shook his head. "Master Billy filled that fish tank using the kitchen sink. You've been boondoggled, Master Kevin."

Several moments of rapid blinking and heavy mouth breathing later, the reaper keeper's words finally sank in. Nella was alive and well—and Kevin had killed Billy in a futile attempt to rescue a few gallons of Harksburg's skunky tap water. The latter would've made him feel hopelessly stupid if the former hadn't already set his heart on fire.

He leapt to his feet and sprinted into the foyer. Several familiar voices cried out from beyond the front doors.

"Nella, let's talk about this!" Ren Roberts shouted. "It's not Driff's fault!"

"Ah, don't listen to that rich pussy!" Abelia Felton growled. "Drain the motherfucker!"

Kevin whipped the glass and gold doors open and hurried out onto the porch. He found his loved ones—and Driff—to his right, gathered on the grass. Nella, naked and blue, loomed over the elf, who lay prone on the ground. A thin tendril of water connected Driff's green right hand to the water nymph's fingers like a liquid leash. Ren and Abelia stood to either side, watching the proceedings intently. Ren's beloved Jag was parked on the lawn behind them.

Abelia spotted him first. "Well, fuck me," she muttered as her pinched scowl spread into a wide smile. Opposite Kevin's mother, Ren's jaw just dropped.

Kevin tackled Nella before she had a chance to turn around, dragging the water nymph to the ground and spinning her in his arms so he could press his lips to hers. Stunned, Nella hesitated for a moment, apparently unable to believe what was happening, and then she responded in kind. Her gills fluttered wildly on the sides of her neck.

"Get a damn room," Abelia snapped. "And then I suggest you make an appointment at the clinic. Lord knows what kind of shit you can catch from fucking a fish lady."

He came up for air briefly before diving right back in. "Nice to see you too, Ma."

"Hey, reaper," Driff croaked, his voice dry and scratchy. "I'm dying over here."

Kevin pushed himself up onto his elbows and turned his attention to the elf. Driff was impossibly pale with bloodshot eyes and cracked, bleeding lips. He didn't look like he was going to last much longer.

"I couldn't feel you anymore," Nella said sheepishly, caressing Kevin's cheek. "I thought you were gone. I thought he had broken his promise to keep you safe, so I took his water xd like I said I would."

"Can you put it back?"

"I can. Let me up."

Kevin rolled off of Nella and rose to his feet. Freed, the water nymph scooted across the grass and took Driff's green fingers gently in her right hand. "This is gonna hurt," she said.

"Of course it is," Driff mumbled.

Nella's entire right arm liquefied, from her fingers up to her shoulder. Driff gritted his teeth and arched his back in pain as water flowed back into his body via his hand.

"So, you're really a reaper now?" Ren asked casually. "How's that going?"

Kevin brushed himself off. "So far, so good. Got the job done with Sweatpants Bob."

"Dude, don't you think that's overkill? All he did was punch you in the face. You ended his entire existence."

"Thought my street cred could use the rub. Gotta lay down the law, make sure everybody knows there's a new sheriff in town." It still hurt, but joking about it helped a little.

Nella stood, pulling the wobbly Driff up to his feet as she did so. A healthy tone had returned to his skin, but he still seemed a little weak and out of sorts. His right hand was no longer green. Nella had released the hex joining his water to her own.

"Good, so it's all over, then," the elf said, trying to come off as official and in charge but really just sounding like he was about to vomit. "Mission accomplished. I'll put out the word to get the dust back into the water supply. Give it a few days, and it'll be like nothing happened." His eyes darted anxiously between the four people standing around him. "Well, mostly."

Driff pushed his spectacles up on his nose, shoved his hands into his pockets, and stumbled forward, nearly colliding with Kevin before righting himself and continuing on. That was it, then: no good-byes, no jobs-well-done, no pleasures-working-with-you, nothing. Classic Driff, really. Expecting more, Kevin realized, would've been foolhardy.

But there was one last piece of unfinished business Kevin felt the need to address before the elf disappeared forever. It was something he easily could've kept to himself and yet, out of some potentially misplaced sense of loyalty, he made the split-second decision to open his mouth and say something he'd been very, very explicitly instructed not to say.

"Rotreego was here," he blurted out. "His sword wouldn't catch on fire."

Driff tripped over his right foot, caught himself, and then stood still as a statue. He turned his head to glare at Kevin in confusion, but his expression softened as he worked to figure out what was going on. Then his jaw dropped, his eyes closed, and his entire body tensed in on itself. Whatever conclusion he'd come to was apparently far worse than Kevin had expected. He faced forward again, shaking his head as he resumed walking away, and he muttered something that sounded kind of like "fucking witch" as he magically hid himself from view.

"Who's Rotreego?" Abelia asked. "Another one of your 'professors?'" She punctuated that last bit with melodramatic air quotes.

"Just some asshole," Kevin replied. Nella leaned in close as he wrapped his arm greedily around her midsection. "Mr. Gregson locked him in the basement and...ah...apparently took his favorite toy away, or something."

"I suppose you're all going to want a ride home now," Ren groaned. "Bunch of freeloaders."

"As long as I don't have to get back in that bucket," Nella snapped, slipping out of Kevin's grasp to sprint for the front passenger seat.

"Don't complain, honey," Ren snapped, following close behind. "That bucket was downright roomy compared to sharing a fucking travel mug with two other people."

"Where is my mug, anyway?" Abelia asked as she and Kevin headed for the Jag. "I won that fair and square in a baking competition and I want it back."

"I'll ask Mr. Pemberton," Kevin replied. An interesting idea struck him then. "Hey, Ren: do extra awesome at getting everybody home and there just might be a brand new job in it for you."

"You couldn't possibly afford my services."

"I'm not sure what the position I'm thinking of pays, but the benefits are great. Full immunity from Tallisker's meddling, for one."

His friend opened the driver side door and looked back at him over the Jag's roof, clearly intrigued. "That might be worth it. What exactly did you have in mind?"

Kevin grinned from ear to ear. "Every reaper needs a keeper."

"I have no clue what the hell you're talking about," Abelia interjected, "but it sounds pretty fucking stupid."

Nella flashed Kevin an amused smile and winked.

"At this point, I'm used to pretty fucking stupid," he said, "and I think you guys can help me deal with the worst of it."

His mother sighed. "You are such a pussy."

**READ ON FOR A SNEAK PEAK OF THE FIRST CHAPTER
OF *SHOTGUN*, BOOK 2 OF THE DEVIANT MAGIC SERIES.**

— CHAPTER ONE —

How would you like to help me change the world?"
Roger had never confronted a burglar before, but he
was pretty sure no trespasser in the history of time had
ever answered the question "What the hell are you doing in my
house?" in quite that way.

The intruder leaned forward from her perch among the empty
takeout containers piled high atop his kitchen counter, her black
dress rustling against the tile. She was a long, spindly thing, her
porcelain skin made even whiter by the long locks of jet-black hair
framing her face. "Come on, Roger," she cooed. "I know you've
got a good heart. I know you want to help people." How did
she know his name? He'd certainly never met her before. Roger
shifted his grip on his old shotgun and took a couple tentative
steps closer. His slippers squeaked on the cracked linoleum. They
were only a few feet apart now. "Who are you and what are you
doing in my house?" he asked, fighting to keep his voice stern and
mostly succeeding. Although the sickly-sweet smile with which
she'd greeted him remained, she clicked her black nails across the
counter in irritation. "Roger, this isn't about me. This is about you.
Are you interested or not?"

"No," he croaked. He never should've come downstairs to investigate that strange, childish laughter. He should've stayed in bed, rolled over, pulled the covers over his face, and pretended nothing was happening.

The tall woman's smile faded and she shook her head. "Are you sure?" She pouted, staring out at him from under her bangs with eyes suddenly gone soft. It was exactly the way Roger's daughter looked at him when she wanted something.

He hesitated before answering. Was this some sort of test? Would things turn nasty if she didn't like his response? "I'm sure," he finally said.

She lowered herself to the kitchen floor like a snake slithering down a tree. Roger stood frozen in place as she confidently closed the gap between them. She took his hand gently in her own and led him into the hallway. He didn't fight it; he couldn't, not because he was afraid, but because her icy touch somehow put him completely at ease. They stopped before the big round mirror Roger's wife often used to check her appearance before leaving for work. Not once did the strange woman so much as glance at his shotgun.

"See how good we look together?" she hissed. "Just the two of us against the world."

What Roger saw was a gorgeous young woman making a man in his late thirties look even older than he felt. She made his brown hair seem grayer and thinner, the crow's feet by his blue eyes the size of railroad tracks, his lean build fat and sloppy, his firm jaw a trio of jiggling jowls. And her simple but elegant dress made his flannel robe and fur slippers look positively stupid.

"Roger," she cooed, turning his face so her shimmering red lips were less than an inch from his chin, "don't tell me you've never wanted to be something. Where's your ambition?" She capped that last sentence with an impetuous giggle.

His heart broke all over again. Those were the last words Virginia had said to him before she drove off with the kids six months ago, taking them to some mysterious new suitor who could better provide the kind of lifestyle she needed. Food and a roof bought with a high school janitor's salary had been more than enough for twenty years. Roger hadn't seen her change of heart coming, and he still couldn't figure out what had caused it.

But whereas Virginia had immediately swung herself into the car and peeled out of the driveway, the strange woman in his kitchen appeared to be waiting anxiously for an answer. Once again, he felt as if he were being tested. Had she been spying on his family? Had she watched his wife abandon him? The answers to those questions were obvious, he decided, and downright chilling—not to mention thoroughly confusing. How the heck was he supposed to help her change the world? He could barely change the ink in his printer.

It was all a trick. It had to be. She'd come to the kitchen to distract him, to mess with his head, to distract him or set him up or otherwise take advantage of him. Roger lowered his eyes to avoid her intense stare. He opened his mouth to demand that she leave, but the words wouldn't come. Opportunity loomed before him. No, more than that—a second chance. A chance to properly answer the question that had been torturing his days and his nights ever since it was first asked of him. Maybe doing so would give him some peace. So where *was* his ambition?

"I did what I had to do," he said, his voice quivering. Roger didn't explain how he could've been a baseball player. Scouts from seven different major league teams watched every game he'd played in his senior year. Consensus pegged him as a good-but-not-great prospect, a solid bench player at worst and a decent regular at best. But then Virginia had gotten pregnant, and the idea of being on the road while she raised their first child alone hadn't been one he could stomach. That jagged hole in his heart where his family had always lived began to throb. He closed his eyes, wishing even more that this damn woman would just go away.

The back of a cold hand caressed his cheek, sending a shiver down his spine. "If you ever feel the need to be more," the woman whispered, her breath hot in his ear, "just look in the silverware drawer."

When he opened his eyes, she was gone. Roger abandoned all pretense of calm or bravery, dashing immediately to the back door beside the refrigerator. It was still locked, as was the tiny window above the sink. He sprinted into the living room, vaulting the mess of old photo albums and empty beer bottles he'd left scattered across the fraying carpet, and tested each of the three bay windows. Locked, locked, and locked. The deadbolt on the front door was shut tight. The windows in the bathroom and the dining room were similarly secured. She couldn't have come in through the basement; the iron bolt on that door could only be opened from inside the house.

He retraced his footsteps through every room on the first floor, searching for things that had been taken. Nothing was missing. The mortgage and his family's birth certificates and Social Security cards were still in the safe under the bookshelf. Nothing was missing from Virginia's jewelry box in the bathroom—not that she'd left much of value. The old green rug in the hall, which usually held footprints for days, showed no sign of tracks smaller than his own. The counter from which the woman had teased him showed no evidence she'd ever been there.

Which left the silverware drawer. Roger stared at it in absolute terror for a few minutes before a small laugh squeaked through his lips. He'd been sleepwalking—that was it. Wouldn't be the first time. After all, what could such a strange woman possibly have wanted with him? And how could she have broken into his locked-up house and then disappeared without a trace? It had been a dream, he decided, a manifestation of his stress and loneliness and perhaps a subconscious need for the approval of an attractive woman. That last part made him feel kind of gross.

He looked down at his shotgun and sighed, thinking how lucky he was that he never kept it loaded. Sleepwalking was dangerous enough; sleepwalking with a loaded weapon in his hands was something he didn't want to think about. He flipped the chamber open, relieved to see that it was still empty.

Roger headed for the stairs and his bedroom, telling himself that the drawer wasn't worth investigating. He wasn't a child who couldn't sleep unless someone checked the closet for monsters. The thought made his heart ache, even though neither Samantha nor Ricky had asked him to do that in years. One night, when his daughter was just four, he decided it would be entertaining to pretend like he'd actually found something. Sam spent the next week sleeping between Roger and Virginia.

The stairs squeaked in protest against his heavy, plodding footsteps. Worn out from his frenzied inspection of the house, he fought to keep his eyes open as sleep tried to reclaim him. A good night's rest, he knew, would go a long way toward helping him put this night behind him. Roger reached the second floor and turned left toward the master bedroom. He stopped in front of Ricky's room to check on his son—then remembered yet again that the little guy was gone. Roger shook his head and stumbled on, wondering if he'd ever break that habit.

He was about to open the door to the master bedroom when a low, guttural snarl stopped him in his tracks. Wood squealed as a dresser drawer was yanked open. Fabric swished as someone rummaged through his clothing.

"Here somewhere," hissed a scratchy, serpentine voice. "Must find it!"

Roger peered around the door, which he'd left slightly ajar. In the darkness, he could just discern a bulky, humanoid shape tearing apart the dresser beside his bed. Moonlight streaming through the window beyond glinted off a scaly hide. Wide hips and a proportionally narrower waist revealed the burglar to be a woman. Roger guessed she was about six and a half feet tall and over 250 pounds—more than big enough to wipe the floor with him. *That's a leather jacket,* he thought. *She's one of those assholes from the biker bar up the highway.* He wondered if his previous sleepwalking dream had been a subconscious warning of some sort or if he were still stuck in the same nightmare. Either way, the meager courage he'd shown in confronting the spindly woman in his dream wasn't enough to make him want to risk dealing with someone larger and probably better armed. A quick call to 9-1-1 would solve this problem. He slowly backed away from the door, his heart pounding in his chest.

In the bedroom, old hinges squealed in protest as the intruder turned her attention to the closet. Roger shook his head at the unintelligible muttering that accompanied the flutter of clothing being tossed every which way. *Drugs,* he thought.

Halfway to the stairs, a sharp corner jabbed his kidney. He spun and righted the table he'd backed into, but the framed photographs it so proudly displayed tumbled to the floor. Roger watched in horror as Virginia, Ricky, Samantha, and their trip to Cape Cod betrayed him in a cacophony of shattering glass and wood.

The sounds coming from the bedroom ceased. Roger raised his shotgun and took aim at the door. The old twelve gauge was a fearsome weapon and there was no way for the intruder to know it wasn't loaded. Roger hoped he'd have the confidence to pull off the deception. He'd never had a particularly good poker face.

Heavy footsteps thudded across the floorboards as the intruder approached the bedroom door. Roger fought the urge to wipe the sweat from his brow, knowing he'd have to make the first move.

The top of the door exploded in a shower of wood and smoke. A ball of flame zipped over Roger's shoulder, colliding with the far wall and setting it ablaze. Three red eyes glared from the master bedroom. The thought of being brave ran screaming from Roger's mind just as quickly as his bladder emptied into his pajamas.

A hissing laugh followed close behind as he scrambled for the stairs and slid over the top step. He grabbed at the railing to try to right himself, which threw off his momentum, and he wound up tumbling down to the first floor. His useless weapon flew from his hands, bounced off the walls a few times, and disappeared around the corner, sliding in the general direction of the front door. Roger grunted as he collided with the opposite wall at the bottom of the stairs. Leaning heavily against the wall, he groaned at the pain in his ribs and back as he hauled himself to his feet. He needed to get to the phone in the family room so he could call the police and the fire department and—

The cold tingle of something metallic and sharp pressing itself to his throat extinguished his thoughts. "Do not move," said a male voice to Roger's left. "Tell me what you saw up there."

Roger took a deep breath, trying to slow his pulse so his quivering carotid wouldn't slice itself open on the blade. "I don't know. It had red eyes, and it spat fire...and I think it had scales."

"I thought so. You've just survived an encounter with one of the most dangerous creatures in the Western Hemisphere," the man explained slowly, as if giving a lecture. "That creature is looking for something very important. She knows it's somewhere in your home, but her limited ESP cannot narrow the search further. If we find what she's looking for first, we get to keep our lives. If we don't..."

Time seemed to freeze as terrible realization dawned on Roger. "It's in the kitchen," he said quickly. Smoke tickled his nose, reminding him of his other immediate problem. "And my house is on fire."

The blade pulled away. "Show me."

Roger nodded and turned toward the kitchen, risking a quick glance at this latest intruder. The man was tall and lean and clothed in black military fatigues. A pair of green eyes burned brightly between high cheekbones and a tight brown crew cut. His posture was stiff and straight, his pace steady and purposeful.

Military, Roger thought, *maybe Special Forces.* He carried a pair of wicked-looking blades, like Bowie knives with bigger guards. The tops of his ears ended in sharp points. Although he didn't seem like he wanted to do Roger any harm, he certainly looked capable of doing so if the mood struck.

Roger flicked a switch on the wall as he shuffled into the kitchen, bathing the room in harsh fluorescent light. He stopped just shy of the cabinets, deeply frightened of whatever was in his silverware drawer. Turning to face the pointy-eared man, Roger spoke in a sad, quivering voice. "Top drawer, to the right of the dishwasher."

"Thank you," the commando replied politely. He stowed his blades in sheaths at his hips and yanked the drawer open.

A golden globe of roiling energy, like a miniature sun, rose up from within the drawer. Thin tendrils of power flared outward from its surface and crashed back down in blinding arcs. Roger stared at it in awe as it continued to rise until it hovered just below the kitchen ceiling. He had no idea what he was looking at, but something told him it was as important as the pointy-eared man claimed.

And then the globe suddenly zipped away from them and streaked down the hallway. It came to an abrupt stop above Roger's shotgun and then lowered itself into the weapon, melted into the steel of the barrels and the wood of the stock, and disappeared.

Jaw agape, Roger turned to the pointy-eared man in search of an answer—but the other merely shrugged. "That certainly wasn't the way this was supposed to go—"

Before he could continue, the ceiling above him exploded downward in a torrent of shattered drywall and lumber. Roger dropped to the floor and covered his head with his arms, cringing as shrapnel pelted his back, coughing against the scratchy dust that filled his mouth and nose. He wondered if the pointy-eared man was all right—not out of any concern for the man's well-being, but because he didn't like the thought of facing the thing in his bedroom alone.

As the dust began to clear, something heavy landed behind him with a dull thud. A predatory snarl sent a tremor through Roger's soul. He was on his feet without thinking, racing down the hall toward the empty weapon he assumed was his only chance. That ball of plasma in the silverware drawer had to have done something to it. Hot smoke streaming down from the fire upstairs burned his eyes and lungs, but he pressed onward. The creature's footsteps followed him like a shadow.

He dove for the hazy shape he thought was his shotgun, gasping as his damaged ribs protested their collision with the hard oak floor. His hands scrabbled across that floor, searching, searching— had the shape just been an illusion of the smoke? —and then his fingers found purchase on the familiar wood of the shotgun's worn stock. He rolled onto his back and brought his weapon to bear on the dark form and the red eyes pouncing upon him, and something in the back of his mind, something he swore came from the weapon itself, told him to pull both triggers.

The smoky room was suddenly and violently illuminated as his shotgun kicked hard into his shoulder. The report was like thunder as a thick ball of blue flame exploded from both barrels. For a brief moment, he could clearly discern the reptilian features of his attacker—bronze scales rippling across a vaguely feminine form, a long snout, a ferocious mouth lined with razor-sharp fangs, a spiky crest of exposed bone where her hair should've been—and then the blue fire slammed into the creature's chest and hurled her back into the kitchen.

Roger dismissed his shock with a quick shake of his head. His home was on fire, and he had to get out before the entire place burned down. He darted for the front door and yanked it open, hoping the creature he'd shot was good and dead and not about to jump him from behind. A dozen scrambling paces later he collapsed on the frozen ground of his front lawn and turned to watch the fire take his small home. The flames roared into the night, hiding the moon and stars behind a curtain of evil black smoke. The harsh siren of a fire truck blared in the distance, but Roger knew there was no hope. He'd lost everything—his family, his home, his every possession except his pee-stained pajamas and the old shotgun in his lap. His lip quivered with rage. Somehow, he knew this was all that strange woman's fault.

Glass shattered as a dark shape crashed through one of the windows on the side of his house. Roger leapt to his feet, weapon ready. It had worked once without any ammunition, so he assumed it would again.

The pointy-eared man stood and dusted himself off, smiling gently. "You've nothing to fear from me, friend," he said with a cough. "That was excellent work."

Roger kept his shotgun trained on the man. "What the hell is going on?" he demanded.

"I'm afraid an otherwise secret affair has spilled painfully out into the public," the man said, casually strolling closer. He glanced at the burning home sadly. "I apologize for the damage."

"You apologize for the damage?" Roger was incredulous. "Tell me what the hell is going on or I'm going to blow your head off!"

The man sighed and stuck his hands in his pockets. He stopped his approach mere inches from the barrel of Roger's weapon.

"Though I'm ashamed to say it, I really don't know why this is happening. My name is Aeric. If you come with me, maybe we can find out."

"I'm not going anywhe—"

Aeric's right hand jerked upward from his pocket and unleashed a handful of silver dust in Roger's face. Roger gasped and turned away, but he inhaled a mouthful of the stuff. It tasted like burnt bread. The world around him spun and went black, and the last thing he remembered as he collapsed was a pointy-eared man slowly prying his shotgun from his paralyzed hands.

— ABOUT THE AUTHOR —

Frustrated with the generic, paint-by-numbers state of modern fantasy writing, Scott Colby is working hard to give the genre the kick in the pants it so desperately needs. Shouldn't stories about people and creatures with the power to magically change the world around them be creative, funny, and kind of weird? Scott thinks so.

Check out deviantmagic.com for more from Scott Colby.